LIES THAT BLIND

TONY HUTCHINSON

CHESHIRE CAT BOOKS LTD

The book is published by Cheshire Cat Books Ltd
Suite 50-58 Low Friar Street, Newcastle upon Tyne, NE1 5UD.

ISBN 978-1-9161349-0-4

In memory of Al Hutchinson
Royal Marine and Raconteur

'The greatest trick the devil ever pulled was convincing the world he didn't exist.'
Roger 'Verbal' Kint
From the film, 'The Usual Suspects'.

Chapter 1

Saturday 31st October 2015

Shattered glass fell like hail on his head and shoulders, the sharp tang of cordite invading his nostrils and rushing down his throat, so strong he could taste it.

The single shot had brought the noise of the battleground to a residential street…shocking, unexpected, disorientating.

Police officer or not, nothing prepares for you that sudden sensory overload…for the sickening fear.

Not when it happens behind you and without warning.

Not when you've just closed the front door and are walking back to your car, the sweat of stolen sex still drying on your skin.

For Paul Adams, self-preservation launched itself on a jet-blast of pure adrenaline, the animal instinct to run, to save his own skin, to let someone else be the hero.

He sprinted down the path, away from where every cell in his scrambled brain was telling him the shot had come, diving head first across the dirty, dusty bonnet of his parallel parked car, dropping onto the Tarmac by the passenger door.

The second shot, when it came, seemed even louder.

Paul realised it was true…gunfire really did sound like an exhaust backfiring.

He crawled into a sitting position, pressed his back against the passenger door, tucked his knees under his chin, and pulled the left side of his jacket away from his chest to fumble inside for his mobile.

His thumping heart thrust panic and concern through his veins in equal measures, the twin emotions colliding in a toxic mix.

Now his sweat ran free and stank of fear.

Was he going to die?

Who was the shooter?

And there, coiling like a knot in his stomach, a different fear…how to explain why he was at Malvern Close when his wife asked the inevitable question.

He doubted she would believe he was at the home of a younger, single woman for professional reasons.

And he doubted his boss, Sam Parker, would cover for him.

Cowering behind the car, Paul bit his lip and berated himself.

He was a police officer. He needed to do his job.

But as irrational as it was, concern was still running fear a close second.

He knew he would be in the shit if this got out.

He should have gone straight home, flowers in one hand, chocolates in the other, and a restaurant booked for his wife's 32nd birthday.

Instead, he'd ignored her calls whilst he'd been with Tara.

Why had he ever listened to her? What could be so important?

Tara had text him the same message three times in less than an hour:

Please, please I need to see you. I can't discuss it on the phone. It's really important. Please I'm begging you. Come as soon as you get this.

Other than rushing him upstairs, what had she needed? Nothing.

But Paul hadn't asked and he hadn't said 'no'.

He never did.

Even then he could have been safely away before all this madness kicked off, driving home with no need for explanations or comebacks.

But hadn't Tara gone and phoned him as soon as he left the house. Christ he was hardly two steps from the door.

'Stand still,' she said, her voice warm, throaty. 'Don't turn around. I'm at the upstairs window watching you. I want to think of you on top of me for a little longer. Don't move.'

She had groaned into the phone as he stood listening. He liked the thought of her watching him, touching herself, her soft moans taking him back.

Those few moments had put him in this shit storm.

Get a grip Paul. Time to do what you're paid to do.

He inched towards the back of the car and dipped below the windows, below the line of a headshot.

At the back wheel, he lay flat on his stomach and slithered forward like a commando until the street opened up in front of him.

The car was facing the cul-de-sac entrance and from his sniper-like position he could see most of the street.

A tall, athletic-looking man, early twenties Paul guessed, with wide shoulders, a small waist, and wearing jeans and a t-shirt to show off his physique not counter the cold, was lying prostrate in the middle of the road.

Was he hit by the first shot? The second? Both?

The slap of rapid, heavy footsteps boomed through Paul's ears and twisting his head, he looked under the car and saw the blur of white trainers.

Don't run into the road you daft twat!

Joey 'Fatty' Sanderson, jogging bottoms and sweatshirt worn for comfort not cardio, was running fast for someone tipping 29 stone and fuelled by a lifetime of lager, cigarettes and takeaways.

Paul, stunned by Sanderson's unlikely speed, had heard fear could do that; give superhuman strength to the weak and now the pace of a sprinter to the morbidly obese.

It also seemed to be stealing, in Sanderson's case, the ability for logical thinking. Why else would he run across the street giving the shooter a target? Why not run up the cul-de-sac on the same side of the street as the gun, each step making the angle of the shot more difficult?

Paul shouted: 'Fatty! Police! Get back here.'

Joey 'Fatty' Sanderson had spent over 50 years avoiding Her Majesty's constabulary. He spoke to them only when absolutely necessary, occasionally providing reluctant information when his own liberty was on the line.

The last time he had bartered 'intelligence' was the high-profile investigation into a missing Asian girl and he still feared the stigma of being outed as a 'grass'.

So whoever was shouting at him now, Sanderson wasn't listening.

Paul pushed himself forward on his stomach until he could peer under the back bumper and see towards the shooter's window.

He watched the thin net curtain dance around the barrel of a rifle as Sanderson launched himself, chubby arms outstretched, towards a privet hedge that topped the brick wall of No. 15.

When the third shot crackled, Paul's body jerked upwards so quickly his head hit the underside of the car.

He hadn't seen Sanderson land like a sack in the garden; no groan, no whimper, just a thud as he hit the ground.

Paul rubbed his eyes and focused on the privet, where small pieces of brain matter dangled from the tightly-knit brown branches.

He blew out air, shifted his eyes downward and acknowledged two things: one, Sanderson was dead and two, whoever was pulling the trigger had to be some shot. Even with his limited knowledge of firearms, he guessed that hitting an airborne human target in the head – even a whale like Sanderson – took real skill.

Had he been able to move closer, Paul would have seen the hole in the back of Sanderson's head. The entry wound may have been small but the exit wound in his forehead was the size of a clenched fist.

Paul's mind was racing. Was Sanderson a target? Was he a wrong place-wrong time random victim?

The security firm Sanderson owned was in essence a small-scale protection racket. Had one of his 'customers' had enough?

Paul's ears felt as if they had been stuffed with Carnauba wax. He had seen movies where soldiers were temporarily deafened after explosions. Now he knew how they felt.

Think Paul, think.

He stared at the window and saw that the rifle had gone.

He waited.

Seconds passed in the silence, a cloak of serenity

fluttering and falling over the cul-de-sac and the two bodies, a Halloween Night tableau turned real.

With the weapon no longer in sight, Paul realised a new fear had been set loose.

Would the shooter leave the house and go on a mobile rampage, firing at whoever or whatever crossed their path?

The street was empty and well lit. The fuzzy glow of a television was visible through some windows, the residents inside oblivious to the nightmare unfolding outside.

Whatever was happening in No. 2 hadn't disturbed them. Not yet.

Bonfire night just round the corner. Probably thought the shots were fireworks.

Paul's mind was racing. He knew he had to do something instead of cowering like a whipped dog.

You're not paid to hide. There is an expectation. You are there to protect.

He remembered the number of the direct line and jabbed at his mobile.

'Inspector Waites,' a clipped voice answered.

Paul Adams took a breath and briefed the Control Room Inspector. He spoke clearly and slowly so future listeners didn't think he was engulfed in panic.

The call would be recorded and played back countless times to senior officers, investigators, the coroner, and if anybody went to trial, a judge and jury. Some of it may even be released to the media.

This was the time to demonstrate a cool head and Paul silently acknowledged the fact that he had even thought about his words being replayed at least showed he was still functioning under extreme pressure.

He gave the shooter's last known location as 2 Malvern Close; said he himself had been visiting No.1 and that the houses in the cul-de-sac went in sequential order from 1 to

17; he had heard three gunshots; the barrel of a rifle-type gun had been sticking out of the upstairs window; an unknown man was in the middle of the street, probably dead; Joey 'Fatty' Sanderson, protection racketeer, was in the garden of No. 15, probably dead; Paul was behind his car with a visual on the shooter's upstairs front window; there were no other upstairs windows at the front, only one downstairs..

'Keep this line open, Paul. Armed Response is en route. You are the forward commander until relieved and told otherwise.'

Every cloud, Paul thought. A chance for glory, an opportunity to get his name in lights and a promotion board talking point.

Yes, I can take command sir; yes, I can remain calm under pressure ma'am; yes, I can make time-critical decisions in major incidents. I demonstrated all those qualities at the Malvern Close shootings.

He still needed to come up with an excuse to satisfy his wife, but that would have to wait.

'I want you to provide a running commentary of what you see but also try to keep people off the street,' the inspector told him.

'Will do.'

'And keep yourself safe. Now, quickly. Do you know anything about the occupants of the house where the active shooter is?'

Paul thought fast, thought clearly.

'Not too much. Male. Early twenties. Zac something or other. Girlfriend called Lucy.'

'Children?'

'Young lad. About four years old. The child doesn't live with him.'

The smashing of breaking glass.

'Hang on…'

Paul shuffled his body to get a better view.

'I can see the barrel of the rifle again. Pointing through the downstairs window now.'

Something moved in his peripheral vision and Paul dragged his eyes away from the gun to look up the cul-de-sac.

Batman and Spiderman.

Only in miniature.

The two youngsters were carrying small plastic, orange buckets in their hands, the kind that make sandcastles. A couple of excited children dressed up and giggling now, doing trick-or-treat for sweets from door to door.

Shit. Shit.

'Any convictions or known associates?'

'Don't know,' Paul said, breathing more heavily.

The two superheroes were making their way towards him. He estimated another four houses and they would be in the firing line.

That gave him maybe five minutes tops if everybody opened the door.

He tried to work out whose children they were; to remember if he had seen them on earlier calls to Tara's, but the combination of costumes and pressure wasn't helping.

All that mattered was getting to them before they knocked at No. 2. He couldn't let that happen. The best-case scenario, the shooter taking them hostage, didn't bear thinking about. The worst…

Paul concentrated on speaking slowly into the mobile.

'Two children, probably no more than six years old, doing 'trick or treat' walking towards me. I need to move,' Paul told the inspector. 'I've got to get them away.'

'You're the forward commander. Don't do anything to jeopardise your safety. ARV ETA 5 minutes.'

Armed Response Vehicle.

Estimate Time of Arrival.

Five minutes.

A lot can happen in five minutes. I haven't got five minutes.

'Roger.'

Paul hung up, despite being told not to, and looked out from underneath the car towards Tara's front door.

Eyes wide with shock, he saw her standing in the doorway.

'Get back inside,' he shouted, pushing himself onto his knees and scrambling towards the front of the car, peering over the bonnet.

His right arm moved back and forth in a blur, a 'get-back-inside' warning, while he hit her speed dial number.

'What the fuck's going on?' Tara asked, answering before he even heard her phone ring.

He dropped back down and rested his back against the front wheel.

'Go into the kitchen and sit tight.' He kept his speech slower than his heart rate. 'Don't leave the house until I know the score.'

'What's happening?'

He wanted to scream, *'how the fuck do I know'*, but he knew that wouldn't help.

'I don't know,' he said calmly. 'Just stay inside. I'll come and get you when it's safe.'

'Are Zac and Lucy okay?'

He took a deep breath.

'I don't know. Just sit tight. I'll get you when this is all over.'

Paul watched Tara quickly turn inside and close the

door then crawled to the back of the car and lay flat on his stomach.

His phone rang. Control Room Inspector.

'You okay Paul?'

'Yes, sorry boss. Had to warn the occupant of No.1 to go back inside. Any update re ARV?'

'Just a couple of minutes away Paul. Keep relaying the information. You're doing a great job.'

The drifting voices of the children were getting louder and closer. Paul watched as they knocked at No. 4.

He scanned the street. No. 3 was in darkness – the occupants either out or playing 'not in'.

He didn't have much time. He knew he had to make his move.

Like a sprinter in the starting blocks he crouched behind the boot, took a deep breath and raised himself into the 'set' position.

He gripped the phone in one hand, the line still open.

He had less time than he thought.

Chapter 2

EVERY BREATH INCREASED Scott Green's nausea. The stench of human sweat impregnated the coarse black material of the hangman's hood over his head, a thick, musty sweat mixing with the dried blood caked around his mouth.

Perspiration bubbled on his forehead, more a reaction to the pounding pain from his knee than the stifling lack of air inside the hood.

He had walked into the backstreet garage in response to a text message but he should have been more careful. It wasn't that long since he had escaped off the boat.

He had shouted 'hello' but heard or saw nothing until he was whacked on the back of his right knee with what he guessed now was something like a pick-axe handle, the blow delivered with the speed, accuracy and force of a professional baseball player.

Whatever hit him, he had dropped.

His dad was right; you can't fight if you can't stand up.

Powerful hands had forced his head into the concrete floor and black-out darkness descended as the hood was dragged over his head. Other hands had searched his pockets for his mobile.

Seconds later he was in a vehicle.

Now he scrunched his eyes shut and willed the van – he knew instinctively it was a van – to go faster, willed fresh air to rush through the gaps in the sliding side door he had heard yanked open and slammed shut.

Every time the van stopped and the engine idled… traffic lights?...the lack of air and the sweat smell increased the feeling of a claustrophobic tomb.

His hands were numb, drained of blood. The ratchet handcuffs dangling from the metal pole overhead dug deep into the wrists of his outstretched arms. The ball and socket joints in his shoulders were on fire, like a prisoner being ripped apart on the rack in some medieval torture chamber.

He sucked in short breaths and shuffled on the wooden bench crudely fitted across the width of the van, trying to restore some feeling into his backside.

His thighs, burning like a cyclist's on an Alpine climb from the effort of balancing on the makeshift seat, threw more pain into his right knee.

Did they know his weakness there? Or was it just chance they had hit the one that had finished a promising rugby career.

His breathing was shallow and rapid, his heart rate off the scale. He had an idea who had snatched him but no idea where he was going. It wouldn't be a happy place and if his captors had their way, it wouldn't end well.

He forced himself to take deep breaths, slow down his breathing, control his pounding chest and concentrate, to focus on the direction of travel.

He knew Seaton St George and knew his start point, but with so many left and right turns and changes in speed he had soon become disorientated. Liam Neeson might have been able to retrace his kidnappers' route through Istanbul in Taken 2, but that was Hollywood not Seaton St George.

Scott was convinced, though, he was still in a built-up area; too many stop-starts to be on an arterial road.

He felt the van slow to take a tight right turn then pull up a short, steep incline.

Another tight right turn, another incline.

Now he had his Neeson moment. He knew where he was.

The roll of panic and his rocketing heart rate was only confirmation.

Tight right turn, incline.

He frantically tried to remember how many levels were on Seaton St George's only multi-storey car park.

Tight right and another climb.

Was the rooftop Level 11?

Scott counted as the van continued skywards, rubber squealing at every turn.

He felt it slow at last to a standstill and heard the engine stop.

He had been wrong about the number of levels.

He had counted 12.

Scott knew instinctively he was on the roof and that could mean only one thing.

He fought the jabbing agony in his knee, the burning in his arms, the fast-flowing river of sweat stinging like acid in his eyes, and the dread that was driving his heart rate to cardiac arrest territory.

Deep breaths. Stop panicking. Search for positives because positives aid survival.

Scott closed his eyes and concentrated.

They no longer had the element of surprise and it had

to be only two against one. He was sure nobody was with him in the back of the van.

Not great odds but not the worst and a fighting chance that was much better than the alternative.

Scott had learned many things in his 33 years but flapping his arms and flying wasn't one of them.

He heard the driver's door open and slam shut, then footsteps.

The sliding side door shook as it rattled across its runners and Scott's nostrils twitched at the sudden sickly-sweet smell of aftershave as the hood was yanked off.

A blast of blinding white from the beam of a powerful flashlight flooded his eyes and like an actor staring out from the stage, Scott could only see the hazy shape of a figure in front of him.

The matter-of-fact voice though, when it came, he recognised.

'Let's make this nice and quick Taffy.'

Scott blinked rapidly, kept his eyes away from the beam and took in as much as he could of what was around him. He was right about the van and saw it was parked close to a high, concrete wall.

The handcuffs were unlocked and his aching arms flopped, blood raced into them as he raised his hands and rubbed his eyes. Strong fingers grabbed his wrist in a tight grip and pulled him up from the bench seat.

The van was so close to the wall there was only room for one of them to be alongside the sliding door.

That was their first mistake.

The second was that the passenger door had been left open and touching the wall. Scott realised his other captor had to be at the rear of the van.

He knew this was the moment. Just one chance. Take

the height advantage that standing in the van gave him and use it now.

Scott rocked back on his heels, tilted backwards and tensed his throbbing thighs, ignoring the pain in his knee.

Do it now!

Suddenly he drove his right foot hard at the small tattooed head perched on shoulders wider than a shed. The searing jolt in Scott's knee as his leather-soled Chelsea boot smashed into the man's nose was excruciating.

But the blow would have felled a prize-fighter, the sickening impact smashing the back of his head into the concrete wall in a spray of crimson blood. He was unconscious before he hit the floor.

Leaping out of the van, Scott ducked his shoulder and charged towards the ski-masked driver, another barrel-chest Scott's granny would have described as being built 'like a brick shit-house'.

The man had two choices – side-step the charge and take his chances in a foot chase or stand his ground.

He stood his ground and was sent flying as Scott sprinted away.

A lifetime ago he had been a promising fly-half. The career-ending knee injury and a 40-a-day self-pity habit had steadily killed off his fitness, but he still fancied his chances of outrunning the stocky 'shit house' struggling back to his feet.

Scott dashed to the yellow exit door, yanked the metal handle and glanced over his shoulder. The driver was running after him now, arms firing like pistons.

Level 12.

He counted as he descended...five stairs to the half-landing, another five to the next level.

Level 11.

Nothing.

Level 10.

He heard a door above him slam. Was he two levels in front?

His chest rose and fell in short, quick spasms, his breathing fighting against the fear. He grabbed the rail with one sweaty palm and leapt the last three stairs, deliberately landing on his left leg.

He howled when he had to put pressure on his right knee.

Somewhere above him, 'shit house' was snorting like a pursuit dog, feet pounding into the steps so loudly Scott imagined the concrete cracking.

Level 8.

The footsteps were louder. He was gaining. Was he jumping the steps five at a time?

Scott silently cursed. Where was everybody? Why did the place have to be deserted? He wondered whether his knee could cope with leaping five stairs. Three was bad enough.

He glanced down through the huge square hole in the wall, a window without glass. The people he could see on the street below were getting larger with every step but they were still too far away to help. And if 'shit house' hurled him through the hole what could they do? Catch him?

Level 6.

Scott's mistake was looking up. 'Shit house' was charging after him, gaining ground, and he knew once he passed Level 1, at the halfway landing, he would leap the banister and land in front of him.

Scott counted again. Identical. Five steps. He could do it. He had to do it.

Level 1.

'Shit house's breathing was so loud and so close Scott

felt he would reach out and grab him. Blood sped through his veins and his head felt like it would burst, but it was his right knee he feared. He knew it could collapse at any moment.

He grabbed the rail with both hands, clenched his teeth and braced for the impact as he vaulted over the side, his cry so high-pitched only dogs heard it. Behind, and still gaining, 'shit house' did the same.

Scott lurched forward, head dropping so low he almost stumbled to the ground. He knew once he was there he wouldn't be getting back up. Instead, he straightened like a sprinter at the start of a ten second dash, slammed both hands down against the long black plastic door handle and launched himself into streetlamp-illuminated drizzle.

Still running, he hurdled a child's buggy that was suddenly blocking his way, chest heaving and lungs burning on empty, the pain in his knee now something alive and vicious.

Behind him he heard a woman's piercing cry and glanced raggedly over his shoulder. He saw the buggy was on its side, wheels spinning with a red-faced toddler screaming and 'shit house' now face down on the pavement.

Scott hoped the child was okay but let a smile spread across his sweat-streaked face, another look behind showing 'shit house' still on the ground.

Scott was still smiling when he ran into the road.

Accident investigators would later establish the liveried blue double-decker that hit him was travelling at a safe 27.5mph. The blameless driver, two weeks off retirement, had never even had time to touch his brakes. Even if he had, the collision would have been inevitable.

From the car park entrance 'shit house' had pushed himself up, his own grin as wide as his shoulders. He stood still, head down and let the rising thrum of gasps and 'oh Gods' from the shocked eye-witnesses wash over him before he walked back into the multi-storey.

He didn't need to look at the body. Nobody could have survived that argument with a double-decker.

But something, maybe instinct, made him stop and turn around.

The old guy outside the newsagent was staring straight at him through the gathering rain.

Chapter 3

Ed Whelan was sat in front of the television watching the closing minutes of Gillette Soccer Saturday, pleased with finishing on time for once.

Telling Sue, his wife, that he'd got an 'early dart' hadn't done him any favours though. She had still gone ballistic, screaming that finishing at 4pm when he'd been at the office before 8am didn't equate to an early finish in her world. Not on a Saturday. Not when he should have been off.

Ed put his outstretched legs on the footstool, closed his eyes and considered the wisdom of swapping his on-call negotiator rota.

He could have gone to watch United at St. James' and had a drink. Getting home after six, stinking of beer, would probably have been unwise given Sue's mood, but at least he wouldn't have been on call.

When his mobile rang, he was imagining Sue simmering upstairs, reading her latest classic and filling her head with perfect heroes Ed could never match, yet another stick to beat him with.

'Ed Whelan,' he said, plucking the mobile from the sofa before the second ring.

On the end of the line, Inspector Waites at the control room requested his urgent attendance at the scene of a shooting on Malvern Close.

Today, Ed was the number 1 negotiator, tomorrow he would be number 2, but in the world of negotiators, rank didn't exist. The number 1 might be a constable, the number 2 an inspector, but there were always two on call and number 1 was in charge.

Ed requested the second negotiator be called out, ended the call and pressed the off button on his Sky remote.

He trudged upstairs, cursing himself for getting changed into his tracksuit bottoms as soon as he had walked through the door. Now he had to go back into the bedroom, to Sue and more shit.

Doubtless the likes of Mr Darcy, with their olde-worlde manners, would never abandon their lady on a Saturday evening. Still, Ed doubted Fitzwilliam Darcy had ever been an on-call negotiator.

Sue remained on her back and put the open book face down on the bed, her voice a snarl.

'If you've come to apologise, don't bother.'

Ed opened the wardrobe.

'Called out. Nego-'

He ducked as the book crashed into the wardrobe at head height, Sue off the bed and moving quickly his way.

'You've just bloody well got in,' she screamed, sending the wardrobe's sliding mirrored door hurtling along its runner like a runaway train.

Ed's fingers tightened into fists, his reflection shaking in tandem with the glass.

'Like it's my fault some fucker's shooting innocent people,' he shouted.

He yanked open the door, snatched a pair of thick blue cords from a hanger, and grabbed a black wool sweater from the shelf.

It would get cold later and for reasons he could never fathom, cords not only kept him warm, they always seemed to calm him. Maybe they brought back memories of his grandfather, one of nature's true gentlemen.

The woollen hat in his 'Go Bag' would protect his shaved head.

'Fine,' Sue told him. 'Go save the world. See if I care.'

She waved her hand in the air, spun round and walked back to the bed.

Ed hopped into the trousers one leg at a time, wary eyes fixed on his wife in the mirror.

Sue was muttering with the book obscuring her face.

Ed felt a jab of sadness. Jane Austen couldn't piss her off. That was his specialty.

DETECTIVE CHIEF INSPECTOR Sam Parker was on her way to Malvern Close at Assistant Chief Constable Monica Teal's behest. The ACC wanted a Senior Investigating Officer – a SIO – at the scene.

Sam rarely had anything to rush home for no matter the day. Halloween, even with the bowl of cheap trick-or-treat sweets she already had waiting by the front door, was no different.

Acting Chief Inspector Mick Wright, universally known as 'Never' to the CID, was already heading to the scene as Silver Command.

The police and other emergency services used the

generic command structure Gold, Silver and Bronze to cover strategic, tactical and operational responsibilities when a major incident kicked off.

Sam knew Ed Whelan, her right-hand man, was also en route as on-call number 1 negotiator.

'You on hands-free?' she asked when Ed answered her speed-dial.

'I am.'

'This doesn't sound great. Three shots fired. Two men shot, possibly dead. I hope Paul's alright.'

'He'll be fine,' Ed said. 'He'll love being Forward Commander. You know what he's like. He'll do a good job, keep people out of harm's way.'

'Jesus, I hope you're right. Guns always give me the willies and he's not long been married.'

Sam glanced in the nearside wing mirror and moved back into the inside lane. 'What was he doing there anyway? I thought he'd gone home. Wife's birthday or something.'

Ed bit his lip and shook his head. Sam Parker didn't miss a trick, a mind much brighter than the modern street lamps that gave off less light than Darcy's candle.

'You still there?' Sam said.

'Yeah, yeah. Shaking my head at these pathetic streetlights. Much bloody use as an ashtray on a motorbike.'

'Cost-cutting and reducing carbon footprint,' Sam could picture his scowl.

Ed shook his head.

'See what shit flies about when a young kid gets knocked down and killed. These lights aren't just useless, they're bloody dangerous. Climate protestors won't be happy until we're all back in the dark ages.'

Not for the first time, Sam wondered what fired Ed's endless rants and rages. No shortage of power there.

'You still haven't told me what Paul was doing?' she said now, sensing even over the phone that Ed was keeping something back.

Ed sighed. It would come out anyway he thought to himself.

'You're right, it was his wife's birthday.' Ed paused, finally deciding. 'But I suspect he took a detour. He's seeing a lass in Malvern Close. Been seeing her for a few months.'

'You're kidding me?'

Ed waited for what he knew was coming.

'Great,' Sam shouted down the phone. 'Absolutely bloody marvellous. All I need...'

She leaned forward, thumped the black plastic dashboard with her left fist, and sneezed twice as a cloud of dust rushed her nostrils.

'Bless you.'

'The dust in these cars.'

'Lot better years ago when the Sunday morning shift had to clean them all,' Ed said.

But sneezes and a clumsy move to change the conversation weren't going to stop Sam on her track.

'Forget the bloody cars,' she shouted. 'He better have a good excuse for being there and not expecting me or the Job to lie for him. Who knew?'

'Only me as far as I know.'

Finally Sam took a pull on her anger and lowered her voice.

'What he does in his own time is a matter for him, not that I condone his behaviour, but I'm not compromising my integrity to cover for him.'

Ed concentrated on the rush-hour traffic and said nothing.

'Never's Silver,' Sam said, breaking the silence.

Ed shook his head again. 'Why need Britain tremble?'

Sam nodded in agreement. 'Air Support are making their way to the scene. They'll provide a live feed into control room.'

They both fell silent thinking about what the live feed might show, what they were going into. Not that there was any likelihood of them getting shot. They would be well back with an inner and outer cordon in place, firearms personnel inbetween them and the shooter's location. But there were already casualties, probably fatalities.

Sam shivered as the thought of a temporary mortuary flashed through her mind.

God I hope not.

The grim make-shift morgues to take multiple fatalities were usually set up in public buildings. There was a school nearby, Sam remembered.

Christ, the last thing I want is a primary school's assembly hall covered in death.

She rubbed her eyes, pushed away the darkness, and hoped the two trick-or-treaters Paul had spoken about were okay.

IN AN IDEAL WORLD Paul Adams would have sprinted up the drive of No.1 into the back garden, hopped over the fences and intercepted the two superheroes out of the shooter's line of sight.

But he wasn't in an ideal world.

What he was, was still in the 'set' position watching Batman and Spiderman frozen to the spot, staring at the athletic figure lying motionless in the middle of the road.

'Run and hide behind that car,' Paul shouted, voice

booming into the silence. 'I'm a policeman. Do what I say. Hide behind that car.'

The youngsters, mouths making small 'o's and trick-or-treat buckets hanging limp at their sides, stayed rooted.

From the doorways of two houses – Paul figured No.5 and No.6 – he could see a handful of residents finally roused by the commotion walking down their driveways.

No, no no…

Paul shouted 'get back' but all they did was stop and stare his way.

He peered around the back bumper, glanced at the window and saw the gun barrel twitch.

Time's up…no choice now.

Legs pumping and head low like a rugby player on the charge, Paul hurtled along the road, past the unkempt lawn of No.2 towards the youngsters.

Without stopping he scooped up a child in each arm, feeling their small bodies writhe and wriggle, and straightened.

Like trance victims suddenly aware, the residents were now moving quickly back down their drives.

'Get back!' Paul shouted again.

The two children in his arms had started screaming, panicked and confused, but not loud enough to drown out the sound Paul had dreaded.

The first shot hit him between the shoulder blades and dropped him in a heartbeat, his mobile bouncing away like a skimming stone as he fell heavily to the ground.

The bullet had ripped through the left side of his back exited through his right arm, and hit Spiderman's right thigh.

The second punched through the window of the house opposite.

Paul had fallen on top of the boys. Batman squirmed

free and ran screaming towards two of the men from No. 5 and No.6.

His wounded friend, trapped and terrified, just screamed.

Paul Adams, face down as warm blood defrosted the cold sheen on the Tarmac, never heard the frantic words of Inspector Waites on his mobile or trembling Spiderman's screams fade to a whimper.

Inside No. 2 a figure watched the reflection of blue flashing lights in the window of the house opposite and a 4x4 screech to a halt at the entrance to the cul-de-sac.

The cavalry are here. Game on.

The next shot blew Paul Adams' head apart.

Chapter 4

Sam glanced at her phone in the hands-free cradle, recognised the control room number, and answered.

'Boss, it's Gary Waites.'

Inspector Gary Waites was unflappable. Sam held him in high regard.

'We've got an update,' he continued. 'Appears three more shots fired. ARV at scene. Inspector, sorry, Acting Chief Inspector Wright at scene.'

Sam fought the urge to let out a heavy sigh.

Gary Waites continued.

'Inner cordon set up at entrance to cul-de-sac, outer cordon set up on Chichester Road. That's your RV.'

'Okay,' Sam said, processing the information, visualising the rendezvous point, voice devoid of emotion. This was a time for cool heads. Police officers were never inspired by panic in the senior ranks.

Sam sounded so calm she could have been conducting a job interview.

'Any update re casualties.'

The pause was only a split second but it was long enough.

'Paul Adams has been shot,' Gary said.

'Shit.'

The line went quiet before Gary spoke again in a hushed voice.

'I heard the shots. Paul kept the line open.'

'You okay?' Sam asked, genuine concern now in her voice.

If Gary Waites was suffering from shock, she would need to question his ability to continue. His role was too important to be compromised by emotion.

'I'm fine.'

'What about Paul?'

Sam heard the deep intake of breath.

'He's not moving, extent of injuries unknown. And there's a child trapped underneath him.'

Jesus Christ…

'Roger that. I'll be there in five.'

Sam made a mental note to maintain a 'watching brief' on Gary's welfare.

'Anything else I need to know?'

'Yes. Chief Inspector Wright doesn't want anybody crossing the inner cordon.'

At a red light she scrolled through her phone and rang Ed.

'What's your ETA,' she asked.

'Two minutes.'

'Paul's been shot.'

'Fuck.'

Ed accelerated hard and overtook a car on the approach to the dual carriageway.

'He's not moving,' Sam was saying now. 'A young child is trapped underneath him. Extent of injuries unknown.'

Ed tried to picture the scene as he concentrated on Sam's words.

'Air Support will provide pictures when they get there. One man is laid in a garden opposite the shooter's address, one in the middle of the road, no signs of movement from either. That's all we've got for now.'

Ed said nothing and ended the call.

He was there in 90 seconds.

———

FRED THOMPSON HAD WITNESSED two fatal traffic accidents in his 69 years and he didn't need all the running and screaming to tell him he had just seen his third.

But as an old boy of the school of life, something this time was making him uneasy as much as sad.

Tours of Cyprus and Bahrain with the 'Paras' in the early sixties had taught him much about human fear, taught him much about being aware of your environment.

The guy who had been hit by the bus was running from someone.

Fred would have guessed it even without spotting the hard man who had been giving chase, but that was the clincher.

He had seen the man and the man knew Fred had seen him.

Fred picked up the blue metal stand showing the day's headlines and prepared to go back into his newsagent shop, turning away as more siren-blaring patrol cars arrived to join the paramedic crew and the gawpers around the bus.

'Nasty accident. People need to watch where they're going.'

Fred had sensed rather than seen him approach, but he knew it was the same man.

'Can I help you?' Fred asked, tugging his green cardigan over fawn corduroy trousers.

Davy Swan was wearing a Ralph Lauren polo shirt stretched taut over what Fred believed to be a steroid-induced torso, the muscle-bound right arm a sleeve of flashy tattoos.

Swan spun his head and looked around the street, a heavy making a little show.

As tough as Fred might once have been, he would be no match for this guy. Not these days anyway and definitely not without a weapon. Best to play the harmless old man.

'Very nasty,' Fred said. 'He never stood a chance.'

Swan turned his eyes back to Fred and gave him an easy smile.

'Whatever you think you saw Mr Magoo, if you're asked, you saw nothing. Understand?'

Fred nodded and watched Swan turn, amble away and slowly melt into the crowd.

Back in the storeroom, Fred buzzed up to his wife on the intercom.

'Let's have a brew,' he told her. 'Something odd's just happened.'

Joyce Thompson listened to Fred's story between slurpy sips of tea and when he had finished, she stretched out her arms and hugged him close.

'You okay?'

'I'm fine,' Fred said. 'Too old to get involved with tough lads like that.'

'You'll call the police, though.'

'Police?'

Joyce gave him a look.

'That poor man was running away from someone.

That someone threatened you. We need help. Sam will know what to do. So, unless you've got a better suggestion Fred Thompson.'

Fred shrugged his shoulders, the familiar resignation on his face, and went to the telephone behind the counter.

'I'll call Sam,' he shouted to Joyce, already walking up the stairs to the flat.

When Fred appeared in their kitchen half an hour later, Joyce was plating up one of his favourites.

She had cooked him liver, pork chop, bacon, sausage, fried egg, fried bread, fried potatoes and beans every Saturday of their married life. Fred insisted she used lard, not sunflower oil and certainly not olive oil, which he had hated since he first tasted it as a young squaddie in Cyprus.

Joyce watched his trembling hands as he sat at the table and reached for the salt, the wall-mounted photograph of him in his military uniform above his head.

'You get hold of Sam?'

Fred aimed his knife and fork at the fry up.

'Left a message on her answerphone.'

Two STATIONARY ARVs, sixty metres apart, blocked Chichester Road and blue tape stretched across the Tarmac like two finishing lines in a marathon.

The entrance to the cul-de-sac was thirty metres away from each ARV. No vehicles or pedestrians were getting past what was now the outer cordon.

Uniformed officers were knocking on the doors within the outer cordon asking everyone to stay inside.

An unmarked police BMW X5 was parked across the entrance to the cul-de-sac. There was no tape there.

Ed had his door open before the tyres stopped rolling.

Two paramedics in their green uniform were sitting in an ambulance next to the outer cordon.

Ed nodded at them as he passed, long strides carrying his broad shoulders and slight beer-belly towards Wright and the black-clad firearms commander.

'What's happening?'

'A shooter in a house firing from the downstairs window,' Wright said, looking up at Ed.

'Do we know who?' Ed asked.

'No.'

Ed waited.

'Any suggestions?' Wright asked.

Ed put his hands in his coat pocket, shook his head. 'I'm not here as a decision maker. I'm the negotiator, I'm —'

Wright didn't wait.

'I was just asking for your contribution,' cheeks already flushing like a blood pressure warning sign.

Ed was in negotiator mode.

'You're in charge,' he told Wright calmly. 'I'm a tactical option like he is.'

He nodded at the firearms commander. 'Alright Fishy.'

Ed liked Gerry Trout: good cop, good laugh, but when it came to firearms operations the ex-Marine was priceless, every possibility carefully considered, as many risks as possible eliminated.

'Sound Ed,' Trout replied, adjusting his police issue baseball cap.

'Can anyone gain access to the cul-de-sac from any other direction?' Sam was quick-marching towards them as she spoke, brown ponytail bouncing against her shoulders.

Ed smiled. In the middle of this her looks and long legs still received admiring glances.

'Potentially,' Wright pointed at the properties to his left.

'The gardens of these houses back onto some of the gardens in the cul-de-sac. The gardens of some of the houses in the cul-de-sac back onto some wasteland. There are two firearm officers there.'

Wright smiled, the supercilious smile of someone saying, 'don't teach your granny how to suck eggs'.

Sam returned the smile. She couldn't think of anyone she despised more.

'How are the casualties?' Sam asked. 'Can we get them out?'

Wright stiffened and thrust out his chest.

'Who made you Silver Commander?'

Gerry Trout bowed his head and took three steps back. Bullets were one thing. He'd been around too long to get caught in verbal crossfire.

Ed didn't move. Before the serious business started, he may as well hang around and watch Sam take 'Never' to the cleaners.

'I'm not Silver. You are. The ACC, Gold, asked me to come here. We'll end up picking this up and one of my people and a youngster are lying in the road injured. So, what do you propose doing about it?'

Wright's face was as purple as a cartoon Ribena blackcurrant.

'We're examining all the options but I will not endanger anyone else.'

Sam knew he was right, as much as it dismayed her to think of Paul and a child left helpless on the street.

Ed spoke: 'Might be worth stepping under that tape and walking ten yards.'

He flicked his head backwards.

Sam and Mick 'Never' Wright glanced behind and saw Darius Simpson, the Seaton Post reporter, striding towards them.

A traffic cop blocked his approach while they stepped under the tape and walked to the inner cordon at the entrance to the cul-de-sac.

Sam swallowed hard at her first sight of Paul Adams in the middle of the road.

She was still staring when a shout came from No.2

'What did he say?' Wright asked.

'I don't know,' Sam said. 'I couldn't hear him. Do we know who's in there?'

Wright shook his head and the same shake followed when Sam asked if he had checked whether there was a landline in the house.

The shoulder shrug when she asked Wright if a no-fly zone had been implemented told her the incident was well beyond his capabilities.

Wright should have demonstrated that he was in command. He should have been making decisions, requesting options from the tactical commanders, drawing up plans to implement those options. He had done nothing.

Sam fought the urge to take command herself. Everyone at the scene needed direction, needed to see the person in charge knew what they were doing, but it was not her role. She would be the post-incident senior investigator.

Sam shook her head, she knew everybody on the ground would be looking at Wright in scorn and despair, a problem when he needed to be leading the solution.

She stepped away, took her mobile out of her pocket and called ACC Monica Teal who was Gold Command.

Sam had a good relationship with Teal, considered her a solid operator with a wealth of investigative experience. She had despised her predecessor, Trevor Stewart, but that slimeball had left to chase the next rank.

Call made, she contacted DC Ranjit Singh and

instructed him to set up an intelligence cell and to use whatever staff was necessary. She told him what she wanted and walked back to the group as Wright's radio crackled into action.

'Control to Inspector Wright.'

Sam heard Gary Waite's calm monotone voice, devoid of any emotion or excitement, come across the airwaves.

'Go ahead.'

'Superintendent Donaldson is en route. He will assume Silver. Can you attend the High Street? There's a fatal. I'll give you more details when you're en route.'

'Roger that.'

Wright glared at Sam.

Sam's poker face stared back.

Chapter 5

THE SHOOTER REMOVED the headgear and flicked on the kettle. The kitchen was in darkness; green blinds drawn, the silhouettes of the A4 sheets of paper covering the walls barely visible.

The Internet was a great resource. No need to watch an American news show or read an American newspaper. Thanks to the Internet and a colour printer, the walls displayed a montage of grief...

32 killed –April 16, 2007 – *Virginia Tech in Blacksburg, Virginia. A gunman, 23-year-old student Seung-Hui Cho, goes on a shooting spree killing 32 people in two locations and wounding an undetermined number of others on campus. The shooter then commits suicide.*

27 killed – December 14, 2012 – *Sandy Hook Elementary School –Newtown, Connecticut. Adam Lanza, 20, guns down 20 children, ages six and seven, and six adults, school staff and faculty, before turning the gun on himself. Investigating police later find Nancy Lanza, Adam's mother, dead from a gunshot wound.*

13 killed – April 20, 1999 – *Columbine High School – Littleton, Colorado. Eighteen-year-old Eric Harris and 17-year-old*

Dylan Klebold kill 12 fellow students and one teacher before committing suicide in the school library.

9 killed – March 21, 2005 – *Red Lake High School, Red Lake, Minnesota. Sixteen-year-old Jeff Weise kills his grandfather and another adult, five students, a teacher and a security officer. He then kills himself.*

8 killed – December 5, 2007 *–In Omaha, Nebraska, 19-year-old Robert Hawkins goes to an area mall and kills eight shoppers before killing himself.*

The shooter poured the hot water over the teabag and walked over to the fridge freezer, put one hand underneath the waist high handle but stopped before pulling it open. The light would illuminate. No point in giving them a shot. Easy decision. Drink the tea black.

———

SAM WALKED AWAY, listened to her voicemail, and then called Fred and Joyce.

Less than an hour ago she'd been in the HQ toilets, day's work almost done, a glass of wine and kids in costumes awaiting. Washing her hands, she'd glanced in the mirror.

It never lied; the face that stared back had lost the vampire pallor and elasticity had finally triumphed over the bags under her eyes. Two weeks off the drink, uninterrupted sleep, and a lack of dead bodies was better than any spa treatment. Who needed a mud bath when you could finally take a break from murder?

Sam accepted the fine lines around her mouth would worsen with age but she couldn't contemplate giving up the cigarettes again. Right now, fighting the cravings was just too much to contemplate.

A non-smoker for four years, the death of a colleague

on another investigation had seen her run back to the welcoming bosom of her nicotine mistress.

'Hi, Fred. Everything okay?

She had met Fred and Joyce when, as a young PC, she attended a robbery in their shop and had kept in contact ever since. The Seaton Post had described Fred as a 'have-a-go-hero' after he bit the knife-wielding attacker.

To this day Sam still wasn't sure who was more shocked; the teenage robber with blood pouring from his forearm or Sam herself. What she found at the shop was nothing she had imagined or expected...and she thought every victim-based scenario had run through her head.

'Hi Sam. Think so.' Fred paused. 'Well, actually not really.'

'What's happened?'

'A man's been knocked down outside the shop. Flattened by a bus. The County Cars are here.'

Sam was struck by the expression. Only fully paid up members of the old school called road policing vehicles County Cars.

'Thing is,' Fred continued, 'he didn't just run in front of the bus. He was being chased.'

The last word focused Sam's mind but she stayed silent, didn't interrupt.

'He ran out of the multi-storey. Proper terrified. Looked like the devil himself was chasing him. Joyce told me to ring you.'

An outsider would struggle to understand, but despite the crisis around her in Malvern Avenue, despite Paul Adams, despite the unknown body in the road, Sam still felt the instant jab of curiosity, the urge that was part of her DNA. She inhaled the cigarette she had just lit.

'About time you were stopping again young lady,' Fred chided.

'Nothing wrong with your ears, Fred.' Sam shrugged, hating the pricks of guilt and failure. 'When did this happen?'

'Just before I rang you.'

So 10 minutes judging by the voicemail, Sam reckoned.

'How long have the police been there?'

'A while. Didn't take them long.'

That makes a change, Sam thought. Response times seemed to be getting worse.

'You're sure he was being chased? It wasn't somebody else just running for the bus?'

Fred's response was immediate. 'The bloke came up to me and....'

'Which bloke? Sam interrupted.

'The one who was chasing. Scottish. Big bugger. Not tall but the bodybuilder type. On the juice no doubt.'

'Steroids?'

'Yeah, that was my thinking anyway. He came right up to me. Told me I hadn't seen anything.'

'Scottish you say?'

'Yeah. Glaswegian. Heard enough of that accent in the Paras to recognise it anywhere.'

'I'll get someone to come and see you.'

Sam turned and saw a Ford Mondeo pull up behind the ambulance. Superintendent Dick Donaldson stepped out of the car, street light catching the silver braid on the peak of his cap as he adjusted it and walked over to Sam. Donaldson's slim 6' foot frame was carried along by shiny black Oxford shoes.

'Fred, I have to dash. I'll come and see you later.'

She ended the call.

'Hi Sam. I thought I'd said goodbye to this sort of thing when I left the Met.'

Dick Donaldson, born and raised on a local council

estate, moved away from Seaton St George to go to university as an 18-year-old, a proud first for his family. From there he had joined the Met and only recently returned to Eastern Police on promotion to Superintendent.

He was a likeable, jovial family man with vast experience, and in the six months since his transfer had already become a favourite of the rank and file.

'I never thought I'd see this in my police career full stop,' Sam said.

They fell silent as they looked at the body of Paul Adams. The whimpers beneath him rose and fell on the cold breeze.

'Right let's get the show on the road Sam. I'm declaring this a major incident and I'm assuming command.'

Sam nodded. She liked decisive people.

'Is that Ed Whelan over there?' Donaldson asked. 'Top bloke. I did my negotiators course with him years ago.'

Together they walked towards Ed and when they were close, Donaldson stretched out his hand in greeting.

'Ed,' he said, stretching out his hand. 'Any contact yet.'

Ed shook his hand.

'Nothing so far other than a muffled shout from the house.'

Donaldson turned to Sam.

'Can you get some of your people to set up an intelligence cell.'

'Already done.'

Dick nodded, smiled, and introduced himself to Gerry Trout.

'I'll just take this,' Sam said and answered her phone. 'Update from the Intelligence Cell,' she said at the end of the call.

'House is occupied by Zac Williams, 22 years, and Lucy Spragg aged 19. She's got no convictions. Williams has form for dishonesty dating back to when he was a juvenile, last arrest two months ago, D and D.'

If Williams is involved he's taken one hell of a leap from drunk and disorderly.

Sam told them Williams was a known cannabis user and that Lucy Spragg had twice made reports of domestic abuse before quickly withdrawing the complaints.

'Williams has a four year-old-son from a previous relationship,' she said. 'No landline in the house and unknown whether Williams or Spragg have mobiles.'

Before Sam could say more, a shout came from No.2.

'What the fuck happens now?'

The voice was controlled, no overtones of panic or rage.

'This is our in,' Dick Donaldson said. 'He obviously wants to speak.

'Ed get your head around what you're going to say to open a dialogue. Gerry, I want a plan for approaching the house.'

They both knew what was coming next.

'I want to get a mobile in to him.'

Chapter 6

DAVY SWAN STROLLED towards the multi-storey, head down, not making eye contact with anyone moving towards the bus and the dead pedestrian. The last thing he wanted was to be remembered and witnesses always remembered runners.

He had stood and watched the activity for ten minutes. The old man hadn't approached the police.

Swan drew on the shaking cigarette until a huge amount of ash dangled from the end. Smoke swirled from his nostrils, a formation of cirrus swirls. He flicked the cigarette away.

The pulse in his neck bulged and he kept balling his hands into fists, the veins in his forearms rising like a 3D road map.

Why had the dozy bastard not waited until they were both next to the sliding door? The whole job would have been clean.

Still, if the old man in the newsagent knew what was good for him, he would keep his mouth shut. And if he didn't…well needs must.

Swan walked back up the stairs.

His passenger was leaning forwards, right arm outstretched, hand pressed against the van for balance, left hand pressing an oily rag against the back of his head.

Swan didn't do sympathy even when he wasn't raging.

'Move away. I'll back out, then jump in.'

Swan muttered 'stupid bastard,' climbed into the driver's seat, turned the ignition key and reversed out of the bay.

Stuck in High Street traffic, he had the driver's window wound down, right elbow sticking out. Blue lights were everywhere, but they weren't interested in them. Not yet anyway.

The congestion meant he had time to watch the police activity: people being ushered away, things written on clip-boards. The newsagent was nowhere to be seen. If the police got around to speaking to the old bugger, the two of them would be long gone.

The police could get a description – years of weights, high protein and steroids made him stick out from the crowd. They may even get the fact that he had a Scottish accent, may even identify him, but so what? Putting him on the street at the same time as the deceased was one thing. Connecting him with the death, something totally different.

He looked around for CCTV. There were cameras but he'd had the foresight to rip off his ski mask and stuff it into his trouser pocket just before he emerged onto the street.

Of course he'd tripped over that stupid kid in the buggy, but whether that was enough to identify him…

The CCTV in the multi storey shouldn't be a problem as he'd kept his head down all the time he was walking back to the van, and the van itself had false plates. The best those cameras would show was a faceless man walking back to the van and a masked man chasing the gimp.

Swan smiled at the bus driver in his uniform sat on the back step of the ambulance, silver foil blanket draped around his shoulders. Thanks to him the fuck up at least had a happy ending.

Time would tell whether The Man would see it that way.

<hr>

ED SQUATTED BEHIND two firearms officers who were in turn crouched behind two ballistic shields. The mini rugby scrum inched its way towards number 2, the helicopter temporarily ordered away from the scene.

Ed, wishing he were six inches shorter, could see nothing other than the backs of the officers in front of him. The officers themselves were looking through a letterbox-sized window near the top of the shield.

I'm getting too old for this, Ed thought, pounding heart thumping against his bulletproof vest.

The vest was one of a number of things in the 'Go Bag' that lived in the boot of his car. Alongside the body armour it contained his ballistic helmet, a woolly hat, pads, post-it notes, pens, cans of pop, energy bars, a packet of cigarettes and matches. Ed had never smoked in his life but could imagine nothing more frustrating than a 'jumper' saying they'd come down in exchange for a cigarette – only for nobody at the scene to have one.

He exhaled loudly. The heavy, pimped, open-faced helmet pushed his neck into his shoulders and his heart continued to pound.

Ed had been stabbed in a surprise attack. That was one thing. Walking towards a firearm that had already been discharged at human targets was something totally different.

He felt like a nervous public speaker: dry mouth, furry tongue, inner cheeks stuffed with cotton wool.

Would he even be able to shout when the time came?

Progress was slow, a hold-your-breath, close your eyes pause after each step, the wait for the crack of a discharged firearm.

It was no more than thirty metres to the point where everybody agreed was close enough to shout, but every forward shuffle ramped up the danger.

Nothing prepares you for this. Training's great, but this is real.

The two firearm officers stopped. The one on Ed's right pushed her left arm backwards and tapped his leg.

That was his cue to start speaking, the reason the helicopter had been temporarily stood down.

Ed inhaled long and slow, ran his tongue around his lips and forced himself to forget the dryness in his mouth. Say the wrong thing now and it wasn't just his life he was endangering.

Another deep breath.

'Hello!' he shouted, keeping his head well below the top of the shields.

They all waited…a 'time stood still' moment where no one was overplaying the danger. They were staring down its throat.

He held his breath and forced his legs to stiffen against the shakes trying to burst from his body.

Nothing.

Another long, slow inhalation of air. He could hear the deep breathing of the firearms pair in front of him and he didn't need to look over his shoulder to know everyone behind him was rigid with tension.

'My name's Ed,' he shouted. 'Can we talk?'

Nothing.

'We couldn't hear what you were shouting. We just want to talk.'

Ed felt two rapid taps on his left thigh, the agreed signal for movement in the house.

He couldn't see the net curtains twitching, but he heard a male voice. 'I said, what the fuck happens now?'

'Look we have a problem here?' Ed shouted. 'Can we talk about it?'

Ed and the AFOs thought they waited over ten seconds for a reply. They waited less than five but five seconds is a long time when you are facing a gun.

'Yeah,' came the reply.

Never assume and never lie…two of the basics of hostage negotiating.

'What do I call you?' shouted Ed.

'Zac.'

Another deep breath.

Use his name as often as possible. Show him he's a person.

'Zac, my name's Ed. Is there a phone number I can call you on?'

Silence.

Ed and his colleagues held their breath, wondering where the gun was, whether they were in the sights of someone who had already killed, someone who in reality had nothing to lose.

'No.'

You haven't got a phone, or you don't want to give me the number?

'Will you allow the uniform officers to bring a phone to your doorstep.'

Another two, three seconds of slow-motion silence.

'You bring it. You've got ten minutes.'

Fuck.

'Okay, one more thing Zac. Can I check on the injured child before I go for the phone?'

Another pause.

'Be quick.'

The athletic looking man was about three metres away from Paul Adams and the youngster.

'Can I check on the other injured?'

'No.'

Bent over and shuffling forwards is difficult; bent over going backwards is even harder.

Ed grabbed the utilities belts of the two firearms officers and guided them. None of the trio wanted to fall over the bodies in the street.

Ed patted their backs when they reached Paul Adams, dropped to his knees, and slowly turned around. There was no need to check if Paul had a pulse. The lifeless eyes staring at him told him everything he needed to know.

Ed blinked away tears and gently rolled Paul to the side. The youngster was breathing but barely conscious.

Ed picked him up, the child's hair, face and Spiderman suit covered in blood and brains, turned to face the backs of his colleagues and began the slow shuffle to the inner cordon.

The other man in the middle of the road wasn't moving, wasn't making a sound.

Once they were inside the inner cordon and out of sight of number 2, the paramedics rushed to take the youngster from Ed's arms.

Ed removed his helmet, bent forward, placed his shaking hands on his knees and gulped in air.

Gerry Trout, the firearms commander, debriefed his personnel. Sam rushed to Ed.

'Jesus Ed you okay?'

She bent down so her head was level with his, relief etched on her face. 'My heart was in my mouth.'

Ed took a few more deep breaths before standing, before speaking. 'I'm fine. How's the bairn?' He loosened his vest.

'Deep flesh wound by the looks. He's lost a lot of blood but he should recover…'

She paused and moved closer to Ed as the helicopter came back overhead.

'Physically that is…mentally? Who knows?'

Even in the poor lighting Sam could see the blood on Ed's hands and chest.

'You should get cleaned up.'

'I'm fine for now.'

Dick Donaldson walked over. 'You okay Ed?'

Ed nodded.

'Great job. I'm sorry you're going to have to do it again.'

Ed nodded again and ran his tongue around his lips. 'Shit happens. We ready to go?'

Donaldson put his hand in his overcoat pocket and took out a basic mobile. 'Just been dropped off by Comms.'

Ed took the mobile, turned to face the inner cordon. 'Ready when you are.'

'I've called out two more negotiators,' Donaldson said. 'Once the phone's delivered another negotiator can take over if you'd prefer. You've already done enough.'

The three of them walked towards Gerry Trout.

'I'm fine. I've started talking to him. Let's leave it like that.'

The tactics were the same. Ed bent down, shuffling behind the two firearms officers and their ballistic shields.

The difference this time was that he was going all the way to the door.

Thirty metres from the house and with the helicopter again out of sight and hearing Ed shouted. 'Zac. It's Ed. Can you hear me?'

'Yes.'

'We are coming to the door with the phone. Is that okay?'

Silence. Was he playing with them? Would he shoot?

Then the voice, a single word. 'Yes.'

Ed closed his eyes, breathed out the fear and signalled to the AFO's with the pre-arranged tap on their backs he was ready to move.

They had already begun shuffling forward when the AFOs' radios crackled.

'Tango 3.'

A firearms officer speaking on the dedicated channel.

'Tango 3 go ahead,' said Control Room.

'Curtains moving in Window 1.'

The front bedroom window of 2 Malvern Close had been designated window 1 in the firearms plan.

'No visual on any persons.'

Ed and the two AFOs paused as planned behind their shields at the path leading to the house.

Ed reached into his inside coat pocket, took out the phone and tapped the backs of the AFOs again.

They had already calculated the length of the path in metres. The video stream from the helicopter had shown there was no debris on the path or in the small garden other than some broken glass. Tripping up was not an option.

Glass crunched under the boots of the AFOs as they shuffled onto the path, the only sound other than their collective breathing.

The plan was simple. Veer left immediately, minimising the shooter's angle of fire.

They reached the corner of the house and got close enough to the door for Ed to slide the phone under the shields and onto the step.

They backed away and carefully inched their way to the inner cordon.

'Tango 3,' crackled the radios, 'Tango 3. Front door opening. Standby, standby.'

The helicopter beamed live feed into the control room. Everyone at the scene held their radios to their ears.

'Tango 3. Door ajar. Stand by...Stand by...What the fuck?'

Chapter 7

FRED THOMPSON WALKED DOWNSTAIRS into the shop in response to the constant knocking. At first he and Joyce thought it was kids, the usual feral gang that hung around the High Street with the sole objective of making peoples' lives a misery, but the knocking went on too long. The little shits would have got bored and looked for a new victim.

He turned on the lights and opened the door to a uniform police officer.

'Mr Thompson. I'm Acting Chief Inspector Wright. Chief Inspector Parker says you have some information about the man who was hit by the bus.'

Fred invited him in, closed the door and told again how he had seen someone chasing the man who was knocked down.

'Are you sure that's what you saw Mr. Thompson?'

Why is he speaking to me like I'm a child?

'Could the other man have been running for a bus?'

He's just going through the motions.

The more Fred thought about it, Wright sounded just

like his doctor, softly spoken and full of concern, but here with a huge dose of condescension thrown in. Another copper not interested, just like the ones who are never interested when you ring about the kids.

'He was chasing the man,' Fred said, 'I know what I saw, but let's just forget it.'

If you showed a fraction of Sam's interest I'd tell you about the guy threatening me, but I'm not sticking my neck out for the likes of you.

'Mr Thompson, stressful events can play tricks on your mind.' Wright wore a smile that tried and failed to look sincere. 'I believe you saw what you think you saw, but whether your interpretation of events was correct, well, that's a different matter.'

He still had the smile as Fred opened the door, thanked him for coming and watched him walk away.

Stressful events? I was a Para. You've got no idea.

⸻

THE TRANSIT WAS BACK in the out-of-town lock-up, false plates removed.

Davy Swan leant against the back doors and tapped out a text.

Package destroyed but not as planned.

He pressed 'send' then turned to Jimmy Marshall, sitting on an old oil drum, rag still pressed against his head. 'You need to go to hospital with that.'

'Screw that. Too many questions. You can sort it.'

Marshall stood up, walked over to an old grey freestanding filing cabinet and opened the top draw.

'Here.'

He handed Swan an almost empty, dusty bottle of whisky and a desktop stapler.

Davy Swan jammed the bottle under his armpit and flicked open the stapler. There were a few staples left.

'Lean forward then. Let's have a look.'

The wound was deep, four inches long.

'Just as well you're a bald bastard,' Swan scowled, no humour just simmering rage.

He poured whiskey into the gash, grinned at Marshall's howl, and started with the stapler.

Eight staples and eight 'fuckin' hells' later he admired his handiwork.

'Good as new,' he lied, imagining the ugly scar that would be Marshall's forever badge to fuck-up and stupidity.

Hard earned and well deserved, shit-for-brains.

Swan opened his phone at the sound of the text alert and read the message.

Speak later.

He turned back to Marshall who was tentatively running his forefinger across the staples.

'Why the fuck did you let him get out of the van before I was there?'

'I fucked up. Sorry, but the job got done.'

Swan put the bottle and stapler back into the draw and slammed it shut.

'No thanks to you,' he shouted. 'How many people have you heard committing suicide by running in front of a fucking bus?'

Marshall bowed his head, the wound like a jagged mountain range.

'None,' Swan was flying. 'That's how many.'

He kicked the tyre of the van, lit a cigarette and let the rant roll out like river rapids.

'Jump in front of a train yeah, no worries, but a fucking bus! He was supposed to throw himself off the multi-storey and he wouldn't have been the first. That was the plan; that's what the Man wanted.'

Marshall stared at the concrete floor as Swan kept lashing.

'The cops will find the suicide note but shit, even the thickest of that lot will think the whole thing stinks.'

'I've said sorry. What more do you want?'

Davy Swan, for the first time, felt a grain of pity.

'It's not me you need to apologise to, is it.'

THE MAGNITUDE of the police response was like a giant machine plugged into the main frame, every last part oiled and lubricated and moving smoothly into action as personnel from the specialist departments joined the siege operation.

From top to bottom, everyone knew their role. Major Incident responses were tested in joint high-pressure training drills with other emergency services, the council-led Emergency Planning Department, and sometimes even trainee reporters to make the whole thing as real as possible.

But nobody could do their job until they were in place and with the right equipment. That was what took the time; that was what caused creaks and groans in the machine.

Two Technical Support Unit officers – the vital TSUs – arrived at the outer cordon driving the Forward Command Vehicle. From the outside it looked like a family motorhome. Internally it was a mobile communication centre.

It didn't take long for TSU to have the command vehicle functioning. A pair of TV monitors showed the live stream from the helicopter and a control room sergeant sat inside to man the designated radio channel for those at the scene.

Dick Donaldson, Sam, Ed and Gerry Trout were hunched around a table in the vehicle.

'Okay,' Donaldson said. 'Ed let's start with the negotiators. They all here yet?'

'In the back office.'

The small self-contained space at the back of the command vehicle would be used by the negotiators, away from everybody else, away from interruption.

Donaldson nodded and continued. 'Ed, you already know the objectives.'

Ed nodded. Nothing needed to be said…prevent further loss of life, prevent further harm, bring about a successful resolution. That was always the challenge and always in that order.

'Sam when this is all over, you're going to be in charge of the post incident investigation,' Donaldson said. 'Please don't think I'm trying to get rid of you, but I suggest you go home and get some rest. Once Ed's brought this to a resolution, you're going to be busy.'

'Agree.' Sam knew he was right.

She glanced at Ed and saw the tension playing across his face. He would be at the sharp end when it came to any 'resolution,' successful or not.

'I'll discuss firearms options with Gerry,' Donaldson was wrapping up the briefing. 'Ed can you go and make contact with Zac?'

'Of course.'

Ed pushed his chair backwards and stood up.

Donaldson shuffled in his seat then sat up straight, back rigid.

'Be mindful of his psychological state Ed. I don't want

any of Gerry's team having to pull the trigger if I can help it.

'We've both done the negotiators course. I don't want a 'Suicide by Cop.''

'You and me both,' Ed said, walking away.

Their negotiator training meant they both knew the stats. The first 'Suicide by Cop' verdict in a UK Coroner's Court came in 2003 and made headlines, something new and shocking.

Ed had been taught to spot the signs; knew the data from American researchers. In 87% of 'suicide by cop' cases, the deceased made prior threats of suicide.

Ed reached the back office. Crammed inside the tiny space were three more negotiators, each with a specific role.

Ed was Number 1. He would speak to Zac.

'Ready?' Ed said, squeezing into a plastic chair opposite Sergeant Jenny Smith.

No words, just nods. They all put on headphones.

Jenny Smith was there, as the Number 2 negotiator, her role to support and encourage Ed.

All four, in passing the national negotiators course, had demonstrated the most important quality needed – the ability to listen.

Jenny pushed her black fringe under her headphones and gave Ed the thumbs up.

Ed dialled the mobile.

It answered on the third ring.

'Is that you Zac?' Ed asked.

'Yes.'

The single word was rapid and Ed heard quick, heavy breathing. Panic could easily follow.

'I can see lots of guns,' Zac panted.

Ed had anticipated this.

A negotiator never lies.

'Of course we have guns Zac,' he told him. 'People have been shot. We want to keep people safe. We want to keep you safe.'

Another thumbs up from Jenny.

Charles Edwards, a Detective Inspector on the fast track promotion scheme, was writing furiously. As the Number 4 negotiator he was the note taker.

Ed wiped his brow. The body heat from the four negotiators squeezed into the tight, windowless space was sending the temperature soaring.

Maybe the cords weren't such a good idea.

'Zac, this can all be resolved by you coming out of the house.'

Silence but the line was still open.

Ed, voice quiet, soothing almost, could have been reading a bedtime story to a child.

'How have we got here Zac? What's happened?'

Jenny gave him another thumbs up.

Everyone in the room knew this was the start of getting into Zac Williams' psyche.

In the heavy silence, the negotiators waited.

When Zac Williams finally spoke, his words were hurried and demanding, like a teenager in a strop.

'I want a burger, make that two, with fries and tomato sauce.'

'Okay I'll ask,' Ed said slowly.

'Why the fuck can't you say yes or no?'

Williams was loud, aggressive but Ed remained impassive.

'I don't make the decisions Zac.'

'Put the fucker on the phone who does then,' Williams shouted.

'It doesn't work like that Zac. You talk to me and I talk to them.'

Ed was laying the foundations.

This is how it works Zac. Everything comes through me, but you get nothing from me.

When he broke another short silence, the edge in Williams' voice had dulled even if the strop remained.

'I want coke as well. Diet. Two. Large.'

'Okay. I'll ask. Zac is anybody else in the house with you?'

The negotiators picked up on the hesitation.

'No'

'What about Lucy?'

Williams' response was agitated, words again loud and fast.

'She's not here. She's at her mother's. No more talking until you tell me about the burger.'

He hung up.

Ed rose quickly from his chair and pushed open the door. They all craved a rush of air.

Dick Donaldson, who had been listening on a fifth set of headphones, popped his head around the door frame.

'Good work everybody. The burgers are sorted and I've got crews out looking for Lucy. Let's see if Zac is telling the truth.'

Jules Merson, the youngest negotiator, was writing on the whiteboards. Her role as Number 3 was to keep the boards up to date.

She had three columns, each with a title.

What do we know?

What do we need to know?

What have we done for the Subject?

The board acted as a quick visual for Ed.

Ed raised his arms high above his head, stood on his tiptoes, and finally asked the question everyone had been thinking. 'Why is he dressed as a white rabbit?'

Chapter 8

SAM DROVE into the town centre, parked the car and called Fred.

She walked past the scene of the fatal, the road still closed while traffic officers took photographs, searched for tyre marks, measured distances. The body had been removed, although the bus was still in situ.

A traffic officer approached Sam with a smile. 'Alright boss.'

'Hi,' she said, trying to remember his name. Jim? John? She gave up. 'Nasty.'

'Didn't stand a chance.'

He glanced over his shoulder. 'Running in front of a bus is never a good idea.'

'Any ID?' Sam asked.

'Nothing on him. No wallet or anything. His clothing's been searched at the mortuary.'

'Strange, not having anything on him.'

'Nothing apart from a suicide note in his pocket.'

Sam had been looking towards the bus but now she snapped her eyes back.

'What does that say?'

'I don't know. I've never seen it. Just what I've been told.'

'Okay,' Sam said. 'Thanks. I'm just popping into Thompsons, the newsagent, check on how they are. I know Fred witnessed it.'

Sam didn't have to tell him what she as doing or where she was going, and the PC was never going to ask, but the decision had been deliberate.

She knew it would get back to Wright.

Sam took five steps, turned around and asked: 'Any suggestion he was being chased?'

The traffic officer almost snapped to attention, hands by his sides, the instant reaction born of self-preservation when a boss was asking a question and you didn't know the answer.

A headshake and an open mouth followed by a six-word reply.

'None that I am aware of.'

Minutes later she was sitting in the kitchen, Fred's empty plate, stained with grease and brown sauce, in front of him.

Still alert and physically fit for his age, Fred told Sam and anyone else who would listen the 'five a day' message was a sham perpetuated by the 'nanny state' and the 'swampy type tree huggers' who would have everybody living on nuts and berries. The only vegetables he ate were potatoes, carrots and peas.

'Good enough for my parents and grandparents. Got through the war on them they did.'

You and Ed Whelan should form a club.

She glanced around the room with its units and décor from the set of a seventies sitcom and smiled as she sat down. The kitchen had never seen spaghetti or garlic bread, all 'Johnny Foreigner muck' in Fred's eyes. Fish and chips, battered in beef dripping, was the only take-away that crossed the threshold. Indian and Chinese was not for the Thompsons. Even on his foreign tours with the Paras, Fred had always lived off the food in the NAAFI.

Refilling the dark brown glazed teapot, Joyce glanced at Sam and the wall-mounted photograph of Fred in his military uniform before carrying the teapot and cups to the table.

'So what happened?' Sam asked, as Joyce joined them.

Fred put his hands on the seat of his chair, pushed himself up and sat to attention. He was speaking to someone in authority and would do it with the respect her rank deserved. Old habits.

He told Sam what he had seen…the man running from the car park, although he seemed to be hobbling on his right leg, the other chasing him, the impact with the bus and the other man turning around and going back to the entrance of the multi-storey car park.

'You sure about him being chased?'

'Not you as well.'

His eyes dropped, he stared at the table, and fidgeted with the frayed cuff of his cardigan. His voice was quieter but firm.

'Come on Sam. I might not be as a young as I once was, but I know what I saw. Don't treat me like that other pillock did?'

'Which pillock?'

'The inspector.'

Sam nodded slowly, realisation dawning, an image of the exchange between Fred and Wright in her mind; Wright paying lip-service and nothing more.

Pillock is the least of it.

'Why were you on the street?'

'Getting ready to close. Bringing the boards in.'

'On the phone you said the chaser looked like he had been on steroids.'

Fred nodded. 'Yeah, not a tall lad, but very broad.

He told Sam again how the man had confronted him, had spoken with a Glaswegian accent, and what he could remember of his clothes,

'Okay, we'll check CCTV,' Sam told him. 'He shouldn't be too hard to spot.'

She was getting ready to leave when she saw a copy of The Post folded in half on the kitchen bench. The front page headline was partly obscured but Sam could see enough to fire that inbuilt curiosity again.

'Can I have a quick look?'

She opened the paper and read the headline.

MY DAD'S DEATH WAS NO ACCIDENT
Grieving daughter slams 'sham' police investigation.

Sam's face didn't alter but she mentally raced through her recent investigations. She couldn't recall any unexplained deaths that had been 'written off' as an accident.

'Nature calls,' Fred stood and hitched his fawn corduroy trousers under his green cardigan.

Sam felt a soft rush of affection when she saw his faded, red leather slippers as he left the room

Joyce spoke once Fred was gone.

'He's adamant about what he saw Sam. Adamant. Wasn't happy with the inspector. Fred might be stuck in his ways but that's no reason to treat him like a child.'

Joyce picked up her china cup but didn't drink.

'I know. I apologise for the officer's insensitivity.'

'No need for you to apologise pet. You didn't do it. I'll make another cuppa.'

Joyce stood up and smoothed her frayed white apron.

'I could do with a new pinny Santa if you're listening.'

Sam unfolded the newspaper, made a mental note to buy Joyce a couple of new aprons, and began to read the story.

THE FAMILY OF BILL REDWOOD, the well-known local yachtsman discovered dead in Seaton St George Marina two months ago, is demanding a review into the police investigation.

Bill's 35-year-old daughter Megan said her father, a qualified Royal Yachting Association Yachtmaster examiner, would never have fallen between the jetty and his yacht while it was berthed in his home marina.

Bill's family and close friends at the Seaton St George Yacht Club have always condemned the speed of the police investigation, claiming it was rushed and focused on a fall and nothing else.

The call for a review has been backed by the family's local MP, Harvey Slattery.

An inquest has been opened and adjourned, but a full inquest has yet to be held.

Eastern Police have remained tight-lipped about the investigation. A spokesman said today they could not comment until after the inquest, but that their investigation was complete and a report had been forwarded to the coroner.

SAM FINISHED the article and took a fresh cup of tea from Joyce. She promised Fred she would get the CCTV checked.

'See that in this morning's paper,' Fred said. 'Patients

paying £30 to have a conversation on the computer with a doctor.'

'Skype,' Sam said.

'Whatever it's called it's bloody ridiculous. All because you can't get in to see a doctor. Health service is a damn disgrace and all the immigration doesn't help.'

Sam didn't have time to listen to another 'state of the nation' speech. She got enough of those from Ed

Her mind was now on Megan Redwood.

Why does she want a review? What does she know that we don't?

Whatever else was going on Sam knew that this would land on her desk.

The piece was written by Darius Simpson. He owed her a favour, especially after the double page spread on the serial rapist. He must know something. He's asking for a review on the family's behalf. She recalled the initial incident and knew that it was Mick Wright's case.

Sam said her goodbyes and left with the copy of The Post.

Back on the street she pondered the headline. She could get Megan's address from Darius. No point in tipping off Wright by getting it from the coroner's file.

She conjured up an image of Wright, full of pompous self-importance and disrespect for an old man who had served his country. The strength of her anger surprised her.

'Leave it with me Fred,' Sam said to herself.

ED and the other negotiators sat in silence in the cramped room, eight eyes staring at the wall-mounted clock, everyone wondering whether its batteries were running low.

Ed was thankful he didn't have to deliver the food to the house. That had been handled by two firearms officers who approached the front door and left the burgers and cokes on the step.

Ed had kept Zac talking on the phone, told him when it was safe to collect the food.

The time for the next call was 20 minutes after the delivery.

Charles Edwards stood up, slipped the fingers of each hand through the handles of four mugs and took them outside. Keeping the small space clinical and clean was vital.

It was time.

Jenny watched Ed.

Jules was stood by the boards.

Charles was back, pen hovering over the notepad.

Ed called the mobile.

'How was your food Zac?'

'Cold.'

Jules Merson raised her eyebrows.

'Sorry about that, but we had to go into the town centre to collect it and then bring it to you.'

Thumbs up from Jenny.

They heard the slurping sound of the last remnants of the coke being sucked through a straw, then a big intake of breath.

'Will Lucy be alright?'

'I don't know Zac. Is she with you?'

'I don't know where she is!' Zac screamed.

The negotiators jumped and pulled the headphones away from their ears at the sudden, piercing volume.

As they all readjusted them, they heard his sobs.

'Zac?' Ed said.

Each word that followed was punctuated by a wet, hitched breath.

'Is she not at her mam's?'

Lucy's mother hadn't seen her today. An officer was with Jean Spragg, firstly, to see if her daughter turned up and more importantly, to stop Jean Spragg storming to the scene and screaming abuse at the man she despised.

Jean had been beaten up every Friday or Saturday of her married life. It was always one of those nights, never both. Every Thursday she would wonder how bad it would be, which night it would happen. She always hoped for Friday. That meant she could enjoy the rest of the weekend with Lucy. Saturdays were never as good if she hadn't been assaulted on Friday. Being spared on Friday only meant she knew what was coming. Sooner or later.

The beatings finally stopped once he developed cirrhosis of the liver. He died an agonising death, although as far as Jean was concerned his last breath came too soon and not slowly enough.

She didn't want Lucy to suffer the same cycle of abuse.

Jean had given the officer Lucy's mobile number but it had gone straight to answerphone.

'She's not there Zac,' Ed said now. 'Her mam's not seen her.'

Ed waited.

The thin hand on the clock inched through seven seconds that felt like seventy.

'Lying cow.'

'Who?'

'Jean. Never liked me. Couldn't lie straight in bed. She'll have seen Lucy.'

'We'll go back and check again.' Ed let his words sink in, allow Zac time to realise that Ed believed him.

'Zac, we think there may be other people injured. We would like to go and check on them. Would that be okay…'

Ed didn't finish the sentence but listened to Zac Williams wail like a hundred mourners at a funeral.

Eventually Zac spoke.

'I see any fucker come into this street and I'll shoot.'

Chapter 9

THE SENSIBLE THING for Sam to do was to go home and rest. Dick Donaldson was right. But she couldn't, not yet. Ed was at the scene and she had staff working in the Intelligence Cell.

She walked into the command vehicle.

'Can't keep away Sam?' Donaldson asked.

'Something like that. I just thought I'd pop in. How's it going?

'He's talking. Don't know if there's anyone else in the house. Can't trace his girlfriend.'

'What does he want?' Sam asked.

'No idea yet.'

Donaldson ran his fingers threw his wispy, ginger hair, the overhead light highlighting the freckles on his hand.

'Why the hell is he dressed as a white rabbit?' he said.

Sam leaned slightly to her left, put her hand on the table and crossed her right foot over her left. The live feed on the screen behind Dick showed two males laid in the middle of the road, another in a garden.

Sam's eyes held on Paul and she involuntarily breathed deep.

Why didn't you just go home Paul?

What did Ed always say to the young detectives?

'Women will pull you further than dynamite will blow you'.

She shook her head, top teeth biting her bottom lip. Paul Adams was dead because he was cheating. She cursed his stupidity. Why did men do it?

Sam had met Paul's wife Erica once at a retirement party. She was nice.

Why hadn't she been enough? Sam suspected plenty of men cheated not just for the sex. For some, the boost to their ego and the thrill of deceit was like a drug. Rarely, Sam reckoned, did love lead them astray.

Visiting Paul's wife wouldn't be easy but she couldn't leave it to others. One of the couple's friends, a serving detective, was sitting with Erica now but it was only right Sam answered the hard question, the elephant in the room question.

'*What was he doing there?*'

Once the affair came out, there was every chance Erica would accuse Sam of knowing about it all along or worse still, engineering his work so he could see the other woman.

And whatever Sam thought of Paul and his choices, the girl he was seeing must have felt something for him, even if it was only lust. Her shock, grief maybe, would be no less real. He had walked out of her house and been killed. Sam would have to visit her too.

Sam blinked and considered Donaldson's question.

'Normally I would say to conceal his identity. But where's he going? This will only end up one of two ways. He gives himself up or he's shot.'

'Let's hope it's the first Sam.'

She stood up straight, eyes firmly fixed on the screen.

'Unless he's sending a message to somebody?'

Sam needed a cigarette and Donaldson was right. There was nothing she could do here.

'On my way home I'll call in and see Jean Spragg. I know her from old. Dealt with a couple of domestics back in the day.'

She left the command vehicle and got into her Audi.

She loved the car but maybe it was time for a change.

Fifteen minutes later a young PC opened the front door of Jean Spragg's house.

Jean had received a phone call telling her to expect DCI Parker and she leapt to her feet as soon as she saw Sam.

'Oh no,' she wailed. 'You being here can mean only one thing.'

She fell backwards onto the brown corduroy armchair.

The heat from the gas fire, overpowering the tiny living room, punched Sam in the gut.

She unbuttoned her coat and sat in the only vacant chair. The young PC stood.

'It's not like that Jean.'

Sam tried to get comfortable in the chair but the springs had long lost their mojo.

'I've popped round because we know each other, nothing more, although naturally we are keen to trace Lucy.'

Jean looked up, rubbed her eyes. 'I don't know where she is and there's no answer from her mobile.'

'Does Zac have a mobile?' Sam said.

'Seriously?' Jean gave Sam her best village idiot look. 'Who doesn't have a mobile these days?'

'Don't suppose you know the number?'

'You suppose right.'

Sam looked at her, a Jean she'd not seen before and it was nothing to do with the shooting.

She'd lost weight and the lines around her eyes seemed to have lessened but it was the striking clothes and make-up that grabbed Sam's attention: red jumper, black pencil skirt, bright red lipstick, heavy, black mascara.

She would never have been able to dress like that when Bobby Spragg was alive and she wouldn't have been able to wear those new mules for long. They'd have been taken off her the first time she did something wrong.

'Anything you can tell us Jean, anything that might help us?'

'I don't know. I haven't seen her today. I hoped she might pop into the pub later.' She shook her head. 'Fat chance. I haven't met her in the pub for ages, not without that bastard in tow anyway. I was going out with some of the lasses tonight.'

Sam smiled inside, pleased that Jean was at last able to go out with friends.

Jean leaned forward, stomach touching her thighs and started heaving. Her back was shaking and then the coughing began, coughing that started in the mules.

Sam watched.

I need to give up smoking.

The coughing fit had barely finished before Jean fumbled in a fake leopard skin print handbag for her cigarettes. 'Want one?' she said to Sam, holding out the packet.

'I'll have one of mine if you don't mind,' Sam said, as Jean's red lips puckered around the filter.

'I don't know anything Sam. I never liked that Zac Williams. Not much better than our lad.'

Jean turned her head away and imitated spitting on the purple carpet.

'Hopefully the devil's making his afterlife a nightmare.'
She grinned.

Sam saw the two front teeth that he'd knocked out years ago had been replaced, something else new, bought no doubt after his death.

They inhaled and exhaled, cigarette smoke making the room even more oppressive. The young PC carefully opened the door and took a small backward step into the hall.

'I kept telling Lucy to leave him. That he wasn't right for her.' Jean leaned forward in the chair.

'She's a good-looking girl with a good head on her shoulders Sam. She can do better than that bastard.'

Jean drew on her cigarette before continuing.

'The lads used to flock around her when she was in the pub you know, not that she gets out these days.'

'I can imagine,' Sam said. 'Did she take any of them up on it?'

Jean sat back in the chair, pushed smoke through her puffed cheeks towards the yellowing ceiling.

'She's not like that, Sam… She wouldn't go behind his back.'

It was Sam's turn to lean forward.

Conscious of the movement, Jean looked away from the ceiling and met Sam's eyes.

'This isn't the time to be taking the moral high ground Jean. We need to find Lucy.'

Sam left the words hanging, stared at Jean.

'If you know anything?'

Jean took a deep breath, tapped the cigarette over the ashtray.

'There was one lad. Marcus. Nice lad. Posh really. She'd seen him a few times.'

'How? I thought she never got out.'

'You can always get out Sam, even if it's only now and then. You just need to be a bit more creative in your lies. Hide clothes somewhere.'

'Surname?'

'I can't remember. Tall lad. Fit.'

She saw Sam's expression.

'Not like that!' Jean said.

She laughed, a throaty laugh that some would call dirty.

'You know. As in played sport fit, not I fancy him fit.'

'Anything else?' Sam said.

'Drove a very nice car. Dropped her off here once. I met him. Like I said, nice lad.'

'What kind of car?'

'Sporty thing, soft top, two door. Sports car. Bright blue. Really bright…more of an electric blue I suppose.'

Sam's face was impassive as she recalled the street and relived the helicopter feed…Paul and the child outside Zac Williams' house, and the bright blue Porsche Boxster parked further up the street.

'WHAT ABOUT SENDING him a drink that's laced with sleeping pills?' Dick Donaldson said.

He was standing in the doorway of the negotiators' room.

Charles was writing his notes, Ed and Jenny preparing for the next call.

'Might work, but if it goes tits-up,' Ed said, 'and we don't know yet if there's anybody else in the house, we put them in danger.'

Ed paused, rubbed his eyes, looked at the clock.

'Let's see if we can talk him out first, he said. 'Try using his kid as an angle. Do we know his name?'

'Elwood.'

The negotiator's eyes locked on Donaldson's.

'Sorry?' Ed said.

'New one on me too.'

Donaldson told them officers had contacted the mother of Zac Williams' child. Both she and the boy were safe. Elwood went to nursery, loved playing with his toy cars.

'Get into his head if you can Ed.'

Ed nodded, picked up the phone. Donaldson closed the door.

Ed looked at his fellow negotiators. 'Show time.'

The phone rang twice.

'Zac, it's Ed. Can we talk about how we got here?'

Silence.

'Zac somebody's been to see Elwood.'

The response was immediate.

'How is he?'

Thumbs up from Jenny.

Charles shuffled himself straight, adjusted his hard-backed 'Black n Red' A4 size notebook.

'All he wants to do is play with his toy cars apparently,' Ed said.

'Yeah he loves them.'

Thumbs up again from Jenny.

Williams seemed keen to talk about his son.

'Four-years-old. Bet those years flew by.'

'Yeah they did.'

'Only seems two minutes ago they were in nappies.'

Zac laughed. 'Yeah.'

Ed resisted asking how often Williams saw the boy.

If the contact between them was minimal, he could get

angry again. Every sentence, every word, had the potential to inflame the situation.

'What do you like doing with him?' Ed said instead.

'He loves football. We go to the park. I just got him a radio-controlled car; he loves that.'

'I bet he does. I love them.'

Williams laughed again.

Charles' pen was a blur across the page, Jules was writing on the whiteboard – filling up the, 'What do we know column'.

'What does he call you? Dad, daddy, fatha?'

'Daddy, but I'm sure that'll change when he gets to proper school.'

'Probably.'

'Can you bring him here?' Williams asked.

Ed was ready for the question, had anticipated it from the moment Dick Donaldson suggested using the Elwood angle.

Various case studies highlighted bringing a family member to the scene was a huge no-no. If the shooter wanted to go out in a blaze of glory, they often wanted to do it in front of a loved one.

'This is no place for a child Zac. People injured in the street, police officers with guns, you in there. What we could do...' Ed paused, let Williams anticipate the rest of the sentence.

'What we could do is fix up a meet once this has been sorted and we're all away from here.'

Another immediate response, aggressive this time.

'You're lying.'

Ed kept his own voice calm.

'What benefit do I get from lying?'

'Well how do I know you're not? I've never met you. What have you ever done for me?'

Jules waved her hand at Ed, pointed at the board once she had his attention. More specifically she pointed at the 'What have we done for subject' column and ran her hand up and down it.

Ed nodded at her.

'You're right we've never met, we don't know each other, but in the short time we've been talking I've done quite a lot for you Zac.'

Ed focused on the boards.

'I got you a phone in there so we could talk instead of shouting out of windows.'

Ed paused.

'You wanted two burgers and coke. I got you them. I didn't lie when I said I had to ask someone, but you got your burgers and coke. Am I right?'

The aggression had ebbed.

'Yeah.'

'I asked if we could look at the injured child. You agreed. I didn't look at anybody else, did I?'

'No.'

Ed slid down his chair, leaned back, stretched out his legs and looked up at the motorhome roof.

'So, I've done quite a lot for you and I've never lied. Why would I lie now?'

'Because you want all this to stop.'

'Me lying to you won't make this stop will it?'

'Suppose not.'

'This will stop when you're ready for it to be stopped. I'm happy to sit and talk to you until you're ready.'

The line went dead.

'BUT YOU CAN'T REMEMBER his surname,' Sam asked.

'No. I think he might have had two surnames; you know like posh buggers do,' Jean said.

'Did Lucy send you any photographs of them together?'

'She might have done. I can check my phone as you leave, it's in the hall.'

Sam smiled. 'Great. Well thanks anyway Jean.'

She pushed herself out of the armchair. 'The officer will stay with you. As soon as we hear anything, we'll let you know.'

Jean was on her feet as well. 'Can I not go down there Sam?'

'It won't help anybody Jean, least of all you. As soon as we hear anything, I'll let you know and I promise we'll keep looking for Lucy.'

'She'll be okay Sam, won't she?'

Sam wanted to say yes, but she was getting a bad feeling about where this was going.

'Let's hope so.'

There was a small table in the tiny hall. Sam hadn't given it a second glance on the way in. She picked up Jean's phone and handed it to her.

Jean scrolled through the iPhone. 'Here.'

She passed the phone back to Sam who stared at the picture of Lucy and Marcus in the Porsche. A young couple, all white teeth and laughter.

'Can I send this to my phone?' asked Sam.

'Sure.'

Sam's fingers danced over the screen and she heard her own phone ping as it received the photograph.

She hit the screen lock on Jean's phone and was putting it back on the table when her eyes went wide.

Sam stared at the image on the Home screen, her pulse quickening the longer she looked.

She turned the phone to face Jean.

'Who's in the photograph?'

'Our Lucy.'

'I can bloody see that,' Sam snapped, her impatience obvious to the nervous young PC hovering in the background.

'Don't you have a go at me,' Jean said, cheeks reddening at the rebuke.

'Sorry.'

Jean took hold of the phone, looked at the photograph.

'Gorgeous isn't she? That was a great outfit, fancy dress party last New Year at the next door neighbour's. Wonder Woman. Got the figure for it don't you think?'

Count to ten Samantha.

'Definitely. Who's that next to her?'

Sam leaned across and pointed at the screen where Lucy Spragg had her tattooed left arm draped across the white rabbit's shoulder.

'Who do you think? Zac. I can't stand the thought of him being on my phone but it's such a good photo of our Lucy, and you can't see his face so I can put up with it. He could be anybody.'

'Can I borrow your phone Jean. Take it away. I'll only have it for a few days.'

'What if our Lucy rings?'

'We'll let you know.'

'Will it help?'

'It might Jean, it might. What's the story about Zac's fancy dress?'

Jean tutted, glanced upwards for dramatic effect.

'All idiots them Williams'. I knew his father… and his grandfather. His father was mad on that film. Zac too. Zac's named after the film.'

'There's a film called Zac?'

'His middle name stupid. Harvey. His middle name's Harvey, after the Jimmy Stewart film.'

Sam face was blank. 'You've lost me.'

'Zac's kid's named Elwood after the character Jimmy Stewart played in that film. Elwood Dowd. Harvey was a white rabbit.'

Chapter 10

SWAN ANSWERED THE PHONE. Marshall, who he'd christened Staples, sat in the passenger seat alongside him. They were parked up in a non-descript Ford Mondeo that had been bought for cash in Scotland a few weeks earlier in a no questions asked deal where Swan had provided a false name and address. He wasn't interested in receiving a DVLA log book and hadn't bothered with tax.

The Man wanted a car that wouldn't attract attention, a cheap car that could be burned when the job was done.

Swan held the phone to his ear, waited, didn't speak.

'What went wrong?'

No 'hello', no 'how are you?' Straight into it, the tone tight with accusation.

'You okay speaking on the phone?' Swan asked.

'Let me worry about the phones. You start worrying about the content of your text message…the package was destroyed but not as planned?'

Swan gulped, explained everything from the kidnapping to the target making a run for it and being splattered by the bus.

The response was short, quiet and aggressive. 'Wankers.'

Swan felt the venom. Best not to respond.

'Were you spotted?'

Swan frantically searched for an answer. Getting the plan wrong was one thing. Admitting there may be a witness was a totally different proposition, one that could see him 'rubbed out' as The Man liked to say.

'Well?' the question wasn't going away. 'Were you spotted or not?'

He couldn't rely on Marshall's discretion. He was responsible for the deceased making a run for it, but if he could deflect any blame he would.

'I had to have a word with the old guy at the newsagent. I knew he'd seen me.'

Swan heard the intake of breath, braced himself for the onslaught.

'Fucking brilliant. This was meant to be in and out. Nobody to know we were even here. Now you may as well have put an advert in the Seaton bloody Post.'

Swan waited for the temper to subside.

'This newsagent,' the voice back under control. 'Will he talk?'

Swan knew the ice beneath him was wafer thin. He didn't want to be thrown off a multi-storey car park...or even a yacht for that matter.

'He was terrified. He won't say fuck all.'

Swan wished he were as confident as he sounded.

Marshall turned his head and stared at him, wide-eyed and open-mouthed. Swan could drop them both in the shit if he wasn't careful.

'Which cops were there?'

'Just uniform.'

'No CID?'

'No. Why would there be? It was just a road accident.'

'Let's hope it stays that way. If the likes of that Parker bird starts putting her nose in then things might take a turn for the worse.'

Swan swallowed hard. Sam Parker was well known in their circles. She'd got the Skinners charged, something that an army of cops had failed to do for years, a proper blow against organised crime.

The Man continued: 'Right, I'll be done in a few hours. Get ready to pick me up. Make sure there's food on board. I don't want to be stopping and getting picked up on some service station CCTV.'

Alright for me to get picked up on some supermarket cameras though, Swan thought. Not that he would say that. Better to pull a hat down low, turn his collar up and do what he was told.

'Anything in particular you want?'

'Surprise me. And get some coke. Diet.'

Thanks a lot. When I buy the wrong stuff, you can have another go at me.

'Wait for my call.'

The phone was disconnected.

'Well?' Marshall asked, licking his lips, shuffling in his seat, wishing he was anywhere but here.

'You heard,' Swan said. 'He's not happy, and just when you think it can't get any worse, you need to think about what you're getting the fussy twat to eat.'

Sam sat in her car and fiddled with the climate control, setting the temperature and fan speed to high.

Jean Spragg was watching, head pushed through the curtains.

Sam scrolled through the contacts in her phone. She needed to make two calls.

'Dick, it's Sam. Just a quick one.'

Dick Donaldson confirmed the Porsche Boxster was still in the cul-de-sac and arranged for an immediate check on PNC – the Police National Computer.

'Comes back to Marcus Worthington-Hotspur.'

'That's him,' Sam said. 'He's been seeing Lucy Spragg.'

'Don't tell me this all comes from a bloody domestic?'

'Do we ever know what starts these, what tips people over the edge?'

Sam reached into the centre console and took a Marlboro out of the packet. 'It's nearly 30 years since Michael Ryan …'

'Don't even go there Sam,' Donaldson interrupted.

In August 1987, Michael Ryan fatally shot sixteen people and wounded another fifteen at various locations in Hungerford, in what was one of the deadliest firearms incidents in British history.

'No, I'm just saying, it's nearly thirty years and we still don't know what really triggered it. Plenty of opinions, but…'

'Well we've got this fucker contained and that's how I want it to stay.'

Sam took the unlit cigarette out of her mouth. 'Back to Marcus. I'll forward a photo of him. He could be the other male lying in the street. You might be able to get an ID from the live feed.'

'Thanks Sam.'

'I'll get the Intelligence Cell to do some background checks.'

'Appreciate it.'

Sam considered her next words carefully. The wrong sentence could prove fatal to her reputation. Hunches that were unsubstantiated and turned out to be wrong were fodder for finger pointers, but sometimes you just had to go with your gut.

'I think Lucy's inside.'

'Go on.'

Sam lit the cigarette and inhaled deeply before continuing.

'Marcus might have gone there to confront Zac, but I feel it's more likely he's gone to see Lucy, or she's somehow been coerced into luring him there.'

Donaldson said nothing.

Sam continued: 'It's too much of a coincidence that he's there at this time and I just can't see him being there without Lucy. If that's the case, where is she?'

'Possibly,' Donaldson spoke at last. 'But then again.'

'I know, I just think you need to be mindful if things escalate.'

'Will do, Sam. But in this case, I really hope you're wrong.'

Me too.

'And Dick, between you and me, keep an eye on Ed. He's not getting any younger and it's not that long since he's blacked out and been stabbed. I suggested he gave up the negotiator role but he wouldn't hear of it.'

'Leave it with me.'

Donaldson hung up.

Sam inhaled again, opened the driver's window a little and blew the smoke out of the gap. She scrolled through her phone again.

Just go home Sam.

It wasn't an option, not with her overwhelming sense of right and wrong.

'Mick, its Sam Parker.'

Acting Chief Inspector Wright was as surly as ever.

'Yeah.'

'Just ringing to see how you getting on. Wondering if you need a hand with staff?'

'All boxed off. Suicide note in his pocket. PM tomorrow.'

'Who's doing the post mortem?'

Sam looked at the house. Jean had moved from the window.

'Jim Melia. A few statements needed: passengers on the bus, a couple of pedestrians, and the poor driver who is in a hell of a state. After that it's just a report for the coroner.'

'You got him identified yet?'

Sam turned down the fan.

'Well there's that as well. Only a matter of time.'

'What about Fred Thompson?'

'Misguided old man. Imagining monsters and bogeymen. God, I hope I'm not like that at his age.'

Sam didn't think Wright heard her low growl but she didn't care if he did. As far as she was concerned, he had one of those faces her arms would never tire of punching.

'He's sharp as a tack usually,' she said. 'You checking CCTV?'

'What for?'

She inhaled long and deep, deliberately letting Wright's question hang.

'Corroborate or discount Fred's version.'

Wright's response was agitated, bordering on aggressive, a sure sign of rising stress levels.

'There's a suicide note in his pocket. What more corroboration do you want?'

Sam knew she was wasting her time. She'd pick this up tomorrow, but she still had time to throw one metaphorical hand grenade in Never's direction.

'Just trying to help Mick. The last death you investigated, the one on the yacht, is splattered over the front page of tonight's Seaton Post.'

Chapter 11

Dick Donaldson was pleased that every neighbour, with the exception of those in the adjoining semi to Zac Williams', had been quietly and safely evacuated, mostly via their back gardens.

The evacuation plan had been drawn up in conjunction with another firearms tactical adviser and a uniform inspector from the Emergency Planning Unit.

Inquiries were still being made to find out who lived in No.1 Malvern Close and whether they could be contacted by phone.

Assistant Chief Constable Monica Teal, sitting as Gold Commander, was chairing strategy meetings with the Police and Crime Commissioner, representatives from the local authority, health, and the fire service. She had already been in contact with appropriate government ministers who were keeping a watching brief.

She had yet to stand in front of the ever-increasing press pack who were waiting impatiently outside the gates of Police HQ.

The Police and Crime Commissioner was holding

meetings with Harvey Slattery, the local Member of Parliament.

The Salvation Army was at the church hall, the evacuation point, providing tea and sandwiches. Whether camp beds and sleeping bags would be needed would be dictated by how long the incident would go on, but people were working on the logistics.

Dick Donaldson wanted nothing more than a peaceful resolution. Time was not an issue, only the end result.

Ed hit speed dial.

'That you Zac?'

'Yeah.' His voice was shaking.

Charles held up a piece of paper upon which he'd written, 'AGITATED.'

Ed nodded.

Jules, whose other role was acting as the bridge between the negotiators and Silver Command left the office to make sure Dick Donaldson was listening in.

Word quickly spread amongst the firearm team that Williams sounded stoked up.

'It's all his fault this,' Williams was shouting into the phone.

'Whose fault?' Ed asked, voice by contrast calm and quiet.

'Him in the road. Who do you fucking think?'

'Which one Zac? More than one person is injured.'

Silence.

'You still there Zac?'

Silence.

'Zac?'

'Fucking flash bastard,' Williams' sobs gave way to a screaming tirade. 'Wouldn't keep away from Lucy. Thought he could take whatever he wanted. Filled her head full of shit. Wanker. Posh car, posh voice, posh twat.'

Ed needed to slow him down, calm him down, bring him back from the edge.

'Okay Zac. Let's talk about it. What's his name?'

Ed feared he was losing him, feared the loud, excited voice was ignoring him, feared whatever rationality was left in the house was rushing out of the broken window

'Tell the guns to move away. I might come out then.'

Slow him down Ed.

'They won't allow that to happen Zac. Not while you're in there with a gun.'

Another loud, fast-fired demand. 'Bring Elwood here then.'

Slow him down Ed.

'I've explained why that can't happen Zac.'

'So,' Williams was raging. 'I can't see my son and you won't take the guns away. Where does that leave me? Fuck this.'

For the first time Ed's voice sharpened to mirror the urgency of the situation.

'No Zac. Stay where you are, think of Elwood. Zac stay where you are.'

———

'Boss, it's Sgt Willings, Road Policing Unit.'

Sam was driving home, mobile on speakerphone between her knees.

'Hi Russell.'

She knew Russell Willings, a well-respected member of the Collision Investigation Unit, who was nearing retirement.

'I'm dealing with the fatal on the High Street.'

'The man and the bus?'

'Yeah. There's a couple of things I wanted to mention. I hope you don't mind.'

'Course not. Just hang on a minute.'

Sam swung into a retail park and pulled into the first available bay. Whatever Russell Willings was going to say, and it must be important for him to be ringing, she didn't want to be distracted by driving.

'Go on Russell.'

'I hope you don't think I'm speaking out of turn, but…'

Sam watched a young mother, face drawn, shoulders slouched, battling with three carrier bags, a toddler and the back door of her car.

Would I have been a good mother?

Something was clearly bothering Russell Willings. He'd gone to the trouble of ringing her, but at the same time he was wrestling with his conscience in a way that Sam knew could only mean one thing; he was going to speak out about a senior officer.

'Russell whatever you're going to say is between us. You've known me long enough and well enough. What's the problem?'

The slight pause and the deep breath were like those of a prisoner getting ready to make an admission.

'There's more to this than meets the eye boss. I've got a witness who says the deceased was being chased.'

Sam's response was immediate, her voice just a little too excited. 'Fred Thompson?'

'Who?'

Sam frowned. 'The newsagent.'

'No. The witness was a pedestrian, a mother pushing her daughter in a buggy. She says she saw the deceased run out of the multi-storey. He jumped over the pushchair, then a squat guy who she was convinced was in pursuit, tripped over the buggy. She saw the first guy get hit by the bus.'

'Did she see where the squat guy went afterwards?'

'No. She was too busy with her child.'

'And the problem is?'

Not that Sam needed to ask.

'Inspector Wright. Insistent that it's a suicide and everything else is just smoke and mirrors.'

Sam watched the mother close the back door and put the shopping in the boot.

'And you think differently. You think like the newsagent, who I've spoken to by the way, that he was being chased.'

'Totally.'

'Okay. Come and see me in the morning. I'll get a couple of Dees…'

Dees – slang for Detective Constables.

'to give you a hand with the CCTV.'

'That'll be great,' Willings sounded relieved. 'There are a couple of other things.'

Sam shuffled in her seat, fighting the wave of tiredness that had sneaked up on her. She just wanted to get home now.

At least you don't have to put a child to bed. Only got yourself to think of. Plenty of women have it much harder than you.

'Go on.'

'He had a SIM card stuffed down his sock.'

A SIM – Subscriber Identity Module – was part of every mobile phone.

'Really?' the adrenalin burst pushing back the tiredness. 'We'll get that looked at tomorrow. Suggests the deceased was involved in criminality.'

'Forget suggestions,' Willings paused. 'It's Taffy Green.'

Chapter 12

Ed swore under his breath.

The line was dead.

He hit speed dial, listened to the beeps as the phone automatically worked its way through the numbers.

'C'mon Zac, pick up,' he said to no-one in particular.

Nobody in the negotiators' room moved, eyes flicking between Ed and the phone. They all knew what was riding on the call. If Williams thought the situation was hopeless there would be no peaceful resolution.

The phones connected. The ring tone began.

Nothing.

'Pick up,' Charles muttered, echoing Ed.

Two more rings.

Nothing.

Nobody moved.

Ed sat opposite Jenny, Charles to the side of her, Jules stood by the board.

Finally Williams answered.

Without taking her eyes off Ed, Jules took the top off

the marker pen. Then, pen poised, she turned to face the board.

Williams' voice was quiet, resigned.

'I'm not coming out.'

'That's okay Zac. You don't have to come out. We can talk some more.'

'What about? Lucy?'

'If you want to.'

Thumbs up from Jenny. She knew Ed had a fighting chance of pulling this back from the brink. Zac was talking again.

'She's here.'

Jules' shoulders slumped; Charles kept his eyes on the pad his face hidden from Ed.

The same word was flashing like neon in their heads.

Hostage.

The tone and pitch of Ed's voice didn't alter.

'I thought she was at her mother's.'

'I lied,' Williams said, venom behind the snarled words. 'Get over it. Caught the slut with him.'

'Is Lucy alright Zac, can…'

'She's fine,' Williams snapped.

'Can I speak with her?'

Jenny half-smiled and rotated her right hand in small continuous circles, a sign encouraging Ed to keep going.

'She doesn't want to talk to anybody.'

'Do you want some more food, drinks?'

Another nod of approval from Jenny.

'We're fine.'

Ed needed Zac to focus on something positive.

'So, what kind of radio-controlled car has Elwood got?'

The switch was deliberate. Ed hoped the thought of his son might calm Williams.

'Funnily enough a police car. He'd love it here, all these police cars.'

Ed was relieved to hear the aggression had gone, at least momentarily, but he didn't want to go down that route, Williams wanting the youngster brought to the scene.

'Maybe when this is all over, we could arrange a trip to a police station. Let Elwood sit in a police car.'

The words earned an almost audible sigh of approval but like Tyne Bridge starters in the Great North Run, everyone in the room knew the finishing line was still far away.

'He'd like that.'

'You sure you don't want any food?'

'No. There's nothing you can do for me. Help's not coming.'

Ed shuffled in his seat, eyes fixed on the circular coffee mug ring on the desk.

'What do you mean Zac? I'm here to help.'

Silence.

The small room felt even more claustrophobic, tension eating up the space, sucking up the stale air.

Charles, bolt upright and rigid, allowed the pen to fall from his hand.

Jules moved away from the board, put both hands on the desk and leaned in towards Jenny.

'Zac?'

Nothing.

Ed wasn't panicking but his heart was thumping.

He was desperate to talk, knowing, like everybody else in that confined room, that the roller coaster ride had taken another plunge.

We're hurtling to disaster here

'Zac?'

Nothing.

'Zac!'

This time a thud and the sound of the line disconnecting.

Nobody breathed.

Nobody spoke.

Nobody moved.

Everyone was caught in a freeze-frame, locked in the moment, breathless and braced for impact.

Hurtling to disaster

Realisation crashed into Ed, catapulted him into action.

He ripped off his headphones and jumped up.

'He's broken the bloody phone,' he shouted.

Jules, flushed and wide eyed, headed for the door to warn Dick Donaldson.

She was still holding the handle when the air exploded and the ground seemed to tremble, the surge of noise deafening in the taut silence.

Gunfire.

SAM RESISTED the urge for a glass of wine. The crime in action at Malvern Close could conclude at any time and her immediate call-out, like an alcoholic's early morning shakes, was nailed on.

Sleep would be a good idea but her head was spinning, the shootings, the siege and Scott Green's demise flying around, vying for attention. Tossing and turning in bed would only increase her tiredness.

She curled up on the sofa with a mug of tea and a box

of Turkish Delight. She couldn't be bothered to cook, even if it was the usual microwave for one. Anyway, the phone would go before the ping. Sod's Law.

Sam flicked through the TV channels. Strictly Come Dancing and its 'Spooktacular' Halloween ballroom battle held no appeal. She would soon be walking into a gruesome scene of death no make-up artist and dancing ghouls could replicate. What she needed now was a distraction not a reminder.

She hit the off button on the remote, the only light in the room now coming from a couple of lamps. Hundreds of channels and nothing worth watching. There was more to watch in the old days when there were only four channels.

God I'm starting to sound like Ed.

She closed her eyes, sleepwalked back to the scene and wondered how Ed was getting on. That he still had the desire to be a negotiator was admirable, but to walk unarmed behind a shield towards a gun was definitely going above and beyond.

Last month he'd talked a 'jumper' down from a bridge, more a cry for help than a serious attempt, but this was an altogether different proposition.

She picked up the latest 'must read' off the small table, a book she'd bought a few days ago from an independent bookshop and opened it at Chapter 1.

Bev had raved about it, read it in two sittings.

The voice of Rachel, the alcoholic narrator, tried to get into Sam's head but Paula Hawkins hadn't counted on a reader waiting to investigate the scene of a mass shooting.

Sam gave up and closed 'The Girl on the Train' at page seven, vowing to get away for a few days and immerse herself in the book.

Her brain, a swirling mass of investigative strategies, was too busy processing Lines of Inquiry, mentally preparing 'To Do' lists based on the information she had.

Of course, that could all change.

No-one knew what secrets the house could be hiding.

Chapter 13

'SHOTS FIRED. SHOTS FIRED.'

Head cool enough to chill ice cream, Gerry Trout's voice sounded like the pre-recorded message on an escalator telling people to keep right.

'Silver Commander to Tango 1.'

Fragments of shattered glass, pursued by a metal kitchen stool, flew from the downstairs window and scattered across the path.

'Tango 1. Stand by Silver,' replied Gerry Trout.

Light flooded the front room.

'Tango 1. Living room light turned on,' Gerry said into his radio.

Ed was out of the small back office listening to the radio traffic.

Does he want to make himself a target? Suicide by Cop?

The helicopter hovered, turned on its searchlights, the house and garden were illuminated like a floodlit football pitch; shards of glass twinkled, light reflected off the metal stool, the dancing net curtains of earlier now horizontal in the downdraft.

'Tango 1 to Silver.'

'Go ahead,' Dick Donaldson responded.

'Two shots fired. Stool thrown through window.'

Donaldson was on his feet in the mobile command unit, voice calm, words brief.

'Silver to Tango 1. Suggestion of at least one other in house. Prepare to implement REP.'

Whilst Ed had been talking to Williams, Gerry and his team had drawn up a detailed Rapid Entry Plan in readiness.

The Emergency Planning Unit, with assistance from numerous agencies, had already delivered plans of the house. Two houses in the cul-de-sac, identical in footprint, were rented to students under House in Multiple Occupancy rules. One had just recently had its licence renewed by the local council housing department.

The REP had been agreed and 'signed off' by both Silver and Gold commanders.

'Tango 1, Roger that,' Gerry replied.

'Silver to Tango 1. Potential for casualties. Potential for murder-suicide.'

'Roger that.' Gerry Trout's eyes had not moved from the front window.

Donaldson was handed a telephone by the communications operator.

'Dick, it's Monica Teal. Implement the Rapid Entry Plan if necessary. Safety of the public and our officers are paramount. There may be casualties inside needing medical treatment.'

'Stand by, stand by,' Gerry Trout said into his radio.

Dick Donaldson and Monica Teal stopped talking, held the phones to their ears as they waited for Gerry to speak.

The white rabbit had appeared at the window holding a rifle.

'Tango 1. Suspect at window pointing firearm into street,' Gerry said.

'Tango 3. Have sight of gunman. Suspect shouting. Inaudible.'

Nobody heard over the noise of the Air Support Unit.

'Tango 1. Appears to be taking aim. Imminent threat,' Gerry Trout said over the airwaves.

Monica Teal spoke to Dick Donaldson without emotion. 'Use of lethal force authorised.'

He relayed the authorisation over the radio.

The snap of two quick shots and the rabbit fell backwards.

———

ED WAS LEANING against the side panel of the Mobile Command Unit ignoring the damp clinging to the shoulders of his North Face jacket. Now would have been a good time for a cigarette if he smoked.

He typed out a text to Sam.

They're preparing to go in, clear the house. Zac Williams shot, presumed dead.

He and the other negotiators were standing in a silent circle, brains in replay mode.

Charles, hands in trouser pockets, eyes fixed on the Tarmac, was the first to speak. 'What happens now?'

'Hot debrief,' Ed said, his voice sounding computer generated, barely above a whisper, devoid of inflection or nuance.

'We'll wait for the coordinator to finish with Silver.'

The negotiator coordinator was the officer who would assign roles and in lengthy siege negotiations, decide when a new Number 1 negotiator would take over.

Changing negotiators was a high-risk strategy and the

decision to do so was not undertaken without serious consideration: any rapport built up between the negotiator and the subject would have to start again and any mistake by the new negotiator could escalate the situation. Something as simple as getting the name of the subject's child wrong could have devastating consequences.

Ed moved off the van and shuffled forward, shrinking the radius of the circle; head down, eyes on the Tarmac, neck disappearing into his ever-more slouched shoulders.

He moved like a defeated footballer waiting pitch-side for the winning opponents to collect the trophy.

Ed scanned the ground in vain. Why was there never a stone or discarded can around when you just wanted to kick something?

He stuffed his hands into the pockets of the blue cords, mentally replaying the phone conversations.

Could he have done anything differently?

Did Zac Williams have to die?

Yes, he'd killed a colleague. Yes, he'd murdered at least two others. Yes, he'd wounded a child.

But Ed's job was to talk him out and he had failed.

He began digging the toes of his right foot into a small hole in the Tarmac.

Nobody sets out to fail he thought. Nobody gets up on a morning with the intention of going to work and making mistakes.

But only certain people, certain professions, work in an environment where errors cost lives.

Ed nodded, raised half a smile, and took the tea from the outstretched arm. He didn't know who the arm belonged to, didn't know how long they all stood there in silence.

'You did what you could Ed,' Sam said, walking towards the negotiators.

The tea was stone cold, untouched.

Momentarily back on the parade ground of his training school days, Ed jerked to attention, shoulders back, chest out, body stiff. The stress of the last few hours fired from his pores like bullets from an authorised firearms officer's Heckler and Koch MP5.

'Try telling that to the firearms team,' he shouted, aggression taking over. 'Tell that to the AFO who shot him, at best suspended from carrying a gun, maybe suspended from the Job.'

Sam didn't interrupt. Sometimes it was better to let people vent when nerves were frayed. Bollocking Ed for his outburst would help nobody. She let him continue. He was on a roll now. Best let him get it all out.

'Investigation into whether the shot was necessary, lefties screaming for cops to be put on trial for murder. Politicians no fucking better. Bottleless bastards; never had to make a critical decision in real time. Run a mile from an angry man. Fucking wankers the lot of them. All the shit that follows a police shooting, and it was my job to stop it.'

None of the negotiators spoke but they were all thinking the same.

Sam took Ed's elbow and walked him away from the others.

Her words were soft, sugar coated.

'Sometimes Ed you can't do anything. Sometimes you enter a battle you never had a chance of winning. You know that. Everybody will be re-evaluating what happened here tonight…negotiators, Gold, Silver, Firearms…everybody.'

She stopped walking and turned to face him.

'But that doesn't mean anybody did anything wrong. He'd killed at least three people. Maybe there's more in the house. If he became a threat again, that threat had to be eliminated.'

She looked into his eyes, saw the film of water in them. 'We didn't start this you know.'

Ed looked away, nodded.

'How's things at home?' she asked, genuine concern in her voice.

Ed didn't turn his head, the words cracking in his throat like dry twigs under a hiker's boot. 'Same old, same old. I'm thinking of leaving.'

Sam's expression remained passive. Highly charged, stressful situations ignite emotions in people that die out like a coal fire when things return to normal.

Ed cleared his throat before continuing. 'I used to think SNAFU was limited to the Job, but it's not.'

It was an old police and military acronym – Situation Normal All Fucked Up.

Ed turned his head. 'My house is the capital of the State of SNAFU. I'm not that long off retirement and the thought of being in that house day in, day out, scares me shitless.'

Sam gave her best empathic smile and nodded, considering her words carefully.

'Look you're tired. I'm going to be here all night. If you want, you can go to mine and get your head down. Do your hot debrief with the negotiators, the higher-ups might want a joint one with the negotiators and the firearms team as well, then get away.

'You sure?'

'Absolutely. Use the back bedroom. There are clean towels in the airing cupboard at the top of the stairs. Help yourself to tea, coffee, whatever you need.'

Sam produced a spare key from her purse.

Ed's brow concertinaed.

Sam smiled at his obvious bewilderment.

'I always carry a spare these days. Lost count of the number of times I've been locked out after a drink straight from work. Car keys on my desk, house key attached.'

For the first time since his arrival at the scene, Ed gave a genuine smile.

'Cheers.'

He took the key from her hand.

Chapter 14

Less than an hour later the house was deemed 'clear.'

Sam was sitting in the front of the Scenes of Crime van next to Julie Trescothick, engine running, heater on full blast.

Julie was a highly regarded Senior Crime Scene Investigator.

They had already agreed on the forensic strategy and discussed the logistics of multiple crime scenes within one overarching scene.

Sam was clear in what she wanted, which other experts she needed.

There were three dead in the cul-de-sac...Paul Adams and two men yet to be formally identified, although in all probability Marcus Worthington-Hotspur and Joey 'Fatty' Sanderson; he was known to the AFOs who found him in one of the gardens.

Three bodies, three scenes, three tents.

There was a dead man in the house, again identity unconfirmed but believed to be Zac Williams in his white rabbit suit. There was also a dead female, possibly Lucy Spragg.

Two more scenes.

The house itself was a scene.

Sam watched the police activity.

She had already liaised briefly with Gerry Trout. Four AFOs had ensured the house was safe, the priority above and beyond the preservation of forensic evidence.

Gerry would inform the AFOs that they might need to hand over their boots to the forensic team. Footwear may have blood on it, tread patterns may be visible in pools of blood in the house. The boots would have to be matched to those tread patterns and identified as belonging to the AFOs.

Everybody's presence in that house – police, suspect, or anyone else – had to be accounted for. Fail to identify everybody and the conspiracy theorists would be all over it… and Sam knew plenty of briefs who loved a conspiracy.

'Maybe the real shooter was the person whose fingerprints weren't identified; whose footprints weren't identified.'

Every case, Sam knew, had to be watertight.

One of the AFOs had made sure the only weapon found in the house had been made safe. Gerry had informed Sam of the type of weapon used by the shooter, its characteristics and capabilities, but guns meant nothing to her. For all Gerry's obvious technical knowledge she only needed to know it was a rifle.

Sam had already spoken with a ballistics expert, who was travelling from the Midlands to conduct extensive tests and answer the questions she had posed.

Were the bullets that killed four people and wounded young 'Spiderman' fired from the same weapon?

Were the bullets that killed 'white rabbit' from the AFO's gun?

Sam exhaled hard, her brain a whirlwind.

Five bodies, five post mortems and she would attend every one.

The AFO who took the shot was himself another scene. His weapon would be seized, he would need to be interviewed at some stage.

Whilst the IPCC – the Independent Police Complaints Commission – had been officially notified of the incident, Sam, as SIO, retained primacy as far as investigating the homicide of Zac Williams was concerned.

Sam walked to the house with Julie, both identically dressed in white paper suits with hoods up and white paper overshoes.

A SOCO was filming an overview of the street, the bodies, the Porsche.

Tents were being erected to give the dead some dignity away from prying eyes and telephoto lenses as well as preserving forensic evidence.

The cul-de-sac looked like a CSIs convention and Sam was responsible for their every move, every examination, every subsequent test.

She knew the weight of expectations placed on her. The expectation from her team, bosses, the Coroner, courts, solicitors and barristers; that every piece of evidence would be recovered in a methodical manner, with no cross contamination, secured for whatever forensic testing she deemed necessary to progress the investigation and to allow any future interested parties to examine the exhibits and perhaps conduct their own tests.

The pressing expectation now was that everything at the scene would be done as quickly and efficiently as possible. Keeping families and young children away from their homes, throwing them together in the confined space of the church hall, was like putting a bullet in a microwave – explosive.

This was not the London Blitz, 1940s strangers spending the night in an underground Tube station. This was modern Britain, a place where many people existed in their own social media bubble, interacting with strangers as alien to them as a bomb dropping on their house.

Sam looked at her watch. 10.30pm.

Personnel at the church hall from a variety of agencies wanted the people back in the houses as soon as possible. Sam knew it had already kicked-off; a guy had demanded he be allowed to return home to get his cigarettes and cans of lager.

It was a balancing act, but nobody else carried the responsibility of the crime scene management. Months down the line if it became apparent things had been missed, nobody would come to her rescue and say 'we were all putting pressure on her to get on with it.'

Sam was anxious to get started, wanted to get into the house, get a feel for where it all started, understand the sequence of events, but she would not be rushed.

The front door was hanging off its hinges, the wood frame no match for the Enforcer, the hand-held battering ram that had been swung at it by one of the AFOs. They nicknamed it 'The Big Red Key' because it opened all doors.

The front garden was littered with broken glass, a metal kitchen stool among the debris.

The walk-through by the SOCO filming the house had been completed. The film showed the front of the house and then the interior of every room, close ups of each body, every blood splatter, everything that looked out of place.

Sam stopped at the door, allowed Julie to enter. The steel stepping plates were already in place, there to enable those permitted entry to walk around without standing on the carpets and stepping in blood, potentially contaminating forensic evidence.

Sam had already asked Julie to call out a forensic scientist specialising in blood pattern analysis. The expert would arrive later that morning.

They both understood the need for such an expert; how the scientist could interpret the blood splatters, inform them and subsequently a court, albeit potentially a coroner's court in this instance, of what the patterns meant.

But it was Sam who authorised their attendance. She held the purse strings and with a ballistic expert, pathologist, and an ever-expanding number of police officers and support staff on overtime, the major incident budget was already taking a hammering.

She walked into the house, hands in her pockets, careful not to touch anything.

She stepped onto the first metal plate in the hallway. The size of a small patio paving stone, the thin rim keeping the plate off the floor.

There was no stair carpet and the white skirting boards were yellow and thick with dust.

Sam loved dust at crime scenes, the SIO's equivalent of a spider's web, where forensic evidence, not flies, were the prey.

In the small square living-room the photographer was taking the last few shots of White Rabbit before unmasking him. The body was laid on its back, two gunshot wounds in the chest.

The room was cold, damp air swooping through the broken window. The window would be boarded up, but only after the net curtains had been taken down, bagged and tagged, and the glass and windowsill had been examined. Same with the one upstairs.

'Presumably the gun's so far from him because an AFO has moved it?' Sam asked, noticing the rifle was at least a metre away.

Julie nodded. 'One of the firearms team kicked it away when they rushed in.'

'Can't blame them for that. I'd have done exactly the same. And it's been made safe?'

Julie confirmed any ammunition had been removed and a check carried out to make sure there wasn't a bullet in the chamber.

'Let's get some photographs of it and then get an AFO to remove it.'

White paper arrows were stuck on the walls pointing out each trace of blood, the arrows occasionally illuminated under the camera flash as another blood splatter was photographed.

The room was a mine of forensic opportunities but like a prospector sieving for gold, Sam knew patience was paramount. Staff would be in this house for days.

She saw the broken mobile phone on the floor, the dent in the wall just below the ceiling suggesting it been thrown with some force.

'Ed was right when he said he'd smashed the phone.'

Sam walked on the plates into the kitchen.

Her eyes locked onto the lifeless body of a blonde, head slumped forward, hands behind her back, tied to a chair, which was pushed tight against the wall.

Sam knew before she bent down that the girl had been shot somewhere in the face due to the massive hole in the back of her head, and the blood and brain matter on the wall behind her. Squatting down, getting her head under the deceased's, she saw that the girl had been shot in the right eye.

'AFOs reckon she's been shot twice in the face,' Julie said.

Sam recalled a lecture when it had been suggested one of the reasons for a previous partner attacking the face was to dehumanise the victim.

'I'm sure they'll be correct but Jim will tell us,' Sam said.

Jim Melia, the Home Office Forensic Pathologist was, at Sam's request, on his way to the scene.

Sam was confident this was 'Wonder Woman' in the photograph on Jean Spragg's mobile phone – same build, same length hair, same female gender tattoo on her left wrist.

Sam stood up, leaned forward, put her hands on her knees and retched.

Julie looked at her, more out of shock than sympathy. Sam Parker never got queasy at crime scenes.

Sam pointed at the stomach-churning smell of years of accumulated black grease on the cooker hob.

'That's disgusting,' she said, wiping her mouth as she straightened.

'Positively gleaming in comparison to the oven,' Julie said, her own bright white smile at odds with the cooker.

'No hidden weapons, but you wouldn't want to warm a pie in there.'

'Pack it in or I'll baulk again.'

Sam's smile vanished as she turned around and saw the copies of the newspapers on the other wall. She read the headlines.

Fuck.

Chapter 15

E<small>D STOOD</small> in the hall and locked the door.

When had he last turned a key without worrying about a verbal ambush? His wife's screeching was like an Exocet missile – you knew it was coming but there was nothing you could do to stop it.

He stood there, eyes closed, savouring the silence. No ambush tonight.

He walked into the kitchen, flicked on the light. It was as he remembered, although walking into the brightness this time was different. That night Sam had been frightened, convinced the serial rapist they were hunting knew where she lived.

He flicked on the kettle and searched the gleaming units for a tea bag.

Two cupboards later he eventually found them; Twinings Assam.

He smiled. *No common brew for Sam Parker.*

He walked across the kitchen to the wine cooler, grinned at the neat bottles, one compartment for red, the other for white, temperature dials showing the white wine compartment was cooler.

He shook his head. He'd never felt the need for a wine cooler, but then again, the £5 bottles he bought probably didn't need it.

He could do with a drink but was worried he would inadvertently open something really expensive. He made do with tea, found the skimmed milk (*what is the point Sam?*) in the fridge and sat at the island.

His conversations with Zac Williams began to play back in his head.

What had he meant by 'Help's not coming'?

Help for Williams?

Help for Lucy?

The AFOs told him there was a dead female in the house. Instinctively he knew it was her.

What help did Williams need?

His help? Not that he had been much help.

Help from anybody else? Who?

Williams never asked for anybody with the exception of his son.

Maybe Ed should have allowed Elwood to come to the house. Things couldn't have ended up any worse. Not for Zac Williams anyway.

He poured the water over the teabag and sat back down, the cogs in his head turning.

Sam had a big job on her hands but would he be on the investigation? He could be deemed too close to it; too emotionally involved.

And who was Paul seeing? Paul told him he had a 'new friend' but didn't mention her name, that he was keeping that under wraps.

Ed had tried to talk Paul out of the affair, telling him he hadn't been married long, but Paul wouldn't listen.

Talk about being in the wrong place at the wrong time.

Ed had never heard of Zac Williams until he spoke on the phone. How did he get a rifle? He'd have expected to know something about the identity of a local criminal who could access firearms.

He sipped the tea, burnt his tongue on the rim of the bone china rose-patterned mug.

He was tired and drained but something was nagging.

'Help's not coming.'

What the hell did that mean?

———

'WHERE IS HE?' Jimmy 'Staples' Marshall was irritated and edgy, glancing at his black-faced G-Shock watch. 10.45pm.

'You know where he is, so just sit tight.'

They were parked in a row of cars outside the cinema on the out of town retail park.

Nothing attracts the attention of the local busybody more than two heavies sat in a car on a housing estate. A car amongst dozens of others on a retail park on a Saturday night doesn't draw a second glance.

'I thought he'd be done now,' Marshall said, glancing at his watch again before looking up at the listings board for the cinema.

'I quite fancy that new Tom Hanks film.'

'Which one?' Davy Swan asked him, not particularly interested in Marshall's movie preferences.

'Bridge of Spies. Looks class. I like spy stuff.'

'Not heard of it.'

Marshall looked at his watch again.

Swan stared out of the windscreen, watched the uniformed security guy waddle along the path toward a burger outlet without the slightest interest in the car park, trouser belt tight under his hanging belly.

'You in a rush?' he said without taking his eyes off the security man. 'Got somewhere else to be?'

'No.'

'Well stop looking at your watch every twenty seconds.'

Swan watched the guard push open the burger place's glass door and shook his head.

'Look at that fat bastard. Unless they're selling Ryvita and salads he should be banned from going in. Fat twat.'

'I hate sitting around,' Marshall said. 'Always gives me the jitters.'

Swan raised his voice in a snarl and turned to face Marshall.

'Go for a walk then. Count the sandwiches. Just shut the fuck up. You're doing my head in.'

Marshall's face reddened. He shuffled in the seat, looked over his shoulder. He was in enough trouble with The Man without cocking up the sandwich order.

In his defence, he might have been instrumental in Taffy Green's escape, but he hadn't threatened the old newsagent and hadn't let himself be seen by a potential witness.

He leaned over to the back seat, picked up the Marks and Spencer carrier bag, and tipped the contents onto the footwell…salmon and cucumber, prawn mayo, and chicken salad pre-packed sandwiches; a Gala pie, sausage rolls, crisps, diet Coke and a selection of bite-sized cakes. A feast.

Marshall put everything back into the carrier and returned it to the back seat.

'Do you think he'll like the food?'

'We'll never hear the last of it if he doesn't.'

'You should have come in with me.'

Then I couldn't blame you.

Ahead, the security guard had pushed open the door with his left hand, mouth already busy on the burger.

'He'll eat his fucking fingers if he's not careful,' Swan said, shaking his head.

'Heart attack waiting to happen. He'll be one of those who need winching out of bed.'

Marshall jumped when the mobile on the centre console pinged.

Swan snatched the phone, read the text message.

Might be a bit longer.

'What does it say?'

Swan showed him the screen.

'Great,' Marshall said, reclining the seat and closing his eyes, thoughts back on sandwiches and cock-ups. 'Fuckin' great.'

SAM READ the news stories on the walls.

The list of locations took in Virginia Tech, Sandy Hook Elementary, Columbine High, Red Lake High School, the Omaha shopping mall.

And she read about the killers.

The oldest at 23 was Seung-Hui responsible for gunning down 32 people at Virginia Tech. The youngest was 16-year-old Jeff Weisse at Red Lake.

Sam stepped back.

The numbers of victims varied but with the exception of Columbine, all the killers had acted alone. All had committed suicide.

She wondered why there was no mention of Dunblane, the deadliest mass shooting in British history.

The print went out of focus, letters blurred, a fog-like mass of grey.

She rubbed her eyes and bit her lip, the memory of the free period when news of Dunblane broke transporting her back to different days, standing off-site with her friends, smoking, weeks away from her 17th birthday and driving lessons. She remembered the lady in the shop repeating the news from the radio, the eerie silence of the walk back to school, collective shock focusing on innocent school children and their teacher.

Nearly twenty years ago. Innocents robbed of their lives by some sick fuck.

She blinked rapidly, refocused eyes and brain, and looked back at the wall.

Stay sharp, Sam

She was dealing with a mass shooting – one location, multiple victims, single event.

Michael Ryan, the Hungerford killer, had been a spree killer – victims in multiple locations–but the murders were still considered a single event because there was no cooling off period.

By contrast serial killers struck at separate times, killing again after a cooling-off period that could last days, months or even years.

She moved in close, re-read the articles.

Each shooter committed suicide.

Was Zac Williams a 'suicide by cop?'

The term had been born in the USA, the tag for those who deliberately and by design left a police officer with no option but to kill them.

Did Williams put his own plan into action? Had he been incapable of taking his own life?

Julie Trescothick poked her head through the doorway. 'Scary isn't it?'

Sam was still staring at the cuttings.

'Yes, but it also shows lots of planning. He hasn't printed these off while we were outside and planning is typical of this type of killer.'

'But why?'

'Why plan or why do it in the first place?'

'Why do it?'

Sam finally took her eyes off the wall.

'That's the six-million-dollar question Julie and we might never find the answer.'

Sam knew the research that found some shooters had experienced a major trigger moment, an event where they saw themselves as a victim. That could be anything...an issue with their partner, something in the workplace. Some, but not many, had an ideological motivation.

Sam inhaled slowly. She needed to keep an open mind. It would be too easy to walk away thinking 'multiple murder and suicide by cop'.

All the signs might be pointing that way but she still had to find the proof.

What had been Williams' trigger moment? Marcus?

Raw jealousy might explain why he killed him and Lucy but the others?

Was there a link between the victims or were they just in the wrong place at the wrong time?

Sam stepped towards the cuttings and focused, on another mass shooting in another part of the UK.

'Remember that spree killer in Cumbria, Derrick Bird? There were a few possible triggers but in every one of them he saw himself as the victim.'

Bird had killed 12 people and wounded another 11 in 2010 before killing himself.

Losing his job and girlfriend, a dispute over a family

will and a tax investigation were all in play, but Bird's 'trigger' had never been fully established.

One thing was certain. Bird had a firearm licence. Zac Williams did not.

So how did Williams get a rifle?

This was Britain not the USA. Guns were available but you had to know where to look and who to ask. Right now, Sam would need some convincing Zac Williams had those kinds of contacts.

Sam's head jerked upwards at a creaking noise, faint but out of place in the house.

'What's that?'

'What?' Julie said, her head following Sam's, eyeing the yellowing ceiling.

Sam moved out of the kitchen, looked up the stairs. Julie followed.

'I heard a noise.' Sam said as they stood in silence. 'We have anybody upstairs?'

Julie shook her head.

Doubt began scratching away at Sam, that irritating itch signaling something was wrong.

Chapter 16

Jɪᴍ Mᴇʟɪᴀ ᴡᴀs sᴛᴀɴᴅɪɴɢ ᴏᴜᴛsɪᴅᴇ 2 Malvern Close watching all the activity when Sam walked out of the house.

'Some Halloween party this. I feel like I'm on a film set and Bruce Willis is about to emerge from a building.'

Sam snapped, didn't bother hiding her annoyance at Jim's insensitivity.

'The 'Die Hard' movies are set at Christmas.'

He picked up on it immediately.

'What have we got then?' he asked, eyes darting away from Sam.

'Two bodies in the house. No official IDs yet. One believed to be Zac Williams who we think is the shooter, shot by the police. Dead female, early twenties, probably, his girlfriend Lucy Spragg.'

'Okay,' Jim said. 'And here.'

He nodded in the direction of the white tents.

'Nearest is Paul Adams, one of ours.'

'Oh, I'm sorry to hear that.'

Sam nodded, screwed her lips together before speaking again.

'Further up the road is who we believe to be Marcus Worthington-Hotspur.'

'You're kidding?'

Jim Melia's jaw had dropped and he stood mouth open.

'Why? Do you know him?'

'If it's who I think it is, his father's a Mason. Same lodge as me.'

Jim stopped, choosing his next words carefully.

'Difficult chap…a tad brash.'

Sam smiled at the pathologist's language, PG Wodehouse suddenly in her head. Jim Melia could have walked straight from the set of 'Jeeves and Wooster'.

'Rumour has it his birth surname was just plain Worthington,' Jim was saying now. 'Apparently added Hotspur to give himself a few more social graces.'

'As in Tottenham?' Sam said.

Jim raised his eyebrows. 'Not football. Well not quite. Henry Percy. Also known as Harry Hotspur. Medieval nobleman. Born Northumberland. Died 1403 at the Battle of Shrewsbury.'

'Wow.'

'His descendants had land near Tottenham's first football ground, hence the Hotspur.'

Sam shook her head, marveling at the history lesson.

'What line of business is his father in?'

'All a bit mysterious, although he does own property, lots of property,' Jim told her.

Sam filed the information.

'Over there,' Sam nodded to her right, 'is Joey Sanderson, known to one and all as 'Fatty Sanderson.' Not exactly original but…'

'Right let's get cracking,' Jim said, walking towards the door. 'I've already got one waiting at the mortuary. Killed by impatience. Thought he was faster than the bus.'

———

SAM SPENT an hour with Jim examining the bodies, the pathologist painstaking and thorough.

His task would be to log all injuries – external and internal – and provide causes of death. Bullet wounds alone didn't mean death by gunfire.

Others would help Sam complete the complex picture. The direction of travel and trajectory of the bullets would be reconstructed by the ballistic experts, which in turn would be corroborated by any forthcoming witness evidence.

Plans and computer 3D imagery would eventually be prepared, providing a visual account to assist both the on-going investigation and any subsequent judicial hearing.

Sam and Jim knelt next to Zac Williams.

'Any reason for the rabbit suit apart from the obvious of hiding his identity?' Jim asked.

'All the family loved the Jimmy Stewart film Harvey,' Sam said, 'He even named his kid Elwood.'

'A classic,' Jim said. 'The story of a Pooka who takes the form of a six foot plus invisible white rabbit.'

Sam looked away, briefly closed her eyes. Was he so obsessed with Harvey he was paying tribute in his final act? No need to disguise yourself if you're planning to die. Disguises only matter if you want to escape.

Given the gallery of slaughter across Williams' wall, you had to doubt he planned on leaving the house alive.

The 'Suicide by Cop' statistic was in Sam's head

again…all perpetrators young males, 87% of them making suicide warnings before or during the incident.

As far as she was aware, Zac Williams had given no such warning.

Most mass shooters also made some sort of threat to someone, either directly or in another's presence. Had Williams?

She looked back at the body.

The crime scene investigators had placed each hand in a clear bag; cable ties securing them to his wrists ensured no forensic evidence would be lost when the body was moved to the mortuary. His skin and the hands of his suit would be swabbed for gunshot residue.

Sam knew that the residue could be lost within hours from his skin but could remain on clothing for years. If there was residue, she reasoned, most, if not all, would be on the fake fur.

Jim lifted Williams' hands simultaneously, turning them slowly, examining each.

The rabbit suit was in pristine condition but each palm had a small clump of fur missing; not a neatly cut patch, too ragged for that, too frayed around the edges, more like a clump of hair ripped from a woman's scalp in a toilet fight.

'What do you make of that?' Sam asked, nodding at the hands.

'No idea,' Jim said. 'That's your department.'

She stood up, walked over to the rifle, and knelt alongside it.

She didn't need a microscope to see the strands of fur on the barrel and around the trigger guard.

Tara Paxman was the only non-evacuated occupant of Malvern Close, her proximity to the shooter's house considered too dangerous to remove her.

'How long have you known Paul?' Sam asked, her direct opening question ignoring the usual effort to relax a witness and build a rapport. Time was too short.

The flared sleeves of Tara's red, silk, knee-length dressing gown danced in tandem with her shaking body. Mascara had run onto her cheeks, her eyes like a panda's.

'He's dead, isn't he? Dead because of that crazy fuck next door.'

Tara's eyes dropped to the floor, her hands ran through her hair.

Sam looked at the bed-hair bob, not a root in sight amongst the jet-black. She took in the fake tan on Tara's arms and legs, the perfectly painted fingers and toes.

Sam wondered what she was wearing under the dressing gown. Something styled for sex not comfort, she reasoned.

Paul Adams hadn't come here for a chat.

The question may have been direct but Sam's voice was full of empathy. 'Have you known Paul long?'

'A few months.'

Tara started to cry.

Sam looked around. The room was clean, the furniture new and a huge TV dominated one wall.

A dozen roses were on the marble fireplace.

Christ, I hope there's not a card from Paul declaring his undying love. Not on his wife's birthday.

Sam changed tack, spoke faster.

'Do you live alone Tara?'

A nod of the head.

The next question was out before the nod had finished.

'Where do you work?'

Tara looked up, rubbed her brown eyes and crossed one leg over the other.

Sam could see the attraction.

'I don't. Dropped out of uni.'

Sam's eyes again drifted around the room…thick red carpet, white sheepskin rug in front of the fire, oak drinks cabinet with an alabaster statute of Aphrodite on top of it.

On the wall above the cabinet were three small provocative prints in gilt frames, Toulouse-Lautrec's decadent Parisian scenes in the late 19th century. Had he stuck to painting he wouldn't have died of alcoholism and syphilis.

'So how do you afford all of this?'

Tara stared at Sam, didn't speak.

'Did Paul pay you for your services?'

The question landed like a punch.

Tara's legs uncrossed in a flash, upper body shooting forward. Her words bubbled with aggression.

'I never charged him,' she shouted. 'Never.'

Sam was the mother figure again. 'Calm down. This is stressful for everybody. So how did you get to know each other?'

They had met in a bar, got chatting and it went from there.

Tara shook her head slowly, cupped her hands around her face, and spoke through the gaps in her fingers. 'I can't live here anymore. Not with all this shit.'

'You called your next door neighbour a crazy fuck?'

Tara looked up into Sam's eyes, her movements slow, choreographed almost. She stuck out her legs, raised her arms above her head and stretched, fingers pointing at the ceiling, toes pointed towards Sam.

I can see how you manipulate men.

'I need another drink,' Tara said. 'Want one?'

'No thanks.'

Tara bent down, took the gin balloon off the floor and shimmied over to the drinks cabinet, hips swaying Samba-style in time to the rhythm of the rattling ice cubes.

You've recovered quickly.

She poured a large measure of Newcastle Gin, didn't bother with tonic. Scooped her hand into the ice bucket.

Sam shook her head at Tara's backside.

You're wasting your time wiggling that at me love.

'So,' Sam said, as Tara sat back down. 'The crazy fuck?'

'Jealous. Insanely jealous. Wouldn't let Lucy go anywhere. And I mean anywhere. Wouldn't even let her go to the Asda by herself.'

Sam nodded, smiled. Why do so many people around here prefix the name of a supermarket with 'the'?

Tara hitched up her dressing gown and scratched her thigh, the painted nails moving smooth and slow.

You certainly know how to work it.

'I've seen a photograph of the two of them at a fancy dress,' Sam said.

'Yeah, that was round here. Lucy's mam said that it's the only photo she'll have of Zac because you can't see his face.'

Tara laughed. 'Her mam's class and Lucy did look mint that night.'

'Why do you think it's him though. Why's he the crazy one?'

The ice clinked against the side of the glass as Tara took a large mouthful.

'Lucy thought he'd found out about Marcus. Decent lad him. I introduced him to Lucy.'

'I thought you said Lucy couldn't go out by herself.'

'I introduced them over the back fence. Marcus used to come to see me.'

'For sex?'

Tara raised the glass again, this time she took a sip.

'Well I like to think he came for the company.'

'And sex.'

'If you say so.'

'Where did you meet him?'

'Can't remember now.'

'Any idea where Zac would get a gun.'

Tara put the glass on the floor.

'No. Whenever he was pissed-up he'd say he'd kill anybody who looked at Lucy.'

'Ever see him hit anyone.'

'Only Lucy. Saw him hit her once when they were in the back garden.'

'Did he ever try to buy your services?'

'Who? Zac? Don't be ridiculous. Hasn't got a pot to piss in. He couldn't afford me.'

Tara flashed her smile.

'He never asked?' Sam said.

Tara reached for the glass, took another sip.

'Yeah he asked. Course he did. But he had no chance and I told him. No money, no soap and according to Lucy, no technique. I wouldn't go with him even if he had the money.'

She swallowed the remains of the gin, got up to refill her glass, and returned with another straight up on ice.

Sam waited, said nothing.

'Mostly it's older men, married, businessmen,' Tara said as she sat back down.

'I'm not cheap and I expect to be taken out. I'm not some slapper from one of the Skinners' clubs.'

Luke and Mark Skinner, part of the infamous crime

family, were in prison on remand, brought down by Sam last December, their trial in two weeks.

'How do you know about them?'

'Who doesn't? Wanted to run me before they went down but I prefer being freelance.'

Sam couldn't believe it was almost a year since that investigation.

'How do you get your business? You've got no record.'

Tara glared at Sam.

'Checked already have you?'

'Of course.'

Sam wasn't getting into a discussion about police intelligence gathering techniques.

'So, how do you get your business?'

'Word of mouth. Plus, discretion guaranteed. You'd be amazed at who I count amongst my regulars. Paul's not the only copper…lowest ranking though.'

It was Sam's turn to lean forward.

'What happened to your discretion? You've just admitted you see senior police officers.'

'But I haven't told you who, or where they're from have I? Or what gender they are.'

Tara let that one hang a moment before continuing.

'I travel all around the country. High-end escort, not some twenty-pound-a-time-prostitute. They buy my company. Buy my intelligence.'

'But you still sleep with them?'

'If that's what they want.'

'No difference in my world then,' Sam said evenly. 'You're still a prostitute, just an expensive one.'

'I make more in a night than you make in a month.'

So why waste time with Paul?

Sam's eyes darted up at the ceiling.

'Did you hear that noise?' she asked.

'What noise?'

Sam looked at her, her voice as impatient as the expression on her face.

'The noise in the roof.'

'I didn't hear a thing,' Tara sipped her gin. 'But sometimes the birds get in.'

Sam stood up. 'Mind if I take a look?'

Another sip, eyes raised.

'I do actually,' Tara smoothed down her dressing gown. 'Don't you need a warrant?'

'I could get one.'

Sam was bluffing and Tara probably knew it.

The magistrate who would sign a search warrant based on a suspicious noise didn't exist

'You best come back when you've got one then,' Tara said coolly. 'This is bad enough without you poking around my house.'

Chapter 17

Davy Swan drove off as soon as he read the text, grimacing at the high-pitched beeping from the dashboard as Jimmy Marshall battled with the seatbelt.

'Where we meeting him?' Marshall asked.

'Pick up in ten minutes. He'll be there waiting. There's no CCTV apparently.'

'Do those streets still exist?' Marshall said, tension drying his mouth.

They cruised towards the pick-up point on sidelights only. Marshall checked the internal lights were switched to off-mode at least five times on the short journey. The Man wouldn't want the car lit up like a beacon when he opened the back door.

They crawled into the designated street, houses and parked cars either side.

A silhouetted figure, head down and dragged along by a panting dog on a taut lead, overtook them.

The Man waited until they had passed then darted from behind a privet, large sports bag in hand. He yanked open the back door and jumped in behind the driver.

'Slow and steady,' he said in greeting. 'No point in attracting attention. Head out of town, south.'

He put his head back, closed his eyes.

Nobody spoke.

Ten minutes later The Man sat forward, head between the two front seats.

'What went wrong then?' he said in a calm, quiet voice, noticing the ugly gash on Marshall's head for the first time.

'He put up a fight and legged it,' Swan answered. 'I sorted Staples here when we got back to the lock-up so no hospitals to worry about.'

'I'm not interested in his cut head. What happened with Scott Green?'

'When he bolted he ran straight in front of a bus,' Swan said quickly.

The Man twisted the black plastic bottle top and turned towards Marshall.

'Go on then, how did you get cut?'

'He kicked me in the head,' Marshall said, 'and I bashed into the wall.'

The Man took three mouthfuls of Diet Coke, looked at the congealed blood around the ridge of staples, and wondered how much blood, how much DNA, was on the wall.

'Turn left here. Get off these main roads. What about the newsagent you mentioned on the phone? Will he say anything?'

Swan glanced in the rear-view mirror, searching for a clue in The Man's facial expression. There wasn't one.

'Don't think so.'

The Man sat back and finally examined the sandwiches.

Marshall stared straight ahead; Swan's eyes darted between the road and the rearview mirror.

The Man discarded two packets before opening the third.

He bit into the Prawn Mayo.

Marshall held his breath. He didn't need to look at The Man to know he'd opened a sandwich.

'Just what the doctor ordered. I'm starving.'

Swan and Marshall exhaled, quiet and slow.

'So,' The Man continued like a managing director chairing a business meeting. 'Scott runs in front of a bus. Not your everyday suicide method. Did you get him to write his own note?'

In the edgy silence, The Man belched loudly. Two things always fizzed him up – Diet Coke and fish and chips. Today it was the Coke. 'Well?'

'He wouldn't,' Marshall blurted out. 'We couldn't get him to do it so I wrote it…looked alright though. Looked authentic.'

'What about his mobile?'

Swan scrambled for approval.

'Took that off him before we went to the multi-storey. It's smashed to bits and dumped.'

The Man took another bite and spoke with a mouthful of prawns, pink Marie Rose sauce on the corners of his lips.

'So the note,' he said, working calmly through the possible consequences. 'It's not in his handwriting is it?'

If the police found the blood, identified Marshall through DNA, it wouldn't be too hard to obtain handwriting samples and tie him to the note.

And the newsagent? One description, link it to known associates of Marshall, and bingo, Swan was identified.

How long before Davy 'The Bull' Swan and Jimmy 'Staples' Marshall were banged up?

How long before they tipped him up in a police interview?

Bull and Staples? Bull and Shit more like.

He unwrapped the Gala pie and bit into it, fighting the urge to snap it in two and get straight to the egg.

Two or three minutes of silence followed, tyres on Tarmac and rhythmical chewing the only interruptions.

Marshall couldn't wait any longer.

'How did it go at your end?'

The Man set his teeth around the pork filling, clamped them together and got a mouthful of boiled egg. He chewed, wiped his mouth with the back of his hand, pastry falling onto the seat. He smiled at the flakes, remembering the young lass this morning pushing the buggy, pasty in mouth and pastry falling onto her child's head…'baker's dandruff' they called it round here.

'My end? Like clockwork. No problem. Take the next turn-off. Find somewhere quiet to pull over.'

Minutes later they turned off the rural road onto a track that within ten metres was blocked by a five-bar gate, high hedges either side.

'Turn off the lights.'

The Man unzipped his bag, put on a pair of gloves and took the mobile out of his pocket. He removed the SIM card, wiped it with his handkerchief, cut it up with a pair of scissors, wiped the phone, got out of the car and then threw all the pieces into the hedge.

Back in the vehicle he drank greedily from the large bottle of Diet Coke. 'Don't worry. It's sorted now. There'll be no comebacks on us.'

He watched two pairs of shoulders in front relax in relief. Like two young scolded children neither turned around; first rule when you're in the shit… don't make eye contact.

The car was in darkness as he leaned forward, put the bottle on the floor and gripped it with his feet. He took the tiny, clear plastic bag from inside his right sock and tipped the powder into the bottle.

———

SAM DROVE into the multi-storey car park opposite Thompson's Newsagents.

She had no idea what she was looking for, but if Scott Green had run out of a car park there were two burning questions: how had he got there, and what was he doing there in the first place?

She slowed on level 4. The old car park attendant was checking tickets on windscreens. She didn't realise they still had staff, presumed they were redundant, replaced by Automatic Number Plate Retrieval cameras.

It was 11.35pm.

Tall and stick-thin, the weight of the uniform jacket pushed the man's shoulders towards the ground.

She pulled up alongside him, wound down her window, and flashed her warrant card.

'Sorry to bother you. I just need to do a check of your car park. Nothing to worry about.'

He adjusted his cap, a mark of respect to authority, old school manners; jacket and tie to visit the doctor type.

Jim McLean, too tired to be curious, old enough to be polite, bent down and put his bony hand on her door. 'That's okay pet. Need a hand?'

'I'll be fine thanks. Tell me, is the car park cameraed up?'

'Normally it is, but it's all down. Maintenance have been working on it all day.'

'You been here long?'

'Since eight this morning. Doing a double shift. Josh, one of the other lads, rang in sick. I'm doing my eight 'til four, and his four 'til midnight. That's when this place shuts.'

Sam's smile turned to pity. The guy must be in his late seventies. Double shift? In this concrete tomb?

'Actually, you probably can help me, but only if you've got time...'

She raised her eyebrows. Old or not he picked up on the unspoken question.

'Jim. Jim McLean.'

'Have you seen anything unusual today Jim?'

She avoided the word suspicious; that invariably led to a resounding 'no'.

People were more likely to tell you about unusual things. 'Unusual' could mean anything, a less loaded word than suspicious.

'No...well apart from the accident outside with the bus.'

'Did you see that?'

'Not the bloke getting knocked down. I heard the sirens. Went out to see what the fuss was about.'

Sam looked at his frail hand, translucent skin, clipped nails and broad wedding ring.

'Tell you what,' Sam said, 'Jump in.'

The higher she drove, the less cars there were.

'Is it always this quiet?' she asked.

'Yeah, not many left now, and only overnighters coming in.'

By the time they reached the upper level Sam knew Jim McLean was 79 years old, married more than half a century, had two children and three grandchildren and would be a great grandfather very soon. He had worked hard at a variety of jobs, never claimed benefits in his life and always believed the state would provide him and his wife with enough money to get by. Working at his age had never crossed his mind.

Sam parked up and they both got out.

'What are you looking for?' Jim McLean asked, adjusting his cap again.

'Not sure. Sorry to sound evasive. I just want to walk around.'

She counted three cars. 'You stay here. If I need anything I'll shout.'

He nodded and watched as Sam looked at the tickets in the windscreens. Each car had been there since around 11 that morning, which explained why they were on the top tier. She touched the bonnets – all cold.

Sam walked to the pedestrian exit door, put her back to it and looked around. Nothing appeared out of the ordinary.

She walked slowly to the perimeter, eyes searching the grey concrete floor and walls. It took her less than five minutes to find red-brown splatters on the wall just below head height, more red-brown drops on the floor.

'Jim. Can you come here please?'

He walked briskly, alert and interested now.

'You know how long that's been here?'

She pointed to the drops. Sam would need forensic scientists to confirm it was blood and if she was right, DNA would hopefully tell her who it belonged to. Blood Pattern Analysis would help her understand what had happened.

Jim McLean shook his head.

'Wasn't here this afternoon. We have to report that sort of thing. Graffiti, vomit. You'd never believe what people do in car parks.'

I probably would.

'We have to keep everything clean as possible. Them up high say it's all about the customer experience.'

He shook his head.

'All they want to do is park their cars. Not stop for a picnic.'

You and Ed would get on like a house on fire.

'How can you be sure it wasn't here this afternoon?'

Jim McLean closed his tired eyes and remembered.

'About four o'clock I helped an old lady with her shopping.'

Sam smiled, wondering if the 'old' lady was younger than him.

'She was parked just here. I'd have seen it.'

'Just excuse me for a minute Jim.'

Sam stepped away and made the call.

Once SOCO had arrived, taped off the area and started photographing and swabbing the walls, she walked every level with Jim including the staircase. Satisfied there was nothing else untoward she thanked him, drove out of the car park and went to HQ to brief Monica Teal.

Sam had plenty to tell her but first and foremost would be remembering to ask the ACC to send a letter of appreciation to Jim McLean's employers.

———

THE MAN HAD HIDDEN in the hedgerow for over half an hour. Two cars had driven past, too fast to notice the car parked on the darkened track.

Swan and Marshall were still in their seats. The crushed Rohypnol tablets had left them semi-conscious. The carbon monoxide had put them in a coma.

Once the Rohypnol had kicked in, The Man had taken

a length of flexi-hose and a jubilee clip from his bag. He had fastened one end of the hose around the exhaust, fed the other through the driver's window and climbed into the back seat.

He had reached around Swan and sealed the window with gaffer tape. The Man wasn't stupid enough to tape the window from the outside. No point in giving the police a bone.

He had dropped the gaffer tape in the driver's foot-well – the gloves he was wearing would conceal his prints – then lifted Swan's limp right hand, pressing his compliant fingers against the tape around the window. He had let Swan's arm fall, checked the car was in neutral, and stretched to turn on the ignition.

Back by the hedgerow he waited and listened, doing his best to tune his ears into everything except the idling engine next to him.

Thirty minutes felt like two hours. The Man was always careful but patience was never easy for him. Finally, another vehicle approached, the sound of the engine slowing over three high-pitched horn beeps as it pulled up just before the farm track.

The Man moved quickly from the hedgerow and put his hands on the warm bonnet of the car still pouring exhaust fumes through the taped driver's window. Through the windscreen, Swan and Marshall were barely visible, motionless ghosts consumed by a fog that churned and boiled with lazy grace.

Satisfied, The Man walked to his pre-arranged lift.

'Sorted?' the driver asked.

The Man closed the door and fastened his seat belt.

'They'll not be talking to anybody,' he said. 'Like the Green Party says, pollution's a fucking killer.'

The Man laughed at his own sense of humour and told the driver to head to York on the A19 South.

The driver glanced back., 'What's in York?'

'I'll find a B and B,' The Man said. 'Bed down for the night then tomorrow catch a train to King's Cross.'

The train might be a bit of a risk but he had business in London that couldn't wait.

'I need to be back home by Monday night,' The Man said, thinking of the rented high-rise, a suburban prison with communal gardens and stuck-up arseholes who thought the weekend trip to Waitrose and a couple of overpriced pints on the waterfront was the good life.

Still it wasn't for much longer.

'The driver accelerated and moved smoothly through the gears.

'There'll be CCTV everywhere at York Station.'

'I'll keep my head down,' The Man said, tired of talking now. 'Nobody will be looking for me.'

The driver concentrated on the poorly lit road, travelled a couple of miles before speaking again.

'You still in that rented place?'

The Man grimaced and stared out into the darkness.

'For now, but Christ I can't stay there much longer. Talk about Stepford.'

The driver glanced at him again.

He thought about explaining the 'Stepford Wives' movie but what was the point? Too young for the original, probably too young for the 2004 remake.

'Do you need me to stay in York tonight?'

Now he let his eyes take in the soft profile of the woman behind the wheel.

'No, just drop me off and get yourself back home,' The Man told her. "And if you get any more visits from the cops, stick to the plan. They've got nothing. They're just fishing.'

He looked at her again.

Tara would be a beautiful distraction, but distractions like her came at too high a price.

Chapter 18

Sam briefed Monica Teal on the Malvern Close shootings, and told her all the post mortems would be carried out in the morning.

'The scene's cordoned off and preserved,' Sam said. 'We'll not be able to speak to many witnesses tonight. The firearms teams, negotiators and everybody else will have had their hot debrief. May as well make an early start tomorrow. Nothing's spoiling.'

'Makes sense. Thanks Sam.'

Sam walked back to her office.

As arranged, Russell Willings was waiting.

She hung up her coat.

'Have you got a statement from the woman in the push chair?' Sam asked, walking to her chair.

'I have, boss,' Willings' eagerness was radiating like cheap cologne. 'Corroborates what the newsagent says.'

Sam sat down, leaned forward, and rubbed her eyes. She could do without this but no way would she let Mick Wright kick the investigation into the long grass.

'Okay. Have you got the suicide note?'

Russell Willings nodded, handed her a scrap of paper in a clear plastic bag. It was written, if that was the correct phrase, in blue ink. The block capitals could easily be mistaken for the handwriting of a child.

I'VE HAD ENOUGH. TO MUCH SHIT TO MUCH HASSEL.
OUR LASS LEEVING WAS THE LAST STRAW.
NO POINT IN GOING ON.
I WON'T BE MISSED.
NOBODY GIVES A FUCK.

SAM READ IT THREE TIMES; each time slower than the time before.

'You spoke to his wife?'

Willings nodded. 'They'd been together over twenty years but she plucked up the courage to leave him three months ago. It wasn't common knowledge. She hadn't told anybody, apart from a few of ours who helped get her into a refuge. She's still devastated, though. Idolised him despite everything'

'She should have got away years ago,' Sam said.

Scott Green was quick with his fists and if there was no other target, Linda would do.

Sam remembered him as a nasty piece of work. She'd interviewed him a couple of times years ago. He was the type who didn't even say 'No reply' in police interviews, just sat there with a smart-arse smile, grinning at every question.

Not that Scott Green had always been an obvious low life.

The son of a Welsh miner, his world had revolved

around Rugby Union since the age of seven. The sport was his past, present and golden future until he did his knee in a game with a touring side from Australia. By the time he met Linda in a pub in St Davids, when she was camping with friends, Scott Green was drifting. He'd shown her around the Pembrokeshire coast and after ten days together, with nothing to stay for, he had followed her to Seaton St George.

Linda's uncle was Billy Skinner.

With no qualifications, no family ties in the north east, and one casual labouring job after another, Green's journey to the bad lands became nailed on.

He had become one of Skinner's trusted inner circle and was loyal to Luke, the youngest son, after Skinner was killed. At one time Green's name carried weight, even fear, but not now. The Skinner empire was falling apart and Scott Green had been finding himself more and more isolated with nowhere to run.

'The SIM card in his sock,' Sam was saying now. 'Did he have a mobile on him?'

'No.'

'Strange,' Sam said. 'We'll see what's on the SIM.'

She told Willings about what she had found in the car park.

'We still have the bus?' she went on.

Russell nodded.

'While we're checking it for faults let's take a look at its CCTV. It might have picked something up.'

Mick Wright appeared in the doorway, face crimson and mouth moving like a goldfish until the words escaped.

'What the hell is this,' Wright was almost growling. 'You've got the suicide note. What more do you want?'

Willings' cheeks reddened but when Sam stood up, she was in control.

'We've also got two witnesses saying he was being chased,' her words measured, assured. Wright's own words were quick, defensive.

'Two people running? So what? You've never seen people running?'

'What were they running for?' Sam asked, like a teacher speaking to a young child. 'They're not likely to be running for a bus if they're coming out of a car park are they?'

Wright glared but the cracks, the awful doubts, were showing.

'I don't know. I'm not a bloody mind reader, but the note's pretty conclusive.'

Like a boxer closing off the ring, Sam kept Wright on the back foot.

'Did you notice anything unusual about the note?'

Wright shook his head and tried to reignite his aggression.

'Such as? He can't spell? Not exactly unusual. Not like the shite are literary buffs.'

Russell Willings shuffled in his seat, wanting to be anywhere but here.

'It's not just the spelling,' he heard Sam say.

'What then?' Wright throwing a desperate counter. 'He hasn't done joined-up writing?'

Sam quick-stepped up to Wright and eyeballed him. Still she didn't raise her voice.

'Scott Green spent his childhood playing rugby. Nothing else mattered, least of all school.'

Sam paused, watching Mick 'Never' Wright's bluster begin to fracture beneath the tough façade.

'If you had one ounce of investigative nous, you'd know not to take things at face value. You know, the ABC of investigations?'

Sam's nose was inches from Wright's.

'Accept nothing, believe nothing, challenge everything. Try doing some checks next time. Check Scott Green's custody records. Check the system.'

Sam turned around, walked to her desk, and delivered the knockout blow with her back to Wright.

'Scott Green can't read or write.'

TARA PAXMAN DROPPED off The Man near the city walls in York and then took ages trying to get out of the place, the one-way system proving anything but one-way; she'd driven in circles for what felt like hours.

She might have got out quicker had she concentrated on the road signs instead of his list of instructions. He dished out more tasks than her lecturers, and she had binned university because it was too much like hard work.

At least with the academics if you couldn't be bothered you just fluttered your eyes, flashed your tits and they drooled a stay of grace. Not him.

Could she really trust him? He was as ruthless as a pit viper. If he felt you had served your purpose or you were a loose end that needed tying off…she shuddered at the thought of a car full of carbon monoxide.

Finally she stumbled across the sign she was looking for and followed the rest to the A19.

She'd known The Man a couple of years now. She had at least met him. Many hadn't. Some wondered whether he was just a myth.

She negotiated the roundabout and turned right towards the A19 north, smiling at the sudden memory of a day out in York with Harry Pullman.

Harry had always treated her well, set her up with a

few locals who had decent wallets. Not that he ever took anything from her. He wasn't a pimp.

He'd even let someone take her into his flat above the pub one night. What did they call him?

There'd been so many, the money too easy.

John, that was it. John. A local councillor. Always getting grief off his wife. She seemed to recall a distant rumour he had finally left her and shacked up with somebody new. What the hell was his surname? She gave up trying to remember and tried to find something bearable on the radio.

Joining the dual carriageway she relaxed her shoulders and settled back into the seat, stress melting away like snow in a sauna.

Her mind went back to John. He was always quick, more time talking than performing, and it was always an easy £300. A slow erotic dance in an Ann Summers red basque followed by a few quick, panting thrusts.

She recalled that night in Harry's flat. She had rubbed his thigh but he'd been more interested in the laptop on the coffee table. And then all hell had broken loose, Matt Skinner smashing glasses and bottles in the bar below.

John's surname, though, still escaped her as the monotony of the drive back to Seaton St George – and the gin – folded tiredness like a cloak around her shoulders.

Back in the house she poured a large gin, no tonic, and turned on the TV. No need to put on her dressing gown. She'd crash in her joggers. She channel hopped before settling on MTV.

She had no idea how long she had been there when her mobile rang. She looked at the screen and answered. 'Lester?'

'Open the door. I'm coming around the corner.'
'Now?'

'Right now. The place is deserted, except for a few Muskas.'

Tara presumed Muska was a cop and tried to shake the sleep from her head. She only had a minute or two. Now wasn't the time to be off her guard.

———

ED SAT up in the chair when Sam walked into the living room.

'Why didn't you go to bed?' she said.

'Knew I wouldn't get to sleep. Too much on my mind.'

'Do you want a cuppa?'

'Go on then.'

Ed followed Sam into the kitchen, sat on one of the stools by the island.

Sam filled the kettle. 'What are you thinking about? Tonight?'

'That…all sorts of things really. Ray Reynolds.'

Sam leaned against the bench.

Ray Reynolds, deceased, had been a Detective Superintendent.

'What about him?'

'In spite of everything I still went to his funeral,' Ed said. 'Puts things in perspective.'

Sam dropped a tea bag into each mug and walked to the fridge for the milk; she remembered Ed dashing to this kitchen when she thought she was going to be attacked. Now it was him who looked worried.

'I used to go to weddings,' he said. 'Then it was christenings, now its funerals. Just reminds you where we're at. More years behind us than in front.'

He took the mug.

'I'm nearly at retirement but what delights does that

hold? Home life up the proverbial creek, not a paddle in sight. Bad enough now, but the thought of being there full time…doesn't bear thinking about.'

Sam sat opposite him.

'Even if she gets half your retirement pot, you'll be okay financially. Sell the house. Buy somewhere smaller. Live your life as you want to live it.'

'Sounds a plan I suppose,' Ed said with no conviction.

He raised the mug to his lips, temporarily lost in domestic purgatory.

'Anyway, how did you get on?' he asked at last.

'Shed load to do tomorrow.'

'What was it like inside?'

'Zac Williams is dead, down to us. Lucy Spragg's dead.'

'Down to Williams?' Ed's tone making it a question not a statement.

'On the face of it.'

Ed gave her a weak smile. Sam challenged everything, even when something looked surer than death and taxes.

'We found internet print outs of newspaper reports stuck on the kitchen wall. All mass shootings in America.'

Sam told him about the grim collection, that all the killers had been young; all had committed suicide at the scene.

'He's been planning this then?' Ed asked.

'Looks like it but that means he must have lured Marcus Worthington-Hotspur there. It can't have just been wrong place, wrong time.'

'So, he takes out Lucy and Marcus because they're shagging behind his back, but why the others?' Ed said.

'Who knows?' Sam had already been going over and over the same question. 'Because he can?'

'Towards the end shots are fired inside the house,' Ed said. 'Is that when he shoots Lucy?'

'Probably' Sam said. 'Well, possibly.'

Ed nodded. 'So it's fair to say, at least as a working hypotheses, that Marcus was killed whilst Lucy was still alive.'

Sam blew across the tea before she answered.

'Are you suggesting he wanted her to know? He wanted to punish her?'

'Could fit,' Ed said.

Sam sipped her tea and when she spoke again her words were slow, thoughtful.

'It could, but what about the others?'

Ed put his mug down. He had a question but had to wait for it to take solid form through the fog in his head.

'Does he even have a printer?'

Sam's sleep-deprived eyes widened.

'Shit!' Her fingers tightened around the handle of the mug. 'That never crossed my mind. Shit. How did I miss something so obvious?'

She jumped to her feet and started to pace the room.

Plenty would excuse themselves for a missing something in the middle of a bloodbath but Sam never needed much of a reason to give herself a kicking.

'Fatty Sanderson had half his head blown off,' she said now, almost subconsciously changing tack.

Ed shrugged. 'That's his suspended sentence permanently suspended then'

This time the sledgehammer wit brought a smile. Sometimes you had to lighten up.

'There's some fur missing from the hands of the rabbit suit, some possibly transferred onto the gun. I've told Julie to have a look at it when they're swabbing for gunshot residue.'

Ed's scrunched face resembled a puzzled Shar Pei. 'What's that about?'

'Not sure,' another question simmering in Sam's mental in-tray. 'It's as if the gun was sticky and when he dropped it some fur's come off with it.'

Ed pictured the scenario, said: 'Can't have been that sticky then.'

Sam stared blankly then fumbled for her mobile.

'Julie, it's Sam. Sorry to bother you.'

Julie Trescothick assured her it was fine.

'When you go back to the house, check to see if there's any glue, you know like Super Glue.'

'Will do,' Julie said. 'We've done the swabs for gunshot residue. There's definitely some sort of gluing agent on both the suit and on the weapon.'

Chapter 19

THE MAN WALKED around the room, naked except for the white towel wrapped around his waist, torso red and tingling after the hot shower.

He bent down, pulled open the mini-bar, grabbed a small bottle of lager and a miniature bottle of whisky.

He gulped the lager, draining the bottle in a couple of seconds, tipped the whisky into the toothbrush tumbler, rolled a little of the fruity liquid around his tongue and swallowed. It burnt more than usual, a sharp contrast to the throat-numbing cold lager.

He flopped on the bed and mentally replayed the day.

Not everything had gone to plan, but when did that ever happen? Improvisation was key.

He stretched out on the bed, took another sip and grinned.

If he had a family Coat of Arms his motto would be the Latin equivalent of 'improvise'.

'THANKS JULIE.'

Sam looked at Ed. 'Hands glued onto the gun?'

She started pacing again.

'Why would you do that?' she said.

'Stop you losing your grip if you're sweating,' Ed said.

He put the mug on the Angel of the North coaster on the bench, carried on speaking.

'He'll be sweating anyway because of the situation. Throw in the fact he's wearing a rabbit suit and he'll be sweating his bollocks off.'

'Possibly,' Sam conceded.

She sat back down. 'Oh, and Scott Green's dead.'

Ed's eyes were as wide as his smile.

'There is a God. What was he doing in there?'

'He wasn't. He was wiped out by a bus.'

Ed let his smile stretch wider.

Sam took out cigarette. 'You mind?'

'Your house. Carry on.'

Sam lit up. 'Strangely though two witnesses say he was being chased and I found blood on the walls on the top deck of the multi-storey.'

'And?'

'Don't know, but he had a suicide note in his pocket and the world and his wife knows…'

'He can't write.'

'Exactly. But if he was killed, who by?' Sam said.

'The Skinners aren't as intimidating as they were. Not with Luke and Mark on remand. Taking out one of theirs is a bit easier now.'

'Even so, they'll still be operating from prison. Every little shit can get a phone in prison. Plenty would want to keep on the good side of the Skinners.'

Ed tried rubbing away the shadows under his eyes.

'I keep thinking of Paul. Poor bastard. Talk about the wrong place at the right time.'

'I know,' Sam said. 'Saved those little kids, killed for his trouble. I saw the girl he was visiting.'

'What was she like?'

'Prostitute.'

'What! You're kidding,' Ed said, voice tailing off.

'Not your skeletal junky street worker, though. High end. And she didn't charge Paul apparently.'

'What the hell was he doing with a Tom?' Ed still couldn't believe what he was hearing.

'I'm not condoning him but believe me I could see the attraction,' Sam said. 'I had a little chat with her.'

Sam looked away, staring at the gleaming granite worktops as if she was searching for inspiration

There was something about her.

She stared a little longer before turning back to Ed.

'I heard a noise upstairs when I was in Zac Williams' place, then heard it again in her house. I wanted to check it but she wouldn't let me without a warrant.'

'Sounds like she's been around the block,' Ed said, surprised a civilian witness would give the cops a hard time when the Wild West had just kicked off next door. 'Who is she?'

Tara Paxman.

Ed knew the name. He looked up at the ceiling, waiting for the fog bank to clear again.

'Tara Paxman. Bugger me!'

'You know her?' Sam said.

'Tara Paxman. Former bedmate of Councillor John Elgin. Well known to our good friend and witness for the prosecution, Harry Pullman.'

SUNDAY 1ST NOVEMBER

SAM ZOMBIED into the en suite, eyes swollen, red and filled with grit.

5.20am. She'd be at her desk by 6am.

Stepping out of the shower she managed a smile; it had been years since she'd dressed to a male snoring concerto. Ed was still in a deep sleep.

They had agreed to tell no one Ed had stayed the night. The rumour mill would be like a bush wire and if Ed's wife spotted the smoke she would go ballistic. The separate bedrooms arrangement would never wash.

Sam dragged her body into clean clothes, eyes on the bed, the duvet like a magnet pulling her back. She had been in there three hours and had no idea when she would feel its warmth again.

On her way out she glanced into one of the other bedrooms. Ed's clothes were neatly piled on the wicker chair; she could see the smudgy outline of his body still wrapped in the duvet. She closed the door silently.

When she reached work a young uniform was waiting outside her office.

'Can I have a quick word Ma'am?'

I hate that. Makes me sound so old!

'Of course you can. What can I do for you?'

She had no idea who he was. Even someone as switched-on as Sam couldn't be expected to know everyone.

The uniform followed her into the office, waited for her to sit down. He was so rigid it looked like someone had rammed a poker up his back.

Sam indicated a chair. 'Sit down.'

He started speaking as he lowered himself into the seat.

'I've been on nights Ma'am. Getting ready to go off duty soon.'

Sam smiled, leaned forward. It was obviously important. Important enough for him to conquer his nerves and wait for her.

'I went to a suicide last night.'

'The one with the bus on the High Street?' Sam asked.

'No, that happened before I came on duty. We were told about that at the briefing. No, mine was another one. A double actually.'

'Two bodies?' Sam interrupted, leaning further across her desk, pulse a little quicker. 'As in potential suicide pact?'

Sam had investigated most things but this would be a new one.

The young officer spoke faster than a job seeker at his first interview. Sam resisted the urge to tell him to breathe.

'I don't know. Two bodies in a car, both male, hose running from the exhaust into the driver's window, taped up from the inside.'

'Where did this happen?'

The officer gave her the location and time, told how he had found the car by chance while he was on patrol and what he had done as 'first officer on the scene'.

Sam knew the uniform, starting to like someone in the early throws of hypothermia, wanted to say more.

'But you think something is suspicious?'

Sam's world revolved around the 's' word and if this wet-behind-the-ears cop wanted to become part of it, he needed to grab his cojones and back his judgement.

'There was a phone smashed to bits near the car,' he said quickly. 'It doesn't make sense. Why destroy your phone if you're going to top yourself?'

His eyes darted left and upwards, worried his choice of phrase wasn't part of any police manual.

Sam leaned back in her chair. The young man's instincts at the scene had been sharp, alright.

'Good point,' she nodded. 'I'll get that looked into. Anything else?'

'Yes. Both had their trousers and underwear off.'

'Lovers?'

'Don't know Ma'am.'

'Any ID on them?'

'No. But I know them.'

Sam waited.

'Davy Swan and Jimmy Marshall.'

Sam pushed her chair away from the desk and stood up. She leaned against the windowsill and stared outside.

She knew them, too. Marshall and Swan, heavies for hire: with links to various crime families and loyal only to cash.

'Write up what you've just told me, Sam told the uniform. 'Put it in an Officer's Report…'

She paused.

'Danny… Danny Unsworth Ma'am.'

'Okay Danny. Write it all up. Put it in an email to me. And thanks for letting me know. I appreciate you taking the time to wait outside my office.'

She followed him out and watched him stride away. 'Good work Danny,' she shouted down the corridor, knowing others would hear. 'Well done.'

Sam walked back to her desk and dropped into her seat.

Three deaths in one night, each trying to lead the police down the suicide route.

She was already convinced Scott Green hadn't

deliberately thrown himself under a double-decker, but Swan and Marshall?

She couldn't see them agreeing to meet their maker in a suicide pact.

And whilst the gentlemen may have been many things, Sam strongly suspected homosexual was not one of them.

Add those three deaths to the five at Malvern Close and this was the kind of carnage that made Seaton St George sound like Al Capone's blood-drenched Chicago.

And what about Bill Redwood, the yachtsman whose death was on the front page of the Seaton Post?

Mick 'Never' Wright had written it off as a suicide but was that another lazy mistake.

Sam was on information overload.

She needed tea.

She needed cigarettes.

She needed a box of new detectives.

Only two of those, she already knew, would be easy to find.

Chapter 20

Sᴀᴍ ᴘᴜʟʟᴇᴅ up outside the outer cordon, anxious to revisit the scene before the briefing.

The bodies were gone, shipped off to the morgue, but the tents were still there.

She stood, hands in pockets, the eerie silence broken by the call of a distant fog horn, and thought about the dead.

What a waste of life and for what?

It wasn't the first time she had asked the same question and it wouldn't be the last, but this was the job she'd chosen. Nobody forced her to take it.

Over the years she had taken part in multi-agency exercises where responses to major incidents from terror attacks to chemical plant explosions were put to the test.

But last night had not been an exercise. Last night was real, a human tragedy the victims' families would never get over. Whatever the police had done yesterday, however well they would have scored if the horror had been just a make-believe test, none of it had helped the dead.

Sam shuddered. Was the smell of gunpowder trapped

in the damp mist or was it still sliding through her memory?

The media would be all over the story, desperate for angles beyond the plain facts, happy to pick away at the police response, drum up a debate on gun crime, and ask why no agency had spotted Zac Williams as a slaughter risk.

Sam knew plenty of that journalism was legitimate – in truth important –but the media was a double-edged sword every SIO knew could land a fatal blow to the most promising career.

It never took long for the police to go from heroes to villains.

There would ultimately be an investigation by the IPCC but for now she retained primacy. Sam wouldn't be judged on last night but her starring role in the spotlight started now. Screw up and she would be the one dodging the blade.

Sam watched a young police officer, clipboard in hand, get out of a marked car.

'Morning Steph,' Sam said. 'You just got here?'

Stephanie Crosby, 25 years old, four years in the Job, had a bright smile that still couldn't light her tired eyes.

'No Boss, I've been here all night. Volunteered for overtime. My relief is on the way now.'

For the past few months Sam had been mentoring Steph Crosby, a promising officer who was now in the CID 'waiting room'. She had passed the interview but a start date to move out of uniform was still to be announced. Like a good quality sponge, she seemed to soak everything up.

'Hope you kept warm?'

Steph grinned and ran her fingers through her brown curls. 'Good heater in the car.'

Sam nodded. 'Anything unusual to report.'

She had chosen the word deliberately again. 'Unusual' was always preferred to 'suspicious' when the request was general not specific. The words meant very different things, even if in the end one could be the other.

'Very quiet. Street empty. The residents aren't back yet. SOCO want to finish in the tents. They've been here since five.'

'Okay,' Sam noted the brevity with a nod of approval. 'Anybody in the house?'

Steph glanced at the clipboard. 'Julie Trescothick went in at 5.15. Just her in at the minute.'

'Anything else?'

'The girl next door.'

'Tara Paxman?' Sam said, interest piqued.

'Well that's the name on the PNC for that car.'

Steph nodded towards the VW Polo on the street.

'She approached me last night and asked if she could go out. I didn't think I could stop her.'

'You couldn't, not really,' Sam said. 'She's entitled to go out. How long was she gone?'

Steph looked at her board again.

'Just over two hours.'

Fine drizzle had come out to play with the mist. Sam pulled up the hood of her berry-coloured Berghaus jacket.

'Did she say anything when she got back?'

Steph shook her head.

'I didn't know whether to let her in but as it was over and she'd never been evacuated I just thought…'

'No problem,' Sam read relief in Steph Crosby's eyes. 'Go on.'

'She thanked me,' Steph said. 'Then a couple of hours later her uncle came to check on her. I didn't stop him because I was worried about her welfare, you know being the only one in the street, what with all these people killed. He wasn't in long.'

'That's fine,' Sam smiled. 'Sound logic.'

Not that I would have let him in...

'You get a name?'

Steph dropped her gaze to the pavement, stomach suddenly rolling in the same direction.

'No.'

Maybe I haven't mentored her enough. Getting his name is pretty basic.

Sam quashed the urge to show her sudden anger and disappointment.

'Don't worry about it. Thanks for everything you did last night.'

Steph looked up, her crimson cheeks a rosy glow on a canvas of dank grey.

'Not sure I'm allowed to do this,' she said, 'but I did get a photo of him on my mobile.'

That's more like it!

'Let me worry about the legalities of covert photographs', Sam told her. 'Text it to me.'

Chapter 21

SAM APPROACHED the house and heard her mobile ping as she pushed open the front door. Steph's text.

'Julie?'

'Kitchen,' Julie Trescothick shouted.

Sam walked in. 'How's tricks?'

'Morning. Getting there. I've concentrated outside so we can let the residents back from the hall. There's a shitstorm going on down there.'

'I bet there is but don't be rushed by whoever is in charge of sorting it. Any problems, tell them to ring me. We only get one chance at this and you know my saying, the crime scene is like a book...'

'But if you destroy the pages you can't read the book.'

They both laughed.

Sam walked back to the wall and looked again at the mass shooting reports.

'They're all American,' Julie said. 'I know we don't have many but why not use British examples?'

Sam re-read each one in turn.

'I've been thinking about this all night. The one thing these have in common is that the shooters are young and they all died at the scene.'

She read another paragraph and backed away before turning to face Julie.

'The likes of Dunblane was beyond awful but…I can't remember his name, not that that bastard is worth remembering…but he was in his forties. The Cumbria shooter was in his fifties. These are much younger. That's the best reason I can come up with. The ones on the wall were all committed by young people.'

'Like our man.'

'Yes. But why put these up?' Sam turned back to the wall. 'To motivate himself? Were these his heroes? Showing him how to get his fifteen seconds of fame?'

She concentrated on another few lines.

'And when did he put them up? Did he know Marcus was coming?'

She turned away from the wall, nipped her nose between finger and thumb.

'It's all too neat. It's like he's speaking to us. Here's my motivation. Now you all know why I did it.'

'Or at least that's what he wants us to think?' Ed appeared at the kitchen door.

'Morning Snore-man,' Sam said, immediately regretting the slip.

She flushed and felt Julie's eyes bore through her like a laser.

'Slept like a top,' Ed said without missing a beat.

'I said to Sue the worst thing she could ever have told you was that I snore. The whole office takes the piss out of me now.'

It was a pretty good lie on the hoof. Time and tongue wagging would tell whether Julie had bitten.

Ed walked to the wall and read the cuttings.

'I've just been saying it's too neat,' Sam said. 'I'll get a team to visit Williams' family, see if he talked about being suicidal. Seems all the rage in sunny Seaton St George.'

'Meaning?' Ed asked.

Sam brought him up to speed on Davy Swan and Jimmy Marshall.

'Trousers down? Forget it! Jimmy's never out of the pubs chasing lasses who like a bad boy and Davy Swan would smack a, a -'

'Gay's the word you're looking for,' Sam stepped in before Ed said something he might regret.

Julie was a great CSI but Sam had no idea how she would react to one of Ed's verbal throwbacks. Not everyone had declared war on snowflakes, the nanny state and anybody who could spell avocado.

'Gay,' Ed said. 'He'd smack them for standing too close, tell them he didn't want to catch something.'

'Hard to believe that kind of attitude still lives and breathes' Sam said, shaking her head.

'Tell me about it,' Julie looked at Ed as she spoke. 'My brother's gay.'

Relief spread through Sam like cool breeze.

Oh shit that was close…

'Jim Melia's s going to be a busy boy today,' she said, happy to step onto safer ground. 'He's got enough to bite a bloody big hole in the major incident budget.

He's had a quick look at them. Marshall's had a bash on the head which someone's generously closed up with the office stapler. Not the neatest of jobs.'

'Beats spending God knows how long in A and E,' Ed said. 'The waiting time's ridiculous. Four-hour targets? Accident and Emergency? More like Accident and Eternity.'

Sam and Julie exchanged a look. Even at this time Ed could summon a rant.

Sam checked they were clear to go upstairs, asked Julie to let her know if she found Williams' mobile or any glue, and set off with Ed in tow.

The torch she had borrowed from Julie was in her right hand.

'Still hearing noises?' Ed said, following her out of the kitchen.

'First I want to see if there's a printer. There's not one down here. And yeah, I want to check the loft. What was Tara's problem with letting me look last night?'

A search for a printer in the two bedrooms drew a blank.

'So the cuttings were ready before the shooting started,' Sam said. 'Goes to the pre-planning I was talking about.'

On the landing Ed stretched to open the loft hatch, relieved to see a ladder.

'Smashing,' he grinned. 'I'm too old to be throwing you up there on my shoulders.'

Sam flicked on the torch and said, 'I'll take a look.'

'You sure?' Ed's voice teasing.

Before she could stop herself, Sam took the bait. 'What, I'm a scared girlie now am I?'

She climbed the aluminium ladder, poked her head into the loft and shone the beam in a slow semi-circle.

The loft had no dividing wall and was almost empty. Almost, but not quite.

'Get a SOCO with a camera up here straight away Ed,' Sam shouted, feet disappearing into the loft.

She shone the beam into the far corner, the corner that was part of Tara's home.

Caught in the light and the drifting motes of dust it looked macabre.

Sam popped her head back through the hatch.
'There's another white rabbit suit up here.'

Chapter 22

THE MAN DIDN'T BOTHER with breakfast, didn't want to give the staff the opportunity to remember him. He'd seen the receptionist last night, Eastern European, pleasant enough, but even less interested in him than he was in her.

He'd kept his head down, hadn't bothered looking for infra-red eyes; he knew CCTV was everywhere.

The reception had been soulless – polished surfaces and fake smiles – and despite the queue, quieter than a sea-front library in a wild winter storm.

He'd stared at the glossy black floor tiles as he waited in line with singles on business, couples on a city break, all happy to get to their rooms without interacting with others.

No different to pubs in London he had thought. Try to strike up a conversation down there and they looked at you as if you were on day release from an institution.

He'd hoped she'd check him in quickly and she did. He'd paid cash, used a false name and was another forgotten face as soon as he took his key card.

Now he stepped out of the hushed foyer into the narrow, quiet Tudor street, adjusted the collar of his coat, pulled the peak of his flat cap towards his eyes and walked slower than a traffic warden.

He headed across Lendal Bridge towards the railway station. He was in no particular hurry. He stopped to admire the pleasure craft moored below, stared fondly at The Maltings pub.

He unwrapped some spearmint gum and chewed slowly as he recalled days gone, days when The Maltings was always the first watering hole on day trips to York. He remembered it as the Lendal Bridge Inn, before the name change in 1992 when Bass Brewery sold it.

He continued over the bridge, towards his train, and rang Tara.

Answerphone.

He rang again.

'Hello.'

Her voice was throaty.

'Woke you up have I?'

'No, I'm up.'

Liar.

'You okay.'

'Yeah.'

'Right. Bin the SIM card on that phone. Hang on...'

He pulled a piece of paper from his inside pocket. On it was a list of handwritten three-digit numbers.

'Use the other SIM I gave you. The number should end in 257.'

'Okay.'

'And do it now. I don't want you forgetting.'

'Okay, okay.'

He glanced again at the paper.

'The next number I'll be calling from ends in 683. You got that?'

'Yes, but who else will be ringing. You're the only one who knows the 257 number.'

He had to admit she was sharp, but he had learned she was inherently lazy, and lazy always led to catastrophe.

'Nothing to report?' he asked.

'No. All quiet. The police are still next door.'

He ended the call, removed the SIM and wrapped it in the warm pliable gum he slipped from his mouth before dropping it in the next bin.

In Malvern Crescent, Tara was already back in her bed.

———

'RIGHT,' Sam barked. 'Next door. Tara bloody Paxman's coming down the nick. Julie have your people wait until we get her before they start taking photographs in the loft. I don't want her tipping off.'

Had Sam banged any harder on the front door her fist would have gone through it.

Tara eventually appeared, looking crumpled in a white knee-length vest-top, wind-tunnel hair, and suitcases under her eyes.

'Alright, alright. Keep your hair on,' she moaned. 'In case you don't remember there was hell on here last night.'

'There's even more hell today young lady,' Sam snapped, pushing past her and stomping into the front room.

'You can't just walk in here!' Tara shouted, spinning around to hustle after Sam.

Ed, grinning, idled after them, hands in pockets, looking forward to watching what was about to unfold.

The women faced each other in the sitting room like street cats with a score to settle.

'Sue me,' Sam said, finger pointing like a rapier ready for the kill thrust. 'Get dressed. Now. You're coming with us.'

'I'm fuckin' going nowhere,' Tara snapped her hands on her hips, 'except back to bed.'

'In that case I'm arresting you –'

Tara shot forwards, the silver crucifix banging against her chest, words flying on wings of spit.

'Arresting me?' she screamed. 'What the fuck for? Living next door to a psychopath? Since when was that a crime?'

Sam leaned in towards Tara until their noses were almost touching. 'How about murder?'

Tara stepped back, words still piggy-backing on those wings, hands back on hips. 'You're fuckin' joking?'

Sam wiped the wetness on her cheek with the back of her hand, took a deep breath, and kept it together.

'What I know is that a person in a white rabbit suit was shooting people last night.'

'No shit Sherlock!' Tara shouted. 'Your lot shot the rabbit.'

Ed, grin still in place, leaned against the doorframe and waited for the punch line.

'They did. But guess what I found this morning?' Sam paused.

'I'm all ears,' Tara said, hands still on hips, body braced, face twisted.

'Another white rabbit suit.'

Tara stood her ground, said nothing.

'And guess where I found that?' Sam said

She looked up for dramatic effect.

'Same place I heard a noise last night. Your loft.'

Tara backed off, sat on the settee, and put her eyes to the floor.

'So, unless these particular suits are in your loft breeding like rabbits…' Sam continued.

Ed bit his lip and tried not to laugh. He would have been proud of that one.

'…you've got some explaining to do.'

Sam walked over to the settee, put her hand on its arm, and leaned into Tara.

'Now get some clothes on.'

Chapter 23

HE'D TOLD Tara he was getting the 12.25 to King's Cross but that was a lie.

Head stuffed into the upturned collar of his coat he boarded a northbound train to Newcastle and sat by the window. There was nobody in the aisle seat, and he was facing the back of the seat in front of him. His only eye contact was with a copy of yesterday's Daily Telegraph.

When the conductor appeared he held his ticket in his outstretched left hand without taking his eyes from the newspaper.

He was a grey man amongst grey people.

The first stop was Thirsk, a north Yorkshire market town, Darrowby in James Herriot's novels about a rural vet.

He stepped onto the single platform and walked, all smiles and outstretched arms, towards the waiting car and its driver.

The small aerodrome, accessed by a five-bar gate with no security, was basically a well-maintained field, the grass cut cricket pitch short, an orange windsock on the boundary. Planes of varying sizes, colours and carrying capacity were lined up like parked cars.

He spotted the white Piper Cherokee with red stripes that he would be flying in, the fairings over the wheels reminding him of Mickey Mouse's feet.

A large wooden hut about the size of two log cabins served as a clubhouse with café and bar, the mic on a small table a rudimentary air traffic control system.

Sundays were popular with recreational flyers and there were already a few pilots standing in small groups outside the clubhouse. A few greeted the driver but took no notice of his passenger.

Above the field a yellow bi-plane was doing aerobatics, buzzing around like an angry wasp.

The Man shook his head. Whenever he came here he always felt he had stepped onto the set of some period drama, watching a University Air Squadron in 1930s England, young, carefree men a few years away from the Battle of Britain.

A glance at the car park and the modern German saloons and Range Rovers snapped him back to the present.

Ten minutes later The Man was in the Cherokee, headphones on as he waited for the pilot to complete his pre-flight checks.

Less than thirty minutes after getting off the train he was airborne.

They flew due east until they reached the North Sea and then turned southwards, flying over the coastal towns of Whitby and Scarborough.

The Man marvelled at how easy it was to fly unnoticed from these fields. Air traffic controllers like to describe flying corridors as motorways in the skies, but he knew these were motorways without cameras or number plate recognition systems. Up here he was an invisible traveller.

When Bill Redwood was alive The Man would sometimes sail with him towards Seaton St George after flying to the field and being driven to one of North Yorkshire's picturesque harbours.

He wanted people to be continually looking over their shoulders, constantly under pressure, never sure of when, or where, he was going to appear. Every move was planned.

His ultimate aim? To be anonymous.

Like a successful Cold War spy, only those who retained their anonymity survived. That meant leaving no traces, electronic or otherwise.

Bill Redwood had been an asset but he got greedy and unfed greed could send men swimming in the police informant pool.

He looked downwards out of the window, the low sun reflecting off the water and the yacht mast below.

His view was better than Sam Parker's.

She was blind.

———————

'LEAVE HER IN THERE TO STEW,' Sam said, slamming the interview room door. 'She knows more than she's letting on.'

'Yep,' Ed said.

Sam leaned against the wall. Her plate was piled Everest-high…post mortems nearly in double digits, a police shooting, press digging around everywhere, and now a second white rabbit.

Ed grinned and flashed his teeth. 'Back in the day, the

only time we'd be mentioning shooting and rabbits in the same sentence was when there were poachers.'

'Poaching?' Sam started to giggle, grateful this time for one of Ed's distractions.

'You had time for poachers?'

'Good old days,' Ed said. 'Didn't happen often, but it happened. More fields in them days.'

Sam shook her head. Ed Whelan was a one-off.

'Issued a lot of pig licences as well back then,' Ed was saying now. 'Cops had to issue them when pigs were being moved.'

Sam giggled harder. 'Remind me when you joined? Top hats, cloaks and lanterns was it?'

Ed smiled, enjoying the sound of her laughter.

'No really,' he said. 'We'd handwrite them at the front desk if a farmer came asking for one.'

Sam looked at him, wiped her eyes, and took a deep breath.

'Funny how things come into your mind,' Ed told her. 'I'd forgotten about those. Job still got done though. Murders still got detected.'

Ed looked around the corridor, making sure he couldn't be overheard.

'Difference was no government targets and efficiency savings in those days. All the cops who sit in offices poring over statistics and preparing reports nobody reads, they'd be on the streets doing police work.'

'Like issuing movement of pig licences,' Sam snorted, the giggles back.

She took a minute to compose herself.

Ed Whelan I needed that laugh.

'Two suits,' she said at last. 'Two suits. You know what that might mean?'

'Zac Williams is not necessarily the shooter.'

'Exactly,' Sam closed her eyes. 'Jesus what are we dealing with here?'

Sam suddenly turned, marched down the corridor towards the exit doors, and rammed them open. Outside she lit a cigarette and inhaled deeply.

'Christ we might have shot someone who wasn't even a threat.'

'Hang on Sam,' Ed was at her side. 'Zac Williams was pointing a rifle. We had three dead in the street.'

'I know, but what if he hadn't shot them? What if there was a second person doing the actual shooting.'

'How would we know that? Who would even consider it?'

They stared at each other.

Ed breathed out slow, broke the silence.

'Bloody hell Sam, any danger that we might get something bog standard to investigate? What you're suggesting wouldn't just take a bit of planning, it would be sophisticated and very, very smart.'

Sam inhaled, exhaled slowly.

'I know and it blasts the 'love rival' theory out of the water.'

She inhaled again before continuing. 'And the cuttings? Were they there to act as motivation, or to point us in a particular direction? You know, crime scene staging.'

Ed didn't respond. He didn't need to. Like Sam, he knew that one of the reasons for staging a crime scene was to lead investigators away from the most logical suspect.

Two quick drags and Sam ground the cigarette into the pavement.

Small trails of smoke were still rising as she pulled out another and lit up.

What if we're looking at this totally wrong?

She stopped walking, flicked ash off the end of her Marlboro, and turned to face Ed. 'Jack Reacher.'

He raised his eyebrows. 'As in Lee Child.'

'Yes, the first film. I can't remember the book it was based on.'

'One Shot?'

It was Sam's turn to raise eyebrows.

'I read a lot,' Ed said. 'Better than watching soaps and it gets me into a different room.'

'Which reminds me,' Sam said. 'Have you rung home yet?'

Ed looked down, shook his head. 'Some things are best put off. It's too early yet anyway.'

'Anything you need…'

'I know.'

'So,' Sam said. 'Jack Reacher, mass shooting, but only one true target. The others were shot to cover it up, throw everyone off the scent.

Ed remembered the plot line.

'What if Zac Williams wasn't the shooter?' Sam went on. 'What if Marcus was shot to make it look like he was the intended target because of his relationship with Lucy?'

'Two huge leaps of faith Sam.'

Sam lifted her head, blew smoke skywards.

'I know, and none of this gets mentioned at the briefing.'

She checked her watch. 'Which is in ten minutes by the way, but let's at least explore the possibility.'

'Okay, but I'm not sure Fatty Sanderson was high enough up the food chain to be the target of such a planned execution. So, for the purposes of this discussion, we can probably rule him out.'

Sam nodded, drew heavily on her cigarette, and spoke as she blew out a plume of smoke.

'Which leaves us with, if not Marcus, then Paul.'

Ed shook his head, eyes wide and lost.

'You think Paul Adams was the target? Why the hell would someone want him taken out? And why like that? This isn't Hollywood. Paul wasn't Bruce Willis.'

Sam pictured Paul Adams, a decent copper who wasn't over flashy or showy.

'Maybe I'm way off here but the rabbit suit's in Tara Paxton's loft. She's a high-end escort. Why was she giving it to Paul for free?'

Chapter 24

'Oh, I've just remembered.'

Sam took her mobile out of her pocket, fingers moving quickly over the keypad.

'Do you know him?'

She held the phone towards Ed who looked at the screen.

'Should I?'

'He told Steph Crosby he was Tara's uncle when he visited last night.'

Ed grinned. 'Is that what they call it now?'

The face of Lester Stephenson stared back at him.

'Doesn't ring any bells. Could be from anywhere. Forward it to me. I'll ask around.'

Sam put the phone back in her pocket. 'She's expensive, so most people couldn't afford her.'

'Something's not right here.' Ed looked away, searching for an answer, seeking inspiration. He turned back to Sam. 'We need to put pressure on her.'

Sam had already planned to turn up the heat on Tara Paxton. Why was she giving it to Paul for free?

'She's not arrested,' Sam said. 'Let's have a chat with her after this is out of the way.'

They walked into the briefing room together and the silence was immediate. 8.30am: the minute everybody lost their voice.

Sam stood at the front, addressed the audience.

'Thanks for coming out. I appreciate it's a Sunday but there's a lot to get through.'

Sam knew they would all be paid well for their efforts; many were due to be on days off and would get time-and-a-half for every hour worked. In reality, on any major job, the constables and sergeants made more money than her; like all ranks of Inspector and above, she didn't get overtime.

Nonetheless, without their commitment, the whole investigation would stall like a £50 junkie.

Sam looked around…fifty personnel, a mix of CID and uniform; detectives from the Major Incident Room; detectives from other police stations who would form Action Crews, the arms and legs of an inquiry; detectives from centralised source units who would form the intelligence cell; the family liaison coordinator; a uniform chief inspector from the Seaton St George management team who would liaise with other agencies; uniform search teams; house to house teams; a firearms tactical adviser; Julie Trescothick from the crime scene investigators; Peter Hunt from media services.

Sam presented an overview before going into specifics.

'Okay…lines of inquiry,' she announced. 'I want the family liaison officers to obtain as much information about the victims as possible, but first I want them all formally identifying.'

There was a short silence, the thoughts of everyone in the room with the victims and their families.

'It's an awful job,' Sam continued, 'but it needs doing.'

Nothing was said. Nothing needed to be said. Most of them had already witnessed grief.

'I know one of our victims is a serving police officer, but we need as much information from his family as we do from the others.'

She paused and made sure all eyes were on her.

'I do not want to hear any speculation about what Paul Adams was doing there, understood?'

Another pause.

'If I hear of anybody starting, or fuelling, rumours then not only will you be off the investigation, you will be facing a disciplinary. Do I make myself clear?'

Nods all around.

'Right, I want a full intelligence picture on Zac Williams. What do we know about him? Get a FLO to visit his family. See if we can establish his mental state. If Zac Williams wanted to go out in a 'Suicide by Cop' scenario, then research shows there's a very high chance he had previous suicidal tendencies.'

The figure was 87% so Sam knew the line of inquiry was solid. She waited until Ed had finished writing her instructions before continuing.

'The rifle is another line of inquiry. Where does it originate from? More importantly, how did Zac Williams get his hands on it?'

She glanced across at Ed.

'And as a matter of priority I want to know Zac Williams' mobile phone number and where his phone is.'

Everybody waited for the next instruction.

'And as if we haven't got enough going on, we had three apparent suicides last night. Whilst I'm not linking them to the shootings, I want us to have a look at them.'

She ran her tongue around her mouth. She needed a drink.

'I want the CCTV checking in the town centre re Scott Green, who was hit by the bus, and I want CCTV cameras and speed cameras checking for the vehicle Davy Swan and Jimmy Marshall were in.'

'Any reason for that Boss?'

Detective Sergeant Russ Chaddick, dickhead and barrack room lawyer, slouched in the chair, legs spread.

'Three suicides in one night is extraordinary,' Sam gave him a stare alive with authority. 'I dislike extraordinary as much as I dislike coincidence. Sgt Russell Willings from Road Policing will liaise with us on this.'

The eyes of the room swerved onto Chaddick, who gave a curt nod.

Back in your box little man

Satisfied, Sam continued: 'The FLOs who visit Lucy's family need to establish what the relationship was like with Zac Williams and any alteration in his behaviour. Jean Spragg, Lucy's mother, has no time for him but dig deep as to why. I know Jean of old. Salt of the earth.'

Sam thought of Jean, how she'd react to the news of Lucy's death.

'See if we can find out how much domestic abuse there really was between Lucy and Williams. We certainly don't have the full picture yet.'

She looked at the Police Search Adviser, Sergeant Ian Robinson.

'Ian there's a questionnaire already prepared in the HOLMES Room for your house-to-house team. For the time being, set the parameters as the cul-de-sac itself and any houses with gardens backing onto them.'

Ian Robinson wrote down his instructions.

'Ed,' she continued, 'I want the youngsters Paul went

to save interviewed by a specialist interviewer and I want them interviewing on camera. We also need to interview the neighbour who helped the lad who managed to run.'

She drew breath, searched out Julie Trescothick in the crowd.

'Julie, keep me updated with any developments and let me know when the ballistic expert arrives. Did you sort a team for the post mortems?'

A nod from Julie.

Sam scanned the room for Peter Hunt and made eye contact. 'We need to have a quick word after the briefing.'

Sam had worked with the press officer enough times to know his importance and value his skill. She would need him more than ever now.

Sam continued. 'I want the mobiles of each victim doing. For speed, just get me texts, incoming and outgoing calls from Friday. If we need to change those parameters later, we can.'

She ran through her mental checklist, satisfied she had forgotten nothing.

'Okay everybody let's get cracking.'

Chair legs scraped along the floor, people stood, chats began.

Sam shouted: 'And for God's sake remember the place will be swarming with media so don't get caught doing anything stupid on camera; that includes laughing, smoking or parking on yellow lines.'

Officers filed out, talking amongst themselves.

Peter Hunt followed Sam into the corridor.

'Shall we do press conference at 10am?' she asked.

'Your call,' Peter answered. Even through a long career as a hard-news print journalist he had never covered anything like this.

'It's a bun fight as you'd expect,' he told Sam. 'All the

nationals are here, a few international as well. It'll be a feeding frenzy. Do you need a hand prepare?'

'I'm not doing it Peter.'

Hunt's mouth dropped a little, his eyes widened a lot. 'Who is?'

Sam explained that ACC Monica Teal would lead the press conference.

'Is she capable?'

'I'm sure she is,' Sam said. 'I've got enough on my plate Peter. Sorry.'

———

TARA PAXTON JUMPED as the interview door burst open.

'Right Tara,' Sam said, 'you're not under arrest. Do you understand?'

Tara stared at the desk, nodded.

Sam sat down, kept her voice deliberately soft. 'I don't know what you're mixed up with here Tara, but you need to start talking to me.'

Tara folded her arms and slunk down the plastic seat. 'Nothing to talk about. I don't know anything.'

'I think you do.'

Ed sat next to Sam.

Tara gave her best surly teenager impression.

'Who's this?' Sam took her mobile out of her pocket, showed the photograph of Tara's 'uncle'.

Tara glanced at the screen and looked at the wall to her left, her words barely audible. 'Never seen him before in my life.'

'Funny, he was at your house last night,' Sam said.

Tara kept her eyes on the wall and her mouth shut.

'Okay Tara, no problem,' Sam said. 'I'll go to the press

with this, get the guy's picture out there, the police are keen to trace…'

Tara suddenly pushed the chair backwards and was on her feet. 'You can't do that!'

Sam smiled, voice still soft. 'Yes I can. Sit down.'

Tara sat and stared at the table.

'Lester Stephenson,' she said sullenly. 'He's a businessman, lives on a farm in the sticks somewhere.'

She paused and swallowed. 'Look the man's nice, married, wife, grandkids. Don't cause him any shit.'

'He should have thought about that before visiting you,' Ed said, speaking for the first time.

Tara gave him 'fuck you' eyes and a pout.

Sam changed tack.

'What do you know about the rabbit suit in your loft?'

'Nothing, that's what I know about it,' Tara sat up, stiffened her shoulders, her voice loud and her words quick. 'That loft goes straight through to Zac and Lucy's. Anybody could have put it there.'

Sam eased back into the chair and kept the smile of satisfaction off her face. Tara had made the classic mistake – spoke faster than her mind was thinking.

'When was the last time you were in the loft?'

Tara's eyes belonged to a bullfrog. 'What?'

'You heard. You've obviously been up there. Otherwise you wouldn't have known there was no dividing wall. So, when was the last time?'

'I'm saying nothing whilst he's here.'

She folded her arms, leaned back in the chair, and stared at Sam.

'What have you got against Detective Sergeant Whelan?'

'He's a bloke. I'm not speaking in front of any coppers with a cock.'

Ed left the room. This wasn't the time for an ego. 'You want to tell me what you've got against Ed?' Sam said when they were alone.

'The only bent coppers I've ever heard about are men. I don't trust any of them. You though, they're always a bit wary of you, so I know you're not in anybody's pocket.'

'I can assure you neither is Ed Whelan.'

'Yeah well, better safe than sorry.'

'So, the rabbit suit?'

Tara looked away.

Sam had witnessed this moment in every interview that started with a denial, the moment when a cough was imminent, the admission that was the light at the end of the tunnel.

Tara started talking.

Chapter 25

Luke Skinner answered the mobile in his remand cell.

The detective monitoring his calls sat upright, pen poised, recording running.

Getting mobiles into prisons was easy – throw a dead bird over the wall with a phone hidden in the carcass, fly them over the wall in a bag on a drone, bribe or blackmail a prison officer – but when your name was Skinner it was even easier; everybody wanted to please.

The covert police team had used the heady mix of fawning and fear to their advantage. When an empire is about to crumble, some foresee the collapse and look for a better deal. So in the interests of self-preservation, a trusted member of the family's inner circle had been coerced to deliver a mobile to Luke Skinner. All the police had to do was wait and listen.

Skinner was two weeks from trial and getting desperate; the prosecution's star witness was still walking the streets.

'Yeah?' Skinner said into the phone.

'In last night's game The Reverend was killed.'

The detective wrote down 'The Reverend' and circled it three times.

Luke Skinner and his associates never used names across the airwaves.

'Fuck,' Skinner muttered.

On the outside he would have shouted his rage. Not in here. No point in attracting attention.

'What happened?'

'We're working on it.'

'Don't take too long,' Luke said. 'Time's running out. Any joy with the…'

The detective then wrote down and circled 'source' three times.

'No.'

'Can Pugsley help?'

'Pugsley' received the same circle treatment.

'Pugsley's status unknown at the moment.'

'What the hell's happening out there? You need to get a move on.'

Skinner abruptly ended the call. No niceties, just business.

Now was the time for a cool head and measured reaction, not gung-ho emotion, something his older brother had never grasped.

Luke Skinner sat on the lower bunk and stared at the magnolia wall.

If Harry Pullman gave evidence he was finished. He stretched out on the bed, hands behind his head, eyes closed.

Pullman could be anywhere, hidden away and mollycoddled by his nursemaid detectives. Each time they moved him it took more time to track him down. And time was running out.

Skinner twirled the phone in his hand, brain turning.

Harry Pullman had more lives than the proverbial cat. Even the North Sea couldn't take him. Overboard in those dark, pitiless waters, but like the fucking Man from Atlantis, Pullman had somehow survived.

Now, betrayed and angry, Pullman was a wounded animal fighting to survive.

The police, the security services, the military…they all relied on intelligence systems. Organised crime families were no different and when an asset is lost, be it a well-placed informant or an undercover operative, the organisational intelligence systems take a hit.

And now Luke Skinner had one whose status was 'unknown'. What did that mean? Dead? Dying? Disappeared?

Whatever had happened to Pugsley, getting a replacement wouldn't be easy.

———

Sam answered her mobile and raised two fingers at Tara, indicating how many minutes she would be out of the room.

'Boss, it's Ranjit.'

Ranjit Singh, Intelligence Cell.

'We've checked the contents of the SIM card from Scott Green's sock.'

Sam stood by the interview room door, gripped the phone between shoulder and cheek, and repeatedly scratched the arm that had suddenly become itchy.

'And?' she said, knowing something revelatory was coming her way. Otherwise Singh would have just fed it straight into the HOLMES room.

'There's footage,' Ranjit Singh was trying hard to keep the excitement from his voice. 'It's not brilliant because it's dark, but you can see an altercation on a yacht, two onto one. The one gets battered then thrown overboard.'

Sam looked around, moved further along the corridor, away from the door, then checked she couldn't be overheard.

'Do we know the name of the yacht?'

'Yeah, the camera zooms in on it. The Conquistador.'

Revalatory was right! Questions flooded Sam's head, a hornet's nest hit with a stick.

What was Scott Green doing with the footage?

Had he been there?

Had he got the recording from somebody else?

Had that person been trying to send a message?

Who to?

If Scott Green recorded it, why?

Insurance?

Blackmail?

Sam thought of Bill Redwood. What was his boat called?

'Get it to the techies, see if you can get the footage enhanced. Anything else?'

'Couple of interesting text messages on Paul's phone.'

Again, Sam glanced around to make sure she couldn't be overheard.

The sense of impending doom turned her stomach into tumble dryer spin mode; her mouth stretched out her next two short words, an almost subconscious effort to delay the response.

'Tell me.'

'Paul gets three text messages in the space of forty minutes on Saturday. Last one is about an hour before he calls in the shooting.'

'What do they say?'

'It's the same message, sent three times:

Please, please I need to see you. I can't discuss it on the phone. It's really important. Please I'm begging you. Come as soon as you get this. '

Sam's body slouched and she leant her right shoulder against the wall.

Was Paul lured there?

'Do we know who sent it?' she asked.

'Well we haven't got the phone that sent it. In Paul's directory the number is listed under the name Jezza.'

'Jezza?' Sam repeated.

'Yes. All the other texts from that number have been deleted but we've already retrieved some of them. It's obviously a woman he's…'

Ranjit Singh fell silent.

'What?'

'A woman he's…'

'Spit it out Ranjit. Having an affair with?'

'Yes.'

'This isn't the time to be coy,' Sam said, already racing through possibilities.

Paul could have used 'Jezza' in case his wife checked his mobile.

'Might be short for Jezabel,' Sam said now. 'That would fit.'

'Jezza for Jezebel,' Ranjit was impressed. 'He would need to keep his wife off the scent, definitely.'

'That the voice of experience?'

Ranjit Singh didn't respond, thankful Sam couldn't see his cheeks burning.

Did she know about him and Steph Crosby? Worse still, did she know tonight he was out with Bev Summers?

If anyone checked his phone, Steph was listed under 'Bing' and Bev was 'Mungo.'

He had always liked 'In the Summertime', Mungo Jerry's biggest hit.

Ranjit wasn't married but he was paranoid about other detectives getting into his phone as a prank.

He concentrated on keeping his voice level.

'And just to confuse things, Boss.'

What, more than they already are?

'Go on.'

'Marcus received exactly the same text, only his came from Lucy Spragg's phone.'

'We've got both of their mobiles. It's word for word identical.'

Sam moved away from the wall and began to process the information.

Two identical text messages to get two men to an almost identical location, both of whom ended up being shot dead.

'Ranjit, what about the times the messages were sent?'

'Marcus got his text first. His only message is at 1.20pm. Paul's first is at 2.05pm.'

'Okay, thanks.'

Sam scrolled through her contacts and made a call, Shane 'Tucky' Walton, 45-years-old, experienced Detective Sergeant and a trusted HOLMES room office manager, answered at the second ring tone.

Walton was 5'9" with broad shoulders, jowls, a beer belly and brown hair styled like a monk because he refused to shave the sides to match his bald head: Tucky to everybody in the office after Robin Hood's friendly friar.

'Shane. It's Sam. Raise an action. I want to know what time Marcus's car is first seen in Malvern Close. Between you and me I want to know if it's there before 2.05pm.'

Sam wondered if Marcus was lured there before Paul received his first text.

'Check CCTV. Have the FLO establish what time family or friends last saw him. And get Ian Robinson to add a question to the house to house questionnaire asking people how long the Porsche has been there.'

'Will do,' Shane said.

She contemplated a quick cigarette, but she'd already left Tara over two minutes.

'Jezzer' she thought, walking back towards the interview room. Jezebel possibly, but would you refer to your girlfriend, even in your phone contacts, as a Jezebel?

She took three more steps before the light went on.

If you were trying to be clever, what about a little word association: Jezzer, Jeremy, Jeremy 'The TV Inquisitor' Paxman, Tara Paxman.

Sam pushed open the interview door.

'What did Paul have you down as in his phone contacts, and what do you know about a man on a yacht?'

Chapter 26

Ed Whelan was on the phone in Sam's office. He ended the call as soon as Bev Summers walked in. Lester Stephenson could wait.

'Morning Ed. I got a text from the Boss asking to meet me here. Do you know where she is?'

'She's interviewing Tara Paxman.'

'Never thought I'd work on one of these,' Bev said.

'Me neither.'

He stared out of the window, replaying his final conversation with Zac Williams.

Bev picked up on it immediately.

'Shit, I'm sorry Ed. I forgot you were there last night.'

He didn't move. 'Forget it. Not your problem.'

Bev's phone pinged. Text alert. From Sam Parker.

I'm downstairs in the interview room.

'I've got to go Ed. Sam wants to see me.'

She got as far as the door, stopped and turned around.

'You ever need to talk.'

'Thanks.'

Ed's phone triggered, the text alert the sound of a hunting horn. He read the message.

'Hold up Bev, I'll walk with you. She wants to see me too.'

Sam was in the corridor outside the interview room, pacing up and down. She started talking while they were still walking.

'What she has to say is so incredible it might just be true.'

Ed and Bev joined her, the three of them in a circle, whispering like conspirators.

'Long and short of it,' Sam said, 'she puts Harry Pullman in the frame and says Paul was the target.'

'Paul?' Ed was thrown.

'What's Paul got to do with it?' Bev asked, like Ed trying to make sense of it.

'All sounds a bit far-fetched if you ask me,' Ed said, thrusting his hands into his pockets. 'Don't you think?'

'I don't know,' Sam said, rubbing her brow. 'I really don't know. It explains the second rabbit suit. She says Harry Pullman was dressed in one, shooting people.'

Ed shook his head. 'Hang on, it was Zac Williams who came to the window with a gun.'

He took his hands out of his pockets, shrugged his shoulders, stretched out his arms, palms facing upwards.

'Otherwise how did he end up dead?' he said.

Sam nodded.

I know, I know. She says Zac didn't shoot anybody, but we need more. All we've got at the minute is her story and you're right, it's hard to believe.'

They each stared at the floor.

'What if,' Sam said, her words quiet, measured, slow, 'the gun was stuck to Zac's hands?'

They all digested that thought.

'Okay,' Ed said. 'But I wasn't talking to Harry Pullman. I know his voice.'

'All staged according to Tara. Harry threatened to kill Lucy if Zac didn't say to you exactly what he was told.'

Ed leaned against the wall, rolled his eyes. 'I don't know Sam.'

'Bev. I want her whisking away…'

'What's the rush?' Ed broke in.

'She's paranoid there are leaks everywhere and she doesn't trust male officers. She keeps going on about Ray Reynolds.'

'Ray Reynolds!' Ed said, moving away from the wall.

'You heard me.'

'Ray's dead,' Ed said. 'What's a deceased Detective Superintendent got to do with it?'

'She's convinced there's a bent cop because she overheard Ray say so to Harry.'

Ed shook his head again.

Bev said nothing.

'To make her feel safe I want her away from Seaton,' Sam told them. 'Anyone any ideas? Ed?'

Ed stared at the wall, wondered absently when it had last seen a lick of paint.

'All sounds a bit on the back of a fag packet to me, but if you're dead set on her going, what about the place we took Harry?'

Sam remembered The White Lion, a quiet pub in The Lake District.

'Perfect. Far enough away and he's not going to look there. Last place he'd think we'd hide her, back to where we took him.'

Sam made eye contact with Bev.

'She can't be left. She's convinced he'll find her. Thinks this place leaks like a sieve.'

'Best get your waterproofs Bev,' Ed said grinning, knowing Bev Summers' idea of the great outdoors was walking outside for a smoke. 'You'll love it. Cracking little boozer, you can stretch your legs on the fells, and Ullswater's bloody gorgeous. A bit wet this time of year, but still…'

'The bloody Lake District!' Bev's face had dropped. 'You're winding me up.'

'Keep your voice down,' Sam said. 'Walls have ears. It's a quiet pub and the owners are sound.'

Bev's whole body seemed to slump and turn in on itself.'

'The Lakes', she said in a muttered whisper, knowing she was well and truly stuffed. 'I'm supposed to be out tonight with a toy boy.'

'Tell the young romeo he's cancelled,' Ed, face beaming, was loving this. 'Least you've still got a hot young date. Just a different gender.'

Bev looked up and stuck her tongue out at him.

'You'll need to stay over there a few days,' Sam said.

Ed laughed. Bev looked like she might weep.

'And…I'm sorry, but I can't send anybody with you. I can't spare the staff.'

'Fine,' Bev said, resigned.

'I want you ready to go in the next half-hour and I don't want anybody knowing where you've taken her. I don't even want anybody knowing we've got her. Anybody on the inquiry asks, let's just say we don't know where she is. It's a free country. She can come and go as she pleases.'

'What about Bev?' Ed said. 'You want me to say she's on the sick?'

'That'll do,' Sam said.

'Thanks a lot,' Bev said. 'Now they'll think I can't cope or I'm swinging one. Nothing too serious Ed, I mean it, and definitely not stress. A touch of flu...what about clothes?'

'Go home and throw a few things in a bag,' Sam said. 'You'll have to buy her some kit over there. Like I said, I want as few as possible knowing we've got her.'

Sam spun on her heels. 'Come on. I'll introduce you.'

She looked over her shoulder at Ed. 'Then you and I are going on a boat.'

Bev's smile was 1,000 watt strong and powered by sweet revenge. Everyone knew Ed Whelan hated being on water.

'Serves you right Pugwash!' Bev's smile was still glowing. 'She who laughs last...'

'Champion,' Ed sighed. 'The day just keeps getting better.'

Sam opened the interview room door and did the introductions.

'Tara this is Bev Summers. She'll be looking after you. Protecting you.'

Tara smirked, loaded up the sarcasm.

'Protecting? Yeah right. That's how this shit started in the first place, because you lot couldn't protect people.'

———

HARRY PULLMAN ANSWERED the front door of the flat, his temporary home within the Gun Wharf Marina complex.

He'd been in the town as a young man when he joined the Royal Navy, but he hadn't kept in touch with anyone. Portsmouth was big enough to keep him entertained, big enough to keep him lost.

He shuddered remembering the Lakes. The pub had been alright, but the place? Christ. Talk about tumbleweed blowing down the streets. It had only been for a couple of nights, but to Harry Pullman, that was two nights too many.

The Witness Protection Officer followed him into the living room with a view over the marina.

'Settled in Harry?'

'I have, but for how long? Sorted the leak out yet?'

'We're working on it.'

Harry spun round, face redder than a poppy field.

'You're working on it! Is that the best you can come up with? You're fuckin' working on it. They've tracked me down twice now. I'm never in one place long enough to find out the barmaid's name.'

'I understand your frustration Harry.'

'Frustration! How the fuck can you understand that! They're not trying to kill you! Two weeks to the trial now. They'll be getting desperate. They found me in Leicester. They found me in Birmingham. I go any further south I'll be in fuckin' France.'

'We're working with Eastern...but they've got a dead police officer on their hands'

'What do you mean?'

'Killed.'

Harry walked to the window, picked up the binoculars and watched somebody abseil down the Spinnaker Tower.

'How?'

'Shot. Where were you last night Harry?'

Pullman spun around again.

'Where was I? I'm in fear of my life and you're asking me where I was? Here! Here all night if you must know, and before you ask, no I haven't got an alibi.'

'Harry it's just routine,' the detective was all patience; part of the job. 'When were you last in Seaton St George?'

Harry Pullman sat and leaned back into the modern

grey leather sofa. He crossed his legs and fiddled with the strap of the binoculars around his neck.

'What, I'm shooting cops now am I?'

He stared at the detective before continuing.

'Oh yeah, let me think. Now I remember. I was in Seaton last night, just nipped down to shoot a cop or two, back here in time for breakfast. No driving licence so I took a private jet.'

'Lose the attitude Harry,' the detective had taken a seat opposite. 'I've got to ask. It's a query from Seaton St George. I'm just the messenger.'

Pullman breathed deep and spoke as he exhaled. 'I've never been back since your lot picked me up in the Lake District.'

'You weren't there last night?' the detective persistent, pushing.

Harry Pullman exploded.

'Tell the daft bastards I've got no car! No access to a car. I'd have to get a train to London. Then up to Darlington. Then train or taxi to Seaton St George. It would take fucking hours. Jesus you people!'

He got up, walked to the window, and put the binoculars to his eyes.

'I bought a newspaper this morning. Check it out with the newsagent.'

The detective saw The Sunday Telegraph scattered across the floor.

Harry stared through the glasses: 'And make sure you tell them that if they sorted their leak out, I wouldn't have to keep moving. You can see yourself out.'

Chapter 27

'HARRY PULLMAN'S IN PORTSMOUTH,' Sam said, pulling away from the police station.

Ed settled into the white leather of her Audi.

'I've just had it confirmed by the Director of Intelligence.'

'Still could be up here. Not like he's housebound,' Ed said.

'He's there now though. Witness Protection just paid him a visit. He hasn't had time to get back there by train. The 12.25 hasn't left yet.'

'Who's to say he went by train?'

'Tara. She even recited the train time.'

'She could be lying, or more likely, he's lying to her.'

Ed looked out of the passenger window at nothing in particular.

'Could be,' Sam said. 'Let's say it is down to Harry, and Paul was involved in tipping off the Skinners where Harry was.'

'Go on'

'If that's right, how did Harry Pullman find out it was Paul?'

'God knows,' Ed said. 'He's obviously been tipped off.'

'But by who?'

'Harry worked for the Skinners long enough. Might know who's on their payroll.'

Sam turned up the radio. The national news was full of reports about Seaton St George. They both listened in a silence that lasted until they reached their destination.

Sam turned off the engine. 'Tara targeted Paul Adams.'

'What?' Ed unclipped the seat belt.

Sam turned her head to face him.

'Tara followed him, got chatting, buttered him up and hey presto. Led him by his balls straight to his execution.'

'Why are we treating her as a witness if she's complicit in Paul's death?'

'It's why she was complicit we need to examine,' Sam had swiveled to look Ed's way. 'She was terrified that if she refused to set Paul up, she'd be killed herself. It's Harry Pullman's house she rents, although she doesn't pay. He comes and goes as he pleases, as do his associates.'

'Cuckooing,' Ed said.

It happened. Criminals would use the homes of the weak, vulnerable or debt-ridden to run their rackets.

Ed let the seat belt retract.

'Another thing that seems a bit far-fetched,' he said.

'Maybe it is, which is why we need to interview her at length.'

Sam opened her door. 'Come on. Let's go and see Megan. Then I've got the post mortems to sort.'

For a woman who was small in stature and a couple of stone overweight, Megan Redwood was very nimble on her feet, grabbing one of the amidship's shrouds and leaping onto 'The Conquistador', a 36' Hallberg-Rassy yacht.

Sam followed her with the dexterity of someone used to boats.

Ed, by stark contrast, grabbed the wire rigging and tentatively placed his right foot onto the yacht. They may have been in a marina, but the boat was gently bobbing. Pedaloes in Skala or bodyboards in Cornwall were one thing; boats were a whole different matter. He always suffered from seasickness and whilst his left foot was swinging in mid-air, he was already regretting not popping a couple of 'Sea-Legs' tablets.

On board, bent over, grimly hanging onto whatever was to hand, he inched his way along the yacht and fell onto the moulded seats in the rear cockpit.

'Thanks for agreeing to meet us Megan,' Sam said, perfectly relaxed around the cockpit table. She introduced Ed, resisting the urge to refer to him as Nelson.

'No,' Megan shook her head. 'Thank you. All we want is for every last avenue to be explored. We don't think it has been. My father was no saint, but…'

Her words trailed away as Megan turned her head and looked across the marina, the steady breeze causing white tops on the waves beyond.

'But what Megan?' Sam asked.

Megan gazed out for a moment more before she turned her eyes back to Sam, a hint of tears shimmering on their surface.

'Great sailing conditions,' she said quietly. 'Dad would have been out today, perhaps making a couple of days of it, maybe sailing down to Whitby, fish and chips at 'Trenchers', then a few beers.'

Sam's nose twitched. She could smell the fish and

chips, hear the gulls. That particular restaurant was a firm favourite of hers.

Megan wiped her eyes and turned back to Sam.

'My father got into something dodgy. I don't know what, but something. He's always had boats. Nothing flash, but he's been sailing since he was a kid, and I mean a kid. Ten maybe.'

Sam looked at the boat. She knew that these yachts were a premier brand. Swedish; very sea-worthy and very expensive. They were flash in her eyes.

Megan caught Sam casting her eyes around the boat.

'Do you sail?' she asked.

Tristram, her husband, came into her mind, grinning and licking sea spray from his lips. Sometimes she still couldn't believe he was dead.

'Not now, but I have done,' Sam said. 'Qualified day skipper.'

Megan's eyes, clearer now, widened and she gave a small smile.

'Oh, well done you. Dad was an examiner. Stickler for protocol. He loved people like you getting trained.'

Megan leaned forward, adjusted her 'Dubarry' sailing boots.

'He got this boat about seven years ago. It was quite a few years old then but he paid nigh on a hundred grand for her. I knew his pension pot wasn't that big, but when I asked him about it, he just told me not to worry.'

Sam glanced at Ed; geisha-girl white face, beads of sweat glistening on his brow.

'What did you think he was into?' Sam pushed.

'I've no idea,' Megan said. 'I tried not to think about it, but he did start sailing to Holland a lot.'

Thought he might, Sam told herself, mental cogs oiled and running smooth.

Megan bit her lip.

'I suppose I wondered if he was running drugs,' she said. 'Things were tough for him when mum died, emotionally and financially, and it crossed my mind that maybe he wanted a bit of excitement and some extra cash.'

Megan put her hands in her white 'Musto' sailing jacket.

'As a mother myself I hoped it wasn't drugs, but I suppose I just turned a blind eye. Ask no questions, hear no lies.'

The questions in Sam's head formed an impatient but orderly queue.

'What do you think happened to him?'

Megan's response was instant, ringing with cast-iron certainty.

'Not for one second do I believe he fell in between the boat and the jetty,' she said. 'On his home pontoon? Not in a month of Sundays. Someone killed him. I'm convinced of that. But as your Inspector Wright continually reminded me, where's your proof?'

Megan shuffled in her seat, summoning up the courage to drive her point home.

'Well pardon me, but I thought proof was your job, sorry his job.'

'Do you mind if we have a look below?' Sam asked.

Megan shrugged and shook her head.

'Be my guest. I'll stay here.'

Ed wobbled to his feet, watching Sam vanish down a short flight of stairs she called a companionway. Why was the language of the sea like some secret society?

He descended the steps slowly like he was going down a ladder. Sam, of course, had all but run down with her back to the steps.

Down below, bent over to stop his head hitting the roof, Ed felt claustrophobic, the eye level mahogany lockers closing in on him. He dropped onto a blue velour sofa-style seat in the saloon.

'Where is it?' Sam said, lifting the desktop lid on the chart table and rummaging around amongst the charts, dividers, pencils and rulers. 'Come on, where are you?'

'Where's what?' Ed said, standing up and immediately lurching to his left as the wash of a passing vessel sent the yacht rocking and his stomach heaving. He grabbed the edge of the seat for support, regained his balance.

'His log book,' Sam said, firm-footed despite the sudden motion.

'We've just been told he was a stickler for protocol. If that's the case, where's the log book?'

'Maybe he wasn't that much of a stickler after all,' Ed said, the bile rising in his throat as the view from the porthole alternated between murky sky and murky water.

Sam turned, looked towards the companionway, bent down and shouted: 'Megan, do you know where your dad kept the log book?'

Megan's head appeared at the top of the companionway.

'Should be in the chart table.'

'I need to go,' Ed said, face now ashen. 'Right now.'

He dashed up the stairs, staggered to the side, and vomited into the water.

Sam popped her head out of the companionway and smiled up at Megan.

'Not one for boats.'

Megan nodded: 'He won't be the last.'

Sam saw a chance to search the boat alone and, in truth, she was enjoying herself, the sounds and smells of the vessel rocking pleasantly beneath her feet.

'There's no sign of a log book Megan,' she said. 'Do you mind if I check out your dad's chart-plotter?'

'Be my guest.'

'Perhaps you could take Ed ashore and get him a cup of tea in the yacht club.'

'Of course,' Megan told her. 'Take as long you like, but his log book should be in the chart table.'

Forty minutes later they walked back into Sam's office.

Ed took a sip from an ice-cold can of coke.

'That's the best I've felt since I got on that bloody boat. Me and the sea don't mix.'

Sam burst out laughing as she hung her jacket on the peg on the back door. 'You were in the marina.'

'Okay then, me and boats don't mix.'

'Right then, while you were drinking your sweet tea with Megan, all sickly and feeling sorry for yourself, I went and examined Bill's chart-plotter.'

'Which is?'

'Think of it as a superdooper Sat Nav,' Sam said. 'His was a nice piece of kit. 'Raymarine'. Like a Sat Nav, if the recent trips aren't deleted, they're stored in the memory.'

She sat down and slowly unscrewed the top on a bottle of sparkling water.

'Planning your journey in a yacht takes a little bit more effort than a car.'

Sam tore a piece of paper from her A4 pad and drew a circle at the top and bottom of the page.

'If I want to go from the top circle to the bottom circle, not only do I have to work out wind directions, I need to work out the speed and direction of the tidal flow, which, like the wind, can knock me off course.'

Ed studied the sheet.

'Yeah, I get it,' he said. 'If the tide is moving

horizontally right to left across the page it would push you off course to the left?'

Sam nodded, took a sip of fizzy water.

'Basically yes. Speed and direction of the tidal flow are taken into account when you chart your route. Skippers programme what are called 'waypoints' into the plotter, so they can periodically check their position against them and alter course if necessary. It's easier than using charts. The waypoints act as a reference. You can put as many in as you want.'

'Okay, I sort of get it.'

Sam smiled: 'Well, without giving you a navigation lecture, I found Bill's record for his trips to Holland, but it's the last one recently to Whitby that caught my attention. This is way better than his log book. He has a waypoint two miles south of Seaton marina. Just off the coast. Why?'

Ed looked at again at Sam's two-circle sheet as if the answer would appear like magic ink.

'You tell me.'

'He doesn't need a waypoint that close to home,' Sam said. 'There would be no issue. He'd know where he was by the coastline and he'd be well aware of any hazards. These are his home waters, plain sailing if you pardon the pun.'

Ed smiled, nodded.

Sam was in full flow, fired by the fuel of a possible breakthrough, her excitement clear.

'For me, that waypoint might not be a waypoint at all,' she said quickly. 'It could be a drop-off point. As in rowing someone ashore.'

She took a longer drink from the bottle.

Ed watched and waited.

The bottle air-popped as it left the seal of Sam's lips.

'There would be no customs or checks to worry about,' Sam said. 'Even if he'd been abroad, he would only tell customs he was back once he was safely at the marina. What if first he rowed somebody ashore?'

'Who?'

'Tara said Harry Pullman used to sometimes arrive by boat.'

Ed worked through the theory and came to a question still floating out of reach.

'So, if Bill Redwood didn't fall, why kill him?'

'That's what we need to sort out. But he didn't fall,' Sam said. 'I'm convinced of that.'

Chapter 28

RANJIT SINGH APPEARED at the open door.

'Got the footage from Green's phone loaded up Boss.'

Sam beckoned him in.

He put the laptop onto the desk, powered it up. The in-house techies had already downloaded the film onto it.

'Have you watched it Ranjit?'

'I have.'

'Let's see it then.'

Ranjit hit a couple of keys and shaky footage began to play.

Sam watched, brow furrowed as she wheeled her chair closer to the desk until her nose was almost touching the screen. A pair of feet appeared at the top of the companionway.

'Whoever's shooting the video must have been onboard before Bill,' Sam said. 'Nobody was seen walking back to the boat with him. Does it have sound?'

Ranjit nodded.

The camera panned around to Jimmy Marshall who was sitting in the saloon, closer to the companionway than the person filming. The camera was aimed low, only occasionally tilting upwards to catch Marshall's face.

'This looks like it's being shot covertly,' Sam said. 'Maybe nobody knows this film exists.'

'Insurance policy.' Ed said. 'Or a message for us.'

Sam, wanting to get the positioning clear in her mind, recalled the lay-out of the yacht.

'The person recording must be sitting at the saloon table, starboard side.'

In her peripheral vision Ed's lips moved, but whatever he muttered was inaudible.

Sam pressed pause.

'The right-hand side as you look to the front of the boat.'

'Cheers,' Ed said.

Sam carried on. 'The recorder is nearest the front cabin, furthest away from the companionway.'

She pressed play.

Bill Redwood's head came into view as he descended into the yacht. Clearly startled, he recovered his composure quickly, his speech scratchy over the recording.

'Everything alright lads? You should have told me you were coming. Drink?'

Ed spoke quietly, his eyes never leaving the screen.

'He's not arseholed is he? He's had a drink, but he's not out of it.'

Sam shook her head.

They watched as Marshall stood up and spoke. 'We need to take a little voyage. This fucker…'

His head indicated towards the camera.

'…needs to take a long walk from a short plank.'

Sam and Ed watched the screen where Bill had looked towards the camera. His face changed. He could see what the camera couldn't, what was silent in the shadows.

When he spoke, the recording was crisper, Bill still calm but now the edge in his voice unmissable.

'Hang on a minute,' Bill said. 'Picking people up, dropping them off's one thing, but I'm not throwing anybody overboard, not for the money you give me.'

The reply was blunt and came from off camera.

'Trouble is Bill, you don't call the shots and you're getting greedy. Not a good combination.'

Sam pressed pause again and moved even closer to the screen.

'Is that the heads opening?'

'The what?' Ed asked her.

'Heads. Toilet.'

'Why can't they bloody call it a toilet then? Yeah the door's opening.'

Sam hit 'play' and on the screen Bill walked past the port side heads' door. It was now between him and the companionway, between him and his way out.

The footage showed a figure duck, and come out of the heads, face not in camera shot.

'Who's that?' Sam said.

'Davy Swan probably,' Ed answered.

They heard Bill's voice, still calm enough.

'I'm not greedy. But I want more than you're giving me.'

On the screen, Davy Swan came into view and suddenly threw his right fist. The few seconds of jerking images looked like they'd been recorded whilst the yacht was sailing through gale-whipped waves, but the speed and power of the punch was clear. Bill did not react. Was that the drink? Or was he one of life's non-fighters?

The blow knocked him off his feet and he crashed into the companionway, his head smashing into one of the steps. He lay motionless on the sole of the yacht, his head lolled to one side.

Sam hit pause. 'He never saw that coming did he?'

When she hit play again it was Marshall's voice they heard.

'Oh well done. Absolutely brilliant.'

On screen, Davy Swan shrugged, climbed the companionway and went off camera before his head reappeared in the opening, obviously lying on his stomach on deck. He reached down and grabbed Bill's collar.

Marshall, back to the camera, took hold of Bill's legs.

Sam and Ed watched as Bill Redwood's unconscious body was hoisted, dragged, pushed, and shoved out of sight. Would the cameraman go on deck?

The camera moved. A voice, trembling and barely audible.

Sam tried to increase the volume, but it was already set to maximum. She turned her ear to the screen.

'What are you going to do now? He's had enough. He's just an old guy with a boat. He's not going to the cops.'

'Who's that speaking?' Sam asked.

'Could be Taffy Green,' Ed said. 'Sounds like him and not many with that accent in Seaton.'

Through the laptop's thin, tinny speakers, Swan spoke next.

'Gone too far. Can't take the risk.'

'Suicide my arse,' Ed said. 'They threw him in. He was dead the second he got back on his boat, he just didn't know it. Poor bastard.'

Sam had stopped the recording, the home screen suddenly bright after the muted footage.

'Let's check the marina CCTV,' Sam said. 'If that was Scott Green he must have escaped,' she said. 'We know he didn't end up in the water.'

Ed was about to make one of his trademark jokes, something about The Great Escape and Steve McQueen on his motorbike, when his mobile rang.

A woman's voice, without a hint of an accent, asked him to, 'pop along' to the Deputy Chief Constable's office.

Ed's throat wouldn't have been any drier if Dyson himself was in there with his vacuum. Summoned without warning by the Deputy Chief Constable would be squeaky bum time for anyone of his rank.

Sam looked at him, raised her eyebrows.

'Deputy wants to see me?'

'Do you know why?' Sam asked, standing up.

'Not a clue. I didn't even realise they worked Sundays.'

'Probably nothing. Might be wanting to pat you on the back for last night. Might even tell you to go for that promotion.'

Sam watched Ed push himself up, chin tucked into his chest, body listless, a man going to the gallows not an awards ceremony.

'On a Sunday? And why's his secretary here?'

He grabbed the knot of his tie, ragged it from side to side.

'Look it'll be nothing,' Sam said, hiding her own unease. 'I'll go to the mortuary. You come over when you're done here.'

Ranjit Singh left the office and told everybody that Ed had been called to see the Deputy. Nobody believed the promotion scenario.

Ed walked, head down, to the Executive corridor, towards the big offices and the thick green carpets.

The secretary was wearing her funeral face; no smile, no greeting, just a slight nod of acknowledgement. She picked up the phone, told whoever was at the other end that Detective Sergeant Whelan was here.

'You can go straight in.'

Ed gulped, wrestled with his tie again, and walked into the adjoining office, the door already open.

Deputy Chief Constable John Winsor, immaculate in crisp white shirt and thin, gold-framed spectacles, was sitting behind his desk. Ed expected that. What he didn't expect was Superintendent Chris Priest and his inspector side-kick Josh Appleton to be with him.

Both stood, leaning against the windows.

Priest, the Head of Professional Standards, was well named; never swore, never married and treated every police manual as a bible, no deviation tolerated.

He wore a navy suit, pink silk tie and pale blue shirt, which covered broad shoulders, pumped arms and a stomach that had never processed a unit of alcohol.

Overweight on day 1 at training school, his derogatory nickname stuck for a while, but he lost four stone in his first year as a police officer and still stuck to a regime of running and weights.

Appleton's ill-fitting jackets, saggy trousers and mismatched shirts were legendary. Today was no exception, an oversized banana yellow jacket, olive trousers and a black gingham shirt. The sky-blue tie had a small blob of egg yolk on it. He hadn't had eggs today.

Officers like Josh Appleton were better suited to uniform, removing the daily decision of what eye-watering fashion disaster to wear.

But underneath the fashion faux-pas lived a ruthless individual who'd batter a pensioner to climb the greasy pole. Priest and Appleton were nothing if not an odd team, the definition of chalk and cheese in the flesh.

DCC John Winsor did not offer any pleasantries or an invitation to sit.

Ed already knew whatever was coming wasn't a pat on the back or promotion.

Winsor's voice was cool and measured.

'Sgt Whelan.'

He eyes locked onto Ed's.

Thighs braced, shoulders back, Ed stood rigid. It was much easier for someone to notice you shaking when you were stood up, and whatever shit was about to fly his way, he wasn't going to allow Twit and Twat – Eastern's odd couple – the satisfaction of witnessing his discomfort.

Ed and Chris Priest had worked together in the CID years ago, before Ed left the Job, but they were never friends. Rumour had it Priest, for all his sanctimony and self-righteousness, still adopted the maxim of his younger days as a detective; take women whenever and wherever the opportunity presented.

Ed glanced at Priest. The tan was deep and undeniably impressive, but if you were a regular visitor to Thailand, as Priest apparently was, why wouldn't you catch a bit of sun?

'Inspector Appleton,' the DCC continued without taking his eyes off Ed, 'will soon serve you with the required Regulation 15 Notice informing you that you are being investigated for offences of corruption.'

Winsor paused.

'An assessment has been made and as the allegations are considered a matter of gross misconduct, insomuch as there is potentially a breach of the Standards of Professional Behaviour so serious as to warrant dismissal, or...'

Another pause.

Sweat rings were beginning to spread under Ed's arms as his deodorant went AWOL.

'...criminal proceedings. The matter will be investigated by the Professional Standards Department.'

Ed's tongue developed a mind of its own, jigging across his lips like a Riverdance out-take.

'You will be suspended from duty forthwith,' Winsor told him.

Ed didn't turn his head. He didn't need to. He could sense the smug, supercilious smile plastered over Josh 'Twat' Appleton's face.

'You will hand your warrant card and desk key to Superintendent Priest,' he heard Winsor saying. 'You will also give him your police issue mobile phone.'

John Winsor wasn't reading from a script. He didn't need to. He'd done this before.

Like every Deputy Chief Constable, he was responsible for all disciplinary matters. Chris Priest, as the Head of Professional Standards, reported directly to him.

Winsor spoke again. 'You will make yourself available for interview at a time and place dictated by Superintendent Priest. You will not access any police building during your suspension. Inspector Appleton will escort you off the premises once all the admin is completed. Do I make myself clear?'

Ed nodded.

'Get out.'

John Winsor picked up his fountain pen and began writing on the pad in front of him.

Ed felt like some insect swatted away as he filed out of the office behind Priest and Appleton, past the secretary who didn't look up from her desktop computer, no doubt already poised to make the 'you'll-never-guess-what,' phone call.

He followed T and T into one of the empty offices. At least he didn't have to travel to their 'secret squirrel' headquarters.

Priest sat. Ed and Appleton didn't.

Ed thrust his hand into his trouser pocket, pulled out the black wallet, removed the warrant card and threw his police ID onto the desk.

Two minutes later, the Reg. 15 in his jacket pocket, he turned and took two steps towards the doorway.

He hadn't spoken since he got the call from the DCC's secretary and would have stayed wordless if he hadn't felt Appleton's hand in the small of his back, ushering him out of the office.

When he spoke, quiet enough to make sure Priest couldn't hear, Ed's words were venom.

'Get your fucking hand off me unless you want to have to sew it back onto your wrist.'

Ed quick-marched along the corridor, leaving Appleton behind.

'I can find my own fuckin' way out,' he shouted.

Chapter 29

Sam answered her mobile as she pulled up outside the mortuary.

'Boss, its Tucky.'

'Hi Shane. What's up?'

'It's Ed. Complaints have just been in the office.'

The older detectives still referred to Professional Standards as Complaints, a throwback to the days when the department was called Complaints and Discipline; some of the younger detectives followed suit.

'What did they want?'

'Ed's been suspended.'

'Sorry?'

Sam got out of her car, balanced the phone between her shoulder and ear and lit a Marlboro Gold.

'They've come into the HOLMES room,' Tucky went on. 'Priest and Appleton. Told everyone that Ed's suspended and then went through his desk.'

'Suspended? What for?'

'They didn't say. Appleton couldn't wipe the smile off his face.'

What a wanker.

'What about Priest?' she asked.

'He came in, made the announcement then left Appleton to it.'

Sam considered ordering Tucky to tell everyone to say nothing but it would get out anyway. Juicy stories like officer suspensions took on a life of their own.

'Okay. Let them do what they have to do. Tell everyone in the room I want no sarcastic remarks towards Appleton. If he starts asking questions, I expect everybody to say nothing until we know exactly what's going on. I'll be back after these PMs.'

Sam smoked the cigarette, called Ed's personal number, and heard raw anger.

'Did you know about this?' he shouted.

'I had no idea. How on earth could you think I knew about it and didn't tell you? Where are you now?'

'On the piss. What else is there to do? I can't go home, can't go to yours, being a suspended officer and all that.'

'There's no point shouting at me. I don't even know what it's about.'

Sam lit another cigarette and waited for a response. She didn't get one.

'Where will you go?'

'I'll sort something and if those twats want to interview me, they'll have to find me first. As for you, remember my phone is probably tapped now.'

'And you remember what you learnt on that Internet Open Source course I sent you on.'

———

ED WASN'T in the pub. Not quite. He had pulled into the car park.

Now he walked through the stained-glass internal door to the bar, rave club decibels pounding his ears.

When he joined Eastern Police in 1978, The Ship, near the harbour, had been a biker's pub; a Harley Davison on the wall, Heavy Metal music booming out of the juke box. Having resigned and left the force for ten years, Ed discovered the bikers had moved on. The new clientele weren't unfriendly like the old days; they were openly hostile.

Most of the seats were already taken. The black stained wooden floor, as old as the pub itself, was already glistening with small puddles of spilt drink. The jukebox was belting out a Bay City Rollers hit and a group of five middle-aged women, sat around a circular table, were screaming the vocals inbetween slurps from their pints of lager.

Men of all ages stood drinking at the bar. Ed checked his watch. 12.05pm.

The music stopped and a few of the men, most sitting alone, made grunting noises. None had the bottle to look at him, all eyes fixed on their pint glasses.

The skinny ginger gob at the end of the bar, washed-out short-sleeved white England shirt, self-drawn ink tattoos on his arms and neck, one foot on the brass footrest, had to be the exception.

'Strong smell of pork in here,' he shouted during the musical lull as the The Bee Gees readied to burst eardrums with 'Tragedy.' The irony wasn't lost on Ed.

The grunters laughed and Ginger looked pleased, at least until Ed delivered a fast and vicious martial arts kick to the knee of his standing leg. Charlie Sneddon had always been an arsehole and today his mouth was in the wrong place at the wrong time and Ed Whelan was in the wrong mood.

The small, thin, wrinkled-faced granny behind the bar,

drying a clean pint glass with a grubby tea towel, didn't flinch.

'You fuckin' wanker Whelan,' Sneddon winced through gritted teeth, holding his right knee with both hands as he rolled on the floor.

'Get over it you skinny little shit,' Ed said. 'Pint of Guinness please Phyllis.'

He turned around, back against the bar, daring anyone else to say anything.

Sneddon dragged himself along the floor. No one went to help.

Betty Rizzo, from 'Grease' replaced the brothers Gibb. The long-haired, peroxide blonde from the table of screamers locked her eyes onto Ed's as she sauntered towards him, hips swaying, arms extended outwards, singing the opening line to 'There Are Worse Things I Could Do', with plenty of lung power but not too much by way of harmony or cadence.

The tight skinny jeans and black thigh-high boots showed off her long legs, the white silk smock completing the impression, from a distance at least, that she was a woman in her early thirties. Up close, her craggy features betrayed the hard life of someone in her late fifties.

Carol Pender was in her early forties, and life had indeed been short on light relief.

'Mr Whelan as I live and breathe. What a pleasure,' she said planting a kiss on his cheek. 'What brings you here?'

'I was hoping to catch you Carol.'

'Ooh, you always were a smooth-talking fucker. Go on then, mine's a vodka and coke.'

Charlie Sneddon struggled to his feet, limped towards a stool.

'Serves you right, dickhead,' Carol shouted, before turning back to Ed and taking the drink from him.

'Thanks love. Come on then, what do you want me for? You were lucky mind. I haven't been out on a Sunday for ages.'

'Let's go to the smoking area out the back. I can hear myself think out there.'

'Hey girls,' Carol shouted above the music, bringing their sing-a-long to a temporary stop. 'I'm just popping out the back with Sergeant Whelan. Must be my lucky day.'

'I saw him first Cals,' shouted a blonde.

'Give's a shout when you're finished and I'll take over,' a black-haired woman with a pink crocheted top cackled.

'Don't take all his strength, leave some for me,' another joined in.

Ed ignored them and their 40-a-day laughter.

The sideways glances from a few of the punters were met by a lip snarl from Carol. Nobody grunted. Nobody wanted to fall out with the Penders.

'What is it then?' she asked, putting a cigarette between her lips.

'You still in touch with Harry Pullman?'

'Long time since I worked with Harry. I'm respectable now.'

'Yeah I believe you.'

She playfully kicked his calf.

Ed smiled, Carol's blue eyes twinkling mischievously at him. 'I didn't ask whether you were still one of his girls. I asked if you were still in touch with him.'

'Bit dodgy these days, being in touch with Harry, you know, since he grassed on the Skinners.'

Ed watched Carol Pender smoke her cigarette, the deep lines around her mouth as she puckered to sip her drink.

'I remember you back in the day,' he said. 'You were a real stunner.'

Carol's lips slid into a boozy grin and she blew him a kiss.

'Always the charmer. You sure you're not trying to get into my knickers?'

Ed laughed. 'Can you get a message to Harry for me?'

She looked directly at Ed.

'Maybe'

'Tell him to call me on this number.'

Ed handed her a piece of paper with eleven digits on it. 'Call him this afternoon.'

'I'll have to try and get a number for him,' she said.

'You'll have a number for him,' Ed smiled. 'You're one of the few he can trust up here. Tell him I've just been suspended for corruption and -'

'Bloody hell Ed,' Carol's eyebrows stretched to their limits. 'I always had you down as one of the good guys.'

Ed shrugged. 'Looks can apparently be deceiving. Tell him I need to see him. Speak to him in the next hour Carol. And when you go back in there,' he flicked his head in the direction of the pub, 'tell them I asked if your lot would sort out Charlie Sneddon if he ever goes to the police about what just happened.'

'Will do.'

She stood on her tiptoes, kissed his cheek. 'Be careful Ed. The likes of me still consider you one of the good guys.'

Chapter 30

SAM WALKED to the tiny office adjoining the mortuary. Two low-slung, high-backed armchairs with thin wooden arms, no doubt recycled from one of the wards, were jammed against the wall. A dirty yellow plastic chair was next to an old table on the wall opposite.

Jim Melia and Julie Trescothick were on the armchairs, the mortuary technician on the yellow seat.

Sam stood at the door, no space in the room.

'Sam,' Jim said. 'Good of you to turn up.' He smiled.

Sam returned the smile. 'Not like I've been getting my hair done Jim.'

'Quite, quite…I've been thinking, and discussing my thoughts with Julie here. To do eight post mortems in one day is a lot and we don't want to miss anything because we're tired.'

Jim watched Sam for her reaction.

'Seems sensible,' she said.

'Good. I suggest we do the four victims of the shooting today and the man in the rabbit suit. Julie tells me the ballistic expert is here and it would be useful to have him at the examinations.'

'Fine with me.'

'I reckon each one will take about three hours.'

Sam nodded.

'What I've done,' continued Jim, 'is call out my two colleagues to speed the process up. Is that agreeable to you?'

Sam considered Jim's proposal. It was unusual for the prosecution to use more than one pathologist, but this was not a usual investigation.

'Fine by me,' she said, before looking at Julie. 'We got enough SOCOs to make three teams?'

'Just waiting for your say-so to call them out Boss.'

'How many of them are on rest days?'

'All of them.'

Sam's face resembled a blow fish as she puffed her cheeks and did the sums. The budget always spiraled upwards when jobs came in on weekends: three teams, six officers all on time and a half. Add that to those who were called out earlier and she'd already clocked up hundreds of hours of overtime.

Pity there was nobody here from the Home Office to see how quickly a major incident budget could evaporate.

'Call them out Julie. I want this show on the road as soon as possible.'

Sam walked outside, lit a Marlboro Gold and rang Bev Summers.

'You on speaker phone?' asked Sam.

'No. I'm 10/8. We've stopped for loo and tea.'

Sam smiled. The good old fashioned Ten Code. 10/8 meant Bev couldn't be overheard.

'Don't speak,' Sam said, knowing Tara must be somewhere near, 'just listen. Ed's been suspended.'

'What!'

'I know, came as a shock to me as well. Look I don't know any details other than he's suspected of corruption.'

Sam heard the huge intake of breath.

'He's angry,' Sam continued. 'Accusing me of knowing, which I didn't. I'm at the mortuary waiting for the PMs to start but I wanted to give you the heads up.'

'Appreciate it.'

'Ring me later,' Sam said.

Bev was a good detective, but she loved a gossip. The news of Ed's suspension would gather momentum.

'WHELAN,' Ed said, phone pressed to his ear.

'Now then cocksucker.'

Ed ignored the insult and the laughter that followed.

Harry Pullman: 'Who's been a naughty boy then.'

It was a statement, not a question.

Ed sat on the edge of the bed, eyes on the yellow-stained white skirting board.

He'd driven to Hartlepool, booked into a B and B a handful of on-line reviewers had referred to as shabby-chic. Ed had to admire their sense of humour. The place was chic perhaps in the 1960s when Seaton Carew was a coastal resort packed with day trippers, a funfair and crazy golf. Now it was just shabby.

'We need to meet,' Ed said.

'Why would I do that? All contact is through my Witness Protection Officer. You know that. They'd go mad if they knew I was even calling you.'

Two small steps and Ed was in the bay window; the sea view blocked by a yellow filament of grime and grease, thick dust trapped in the folds of the long, faded red curtains.

Ed sneezed.

'Bless you,' Pullman said.

'Thanks. Firstly, don't forget who spirited you away to safety in the first place.'

'And you know I appreciated that, but this life in protection is not all beer and skittles Ed.'

'Better than the alternative. If the Skinners had their way you'd be at the bottom of the North Sea by now.'

'And they're still trying to do me,' Harry sounded bitter. 'Remind me. Why should I meet up with you?'

Ed counted the dead flies on the windowsill while he thought about his answer.

'Two reasons,' he said finally. 'The cat's out the bag as far as Tara's concerned and nobody's buying the suicide pact.'

Harry Pullman's tone hot-wired to enlightened excitement, a child who suddenly grasped trigonometry.

'What are you telling me you bent bastard? You know Ray Reynolds always thought you were bent. Too close to that twat Brian Banks amongst other things.'

Ed didn't respond. He'd known Brian Banks, a scrap metal dealer, property developer and suspected drug dealer, since he'd joined the force; over the years Banks had provided a lot of information.

Pullman continued. 'You're the fourth man.'

'You what?'

'After that corruption inquiry years ago, the 'Seaton Three'. Ray always talked about another bent copper. Always asking if I knew anything. He called the bent bastard 'The Fourth Man'.

Ed's jaw clenched at the reference. Anthony Blunt, a member of the Cambridge Spy Ring providing information to the KGB along with Donald Maclean, Guy Burgess and Kim Philby, was publicly revealed to be the 'Fourth Man' in 1979.

'I'm not bent and I'm no fourth man.'

'What you talking to me for then? Your chickens have come home to roost and you're in the shit big time.'

Ed sat on the edge of the bed, the thin nylon duvet cover a yellow floral number pock-marked with clicks.

'Do you want to meet or what?'

'What's in it for you Whelan?' Harry Pullman on his guard, playing hardball. 'That' the question I'm asking myself.'

The knock was so quiet Ed almost missed it.

He turned to see an elderly soul who should have been in a retirement home years ago.

'Sorry to disturb you Mr Smith,' old school polite like she was running the Ritz not this broken down relic. 'What time will you be wanting breakfast?'

'I won't thanks. I'll be leaving very early, but thank you.'

He closed the door.

'Is that the best name you can come up with?'

Ed pictured Pullman shaking his head with a wide smirk on his face.

'Look,' Ed snapped, 'do you want to meet or not?'

'Tell you what. I'm curious. I'm not due to see my protection officers —'

Ed's anger finally snapped.

'You're not a member of the Royal Family you cock, you're a frightened nobody on the run from the bogey men.'

'And you're a soon to be ex-cop jailed for being bent,' Pullman fired back. 'It's true what they say about jail and the police.'

He let the words hang before continuing. 'Now we both know where we stand…I'm not due to see my protection people until Wednesday.'

'Fair enough. I can drive to you. Where are you?'

'Like I was born yesterday,' Pullman's voice was thick with scorn and disdain. 'For all I know you're working for the Skinners you bent bastard.'

Ed walked back to the grime and flies.

I'll remember this knobhead

'So how do you want to play it then?' Ed asked.

'You still got that campervan?'

'Using it now.'

'Drive to Robin Hood's Bay, it's just outside Whitby.'

'I know where it is.'

'There's a campsite above the village.'

'That might be closed. It's out of season.'

'Find somewhere to pull over then.' Pullman was enjoying calling the shots. 'Be there tomorrow. I'll call you at 8am.'

'You somewhere near there?'

'Nice try Whelan.'

Chapter 31

HUGH CAMPBELL WAS NOT a man to cross; politeness personified and pleasant when he wanted to be, but so were the Krays.

Campbell's last pair of school shoes would still fit him and he hadn't been inside a classroom since he was 14. But size never equated to aggression.

He swayed back and forth on the canopied swing, thoughts drifting in tandem with the motion, watching birds fly across the moorland, his hand occasionally touching the heads of the two black Labradors beneath him. Rocking on the veranda, he reflected on his journey from Seaton St George poverty to landowner.

He had left school with no qualifications; boys like him didn't do homework, boys like him fought and got involved in petty theft. The lucky ones got to run errands for criminals, not low life bottom feeders, but the serious figures who ran Seaton. They were players, and Hugh Campbell always did what they asked.

He had got his chance early, an opportunity to show he was the right sort, when he picked up and hid a discarded handgun used in a gangland hit. He was 12 years old. He shouldn't have been playing on the diggers that Sunday night, shouldn't have witnessed the execution of one of Kenny Skinner's boys, but he had, and more importantly he knew who had pulled the trigger.

Hugh Campbell had three choices…say nothing, go to the cops or go to Kenny Skinner.

Saying nothing was not an option.

His own father, useless and absent as he was, had always told him never to speak to the police.

So the answer had been easy. He went to Kenny Skinner and showed no fear, even at that young age. Fear was something he had conquered long before. His father's belt had seen to that.

Campbell closed his eyes now, the gentle movement of the swing transporting him back to his childhood. The peaty richness of the moorland became the smell of fried food, the noise of the birds overhead was replaced by aggressive drunks shouting the odds, the light patterns behind his eyes were suddenly the glint of flick-knives under cold street corner neon.

He shivered as he remembered the snow and freezing temperatures of the December childhood that changed him forever. 'Can I speak to Mr Skinner?' He wasn't much older than Kenny's son Billy. 'I have something important to tell him.'

A shaven-headed bouncer with angry tattoos and a boxer's nose had blocked his way to the back street pub that was Skinner's office back then.

Hugh Campbell refused to say why he needed to speak with the boss. His cheap, shiny, black tracksuit and worn, white plimsolls spoke of poverty; his bright eyes glistened with defiance.

Kenny Skinner gave him two twenty pound notes in

exchange for the location of the gun and the name of the killer.

It became the best Christmas of his life, the first time the family hadn't been short, the first time he bought presents for his mother and younger sister, the first time they enjoyed Christmas dinner with all the trimmings. After that, his mother and sister always had presents and a turkey at Christmas. His father could go fuck himself.

He didn't know what happened to Albert Craig, the guy who had pulled the trigger, not then anyway, but he never saw him again. Twelve years later, when he was one of Skinner's trusted confidantes, he found out.

Albert Craig's death came after two days of prolonged punishment beatings, entry to the afterlife via the stomachs of the local pigs.

By the time he was 18, Campbell was running Kenny's snooker halls with Billy Skinner and at 21 they were managing a string of nightclubs.

Before he was thirty, Kenny Skinner allowed Hugh to break away and form his own businesses. Hugh had nothing to do with clubs and drugs, preferring instead to concentrate on the two loves of his life: gambling and girls. A life surrounded by fillies, he'd boast; betting shops and massage parlours with some lucrative loan sharking the vinegar on his chips.

If anyone crossed him he was ruthless. Nobody fucked with Hugh Campbell.

That life was behind him now, the advent of internet betting securing him a pension fund big enough to make even the greediest banker happy and letting him step quietly into gilded retirement.

He still had the scars, the physical ones anyway. Hugh Campbell had no lingering emotional issues; business had always been business. The vivid scar on his cheek, running from the lobe of his left ear to the corner of his mouth, had earned him the nickname 'Scarface'. Not very original but he liked it, or at least he did when he was still in that life, the aura of violence it created.

The mistake his attacker made was to just maim him. Three nights later he was found dead on the street, one bullet in the head. No one was ever convicted. Those who knew who was responsible said nothing.

At 59 and after a life of crime hidden behind a veil of respectability, his total jail time was a single 18-month stretch. Even that had been enough to make him realise there was no loyalty in the underworld. Too many were ready to grass when their backs were to the wall, and the bigger the fish...

He wasn't about to be taken down in the next police operation. No point in tempting fate this late in the game. Get out with the money while the going was good.

And for Campbell, that going had been better than he could ever have dreamed. He fell in love with country life, shooting and fishing like a man born to it, walking the moorland paths, never tiring of the sight of the heather and grasses that thrived on the dense layers of peat.

More than anything, Hugh Campbell was determined to remain at liberty to enjoy the life his old world had delivered.

These days the police seemed to have the power to confiscate anything they deemed proceeds of crime. Forensic Accountants were springing up everywhere, leeches tracing people's assets for a tidy fee.

The police had been an occupational hazard back in the day. Now, he didn't want them anywhere near him.

He also had sons of his own to think about. Shirley had died nine years ago, radiotherapy and chemo finally losing their rearguard action against the tumors that spread like weeds through her broken body. His sons didn't want betting shops and massage parlours, not now. Campbell knew his sons' sights had risen, the lure of their own empire suddenly so close they could taste it. They wanted excitement and saw an opportunity, the only one potentially standing in their way that grassing snake Harry Pullman.

If Pullman didn't give evidence Luke and Mark Skinner were out. If he made it to the witness box and delivered, the Skinners would grow old in their prison cells and Harry Pullman might like his own chances of taking over.

Hugh Campbell rocked back and forth, accepting now what the scrawny 12-year-old had accepted a lifetime ago. Doing nothing was not an option.

SAM TURNED UP HER COLLAR, lifted her face skyward and allowed the drizzle to wet her face. Five down, another three tomorrow.

The PMs revealed Lucy Spragg, Marcus Worthington-Hotspur, Joe 'Fatty' Sanderson and Paul Adams had all died as a result of gunshot wounds. No surprises there.

The ballistic expert had confirmed the wounds were consistent with the ammunition used by the rifle recovered at the scene. He had taken pages of measurements to allow him to reconstruct the trajectory of the bullets.

Zac Williams had been killed by police issue ammunition.

Sam pressed the button on the remote and lit a cigarette. Her head was a whirling tornado of questions and plenty of them had been airborne without answers since all of this started.

Sam rattled through the list in no particular order.

If Zac Williams was the killer, how had he got a rifle?

Was Tara's story true?

In light of the video on Scott Green's SIM card, was his death an accident, or were Fred Thompson and the mother pushing the buggy right when they claimed he was being chased?

Had Davy Swan and Jimmy Marshall killed him as they had Bill Redwood?

Had they themselves been killed and the scene staged to make it look like a suicide pact?

Was Paul Adams the real target and if so, why?

How was Ed?

She climbed into her car, reached into the glove compartment and sprayed her clothes with Yves Saint Laurent's 'Opium', fruit and spice notes battling with the smell of cordite and death.

She turned on the radio in time to catch the last few seconds of the 4pm news and Monica Teal's press conference.

Back at HQ she popped into the toilets. On her way out she walked straight into Mick 'Never' Wright.

Dressed in cheap jeans and a hideous ill-fitting shirt he wore a smirk Sam wanted to batter off his face.

'See they finally caught up with your partner in crime,' he said.

The pressure cooker inside Sam exploded.

'If I was you, I'd be more concerned about how you're going to keep yourself out of the shit.'

Wright kept the smugness on his face but a trace of doubt flashed briefly in his eyes.

'You what?'

'Bill Redwood.'

Wright shrugged his shoulders. 'Old man. Lost his footing. Shit happens.'

Sam closed the gap between them, her words quiet but menacing.

'I've got information to the contrary.'

Mick 'Never' Wright glared at her, mottled spots of anger colouring his cheeks.

'You never found any evidence of an argument, did you?' Sam said it as a challenge. 'No evidence that Redwood wasn't alone?'

Wright's mouth was a tight line.

'Thought not. You were too quick to write it off. We'll follow it up. Coroner will be interested. So will his daughter. And the Seaton Post.'

Now the fleeting concern that had washed through Wright's eyes had taken up permanent residence.

'What have you got then?'

Sam took a second to enjoy the moment.

'Just a video of him being beaten up on his boat on the night in question.'

Mick 'Never' Wright's face went from blood-red to ghost-white in a heartbeat.

'You really should have checked the CCTV before Bill went on board,' Sam drove home the blade. 'It's called being thorough.'

Now she leaned into his ear.

'You might have seen other people on the pontoon. If you'd looked fifteen minutes after he got on his boat, you'd have seen Scott Green, he's a criminal by the way, running away from the boat.'

Sam turned, took two steps, then spun back quickly. Wright hadn't moved.

'So instead of gloating about other peoples' problems, worry about your own. If I have anything to do with it, you'll have enough Regulation 15 Notices to decorate your bathroom.'

Sam came forward again as she spoke, only stopping when she was inches from Wright's beer gut.

'For starters there's failing to investigate Bill Redmond's death, and all the shortcomings are neatly presented in the file you submitted to the coroner.'

She leaned forward. Any closer and they would be Eskimo kissing.

Wright could feel Sam's hot breath on his lips.

'I hope you get busted back to PC. If it was down to me you wouldn't be supervising a school crossing.'

She spun around again. This time she didn't stop or look back and was still walking when she answered her ringing mobile.

Julie Trescothick.

Sam listened.

Her head was pounding, the pressure of the investigations, the confrontation with Mick Wright and her fears for Ed pushing her to the limit.

Ninety seconds later when she ended the call, Sam was on information and interpretation overload.

Julie's report had been, as always, to the point: no gunshot residue on the hands of Zac Williams' rabbit suit; fibres found on the stock and barrel of the weapon; sticky substance on both the hands and on the stock and barrel.

Maybe Tara's story wasn't so fantastical after all.

LUKE AND MARK SKINNER were playing pool. Not as nice as the table on the raised area in their mother's house, but better than nothing.

'Association' inside didn't mean they had to associate with anyone other than each other.

Other remand prisoners were standing in twos and threes talking football, women and grasses. A pair of old-timers, career criminals who'd spent longer inside than out, were playing chess.

The case against the Skinners revolved entirely around the evidence of Harry Pullman. There was nothing else.

The trawler skipper who'd navigated the beaten victims to their salty graves never said a word to the police. He preferred to take his chances with the Crown Prosecution Service rather than the Skinners.

Without their star witnesses the prosecution wouldn't get as far as an 'opening statement'. The defence would make an application to discontinue proceedings before the jury had even warmed their seats and they would win. No Harry Pullman meant no evidence and no case to answer.

Two more weeks and they'd be back on the outside.

Luke smiled as he potted the final red, walked around the table, and lined up his shot on the black, an easy kiss with the ball already in the jaws of the pocket.

He bent over his cue and called it.

'Top left.'

From behind a hand grabbed his hair, yanked his head up and rammed his nose onto the side of the table. Blood sprayed onto the green baize.

Luke tried to run but a single kick to his right knee sent him crashing chest first onto the table. Strong hands pulled his head back and held it there.

Mark had rushed forward but two thick-set heavies blocked him and pinned his arms. A third kicked the back of his left knee. Mark staggered like a newborn calf before his weakened leg collapsed. Like Luke, he felt his hair grabbed and his head yanked back.

By the time the head pullers reached into their pockets, took out a toothbrush with a razor blade taped to the end and sliced the Skinners' throats wide open, the onslaught had lasted less than 20 seconds.

The brothers dropped to the floor, hands gripping their wounds, dark blood bubbling between their fingers.

One of the chess players walked away, toothbrushes in his pocket, while the attackers watched two pools of red rushing to meet in a final act of sibling solidarity.

Chapter 32

SAM SAT down behind her desk. She needed five minutes. She got one before her mobile rang.

'Can you speak boss?'

It was one of Luke Skinner's phone monitors.

'Yes.'

'Interesting call to Skinner's phone.'

'I'm all ears.'

'Three points of interest.'

Sam shuffled in her seat, the power of three raising its head again; three forensic issues, now this.

'Firstly, the caller says, in last night's game the Reverend was killed.'

Sam wrote it down.

'Next we've got, any joy with the source?'

Sam wrote it on a new line.

'Skinner then says, 'Can Pugsley help out?' and the caller replies, 'Pugsley's status unknown at the moment.''

Sam wrote everything down, stood up and paced her office with the mobile pressed to her ear, silently cursing Ed. He was always good with cryptic clues.

'Any joy with the number of the incoming call?'

'We're working on it, but don't hold your breath. Anyone ringing Skinner in prison isn't going to be daft enough to use a contract phone.'

'Okay thanks.'

She put the phone down, stared at her handwriting.

Pugsley. The Addams Family. She recalled watching reruns of the 1960s programme. Pugsley was the son.

That had to be Paul, didn't it?

She stared at the sentence, 'Can Pugsley help?'

If Pugsley was Paul Adams, Luke Skinner asking if he could help could only mean one thing.

Her hands covered her face, her shoulders slumped. Bent cops were worse than criminals, but a bent cop on your team…

She sighed and looked back at the paper, staring hard at 'Reverend' and 'the source'.

Nothing. A total blank.

Her desk phone rang.

'Sam Parker.'

'Sam its Darren.'

Darren Halshaw was the DCI on Organised Crime.

'Hi Darren. What you doing out on a Sunday.'

'Luke and Matt Skinner are dead.'

'What!'

'My response as well. Seems they had their throats cut whilst playing pool.'

'Jesus.'

Sam was instantly relieved the prison was in a different Force area. At least she didn't have another multiple murder investigation on her hands.

'I'm just giving you the heads-up Sam. You might want someone to prepare a Community Impact Assessment.

There's a chance of reprisals. Maybe someone's getting ready to launch a takeover bid.'

'Any ideas who's behind it?' Sam asked.

'Killing the Skinners? Sketchy at the minute but the two we fancy are on remand with shedloads of evidence against them for murder. They're connected to a crime family in Newcastle. As for who ordered time on the Skinner boys…plenty of potential suitors.'

'The crime family you mentioned,' Sam said. 'Are they looking to expand?'

'If they are we'll never prove it,' Halshaw told her. 'But there are families on Teesside, teams in Leeds. Could be anybody. And obviously you've got the Campbells on your patch. Hugh might be the country squire these days but his sons aren't.'

'God, we don't need a gang war in the middle of this shit,' Sam groaned.

'I know. But live by the sword and all that. Listen, if you need any staff I can probably help out for a couple of days.'

Sam tilted her head into her free hand.

'Cheers mate. You know what it's like trying to get bodies on seats these days.'

Sam opened a desk drawer, found an oat bar, ripped it open with her teeth and took a small bite. She was too hungry to check the 'best before date'. Just as well.

'I've even gone through the admin cupboards, looking for a new box of detectives but I can't find any,' Sam said. 'Must be lost in the post.'

Darren Halshaw laughed. 'Grab me a few if you find any.'

The next question she knew would be coming.

'What's happening with Ed Whelan?'

Well it was always going to get out.

'You know as much as me,' Sam said. 'Suspended. I was on my way to the mortuary when it happened.'

'He kept some bad company.'

Sam kept her tone conversational. There was no point in losing her temper. Speculation would grow whatever she said until everything was resolved.

'C'mon Darren. Every detective who ever had an informant keeps bad company. It goes with the territory. You know that better than me.'

'It's when people cross the line there's a problem,' Halshaw said. 'There are so many rules these days. Not like it was back in the day.'

Sam heard Darren take a slow breath.

'Not like it was in Ed's day,' he said.

Sam switched topic.

'Did Paul Adams' name ever crop up?'

'The DC on your team?'

'That's him.'

'Not to my knowledge. Why?'

'Just one of a number of theories I'm exploring.'

'You think he should have cropped up?'

'Not sure.'

'Sorry Sam, can't help you there. I'll keep you posted re the Skinners.'

'Cheers'.

She hung up, walked to the Deputy Chief Constable's office.

'Come in Sam,' John Winsor said as she appeared at his door.

As he was the on-call chief officer she took the indicated chair, briefed him on the prison murders and that she had just spoken to the on-call superintendent about a Community Impact Assessment.

There had been no request so far to provide family liaison officers to the mother, Marge Skinner.

'Thanks Sam. Have you seen Whelan?'

'No sir, I was going to the post mortems when he came to see you.'

'Look I apologise if Appleton seemed to be gloating. I know there's no love lost between some uniform officers and the CID.'

'I didn't know he was gloating sir, although it doesn't surprise me.'

She pictured Josh Appleton. Josh the shit: another desk jockey who couldn't investigate a bad smell. Never been in the CID. Thought a stint investigating his own would look good on his CV.

Sam smiled as an image of Ed in full flow slipped into her mind, the mention of Appleton's name enough to ignite the burners.

'This is a very serious investigation Sam.'

Shit. He saw me smile.

'I want minimum collateral damage. You need to bite your tongue, exercise maximum discretion around Appleton.'

He adjusted his glasses. 'This is incredibly delicate.'

'Sir.'

'Now, how are we getting on with the shootings?'

She briefed him on the forensics, the newspapers, Tara Paxman and the rabbit suit.

'You think it was a set up? This Tara girl might be telling the truth?'

'Possibly. I've fast-tracked the second rabbit suit for DNA examination. Hopefully, if someone has worn it, their DNA will be all over the inside. Then it's just a case of hoping whoever was wearing it is on the DNA database. First DNA profile to be checked will be Harry Pullman.'

Winsor removed his glasses, pinched his nose.

'What you're suggesting is that we've potentially shot an innocent man.'

Sam took a deep breath.

'It's early days yet, but that is a possibility, given what we know at the scene. No residue on the suit Zac Williams was wearing.'

'Are we sure we were even negotiating with the man who got killed?'

Sam paused remembering Ed's reaction.

'Ed was certain, and we can get comparisons between the voice speaking to Ed and previous interviews we have with Williams.'

'Good.'

'We'll listen to the tapes of Ed negotiating with him again. There were times Ed felt Williams' responses were a little slow. That could be down to the stress of the situation…'

Winsor put his glasses back on.

'Or,' he pressed, sensing something was coming.

'Or,' Sam hesitated, 'it could be that someone was telling him what to say and he was under duress. The duress of a gun being pointed at your girlfriend.'

Winsor nodded, then spoke.

'Keep me posted Sam. As for interviewing the firearm teams you retain primacy until you're satisfied that there are no murder or manslaughter issues.'

'I'll speak with the CPS first thing tomorrow, before we interview any AFOs,' she said.

Whilst the Crown Prosecution Service was responsible for authorising any charges after the evidence had been gathered, many SIOs liked to get them involved very early in a major inquiry.

FIVE MINUTES later and after sneaking a Marlboro moment, Sam walked to the HOLMES office.

'Listen up,' she shouted as she burst through the doors.

Necks turned and fingers stretched, glad of a disconnect from the keyboard.

'Nobody has any contact with Ed. Understand?'

It wasn't a request and Sam watched a wall of nodding heads.

'If he rings you, hang up and notify me, and before you ask, I have no idea what he has allegedly...'

She paused, letting the word *allegedly* resonate across the room.

'...done. We all know these things can take bloody years. As much as it hurts to say it, even if the allegations are unfounded, by the time the investigation is complete, Ed will no doubt retire. He's worked his last murder.'

Sam scanned enough sad eyes to grace a funeral and headed for the door.

The whispers would start as soon as she closed it.

Chapter 33

Rain was lashing against the windows when they pulled up, the kind the Lake District wears like a badge of honour.

The car park was diagonally opposite the White Lion, but in this monsoon, it was still far enough away to have them drenched by the time they reached the door.

Inside, much to Tara's disappointment, they had gone straight to the room; she'd hoped to dry off with a gin and a roaring fire.

But Sam had already marked Bev's card and she wasn't going to let a witness, especially one who enjoyed a drink, anywhere near a bar. Not yet anyway. Maybe later.

Sam had spoken to the owners before Bev's arrival, telling them that it was a delicate situation and that Tara was fleeing domestic violence. Sam hated lying to them, but sometimes it had to be done. Tara's safety was paramount. Mentioning protective custody would lead to a shed load of questions and the fear that the wrong people would be alerted.

Showered and changed, Bev wore clean jeans and a dry sweatshirt.

Tara stomped out of the en suite wearing a tracksuit Bev had bought her and leaned against the doorframe, one leg bent, hand on hip.

'I wouldn't be seen dead in this.'

Bev hid her grin under the towel, rubbed her hair harder. That was exactly why she had bought it; four coast-to-coast walkers were staying in the pub tonight and she didn't want Tara flashing her eyes when they went down for food.

Bev put the towel on the bed, tapped out a text and pressed send.

The message was refused passage into cyberland.

She cursed the fells, the thick stone walls and the impassive rain.

Bev walked to the window, held the phone aloft and pressed send again. This time the apologetic message cancelling the date pinged on its way. Probably for the best. He was too young for her.

'Right, let's crack on,' Bev said.

She put two cassettes into the portable tape machine, pressed the button and waited for the long beep to finish.

'Okay Tara. The time is 6.05pm on Sunday 1st November 2015. I am DC Bev Summers and for the benefit of the tape, you are?

'Tara Paxman'

'Okay Tara. I want you to tell me exactly what you told Detective Chief Inspector Parker.'

———

THE SECURITY LIGHT above the double garage illuminated

the lush green lawn either side of the path, the grass straight out of an advert for chemical feeds.

Megan Redwood had a houseful of people and the noise from the back garden hinted that the party was bigger than the parked cars in the street suggested.

Normally, Sam wouldn't be dragging Shane 'Tucky' Walton out of the office, but after Ed's suspension nothing was normal.

Knocking would be futile. Sam guessed the front door would be unlocked and it was. She stepped inside. Shane followed.

A skinny, giggling forty-something blonde ran along the hallway chased by a man half her age. They both skidded to a halt when they saw Sam.

'Megan,' the blonde shouted. 'New people.'

The young guy slapped her on the backside, and she was off running again, this time up the stairs, shrieking as she took them two at a time.

'Hi,' Megan said, walking towards them, a large glass of white wine in her hand. She glanced at the stairs.

'I see you've met Frances. Lives next door. Husband left her for a younger model, and now she's taking a few younger models of her own for a spin. Always seems to have plenty, but whether that's her or her money…' Megan grinned. 'What a bitch I am. And it's not Frances now, it's Franky.'

Megan snorted then giggled, a cocktail of drink and nerves.

A twenty-something girl appeared, iPad in hand. She tapped it a couple of times and 'Hi Ho Silver Lining' started belting out from some distant speakers.

'Is there somewhere we could have a private chat?' Sam asked, wondering whether it was a little early for Jeff Beck.

Megan nodded. The giggles had gone. Only the nerves remained.

The small study off the hallway was private, if a little compact for the three of them. Sam spun the chair away from the desk and asked Megan to sit down.

Sam noticed the screensaver on the desktop Apple Mac, a photograph of Megan and her father on a yacht.

'I'm sorry. We were wrong. You were right. Your dad didn't fall.'

Megan's hand shot over her mouth; her head moved slowly from side to side. She stared at the floor for what felt like five minutes to the detectives, but was probably less than one. Then she rubbed her eyes, looked up at Sam, and spoke. 'Thank you so much for believing me, I knew he hadn't fallen in. How did you catch him? I presume it's a him?'

She rubbed her eyes again.

Sam dropped onto her haunches and took hold of Megan's hand.

'It's a them,' she said quietly. 'It's part of a wider investigation. I can't go into too much detail now. I just wanted you to know that things are progressing.'

'Do you think they'll admit it?'

'It's early days. I'll keep you posted.'

'Okay, but what's your gut instinct?'

'Let's just wait and see Megan,' Sam said, understanding Megan's need for information. Every relative of every homicide victim wanted every detail.

Megan stood up. 'Thank you again. I'm just so glad you listened.'

She wiped her eyes, sniffed, and took a huge deep breath. 'Now, can I get you a drink?'

'Best not,' Sam said, moving towards the door, 'lot to get through yet.'

Sam walked into the hallway, opened the front door, turned to say goodbye, and was caught off-guard by the lunge and smothering tightness of Megan's arms around her neck.

'Thank you again. Thank you for believing me.'

Sam dodged the hanging baskets as she stepped outside and headed for the car, Shane in tow.

'What do you think?' she asked him. 'And before you answer, I'm not asking about the blonde.'

She blinked, focused on the car keys, and kicked herself for mentioning the blonde. Ed would have come back with some quip but she wasn't with Ed, she was with Shane and he wouldn't dream of making sexist comments, certainly not to her.

'Megan?' Shane asked. 'Seems a nice woman. Think she'll make a complaint when it's all out in the open?'

'Probably. It was all set to go to the coroner and get written off as a suicide. What would you do?'

Sam pressed the remote, the car beeped and the lights flashed.

She might be wrong but no one could blame Megan given the justification and the failings of the initial investigation.

'Why are we bothered anyway Boss?' Shane asked now. 'It's Mick Wright who's in the shit.'

Sam had opened the driver's door, about to step inside.

'Because Shane, from the outside looking in, it damages the reputation of the Force, not the individual, and I don't like…'

Ed's voice flashed into her head. 'I thought it was a Service Sam, not a Force.'

She paused. One hand still on the open door.

'Let's turn it on its head,' Sam said, 'What if Wright's

not as incompetent as we think? What if he just wanted this to go away?'

Shane 'Tucky' Walton felt out of his depth. He had no idea what Sam was thinking.

'Uhmmm.'

Sam ducked into the car.

'Oh, just ignore me Tucky. It's the sleep deprivation. I'm seeing corruption everywhere.'

Chapter 34

BEV LAID on her back in bed, hands behind her head, her mind on Ed Whelan.

She glanced at the two plates on the bedside table, smears of tomato sauce around the edges, and burped back the fish finger sandwich and chips.

Her fault. She ate too late.

Bev had known Ed for more years than she hadn't. Could he really be bent?

She kicked off the duvet, her body overheating in the small room, she guessed a consequence of the large radiator and that time of life. Typical that the pub Sam insisted they stay in had only one room available.

Tara hadn't mentioned Ed by name, but she had a real downer on male police officers. She'd often overheard conversations about bent cops, no names but always the references to 'him' and 'he'.

There had been only one exception. Paul Adams.

Bev couldn't believe Paul was corrupt; 'Jack the Lad' as far as women were concerned, but corrupt?

She was still trying to make sense of it all. Could she work with corrupt officers and not smell them?

Tara claimed she had been told to target Paul, said he'd been easy: swayed past him in the pub, made eye contact going to the toilets, more eye contact on the way back and he had followed her to the high bar table and two Manhattan bar stools.

Bev could believe it. Paul wouldn't be the first to be led by his trousers.

Tara had been told he was in there, what he looked like, even what he was wearing.

They had gone back to her house that night.

Tara was loyal to Harry Pullman but where did Paul Adams hang his allegiance? Tara didn't know the answer. At least that's what she claimed.

At first blush, Bev knew the allegations against Ed couldn't be anything to do with last night's shootings – too soon after the event.

But what if Ed knew Harry Pullman's plans in advance? What if he was in on it? Easy enough to set it up it for a night when he was on-call lead negotiator. Ed wasn't on call last night, that much she'd established, so he'd arranged a swap. Did that mean something had happened to bring the shootings forward?

Bev closed her eyes, tried to concentrate.

Paul was maybe going to expose Ed, but what would be the sense in that? Was Ed loyal to a different firm?

Bev expected sleep to move over her like a warm summer breeze, for tiredness to pull her down to a dreamless dark.

But her mind wouldn't let up, the questions snowballing.

Nothing made sense but one thing was clear. The best way to have someone rubbed out was to get the police to

do it for you. Okay, the police hadn't killed Paul Adams…
but they may have killed the person who did.

Bev rolled over onto the other side, Tara asleep in the
other single bed.

She had watched her peel of the tracksuit. Like Sam
she could see why Paul had taken the bait.

Finally Bev slipped out of bed and stretched. She may
as well smoke as toss and turn. She pulled on jeans and a
top, walked out of the room, down the stairs and out of
the back door. There was surface water everywhere but at
least it had stopped raining and it was blissfully cool after
the sauna that was masquerading as a bedroom.

Ed had always got huge amounts of information from
informants. Now Bev wondered if that was all part of
some grander plan… sacrifice the small fry to keep the
bigger fish free.

She shuffled her feet and savoured her cigarette.

Then there were the years between Ed leaving the Job
and returning. He was out for a decade. Had he really left
because his wife wanted him to work in the family-run
company? And why come back after so long away?

Bev could just pick out the outline of something
towering above her, dark and foreboding. She couldn't
have named Place Fell for a small fortune, but the vision
made her uneasy, something so big and still in the pristine
silence.

Bev Summers was arrow straight but the rank stench
of corruption had found her years before.

She was a probationer, still within her first two years,
the point in service when your career could be terminated
for 'not being likely to become an efficient officer'. Nothing
to do with pass marks or fitness tests. Just someone who
mattered sniffing the wind and deciding your future.

That was the time Bev had found herself mixed up in

the biggest anti-corruption inquiry Eastern Police has ever seen.

Three officers were convicted of taking bribes. The backhanders were big, each worth more than a month's salary, and as the Crown Court heard and the Seaton Post faithfully reported, there had been plenty of dirty money to go round.

Bev's crime? To be young, naïve and attractive...and to fall for a smooth-talking married detective who was dynamic, exciting and, unknown to Bev, absolutely corrupt.

She had spent fraught hours in interview rooms pleading her innocence to Complaints and Discipline. The threat of jail was terrifyingly real, the off-stage whispers a soundtrack that seemed to follow her for years.

No charges had ever been brought against her and now, after so long, Bev almost felt like it had happened to someone else.

Shivering in the soft rain that had drifted from the fell she looked up towards the summit, sucked hard on the cigarette, and remembered how it had ended.

The corrupt detectives all worked in the same CID office as Ed Whelan.

They went to prison. He went to work in the family business.

SAM WAS CURLED up on the large white leather settee, feet underneath her, staring at the latest copy of Yachting Monthly, staring at the same page she had turned to ten minutes ago.

She had eaten as soon as she got home – overcooked roast beef and soggy mash that took the microwave meal for one to a new culinary low. No point in doing a Nigella for yourself was there?

At least the bottle of Cabernet Sauvignon from Beaulieu Vineyards in Nappa Valley would be savoured for an hour or two; the meal was already forgotten.

Sleep wouldn't come easy tonight. It never did this early in an investigation.

She pushed herself off the sofa, walked back into the kitchen and poured another glass, remembering the wine moments she shared with Tristram.

Why aren't you here? I could talk to you…watch you nodding your head as you listened. Then you'd speak in that deep, soothing voice, a hypnotist's voice, the sound of reason, easing my fears. Instead I'm left behind. Widowed. Alone.

What have I got to look forward to? We were going to retire together, sail away. Now what? Nothing. Absolutely nothing but the job and shitty food.

'Fuck the yachts. Fuck the sea,' she muttered before stomping into the lounge, snatching the magazine off the settee, and throwing it against the wall.

She made sure her tears didn't drop into the wine.

The only light came from the TV, a period drama that held no interest but broke the silence. Tears and wine flowed, sometimes at the same time, until the bottle of Cabernet Sauvignon was empty; the clean ashtray of a few hours ago now home to nine cigarette butts.

Sam replayed every decision she had made throughout the investigation, questioned what, if anything, she could have done differently.

She lit cigarette number ten.

Chapter 35

Ed left the bed and breakfast at 6am, 'Doris', his 1972 fully restored VW campervan, now in a car park opposite The Victoria Hotel.

Located about 5 miles south of Whitby on the North Sea, Robin Hood's Bay and its narrow, cobbled streets twist and turn steeply downwards from the car park to the sandy bay where coast-to coast walkers at the end of their journey drop a pebble they've carried from St Bees on the Irish Sea.

Descending the eerily quiet streets on foot, Ed imagined sailors and fishermen, smugglers and press-gangs, roaming the bay hundreds of years ago.

He stood outside The Bay Hotel, breathed in the sea air and drizzle and strolled back up to the car park. He winced at the dirt on Doris' Porsche Fuchs wheels.

Inside he made a coffee, picked up a Raymond Chandler paperback and waited.

He didn't wait long.

Five pages into 'The Long Goodbye' he looked up and saw a local taxi pull onto the car park. Harry Pullman stepped out.

'Kettle on?' Harry said, opening the side door.

'It is.'

Harry stepped inside, sat down behind the table.

'So, what's this about?'

'You know exactly what it's about,' Ed said, putting a mug of coffee in front of Pullman.

'I've got no idea what you're talking about.'

'Tara Paxman.'

'A daft tart who'll say what anybody tells her to say, your lot included. What about her?'

Ed sat next to him.

'Why did you come then? Something must be bothering you.'

Harry blew across the top of his mug.

'Maybe I just wanted to look into your eyes, see what a bent bastard looks like.' He slurped on his coffee. 'Maybe I want to tip off the local press. Your lot sure as hell won't.'

'It'll be in the press soon enough so crack on. See if I'm bothered. But maybe you're here because you know you're in the shit? We've got Tara.'

'Like I said, a daft tart.'

Ed tried to read Harry Pullman's eyes, find the tell-tale tics of doubt, the shadow of fear. 'A daft tart with a second rabbit suit in her loft.'

Pullman sipped the coffee. 'What are you on about?'

He had held Ed's gaze, eyes steady and clear, but now he looked away.

'Maybe your grand plan hasn't quite worked out,' Ed said. 'Maybe Tara is telling the truth.'

Pullman looked out of the window, stared at the drizzle.

'It's too cramped in here for me.'

He leaned forward, pushed open the door, and moved out of his seat.

'What grand plan?' he said, stepping out of the van.

Ed hadn't moved, just raised his voice a little. 'We could start with the shootings on Saturday night.'

Harry Pullman turned to face him so quickly it caught Ed by surprise, veins bulging in his forearms, hot anger coating his words.

'What, the one that's been all over the news? You think I've got something to do with that?'

Ed's tone was as laid back as his posture. 'You have according to Tara.'

Pullman let the rage melt away, smiled as he shook his head, and sipped his coffee.

'Fucking hell Ed this is bollocks,' he said. 'Don't tell me you think I'm involved because of some shit Tara's feeding you. What's she saying now?'

'Plenty.'

'How will that ever stand up? I'm living at the other end of the country in case you've forgot. And I've got an alibi.'

Ed was still searching for fear to betray Harry Pullman's eyes but saw nothing but confidence and calm.

'And we…' Ed said, before Pullman cut him off.

'Last time I checked you weren't part of the 'we' anymore so cut the bullshit.'

Ed took a deep breath. 'Big mistake not getting rid of the suit. Hot as hell them things. Make you sweat a lot I would imagine.'

Ed drank some coffee. Pullman would know where this was going.

'And where there's sweat, there's a boatload of DNA.'

'What suit?'

Ed smiled.

'Big white rabbit suit.'

'I have absolutely no idea what you're talking about.' Pullman sounded bored but Ed thought it was put on.

Are you starting to wobble you cocky twat?

'Fancy dress costume?' Pullman nodding now, eyebrows pinched in concentration. 'Come to think of it I did wear one of those suits but that was months ago. Left it at Tara's. Forgot about it to tell you the truth. Is that what this is about? A fucking fancy dress costume?'

Ed stood up, reached into an overhead locker, and took out a pack of stem ginger biscuits.

'Want one?' he held out the packet.

'No thanks.'

Ed sat back down, dunked the biscuit in his coffee.

'Well good luck standing in the dock running that gem to get you off the hook,' he said. 'Even juries aren't that daft.'

They sat staring at each other through the door.

Ed bit into the softened biscuit.

Harry was first to speak.

'This won't get to court. You should know that better than most. You've been getting away with it for years. Avoiding court, I mean.'

Ed said nothing, stared at Pullman over the rim of his mug.

'You mentioned a suicide pact when I called you,' Pullman changing tack. 'What's that all about?

'Finish your coffee and then we can both be on our way,' Ed told him 'I've got enough of my own shit without taking yours. You take your chances with Parker.'

He dunked the biscuit again. 'And good luck with that as well. She'll have you done up like a kipper.'

'How do I know you're not working for the Skinners?' Pullman asked.

'If you thought that you wouldn't have come.'

'Maybe, but who are you working for? You must have been working for somebody? And if it's not them, who?'

Ed said nothing, held Pullman's gaze.

'Ray Reynolds always thought there was something dodgy about you,' Pullman was fishing. 'And that Brian Banks.'

Ed smiled.

'So, what do you want?' Pullman asked.

'That depends on you, but make no mistake, where you are now is right in the shit.'

Pullman leaned his head into the van.

'You still haven't told me what you want?'

Ed knew it was the right time.

'Ok Harry, we've known each other for years so cards on the table. I'm suspended but any investigation will take years and they'll still find nothing.'

Ed paused, let those words hover.

'Then I'll retire. But in the meantime, I don't want to be hanging around here. I may as well wait in the sun.'

'And you want what from me exactly?'

Ed laughed. 'I want fuck all from you. I'm not the one going to prison for multiple murder.'

'Neither am I,' Pullman growled. 'And you fucking know it.'.

Ed sat back, laced his hands behind his head and grinned.

'Well if you want to make sure that stays the case it's a matter of what I can do for you, and more importantly, how much you're willing to pay for your liberty.'

Chapter 36

Bev and Tara ordered the full Lakeland breakfast.

Other guests were already eating, rucksacks by the door, ready for the next leg of the coast-to-coast.

Bev had warned Tara to speak about nothing other than the weather, the scenery, or general chit-chat.

They had each said 'good morning' to the others in the room before they took their seats.

The friendly waitress gave them a pot of tea, returning not long after with their food.

Apart from banalities about the chances of rain – high – they ate in silence and watched the hikers hurry into waterproofs, keen to make a start.

Bev shook her head, voice barely audible. 'Why?'

'What?' Tara whispered, looking around.

'Why would you walk from one side of the country to the other?' Bev said. 'I honestly don't get it.'

Tara shrugged, watched the last of the hikers load up and head out.

'Loads of reasons I imagine… sense of achievement, test yourself against the elements, enjoy the scenery.'

Bev cut into her poached egg. 'Plenty of roads if you want to see the countryside. Just drive for God's sake. Anyway, once you've seen one hill, you've seen them all.'

They finished their breakfast in silence.

They walked across the road towards the car park and picnic tables, the black sky casting a shadow over everything underneath it.

'I'm just popping into the shop,' Tara said, emerging soon after with cigarettes and one of Alfred Wainwright's legendary guidebooks.

Minutes later they had both lit up and were watching a Mazda MX5 drive past.

'One of my old boyfriends used to have one of them,' Tara smiled. 'You ever had sex in a two-seater?'

'Can't say I have,' Bev thought about the logistics, doubted she was supple enough these days.

'The man used to say you couldn't beat sex in a convertible.'

'The man?'

Tara exhaled. 'My ex.'

Did she call every male 'the man'?

Bev stubbed her cigarette out in the ashtray. 'Right, finish up and then we can crack on.'

She fished the ringing mobile out of her coat pocket, not daring to move in case she lost the signal.

'Hi Sam. Yeah we're just about ready to start. We're both outside having a smoke. Just finished a cracking full English.'

Sam would realise Bev wasn't alone.

Bev listened as Sam brought her up to date with all developments including the murder of the Skinners, the last call to Skinner referring to the 'Reverend' being killed, 'Pugsley's unknown status, and the mention of the 'source.'

Across the road Tara was watching a hawk hovering above a stone-walled field.

Bev agreed with Sam that 'Pugsley' was probably code for Paul Adams.

'But what about the 'Reverend'?' Sam said.

'That'll be Green.'

'Scott Green?'

Bev lit another cigarette, laughed. 'You know all about posh wines and yachts but you don't know Cluedo? Reverend Green's one of the characters…you know…it was Reverend Green in the library with the candlestick. A classic.'

'Jesus I'm so wide of the mark at times,' Sam said, squashing her embarrassment. 'Cheers Bev.'

Sam took a deep breath. 'Ed was always good at the cryptic stuff,' she said, Ed washing into her mind. 'If he was here he might have worked out who Skinner's 'source' was.'

There was a moment's silence before Bev spoke. 'I couldn't get Ed out of my mind last night. Couldn't get to sleep for thinking about him.'

'We'll just have to see what happens. No point in trying to second guess. I'll have to crack on Bev.'

Bev got the message. Sam wasn't getting involved in any speculation.

'No bother boss.'

Bev smoked her cigarette and wondered whether Sam knew more than she was letting on.

Cigarette finished she called to Tara, who walked back across the road.

'Missing your boyfriend then?' Tara said, chewing on a piece of Kendall Mint Cake she had bought in the shop.

Bev snapped her head towards Tara. 'Sorry?'

'You said you couldn't get to sleep for thinking about him. You shagging Whelan?'

Bev hadn't realised Tara could hear her from the other side of the road. But what was there to make noise in this wilderness?

Shit!

'No I'm not,' Bev said. 'And didn't anyone tell you it's bloody rude to listen to private conversations?'

'Couldn't help it could I,' Tara grinned. 'Not exactly buzzing with noise round here. Who was on the phone? Nosey?'

'Who?' Bev asked.

'Parker. Nosey Parker.'

Bev pushed open the pub door, stopped in the small vestibule, turned and glared at Tara.

'Show some respect. She's the one who's trying to save your neck.'

'Alright, keep your hair on,' Tara at least looked guilty. 'Everybody's got a nickname.'

'Do they?'

They walked into the pub.

'What's mine?' Bev asked.

'I don't know, but you'll have one.'

'What's yours?'

Tara ran the tip of her tongue around her lips. 'Whatever they want it to be.'

'And Harry Pullman's?' Bev asked, smiling at two women helping each other with their backpacks.

'Sauce,' Tara said.

'Sorry?'

'Sauce.'

Bev's face was a blank as Tara shook her head.

'Keep up with the programme. Harry Pullman. HP. HP sauce!'

Chapter 37

S AM MADE DO with coffee and a cigarette, envious of Bev and her cooked breakfast.

She blew smoke upwards, aware of how much there was to get through today. Bev would get a full, comprehensive statement from Tara but they'd need plenty of corroboration.

She perched herself on a stool at the kitchen island, tapped ash into the glass ashtray.

The next few days would be difficult enough, but being without Ed, her 'sounding board' and the person whose opinion she valued above all others, would increase the degree of difficulty.

She moved to the kettle, flicked it on.

'Sounding boards' and 'degrees of difficulty' reminded her of Olympic divers. Whatever she was diving into she had to do it without Ed, and as much as she worried about him, she couldn't afford to get distracted.

She made another cup of coffee as she finished her cigarette, watching the smoke and steam curl upwards.

Placing the mug on the island she sat back down and began jotting things down on a pad.

The forensics from the scene would take their course. She'd already told Julie Trescothick the priorities.

She needed someone to visit Lester Stephenson. Was his visit just a badly-timed need for Tara's sexual services, or was there a more sinister reason?

The decision was who to send now Ed was out of the picture.

She took one final drag of the cigarette and stubbed it out.

Not Russ Chaddick. God she couldn't stand him. The sooner she got him off the investigation the better. He was negative to the point of being poison. What did Ed used to say? Negativity is like a cancer. Stop it before it spreads, cut it out like a tumour.

She put the pen down, held the mug to her lips with both hands.

She would visit Paul Adams' wife. If Tara was right and it was Paul who was tipping off the Skinners on Harry's location, how had Paul got the information in the first place?

Bev's last call was interesting.

If Luke Skinner had been talking about the 'sauce' not 'source' then the Skinners wanted Harry Pullman dead. She got that.

But in retaliation could Harry Pullman really organise a series of targeted killings and then take out everybody connected with them.

She put the mug down, wrote 'Tara' on the pad.

If she'd dropped him in York as she said, how had he got back to Portsmouth so quickly? Did he meet someone in York who drove him back? Did they have time to drive back?

Sam wrote 'danger?' next to Tara's name, circling it to the point that the pen almost penetrated the paper.

She stood up and paced the kitchen. Pacing helped her think. It had since her days at Durham University.

Why had no police officers at Malvern Close or the surrounding area seen Harry Pullman?

Had he been hiding in the loft? Had he made the noise she'd heard?

She understood why Pullman couldn't risk taking the rabbit suit with him when he left Tara's. If he was stopped and checked by the police, he would be straight down the station. But what if Harry Pullman was never there? What if someone else was in the loft? What if Harry Pullman was as much a patsy as Zac Williams?

She called Julie Trescothick and told her how to progress the unidentified DNA profile on the second rabbit suit.

Harry Pullman was back in his seat inside 'Doris' drinking his second cup of coffee.

'So you're saying you want me to pay for you to swan around in the sun somewhere?'

'I'm not saying that at all,' Ed was standing by the sliding door. 'What I'm saying is that I'll wait out my suspension abroad.'

'And what would be in it for your's truly,' Pullman interested now. 'How can you help me, if of course I need and want your help.'

'I've told you. Sam Parker's got Tara.'

'And I've told you she's just a lying tart.'

'A lying tart living in your house.'

Pullman put the mug on the table.

'Making me easier to set up,' he said. 'The Skinners will do whatever it takes to stop me going to court and in case you forgot, she used to work for them.'

'She'd dispute that. We've got a -'

'Stop saying 'we',' Harry snapped. 'You're not in their gang any more.'

Ed ignored the slur and carried on.

'The rabbit suit from the loft. If you've worn that, your DNA will be all over the inside.'

'I wore it ages ago. I told you that…hang fire.'

Harry Pullman picked up his mobile, scrolled through the photos and smiled as he passed the phone to Ed.

'There you go.'

Ed took it.

The first photograph showed someone wearing a full white rabbit costume, which could have been anybody.

Ed flicked onto the second photograph; Harry in the white suit holding the rabbit head.

'Accounts for my DNA being in one if that's what your tests show and unless I'm mistaken, you can't date DNA.'

Pullman slurped on the coffee before continuing. 'No way you can say how long it's been there, so you've got nothing.'

Ed stepped inside from the doorway.

'So none of this has anything to do with you then?'

'Absolutely not. How many more times?'

Ed sat down.

'Bollocks…but if that's your attitude you may as well head home. By the time you get there Sam Parker will have a team waiting to lock you up. Take your chances at court. Your DNA, Tara's evidence…'

Pullman set down his mug and shrugged.

'DNA you can't date and the word of a prostitute

who's probably on the payroll of a crime family. I'm shitting it.'

Pullman stood up. 'I'll be on my way then. It'll be a pleasure watching you go down. Bent as a nine-bob note Whelan.'

Pullman stepped outside the van.

'Sam Parker's not just investigating the shootings,' Ed said.

Pullman hesitated, stopped and put his head back in the van. 'I'm pleased for her.'

'She's also looking at four suicides which she believes are murders and the finger's pointing one way. Towards you.'

'Is she on glue?' Pullman said, stepping back into the van. 'Who am I, the big cheese coordinating everything, killing people all over the place?'

Pullman sat down. 'For fuck sake why would I do that?'

'Takeover bid.'

Pullman laughed. 'Take over from the Skinners? At my age? I just want a quiet life living somewhere with a new identity and a few quid in my pocket. I'm not going back to Seaton St George. Ever!'

Ed took out his mobile and scrolled through his photos.

'Do you know him?'

He handed Pullman his phone.

'Should I?'

'Just wondered.'

Harry held the phone closer to his face.

'Is that Tara's house?'

'Well it's where she lives. It's your house remember.'

'When was this taken?'

'Nothing to do with you.'

Pullman handed the phone back to Ed.

'I know him. Well, know of him. Only met him the once.'

'And?'

Pullman grinned. 'He's an accountant. Retired now but still does a bit part time. Boring as fuck.'

'Aren't they all?'

'Not as boring as this old fart. I met him once. Spoke about his wife, kids, grandkids non-stop. Twenty minutes of my life I'll never get back. Showed me a picture of them all on his phone. Pack of in-breds, all ugly as fuck, especially the wife.'

Pullman scrunched his nose, wincing at the memory. 'I wouldn't touch her with yours.'

'Where were you talking to him?'

'Some party. As soon as I introduced him to Tara he forgot about his wife. Dribbling all over her he was. Dirty old bastard must have got her number.'

'What's his name?'

'Do you remember the names of the boring bastards you meet?'

Ed shrugged his shoulders. 'I remembered yours.'

'Fuckin' comedian now,' Harry scowled. 'When was that photo taken? Before or after the shootings?'

'It's irrelevant.'

'Might not be. Especially when I tell you who his only client was…maybe still is.'

Ed knew who he was. He wanted to test Pullman. Make sure he was telling the truth.

Chapter 38

SAM WALKED into the briefing room, the assembled crews with their backs to her. Unfortunately for Detective Sergeant Russ Chaddick there was a lull in the conversations when he said Ed Whelan was a dinosaur who should have gone years ago.

Sam's raised voice had heads jerking over shoulders.

'You couldn't lace his boots,' she said, eyes following her as she walked to the front of the room.

She wanted to eyeball Chaddick but as he had found something riveting on the floor, she glared at the thinning hair on the top of his head.'

'I told you all I didn't want to hear any speculation about Ed. I certainly don't want to hear people slagging him off when the reasons for his suspension aren't known and he's not here to defend himself.'

Chaddick kept his eyes on the floor in the silence.

'Right, we've got plenty to do today and time is short. Russ, would you mind waiting outside please.'

Eyes bore into Chaddick. They all knew what would follow – his dismissal.

Sam waited until he left the room, then gave an overview of the investigation and the reasons why they were looking at the circumstances surrounding the deaths of Bill Redwood, Scott Green, Davy Swan and Jimmy Marshall.

'Let's take one thing at a time. Malvern Close. Three dead outside including one of our own, two dead inside, one shot by us.'

She paced the stage; all eyes followed her.

'I spoke with the Chief and Deputy Chief earlier. I've told them we will review the footage from the helicopter, the negotiator tapes and everything else regarding the police actions at the scene.'

Sam sensed the collective slump; nobody wanted that job.

'Today.'

The sighs were audible.

Sam stopped in the centre of the room and let the silence become deafening before she spoke again.

'You are on one of the biggest investigations in the history of the force. The eyes of the country are watching you. There is no room for error, no room for half-baked concentration. If you get a shit job…tough. Shit jobs have got to be done and done effectively and efficiently. We can't afford to miss anything.'

She let her words sink in before continuing.

'Be under no illusions. I am not convinced the shooter is Zac Williams. There are inconsistencies with the forensic evidence. Now what I am about to tell you does not leave this room.'

Bums shuffled on seats; backs straightened.

'We have a witness who throws doubt on Williams being the shooter although in fairness, I'm far from convinced that the witness is 100% truthful.'

Sam started pacing the stage.

'It may be the witness is more frightened of other people than of us.'

Sam turned to Lester Stephenson, the man who visited Tara Paxman not long after the shooting. 'We know she is a high-end prostitute so is this man just a punter or something more sinister? I want background checks on him and I want to know everything there is to know about Tara Paxman.'

Sam paused, her head on the point of exploding, a balloon overfilled with information not air about to burst.

She glanced at Shane 'Tucky' Walton, hard-backed A4 notebook in hand, ready to write down her instructions.

'I want the FLOs to establish why all victims were in the vicinity. We need to establish if they were random targets, wrong place, wrong time. Remember, the more we know about the victim, the more we know about the killer.'

All eyes remained on her, heads nodding.

'I want house to house to establish if anyone saw anything unusual in the days leading up to the shootings, if they saw anything unusual before they were evacuated from the area.

I want us to speak to the Domestic Abuse team, see how often we've been called to 2 Malvern Close.'

Sam paused, took a breath, gathered her thoughts.

'I want Zac Williams' computer examining. Check his search history. Where and when did he get those newspaper articles? If you haven't seen the newspapers in question, there are photos of them in the Room.'

Sam looked around. Everyone would share the success if everything went well; she would be out on a limb if it all went wrong.

'Moving on. I want a fingertip search around the car

277

where Swan and Marshall were found. If someone else was present let's see if they left anything behind.'

Tucky wiggled his wrist.

'We'll let Detective Sergeant Walton have a breather. His shorthand's not as good as it used to be.'

A ripple of laughter, like a Mexican wave, worked its way around the room.

Shane looked up from his pad, smiled at Sam's sarcasm.

'Ready Shane?'

He nodded.

'Scott Green. Any updates on CCTV?'

Sergeant Russell Willings spoke quickly: 'Green sprinted straight in front of the bus. He was being chased and his pursuer can be seen tripping over the pushchair. As you know I have a statement from the mother. CCTV didn't capture his face.'

'Build?'

'Stocky. Would fit Swan or Marshall.'

'Anything from the CCTV on the bus?' Sam asked.

'Not at the moment,' Russell said.

She paused, looked around the room, everyone waiting for her next words.

'Be aware that you may be in and around the property in Malvern Close for some time. Media interest will be intense. They won't be able to get near the house but they'll have their helicopters up, maybe even drones. They'll come scurrying around corners with their cameras, like lurchers chasing rabbits.'

A laugh and nods of agreement went around the search team.

'Don't get caught in their telephoto lenses doing something you would rather the world and their wife didn't see in the newspaper or tv news...so that's smoking, eating, scratching your backside…you all know the drill. Look professional at all times.'

Briefing finished she called the Detective Chief Inspector in charge of Seaton St George CID and informed him of Chaddick's comments about Ed.

Sam explained her proposed course of action.

Ten minutes later Chaddick was standing in her office. No doubt he had a good idea what was coming next.

'I'm not having the likes of you publicly slagging off Ed Whelan and I'm not having people on this inquiry thinking I don't stick to my threats.'

Sam watched Chaddick's face burn like an overheating engine.

She stood up, put her coat on. 'You're off the inquiry. I've spoken to your DCI. He's expecting you back pronto.'

Sam walked past him without another word. No point in launching into a tirade. Mission accomplished as far as he was concerned.

Chapter 39

'So, THE ACCOUNTANT,' Harry Pullman said, breathing in the damp sea air. 'Maybe I can help you with that retirement fund.'

They had both walked across the car park.

'How's that?' Ed said, pulling on a blue woollen hat.

'You tell me where Tara is.'

'Why would I do that?'

'Five grand. No questions asked.'

'Why do you want to know?'

Harry Pullman's smile had something unpleasant at the edges. 'Five grand loses you the right to ask, but let's just say the accountant's employer might be interested in her whereabouts.'

Ed stared at The Victoria Hotel.

Or you want to know where she lives.

'How would I get the money?'

'I'll pay it into any account you want.'

Ed ambled across the car park back towards 'Doris', hands in pockets, deep in thought.

'My taxi's here in five,' Pullman shouted. 'You better decide sharpish.'

Ed turned and walked back.

'Ten grand.'

He put his hand in his pocket, pulled out a slip of paper, and handed it to Pullman.

Harry examined it. A handwritten note, in blue ink: account number, sort code, mobile number.

'You had that ready you bent bastard.'

'We both knew what you were coming here for. You want to know where she is; it'll cost you ten grand. But don't take too long. She won't be where she is forever.'

'How the fuck did you get an account in the name of Chris Waddle?'

Ed smiled. Years ago, as a young detective, all of his informants had the names of Newcastle United players.

'Easy when you know how. And before you ask, the answer's no. You get nothing until I've got the cash. Ring that number when the money's in and I'll tell you where she is.'

SAM HAD TRAVELLED to see Paul Adams' wife with the three post mortems of the apparent suicides complete by lunchtime.

Swan and Marshall had no physical injuries, just smoke inhalation in their lungs. Sam wanted toxicology reports to establish if there were traces of any substances in either body.

Scott Green had suffered multiple fractures to his right arm, ribs, and right leg and a head injury had caused massive bleeding on the brain. The injuries together resulted in a heart attack.

Erica Adams, thin, arms pasty white and with red blotches all over her face, was sitting in an armchair leaving the grey fabric settee free for Sam.

Sam doubted she'd slept since Paul's death.

'Nobody's told me what he was doing at that house,' Erica said. 'Is it a big secret?'

Sam had known the question was coming. The answer might be better heard from someone close to the couple but lying was not an option.

'It's not a secret Erica. Truth is we don't know why he was there. Not really.'

'What does that mean? Who lives there?'

Erica's questions had the frantic air of a parent looking for a lost a child. Without drawing breath, she continued. 'On television it said a young woman lived there. Why did she say Paul was there? It can't have been police business if you don't know so what business was it?'

'We're still checking.'

Erica stood up and took her tall, gaunt frame to the window. 'I'm not stupid. If he wasn't there as a detective, was he sleeping with her?'

Sam couldn't find it in herself to forgive Paul Adams in that moment.

'I don't know.'

Erica turned and lunged forward, face contorted, lips trembling.

'Does she say they were sleeping together,' she shouted.

Sam looked up from the settee.

'Yes. I'm sorry.'

'Thank you!' Erica's bean-pole body sagged. 'Thank you for being honest. More than that bastard was.'

'I'm sorry I'm having to tell you this.'

Erica nodded; her shoulders heaved under the weight of the tears that finally fell.

When Sam stood up the raised palm of Erica's outstretched arm almost hit her nose. Sam took the hint, sat back down.

'How long?' Erica demanded.

Sam slowly shook her head, voice quiet. 'I don't know.'

'How long,' Erica screamed, the blotches on her cheeks gone, her whole face now a mass of red.

'Not long according to the girl.'

Erica's next two questions came in a whisper.

'What's she like, the girl? Have you seen her?'

'I've met her...but I'm not sure what you want me to say'

'Is she attractive?' Erica asked, voice a little louder.

'That's subjective Erica and not helpful. Some people would say she's attractive, some wouldn't. Same goes for you and me.'

Erica sat back down, took a tissue out of the box on the floor, blew her nose.

'Excuse me.'

She bowed her head, clasped her hands, and cried.

After a few minutes she cleared her throat.

'Sorry to take it out on you.'

Sam relaxed into the back of the settee. 'That's okay.'

'Would you like some tea?' Erica asked.

'I'm fine thanks but...can I ask some questions. I don't want to be insensitive but it might help.'

Erica nodded.

'How was Paul these last few months? Was he himself?'

'He seemed tired, stressed, but I thought it was the job not that he had another woman.'

Tears ran down her face.

Sam waited while Erica blew her nose into a tissue and took another out of the box to wipe her eyes.

'None of this is your fault,' Erica voice shaky. 'Paul told

me how good you were. Great detective, great boss he used to say.'

Sam's nod was barely noticeable as Erica's raw-rimmed eyes travelled up and down her.

'He never told me you were gorgeous as well.'

Sam shuffled in her seat. Her cheeks were burning now.

'Ask me anything you want,' Erica said now. 'My husband's dead. Whatever he was doing before he died doesn't really matter does it? Not like I can scream and swear at him is it, tell him to get out, tell him he's destroyed his marriage? It's cost him his life.'

Erica suddenly jumped up and rushed from the room, her 'sorry' a barely audible whisper as she flew out of the door.

Sam heard retching; a tap running. She sat and waited.

When Erica Adams returned she was holding a blue fluffy towel against her face.

'I suppose I can have pink towels now,' she said, sitting down. 'Paul would never have pink towels in the house. Too girlie he used to say.'

Sam let Erica finish, waited until the towel was on her thighs, fingers playing with it like a child curling the edge of a comfort blanket.

'Suppose I can do what I want now. Only me here.'

Sam felt sorry for her, was touched by her pain, but she couldn't be her counsellor, couldn't even be her FLO. Sam needed information and she needed it now.

'You said Paul seemed tired, stressed. Any idea what that was about?'

'Not really.'

Sam scanned the birthday cards on the windowsill, eyes honing in on the big one in the middle that said, 'To the Woman I Love'.

Fucking hell Paul what you were thinking?

Erica saw Sam looking at the cards.

'Crazy day of all days for it to happen, but I'll never forget the date will I?'

Sam shook her head. She had no words.

'Did you have any money worries?' she asked, needing to get Erica focused.

'No.' Erica dabbed at her eyes, shook her head. 'Quite the opposite really. We always had plenty and we never skimped. Paul was always taking me to nice places, smart restaurants and lovely hotels for weekends away. Whenever I asked if we were okay money wise, he just used to laugh and say 'of course'.'

'Did Paul look after the finances in the house?'

'Yes.' Erica smiled, glanced at her parents' wedding photograph on the occasional table. 'Not like my mother. She took dad's wages off him every week and then gave him pocket money.'

Sam nodded. Shock, stress, and emotion often caused people to babble about nothing in particular. She would let Erica continue, her questions could wait a few seconds.

'Dad was still getting pocket money the day he retired,' Erica said. 'Mam looked after the money. The chancellor with the iron fist dad used to call her.'

'But you didn't take after her, running the finances?'

'No, I just left it to Paul. He always said he'd look after me and I believed him. He was always surprising me. Nights out, fancy holidays.'

Erica stood and picked up a shoe box Sam had already noticed by the side of the armchair.

'I found this at the bottom of his washing basket,' Erica said. 'I wanted to smell his clothes.'

Sam didn't need words. Her face asked the question.

'We had separate baskets. Paul didn't like his clothes mixed up with mine.'

She passed the green 'Crockett and Jones' shoe box to Sam and sat back down.

It felt heavier than a pair of shoes.

Sam remembered reading somewhere that Daniel Craig wore a pair of Crockett and Jones in 'Spectre', the James Bond movie that had just been released.

She put the box on her lap, lifted the lid, and clamped her mouth tight to keep her face from showing emotion.

'Have you seen this before?'

Erica, hands clasped again, shook her head.

'Do you know where he got it?'

Erica's hands shot up to her eyes as the tears returned, her breathing so fast Sam thought she was hyperventilating.

'What's he done? Where's that from? Who's he mixed up with?' the words a torrent.

Sam was staring at a safety deposit box. It wasn't long and thin, it wasn't made of metal and it didn't need two keys to open it, but it was full of neatly stacked, banded bundles of red fifty pound notes.

Chapter 40

'CAN WE JUST GO FOR A WALK?' Tara had pleaded. 'I'm getting cabin fever in here.'

Bev had switched off the tape. An hour's break wouldn't do either of them any harm.

'It's beautiful,' Tara was saying now as they turned right out of the pub. 'I could be really happy here.'

The footpath was damp, the mist low over the fell tops, but it had stopped raining.

Bev looked around.

'In the middle of nowhere? Not for me thanks.'

Tara spread out her arms. 'Quiet, fresh air and best of all, a gangster-free zone.'

Bev smiled. Tara might be brash, cocky even, but she was the one with a price on her head.

They walked past a primary school, gaudy paintings stuck to the windows, the perimeter fence newly varnished and heavy with moisture.

'Imagine going there,' Tara said. 'Beats the shit hole I went to. Not a needle in sight I bet. We had dealers at the school gates selling tenner bags of heroin.'

They continued towards Glenridding.

'What was your childhood like then?' Bev asked.

'Usual I suppose.'

Bev put her hand on Tara's. Both stopped, faced each other.

'Dealers at the school gate? Not what I'd call usual.'

'Usual for me and my mates. My mum was on her own but she did her best… at the beginning.'

Tara walked, linked arms with Bev.

'I never met my father,' she said. 'Don't know anything about him. My mother wouldn't talk about him.'

Tara looked up at the fells to her right, the mist moving like a slow motion sea.

'Your mother have boyfriends?' Bev said.

They walked a few steps, Bev waiting for an answer, Tara considering what to say.

'A few. Only one interfered with me if that's what you mean.'

Bev hadn't expected that answer but when it came she wasn't surprised. Too many years in the Job to be surprised by anything anymore.

'Want to talk about it?'

'Not really.' Tara turned her head, looked straight ahead. Bev did the same.

They walked in silence for about twenty metres.

'I was thirteen.' Tara's voice was steady, quiet.

She broke away from Bev, put her hands in her pockets, rested her chin on her chest.

'Usual shit I suppose. They came home from a night out. My mother crashed out on the sofa pissed. He came into my bedroom. Told me to be quiet.'

Tara let the memory replay in a monotone..

'I was in bed. He knelt down, kissed me, shoved his

tongue down my throat. I still remember his beer breath. Fuckin' disgusting. Shoved his cock in my face. You can guess the rest.'

Bev nodded, said nothing. She'd spoken to too many victims of sexual abuse over the years. If a victim wanted to talk, they would.

'That was the start. Every time they went drinking my mother would pass out and he'd come upstairs. Not kidding Bev, got to the stage where I was convinced he was spiking her drinks.'

Bev was taken by Tara's strength of character, throwing out a one-liner in the middle of all that horror.

'He must have been putting something in her drinks because my mother could drink the skinny twat under the table.'

Bev bit her lip to stop herself laughing.

'What happened to him?'

'Still there. Full-blown alcoholic now, like my mother. The pair of them were made for each other.'

A pile of wet leaves in the gutter, pushed there by nature or man, flew upwards as Tara kicked them.

'I told my mother once,' she said quietly. 'Got accused of being…what did she call me…a vindictive cow.'

Tara rubbed at her eyes again. This time tears ran down her cheeks.

'She fucking told him and guess what? He just did it more. Said at least he knew now she'd never believe me.'

Bev bit her lip again, this time to stop herself saying something inappropriate. Tara's mother had hung an 'open for business sign' around her own daughter's neck.

Experience had taught Bev that the unforced reveal was over, for now at least.

The easy option would be to ask Tara if she wanted to

make a historical child abuse complaint but now was not the right time. Bev needed to build up trust, become a confidante, not dive in like some overzealous authority figure.

'You still see them?'

'God no,' Tara's tone all 'are you mad'. 'Got out when I was sixteen and never went back. What mother stands by and lets her daughter…'

Another pile of leaves, another kick.

'You know what I mean.'

Bev nodded, said nothing.

'He used to tell his mates how I had no stretch marks, no fat, was nice and firm. I'd hear him when he started to bring them back. Mother out of it on couch. Him renting me out.'

Bev shook her head but it wasn't an evil she was hearing for the first time. Some children, some women, had dreadful lives, suffered experiences people would never believe, never know was happening almost under their noses.

'As soon as I could, I got a flat. Even went to university, but that was shit.'

'You didn't stick it then?'

'No. I remembered he'd give me a fiver if one of his friends had sex with me. You just switch off, don't let them kiss you. After a while it's no big deal. Made it easy when I got involved with the Skinners and Harry. Got more than a fiver then. Fucking way more.'

Tara laughed out loud, Bev gutted by the empty sound.

What you've had to go through.

When they reached Glenridding Tara stopped to admire the boats bobbing on their moorings.

'I'd like to learn to sail.'

'Ask Sam,' Bev said. 'She sails big yachts.'

'Really? Wow! I'm suddenly impressed.'

They stared out across Ullswater, grey and vast and ancient.

'Where do you learn?' Tara said.

'No good asking me. I've got no idea. You need to ask Sam.'

'Will you get me away then? You know, to start again somewhere new.'

'I'll do whatever I can to help you.'

They walked in silence, Bev reflecting how this young, intelligent woman never had a chance. Until now.

'Can you just leave me here,' Tara said. 'While you're sorting things out, can I just stay here?'

Up ahead, a man in a lime green windbreaker strolled into the village store; a couple, boots mud-splattered and leading an exhausted-looking dog, trudged towards wherever they were going. The thickening mist seemed to suck the light from the heavy sky.

You must be mad

'I'll have a word with Sam but don't get your hopes up,' Bev said. 'I'm telling you she'd want some massive assurances. Like no getting pissed for starters.'

They turned right onto the driveway leading to the Inn on the Lake, a hotel with manicured lawns and gardens running down to the water.

'Sam's stayed here,' Bev said. 'Said it was beautiful.'

'She was right.'

'Before you ask, no you can't stay here.'

Tara stuck her tongue out.

'Spoilsport.'

They walked to the sparkling glass doors, into reception and through to the bar, the ambience all luxury, the staff all models of discretion.

'Grab that table. I'll order the drinks.'

Tara dropped into the fabric tub chair in the bow window and looked across the lake while Bev spoke with the barman.

'Beautiful isn't it?' Tara said, when Bev joined her.

'If you like that sort of thing,' Bev said, sitting down opposite.

A small yacht sailed past, powered by its white main sail.

'So, Sam Parker could sail one of them?'

'She sails them bigger than that,' Bev told her. 'Used to live on them for a couple of weeks in the holidays.'

'Wow.'

A white-shirted arm carrying a small, circular tray appeared inbetween them.

'Ladies.'

The young, short-haired barman placed their drinks on the wooden circular table: two large gin and tonics.

'He's fit,' Tara stage whispered as the barman walked away.

'You behave yourself young lady. You're here for safety not fun.'

'Just saying.'

Bev stood and walked towards the foyer as her mobile signalled a call, the screen telling her it was Sam.

'Hi Sam.'

She made sure this time Tara was too far away to hear.

'Yeah we're at the Inn on the Lake. She needed a break bless her. So did I.'

Bev brought Sam up to speed before returning to the table.

'Sam's hoping to get across here soon. And if you behave yourself, she might let you stay.'

'When do you go back?' Tara asked.

'Tomorrow lunchtime probably. We can possibly leave you here tomorrow night, move you Wednesday.'

'I'm not being funny but thanks, I mean it.'

She sipped the Hendricks with the slice of cucumber.

'I love it here and where's better to hide? Nobody will find me here. Who would think to look?'

Chapter 41

THE CAMPERVAN ROLLED along the farm track a Roman would have been proud of, curiosity causing the grazing sheep to look in Ed's direction.

Three hundred metres of arrow-straight, black Tarmac led to the only house for miles. An electric vehicle may get to the house unannounced, an air-cooled VW would not.

Hugh Campbell walked out of the old grey coloured farmhouse and planted one red corduroy leg on the ranch-style fencing.

'Ed Whelan as I live and breathe,' Campbell said, as Ed got out of the van. 'What brings you here?'

'Was just passing and thought I'd pop in.'

'Yeah, right. Pull the other one.'

'It's true.' Ed was walking towards him. 'I've been down to Whitby. Thought I'd come across the moors, then thought, I know, I'll call in on Hugh.'

'Best come in then, not that I believe a word of it.'

Unlike Hugh, Ed had to duck under the doorway lintel. Houses over two hundred years old were built for a smaller generation.

Ed followed Campbell into the farmhouse kitchen: black slab floor, black Aga, large pine table.

'I hear you've been suspended.'

'News travels fast,' Ed said, pulling a wooden chair out from the table. 'Milk, no sugar.'

'Tell me, what brings a disgraced detective to my door?' Campbell flicked on the kettle, leaned against the bench.

'Lester Stephenson,' Ed said.

'What about him?'

'I was wondering what your long-term accountant was doing at the scene of a mass shooting.'

'Lester? Mass shooting? Don't be ridiculous.'

Campbell spooned instant coffee into two mugs, one white, one green, and added boiling water.

'Things aren't as clear cut with that shooting as they first appeared,' Ed said.

Campbell carried the mugs to the table, sat down opposite Ed. 'And you're bothered because of what exactly?'

'Just because I'm suspended doesn't mean I don't think. I knew immediately it was your man Lester as soon as I saw the photograph. Sam Parker doesn't, but she'll find out.'

'He paid for a shag. So what?'

Ed raised the mug to his lips, stared over the brim at Campbell.

'I never said who he went to see.'

'Bully for you. The street's been all over the tele. I know Tara lives there. Lester's met her before. Obviously fancied a dabble.'

'In Harry Pullman's house?'

'Harry's a landlord. Entitled to rent his property out to whoever he wants.'

Ed drank some coffee.

'But let's say somebody thought it might be an opportunity to set Harry up. Lead Sam Parker to think Harry was responsible for the shootings.'

It was Campbell's turn to look over the rim of the mug. He blew across the liquid.

'I thought the lad who your lot…' Campbell stopped, a barrister before the jury, pausing for effect. 'Your ex-lot I should say. I thought the lad your lot shot was the gunman.'

'Maybe he was, maybe he wasn't.'

'This is all fascinating stuff, but I'm not sure where I come in.'

Campbell sipped the coffee.

'The Skinners have gone. Anybody fancying a take-over is only really left with Harry Pullman as an obstacle,' Ed said.

'I'm retired,' Campbell let his lips form a faint smile. 'Successful businessman enjoying the fruits of his labour. If Harry Pullman still wants to be in the game at his age, that's a matter for him.'

'But your sons aren't retired,' Ed watched Campbell's jaw tighten. 'Maybe they fancy a bit of action.'

Campbell put his mug on the table, shook his head.

'What is it you want Ed?'

'Lester may have gone to get his leg over, or maybe he was going to check on proceedings.'

'You always did tell a good tale, but that imagination will be the death of you one day.'

Ed pushed his chair away from the table and stood up, leaned towards Campbell.

'You threatening me Hugh?'

Campbell didn't move, didn't speak.

'I'm warning you. Don't threaten me Hugh. Ever.'

Ed backed away from the table.

'Well I'll be off then. Sorry to have wasted your time. Obviously, the fact that Tara's been whisked away into protective custody doesn't concern you.'

Campbell's face stayed poker straight.

Ed walked to the kitchen door, stopped and spun on his heels.

'But of course, if you or your sons are involved, and it's been an exercise in double patsies, Tara Paxman would know it,' Ed said. 'Her place was used to slip into the shooting site. See you later.'

Ed walked outside. Campbell caught up with him by Doris.

'What is it you really want Whelan? You were never one for social calls, not unless there was something in it for you.'

'What I want is out,' Ed opened the driver's door. 'I've had enough. Time I put me feet up somewhere warm. You ever been to Kefalonia? Greek island. Gorgeous.

'Right, but I still don't understand why you're here.'

'Simple,' Ed said, sliding behind the retro Banjo steering wheel. 'If Tara can't drop you in it you've got nothing to worry about, but…'

'But what?'

'If she can, you're in the shit.'

Ed turned the ignition. When the air-cooled engine sprang into life, a herring gull flapped off a wheely bin, a piece of steak pie in its yellow beak.

'If she can turn Harry Pullman, Sam Parker will have no problem turning Tara,' Ed went on. 'And Tara might have all sorts of interesting things to tell the police.'

Ed closed the door, wound down the driver's window, and watched Campbell.

In truth, he wasn't sure Tara Paxman would be easily

persuaded to turn informer but he was pleased to see the tension in Campbell's eyes.

He selected reverse.

'Where is she then?' Campbell tried to make it casual.

Ed put the gear stick back into neutral, raised his backside and produced a piece of paper from his trouser pocket.

'Call the number on there when you've deposited eleven thousand into that account.'

Campbell laughed. 'Eleven grand?!'

'Makes no odds to me if you or your sons rot in jail,' Ed smiled. 'Eleven grand, then I'll tell you where she is.'

Campbell came closer to the window, the violence in his past bubbling back to the present.

'I always knew your mates were bent bastards, but I could never decide about you,' his mouth twisted. 'Until now. So do me a favour and fuck off, the smell of police corruption is upsetting my sheep.'

Ed reversed slowly, stuck his head out of the window.

'You want to know where she is, call that number after the money's deposited. But better hurry Hugh. She won't be where she is forever and once she moves, I won't be able to find her.'

Ed did a three-point turn and drove off.

Maybe he was closer to life in Kefalonia than he thought.

Chapter 42

SAM PARKER DROVE to the sea and walked along the pier. She relied on Ed more than she cared to admit. He would have a view on the money – £60,000 when the counting was done – stashed in the shoebox. What was Paul Adams mixed up in that warranted that kind of cash?

Sam leaned against the railings and looked out across the flat North Sea, an off-shore wind on her back.

She popped a Marlboro Gold into her mouth, ducked her head and cupped her hands around the lighter. She lit up on the fourth attempt.

She had stayed at Paul's house until the CSIs arrived. She had them photograph the laundry basket, the shoe box with the lid on, the money in the shoe box, the money laid out on the table.

Three of them counted the money in front of Erica.

Each elastic band was tied around twenty notes; £1000 bundles. There were 60 bundles.

£60,000 bought a lot of information.

If Paul was the target then Tara's 'cuckoo' was responsible. But what had Paul done? Had he found out where Harry Pullman was hiding? How did he come by that knowledge? And was Harry Pullman really capable of pulling off such an elaborate revenge hit?

Bloody hell, Ed. Where are you when I need you?

She fiddled with the sleek iPhone in her coat pocket and took the battered Nokia out of her trouser pocket. The Nokia had become temperamental in its old age, three presses per button for texts, but the battery lasted days before it needed a recharge.

She called the only number stored in its memory.

'It's me,' she said.

'So you haven't forgotten about me then.'

Sam ignored the jibe.

'How are you?'

'Can't stop laughing. You?'

'Surviving. Christ Ed there's so much going on and I've got nobody to bounce ideas off.'

'What's happened?'

Sam told him about Paul Adams and the money.

'What was he selling that was so valuable and how the hell didn't we know?' Sam said. 'But listen I haven't rung to talk about work. I just wanted to see how you were getting on.'

'Fine,' Ed answered. 'Don't worry about me. Listen, I'm sorry I jumped down your throat.'

Sam was distracted by a tractor towing a coble on the beach below, a boat she recognised, its faded blue and white paint worse than she recalled.

The elderly driver looked up, raised his arm, and doffed his Breton cap.

She waved back. The memory of the search and rescue mission was brighter than the coble's paintwork, and the old man had been so eager to help. If she knew where he lived, she would buy him a new cap for Christmas; the one he was wearing looked more ancient than him.

'You still there Sam?'

'Yeah, sorry Ed…forget about apologising. Just look after yourself. Keep your head down.'

'So the £60,000…' Ed said.

Sam was still watching the tractor and coble, surprised at how easily the man jumped from the driver's seat like someone half his age.

'Sam?' Ed said.

'Sorry. What?'

'The money.'

'Yeah, the £60,000,' Sam said, suddenly regretting calling Ed.

Were her calls being monitored? Did they know about this phone?

'Listen Ed, I better fly,' Sam told him. 'Shedloads on. I just wanted to check in. You sure you'll be okay?'

'No other choice,' Ed said. 'You get cracking. Speaking of okay, how's Tara?'

'Fine.'

'Bet Bev is spitting feathers she's missing some fun and games with her toy boy.'

Sam waved at the old man as he put out to sea.

'She'll be home tomorrow.'

Josh Appleton burst into his boss's office, words faster and more excited than a child on Christmas morning.

'Sam Parker's just rang Ed Whelan.'

Chris Priest looked up from his computer. 'What did she say?'

Appleton, mouth wide open, was suddenly the kid who hoped for a racing bike and got a plastic scooter.

'Well we don't know that. We haven't got an intercept on it, but she's rang him.'

Priest wheeled his chair away from the desk, remained seated.

'What you're saying is that Sam Parker's job phone—'

'Not her job phone. A personal number.'

'Okay, so we've got a phone registered to Sam Parker that calls Whelan's number, but no idea who made or who received the call.'

Appleton said nothing.

'Not much is it. You'll need to dig deeper than that.'

'I'll dig to Australia if I have to.'

Priest walked to the metal filing cabinet, opened the top drawer and retrieved a manila folder. He stared at the wall as he spoke, his back to Appleton.

'Look just leave it for a while. Let the dust settle. And never, ever underestimate either of those two. They'll chew you up and spit you out.'

'He's bent and she's protecting him,' Appleton spat out the words. 'Shagging him if the rumours are right.'

Priest spun round, words matching the speed of the turn.

'Don't make this personal and don't listen to tittle-tattle. Nobody was ever convicted on tittle-tattle.'

Priest put his hands on his hips.

'Do you seriously think they'd use their own phones if they were up to no good? So back off and don't end up looking a tit.'

Josh Appleton skulked out of the office.

A uniform officer all his life he had been in Professional Standards for six months. He saw the posting as short term, a CV builder, but if he could sort out Whelan and maybe even throw a bit of collateral damage Parker's way, he would finally get noticed.

Priest could go fuck himself.

Mick Wright, his sergeant when he first joined, had become a friend and they regularly went out for a beer. When the pints made way for whisky, talk always turned to their mutual hatred of detectives.

Maybe he could do Mick a favour and stitch these two up good and proper. Whelan was as bent as they come and Parker had looked after him for years.

Priest might be willing to let the dust settle but he wasn't.

He hurried out of the office, climbed into his car and raced to Brian Banks' yard.

Banks stood amongst mountains of scrap, hands thrust in his tweed trouser pockets, taut red braces stretched over his barrel chest, a chest which looked like he spent hours bench pressing and drinking whey protein.

Seaton St George's very own Iron Man, although not many would class Brian Banks as a superhero.

He didn't wait for an introduction.

'What do you a want?'

Even in his atrocious clothes, Appleton didn't look like he was weighing in scrap metal.

'A word.'

'And you are?'

'Detective Inspector Josh Appleton. Professional Standards.'

Appleton extended his hand; Banks kept his in his pockets.

'Well I've got fuck all to say to you,' Banks said. 'Goodbye.'

'You won't be able to protect your mate forever,'

Appleton fired back. 'You might have him in your pocket but you haven't got me.'

Banks stepped forward until his chest was inches from Appleton's.

'Listen you snotty nosed little twat, I don't have mates in the police and I've got nothing to say to the likes of you, so fuck off before I take my hands out of my pockets and lose my temper.'

Appleton, small in stature, big in self-importance, wasn't ready to retreat.

'What exactly is your relationship with Ed Whelan?'

Banks' right hand shot out of his pocket, grabbed the vile patterned tie and yanked Appleton closer, the Windsor knot shrinking as it tightened.

Banks' breath warmed his ear.

'You're on private property. If you've got a search warrant, show it. If you haven't, walk away before I put my boot up your fuckin' arse.'

Appleton slinked to the gates before turning around. 'I'll be back and you'll be in the cell next to Whelan.'

'Good luck with that you fuckin' knob. When you come back, bring some proper policemen with you. Ones I'll go quietly with.'

Banks watched him drive away before making a call on his mobile.

'Ed? Banksy. Some snotty-nosed twat just turned up asking questions about you. I put a flea in his ear and sent him packing.'

Brian Banks listened then said, 'Apple something or other. Right cock.'

Chapter 43

SAM CALLED A BRIEFING FOR 4PM.

The room, full when she walked in, hushed as she approached the chair at the front.

'Okay, let's see where we are. Zac Williams' computer? What's on it?'

'Not a lot,' said an officer at the back of the room. 'Looks like it's used for video games, porn and some social media. Mainstream porn sites, nothing illegal. Has Facebook, no Twitter, no Instagram. Doesn't post much. Nothing of interest to us.'

'Newspaper research?' Sam asked.

'Nothing. Search history is all around You Tube, porn and daft videos. There is nothing on the computer to suggest what he was going to do: no violent posts, no posts about suicide, nothing remotely resembling 'I Don't Like Mondays.'

There were a few smiles, a couple of chuckles.

The Boomtown Rats recorded the track, a big hit, after Brenda Spencer opened fire on Cleveland Elementary School, San Diego, in 1979.

'Okay lose the wisecracks,' Sam said. 'I get the analogy but it's not exactly appropriate. Comparisons like that get out and the next thing we're heartless bastards making insensitive remarks about mass shootings.'

She didn't need to repeat the warning.

'Anything from the helicopter feed?'

'Nothing new,' came another voice from the back of the room.

'Victims of the shooter?'

This time the Family Liaison Coordinator spoke. 'The teams are still out and about but I've got verbal updates off them.

'Great. Let's hear them then.'

'Okay. I'll just go in the order the teams rang in.'

He glanced at his notepad.

'Joey Sanderson. Just walking home. Family don't think he knows anybody in that street, but by their own admission anything's possible with Fatty. They don't think he knew Tara Paxman or Zac Williams or Lucy Spragg. Looks like wrong place, wrong time.'

'That's what we've got boss,' Ranjit Singh, from the Intelligence Unit, joined in. 'No intelligence at all to suggest Sanderson knew anybody involved.'

'Okay,' Sam said. 'Next?'

The coordinator spoke again. 'Marcus. Mother, Pippa, well- spoken, expensively dressed, no time for Lucy. Calls her...'

He paused, glanced at his notepad. 'No good trailer trash –'

'Charming,' Sam interrupted. 'What does she do for a living?'

'Marcus's mam?' asked the coordinator.

Sam nodded.

'Nothing. Stays at the family smallholding all day.

Husband's in property. She drinks gin and watches American TV all day. Stated Lucy Spragg was trying to move up the social ladder, trapping Marcus by dragging him up the aisle by his…'

Everyone in the room waited, knowing the gist of what was going to be said, but intrigued how Pippa Worthington-Hotspur would describe it to a police officer.

'…his overactive love stick.'

The room burst into fits.

Sam wondered what Ed would have said, wondered how a 1980s CID briefing would have responded to 'love stick.' She had a good idea.

When it quietened down the coordinator continued.

'His mother said he got a text and flew out of the house.'

'That'll be the one from Lucy,' Ranjit Singh again. 'The message read…'

He flicked through his A4 hardbacked book, found the page he needed.

'Please, please I need to see you. I can't discuss it on the phone. It's really important. Please I'm begging you. Come as soon as you get this.'

'So,' Sam said, 'Marcus responded to a message from Lucy's phone, not necessarily a message from Lucy herself.'

Sam paused. The room fell silent.

'How much longer are you going to be in there with the forensics Julie?'

'Probably another two days.'

'Any sign of Zac's phone?'

'None. I know you'll want to get the search team in after we've finished, but we've not found it.'

Sam looked at Sergeant Ian Robinson. 'While you're waiting for access to the house, and while you're doing the house-to-house, get some of your team to search the bins, rooftops and drains in the street. We need to find that phone.'

Ian Robinson made a note in his pocket book.

'I wish I could open up a new box for you,' Sam said.

Ian smiled, nodded.

'Bear in mind,' Sam continued, 'we had the place cordoned off, so the first place to look is in the street itself. Start off at Zac's, then do Tara's.'

Sam looked at the coordinator. 'Sorry, carry on.'

'Lucy Spragg's mother's devastated. She hoped Lucy was going to leave Zac. Says she met Marcus once. Describes him as a nice lad. Liked him.'

'A bit more charitable than Pippa then,' Sam said.

'Jean Spragg always thought Zac was violent and that Lucy was on the receiving end. She knew about two police visits in the last six months for DV.'

She glared at the coordinator.

'It's not called domestic violence these days.'

The coordinator blushed. 'Sorry boss.'

Old habits die hard and it had been called DV for years. Everyone in the room felt for him. It was a full-time job keeping up with the ever-changing language.

Ranjit Singh confirmed police had attended fifteen times in response to reports of domestic abuse in the last twelve months but, as Jean said, only two in the last six.'

'Interesting,' Sam said. 'Is that because she's not bothering to report or he's changed his behavior? Anyway, carry on.'

'Moving onto Paul,' the coordinator said.

He didn't tell Sam anything she didn't already know. She knew plenty he didn't.

The search team informed her that house-to-house had not found anyone who had seen or heard anything suspicious.

All the phones in the office were off the hook with the exception of one. That one rang.

'Boss. Lester Stephenson is downstairs.'

'Interesting,' Sam said. 'Anything else? Fingertip search around Marshall and Swan's car.'

Ian Robinson spoke again. 'There's a SIM card in the bushes near the car.'

'Let's see what we can get off that then.'

'It's in pieces. Been cut up.'

ED DROVE Doris over the moors to Helmsley, the only market town in the North Yorkshire Moors National Park, parked in the square and walked into The Feathers.

Nursing a pint of craft ale in the Pickwick Bar he scrolled through his phone.

His suspension had already made the local newspaper's website. Whilst Eastern Police declined to comment on the identity of the suspended officer, the Seaton Post reported that 'sources' believed it to be Detective Sergeant Edward Whelan.

The story had caused two reactions.

Firstly, he had thirteen missed calls from Sue, three from players in the local football team and two from Darius Simpson at the Seaton Post.

The only calls he'd answered were from Sam and Brian Banks.

Secondly, the newspaper had trawled through the archives and dug up the court reports from the three officers who were convicted of corruption in the late eighties.

Whilst that story wasn't directly linked to him, it

alluded to the fact that this latest suspended officer worked with the convicted three.

Under the headline, 'The Seaton Three: Eastern Police's Darkest Day', three black and white passport-style photographs stared back at him: no smiles, wide shouldered double-breasted pinstripe suits, permed hair.

Ed hadn't seen them for years. One was dead, two used their criminal connections on their release to move out to Tenerife where they made a killing in the unregulated Timeshare holiday boom. As far as he knew they were still there.

Ed stared back at them – different era, different job.

In 1981 he was the new detective joining an established team. The Detective Sergeant nearing retirement took scant interest in their work, preferring to be at his desk by 8am, in the pub by 11am and home by 5pm. As long as arrests were being made, crimes cleared up, he didn't question the methods.

For a while Ed was the youngster of the group, but they had all been inseparable: worked hard, played harder.

It was a time when food – burgers and chips had replaced chicken in a basket – was still served in some nightclubs, armed robberies on security vans were regular and drugs mostly limited to a few would-be hippies and their cannabis haunts.

That was all about to change. Ecstasy would soon hit the UK, demand for cocaine and heroin would soon soar.

Ed saw the new world take shape as career criminals saw a new opportunity. No longer did they need to risk ten years or more in jail for toting a sawn-off shotgun, staging ski-masked hold ups at village post offices and Securicor vans.

Instead they could import and sell drugs on a huge

scale with so many layers of criminality beneath them their chances of being convicted fell dramatically.

But like every business, and to them it was a business, averting risk was a vital. Paying police officers for information was a key component of their strategy. And there were corrupt police officers prepared to get their hands dirty in exchange for cold cash.

Ed looked up from his phone, glanced at an elderly couple in matching tweeds order a pint and a gin and tonic, then stared at the carved mouse on the stool opposite.

His mind drifted back to the custody office of the early 1980s; charge office as it was known then. A time before computers, when A3 detention sheets were handwritten, yellow sheets before charge, white after charge.

A time before the Police and Criminal Evidence Act, DNA and mobile phones.

He vividly recalled hearing a uniform sergeant, a known Freemason, talking to one of the three during an argument over the detention of a prisoner. 'Watch your back,' the sergeant had warned. 'I know people in high places.'

Ed smiled at the memory of the nose to nose reply: 'I know plenty in low places and they'll cause more fucking damage than your friends in high places could dream of.'

By the late eighties he was still considered one of the youngest detectives in the office. Complaints and Discipline concentrated a lot of their efforts on him and the even younger DC Chris Priest; their interview strategy consisting of nothing more than a simple but effective tactic… 'break the weak links'.

The interviews weren't taped, weren't conducted in the spirit of the relatively recent Police and Criminal Evidence Act, and at times were overtly oppressive.

Ed maintained his innocence and all evidence of dirty money pointed towards the 'Seaton Three', not to him.

They were all living way beyond what they earned from The Job.

Ed's situation was different. Sue came from a wealthy family and his comfortable lifestyle dovetailed with the world of successful self-made business people.

When Complaints came for him, he gave them the same line throughout the interviews: why would he risk jail for a couple of grand here, a couple of grand there?

At a time when the pay rise between Chief Inspector and Superintendent was about £5000 a year, Ed's answer was petrol to the fire.

Many on the force, some still serving now, were convinced the 'Seaton Three' was in fact the 'Seaton Four', with Ed the tainted missing piece. That, coupled with Sue nagging about how he could make more money in her family's business, had led Ed to resign. It was ten years before he rejoined. Now the Seaton Three was back to haunt him.

He swallowed the last of his pint and was contemplating a second when the text alert sounded.

He put his registered phone down on the table, read the text on the unregistered one.

Check your account. Will expect information within 15 minutes.

Internet banking gave everyone immediate 24-hour access. Ed went online. The money was in the pending transactions.

Ed tapped out a reply:

Subject will be alone tomorrow evening. More details to follow tomorrow morning.

Chapter 44

SAM WAS SITTING in an interview room looking at the man opposite.

Lester Stephenson was gaunt, jaundiced and with dyed jet-black hair contrasted with the matt grey frames of his glasses.

His blue chalk pinstripe suit came with creases that could hand out paper cuts.

Sam knew the sixty three year old hadn't walked in of his own volition, hence the reason for keeping him waiting. Make him sweat.

'What can I do for you Lester? Can I call you Lester?'

'Yes,' he stuttered, tongue running around his lips. 'I felt it prudent...'

He took a crisp white handkerchief out of his inside jacket pocket, wiped his forehead.

'In view of the events at Malvern Close, and the fact that I spoke to a female police officer, I felt it prudent...'

Sam doubted he would sweat, squirm and wring his hands more keenly had his wife been interrogating him over an affair. Lester Stephenson wanted to be anywhere but here.

'I thought I would visit you Chief Inspector before you sent someone to visit me.'

'And why would I do that?'

'I just thought, well, you know, the fact that I visited that young lady…'

'Your niece?' Sam interrupted.

Lester glanced sideways, put his hands over his mouth and coughed.

'To save any embarrassment Chief Inspector I thought if I paid you a visit, in what would be more convivial surroundings than my house with my wife present, perhaps we could avoid the necessity of you visiting me at home and all the unpleasantness that would entail.'

'First time I've heard a police interview room called convivial,' Sam said. 'So…she's not your niece then?'

'Chief Inspector, we both know that the young girl is a commodity…'

Stephenson paused.

Sam said nothing, fighting the urge to leap up and slap his ashen face.

'…for lonely men whose wives have…what's the words I'm looking for?…lost interest.'

Sam stared at him. Crank up his embarrassment. Let him fill in the silence and see if discloses more than he intended. It was a useful tactic, one that police and TV interviewers alike had used for years.

'So, I went that night, after calling first to make sure it was convenient, to… how shall I put it?…have a mutually beneficial liaison.'

Sam leaned across the desk.

'You get a shag and she earns a few quid.'

Lester Stephenson shuffled in his seat. 'I'm not sure I would put it quite as coarsely as that Chief Inspector.'

Sam spat her words at Stephenson.

'You call a young woman a commodity in one breath and me coarse the next. Hypocrite. Now what the fuck do you want?'

Stephenson recoiled in the chair. 'Only to save you and your men time.'

Sam pushed her shoulders closer towards him, maintained the anger.

'We're a modern service now Mr Stephenson, and guess what, we even have women working as senior police officers,' Sam said. 'Not where you think a woman belongs?'

Stephenson removed his glasses, wiped the lenses with the handkerchief.

'A slip of the tongue, chief inspector. I meant no slight.'

Sam leaned back, hands behind her head, voice softer.

'You're here so that we don't visit you at home. Might take some explaining to your wife. Remind me why you were at Malvern Close?'

'I've just told you. Sex. Nothing else.'

'Why did you lie to the police officer at the scene?'

'I said the first thing that came into my head.'

'And that was the only reason you called around?'

'Yes.'

Sam dropped her hands onto the table and pushed against it, simultaneously forcing the chair backwards. The sudden movement and the high-pitched grating noise of metal legs against wooden floor caused Stephenson's creases to leap and hit the underside of the table.

'Then I thank you for coming in. You are free to leave.'

Stephenson stood up. 'Thank you for your understanding chief inspector.'

She opened the door and waited for him to make a move towards the threshold before blocking his exit with her arm.

'One more thing.'

She leaned into his ear.

'I find out you're lying, discover you went there to pass on a message, your wife won't have to slice your balls off. I'll gift wrap them for her and send them recorded delivery.'

She dropped her arm, flashed her teeth. 'Have a pleasant evening.'

———

'IMAGINE DRIVING up here every bloody day,' Bev was navigating the challenging twists and turns of Kirkstone Pass, a sub-conscious reflex throwing her foot off the accelerator whenever a set of headlights came towards her.

They had both wilted under a heavy dose of cabin fever, an overwhelming urge to escape the bedroom and the incessant whirring of the tape machine.

Bev was never a one for walking if there was an alternative. It was why she loved holidaying in America: straight, wide roads, no roundabouts and drive-thru ATMs.

The hotel owner had suggested a drive into Ambleside.

'If he'd told us the road was like this I wouldn't have bothered,' Bev said, head shaking from side to side, the car in second gear, dry-stone walls closing in on them at every turn. 'Light me a cigarette please.'

Tara handed her a Players Crushball. 'Look at that. A pub. Right up here. Can we go in?'

Bev glanced to her left, saw the pub.

'Why not.'

She swung into the car park on the right, cigarette clamped between her teeth, pleased to be off the torturous road, a view confirmed when she saw the sign. The descent into Ambleside was called 'The Struggle.'

No shit Sherlock…

Tara had hopped from the car and rushed across the road, casting an admiring glance at a black VW Golf at the top of the car park. Now she was pointing at the sign above the door to the Kirkstone Inn.

'Look at that,' she shouted as Bev walked towards her. 'Been here since 1496. Imagine that. Imagine all the people who've walked through these doors.'

Bev blew smoke out in front of her.

'Let's hope they were happier out here than I am, otherwise there's going to be some pretty pissed-off ghosts wandering about.'

Bev finished the cigarette, stubbed it against the wall and put it in the bin.

'You're not interested in history then Bev?'

'I'm only interested in the here and now, and right now, I would rather be in the office arse deep in paperwork than here.'

'Charming,' Tara sounded hurt.

'Nothing to do with you. It's this place. The Lakes. Middle of nowhere. More life in a tramp's vest. I guess I'm just a townie at heart. I don't get what all the fuss is about.'

They stepped inside.

'To think,' Tara said, 'this was built when Henry VII was on the throne.'

Bev glanced at the beamed ceiling, ordered the drinks and sat down on a red upholstered chair close to the blazing fire leaving Tara talking history with the barmaid.

The ice rattled in the balloon-shaped 'copa'. Bev preferred highball glasses. More gin, less ice, minimal tonic. These days, though, it was all high-stemmed styles where the drink never seemed quite right.

She took a sip, more tonic than gin, and checked her mobile, smiling at the signal.

She typed '**all done here**' and pressed send.

The reply was almost instantaneous.

Ring when you get a chance

She finished her drink, dragged Tara away from her local history lesson, and drove them back to the White Lion.

One large glass of white wine later she was standing outside the pub. Tara had gone to the room to read her Wainwright book.

Bev called Sam.

'Like I said in the text, we're all done here. Nothing more to get out of her. How's things at your end?'

'Moving slow but steady. Tara still okay to be left alone tomorrow?'

'Yeah, she's looking forward to it. Got her nose in guide books and her mouth around that Kendall Mint Cake stuff. Seems quite taken with the place.'

Bev sparked a cigarette.

'It is beautiful,' Sam said.

'A matter of opinion,' Bev said, remembering the wall-lined turns of The Struggle. 'Any thoughts where we'll put her on Wednesday.'

'Somewhere that's easily accessible,' Sam had the question on her endless list. 'We'll need her close once we make arrests.'

Bev blew out smoke slowly.

'You're making the arrests on her say-so?'

'It's not just her is it?' Sam said. 'She's saying it's down to Harry Pullman and if his DNA's inside the suit we've got to lift him.'

'Suppose so,' Bev said. 'Where will we put her when it's all sorted?'

'Long-term? It's something we can discuss with her. Has she said anything to you about her future?'

'I think she wants to move on with her life and she definitely loves it over here. Maybe somewhere rural will appeal.'

'I'll see what I can do,' Sam said. 'Before you leave, ask her again about Lester Stephenson. He came in to see me. My big question is this…did he go to her for sex or did he pass a message?'

Chapter 45

Sam walked along to the office of the Director of Intelligence and had a forty-minute conference behind closed doors with the Detective Superintendent.

Paul Adams' cousin, Rob Conlon, a member of a regional team assigned to the Protected Persons Service under the umbrella of the National Crime Agency, had been interviewed.

He denied passing information onto Paul about Harry Pullman's whereabouts but his interrogators were far from convinced he was telling the truth. The feeling was that any information passed would have been the result of family loyalty and naivety. A search of Conlon's home and bank accounts had not revealed any cash piles or unusual payments.

He didn't believe his Paul was corrupt, but admitted that even as a child Paul was manipulative and always got his way.

Conlon had not yet been suspended but that was under review.

Sam walked along the deserted corridors, pondering

the information. When she reached her office, she closed the door and kicked off her shoes.

She leaned back in her chair, staring up at the ceiling. If Paul was the one who always got his own way how had he been so easily manipulated by Tara?

Was it really so easy to lead men by their balls to their death? Did Paul's brains drop below his waist as soon as a pretty girl threw herself at him?

Sam stood up and paced the floor in her bare feet.

Tara was an itch she couldn't scratch, the itch in the middle of your shoulders that you just can't reach. Something wasn't quite right with her. Something was missing.

Sam rubbed her face with both hands, hoping to conjure up a piece of the jigsaw.

She considered what Tara had told Bev about her childhood. Was that a true account or a sob story designed to get sympathy and lower Bev's guard?

They had, so far, been unable to trace Tara's mother.

Had Tara really been coerced and threatened into meeting Paul then finally luring him to her house that night? How long had the second rabbit suit been in her loft?

Was Tara a pawn or a player?

Investigations were always more difficult when you questioned the honesty of the witnesses, but Sam rarely took anything at face value. Tara Paxman was no different.

***

TUESDAY 3RD NOVEMBER

'BEV, ITS ED.'

She always ignored 'unknown number' calls but had answered this time without thinking, mind elsewhere as she contemplated her great escape from The Lakes and a possible meet with Ranjit Singh.

'Hang on.'

Scrambled eggs abandoned, she rushed outside.

How can you love this place when it's permanently pissing down?

Legs quick-marching, she scrunched her shoulders against the rain and hurried towards the deserted car park where there was no chance of being overheard.

'Jesus Ed, you okay? What's happening?'

'I'm fine. Listen I haven't got long. I'm going away for a while but I need someone I can trust.'

'What do you need?' Bev panted, lungs losing the battle with the car park's uphill access road.

'Keep an eye on Sam. She's under a huge amount of pressure and I'm not there to help shoulder the burden.'

Bev stood under a tree, seeking shelter. A couple of hikers walked past her on the other side of the road, laden down with waterproofs, rucksacks and walking sticks.

'I'll do what I can,' she said, shaking her head, wondering why anyone in their right mind would walk anywhere in this weather. 'But I don't know if she'll listen to me.'

'Just ask her how she's doing. Be her sounding board. Take her out for a drink.'

'I can do that.'

'Tonight?'

Bev watched the walkers, heads down, heavy drops of water falling from the hoods of their brightly coloured jackets.

Mad as trout…

'Can't tonight. Got a date.'

'Toyboy?'

'Something like that.'

Bev wondered where the walkers would be tonight. She hoped she'd be in a warm pub deciding whether to invite Ranjit Singh back to her house.

'What about Tara?'

'We'll leave her here tonight. Move her tomorrow.'

'You still leaving her alone?'

Won't do her any harm. She gets plenty of company normally. Hopefully, tonight, it's my turn. That'll make a pleasant change.

'She'll be fine for one night.'

'Look I have to go, and Bev.'

'Yes?'

'Don't mention this call to anyone.'

INSPECTOR JOSH APPLETON was in the office at eight, back in the car within fifteen minutes. He wasn't hanging around for Chris Priest. He knew the superintendent would block his proposed course of action.

He checked his bloodshot eyes in the interior mirror; Inspector Mick Wright's collection of red wine had taken a hammering last night. So had his Jura whisky.

Appleton burped stale Scotch fumes against the windscreen.

He turned on the engine, opened the window and drove off.

Last night's conversation had been all about that bent bastard Whelan and the self-righteous, know-it-all Sam 'Nosey' Parker.

Booze flowing, they had grudgingly agreed they would 'give her one' but that she needed shoving off her perch.

Appleton said it was simple. Bring down Whelan and Parker would fall too. The more he had drank the more he saw Mick Wright as the victim. The death of that sailor? Anybody could have made the same mistake Mick had made. As for Taffy Green, even if someone was running at the same time he ran in front of the bus, it didn't mean Taffy was running away from them. And who was to say Taffy Green couldn't write? He could have conned the police for years.

By the time Appleton pulled up outside Ed Whelan's house he was raging.

Nice house, nice village. Here Appleton was, an Inspector who worked the hard yards and he could never afford this. How could Whelan? The answer was obvious.

Bent bastard.

He slammed the car door, marched up the drive, and hammered on the front door. He ignored the bell. He wanted to feel his fist hitting something.

'Mrs Whelan?'

Sue Whelan had opened the door in lime green joggers and white t-shirt, hair uncombed, no make-up.

'Yes.'

He flashed his warrant card. 'Inspector Appleton.'

'What's this about?'

'Can I come in.'

He moved towards the door.

Sue half closed it, wedged her foot against the bottom.

'Is it about my husband?'

'Yes. Can I come in?'

'I don't know where he is and I don't particularly care. Check Parker's house. He seems to spend more time there with that fawning slut these days.'

She slammed the door.

Appleton stared at it, grinning.

Well, well, well. From the horse's mouth.

Juggling car keys and mobile he hit the remote, then called Mick Wright.

'Can you speak? Listen.'

He ducked into the car.

'I've just been to Whelan's house. His wife thinks he's shagging Parker.'

'Jackpot.'

'I promise you Mick I'm going to nail the fucking pair of them.'

Twenty minutes later he walked into Chris Priest's office.

'Can I have a word?'

Priest looked up from his computer.

'I've just been to Whelan's house.'

There was a steaming mug of tea on Priest's desk. He wouldn't have been out of his seat any quicker if he had spilt the lot over his crotch.

'What the hell for?'

'Even his wife thinks he's shagging Parker. So much for tittle-tattle.'

Priest got his emotions back under control and sat down.

'So they're having an affair?' Won't be the first. Not exactly against regulations, unless they've been doing it in the office and you can prove it.'

Appleton bent over, put the palms of his hands on the desk and leaned in towards his boss, the whisky fumes making Priest wince.

'No, it's not against regulations, but it tells us why she's been protecting him.'

'Get out of my face. You smell like a fuckin' brewery.'

Appleton took three small backward steps and spoke again.

'There's more. After the stuff in the Post last night I've asked around about that corruption inquiry…'

'Enough!' Priest put his hand up, palm facing Appleton like a traffic cop ordering a driver to stop. 'Don't get involved with bitter and twisted retired cops with a score to settle. You'll end up running off at a tangent and making yourself look like a prat.'

Priest drank from the mug.

Appleton waited.

'Leave this investigation for another couple of days. I'm warning you.'

'But…'

'No 'buts' Josh. If I hear of you doing anything on this investigation you'll be out on your ear before you know what's hit you. Understand?'

Appleton's face reddened: hangover plus unfair bollocking equaled rage. He wasn't finished yet.

'Did you consider Whelan swapping the negotiator call-out might not have been a coincidence. He swaps and just happens to be the Number 1 when the wild west comes to town.'

'I'm warning you,' Priest snapped. 'There are things happening in the background on a need to know basis. You don't need to know, so at the risk of repeating myself, back off.'

'But…'

'Drop it Josh. And leave that corruption inquiry where it needs to be left. In the past.'

Chapter 46

ED ENDED the call with Bev and tapped out a text.

She's in the White Lion, Patterdale. Will be alone this evening. Moved tomorrow. Tonight's your only chance.

He didn't know who would receive the message. Even if he was at his desk with all the force's investigative tools at his disposal, he would struggle to get a lead on what would undoubtedly be an unregistered phone.

But the number had informed him of payment into the correct account, the deposit confirmed by the bank.

£10,000.

Not £11,000.

He may not know who was holding the phone but he knew who was behind the payment.

He lit both rings on the gas burner, put the kettle on one, the frying pan on the other: bacon sandwich and a mug of tea.

'Doris' was in a car park high up on the North Yorkshire Moors giving Ed a view of Whitby Abbey and the North Sea.

His had been the only vehicle there last night and this morning the only noise was coming from herring gulls. The amount of them flying in raucous circles was a warning of a big storm on the way. At least that's what Sam had once told him, that gulls responded to changes in air pressure they could detect.

He turned on his personal phone, scrolled through the site of the Seaton Post. Nothing new about him.

There'll be plenty in tomorrow's edition.

He put the phone on the table and looked through the drizzle at the abbey.

———

SIXTY GRAND, Sam thought as she sat behind her desk, hands covering her face.

Who wanted Harry Pullman dead?

Was it the Skinners?

Had he got to the Skinners first?

She felt like she was going around in circles. She stood up and paced.

Harry Pullman's down to give evidence; Luke and Matt Skinner need to stop him; they pay Paul to find out where he is.

That would work…

Pullman finds out Paul is selling him out to the Skinners; uses Tara to lure him to her house; sets up Zac Williams to come across like a wannabe mass killer with the cuttings all over his wall.

Still holding up…

Bill Redwood killed because of his connection to Harry Pullman; Scott Green a 'get in first' victim because he's a Skinner associate; Swan and Marshall taken out to tidy up the loose ends. No evidence against Harry

Pullman. Neat and tidy. Only person left to clean up…
Tara Paxman.

Why does it all feel too tidy?

Questions were bouncing around Sam's head like balls
in a bingo caller's wheel.

Was Tara telling the truth?

Could somebody else be preparing a takeover?

Could Tara be involved with them?

Was Harry Pullman set up? Does he even have it in
him to plan this?

If Paul was tipping Harry Pullman's location, how did
Harry find out it was Paul?

Did Harry know of Paul from his days working for the
Skinners, the time before Luke and Mark planned to leave
him for dead in the North Sea?

How long has Paul been bent?

Was he bent?

Or in the end, was Zac Williams just an angry maniac
and the conspiracy theories all bull?

Sam returned to her desk; the questions endless.

Accept nothing, Believe nothing, Challenge everything.

Sam's ABC, a mantra that had always served her well.

She sat down, turned on her computer, glanced at her
inbox. Seventy-seven emails. Scanning the list there was
nothing regarding this investigation.

She resisted the urge to hit the delete button, sending
details of this meeting, that meeting into cyberspace, and
looked out of the window.

'Coffee, boss?' It was Shane Walton.

'Cheers. I'll come through soon. Just got to sort a
couple of things out first.'

'No bother.'

Shane walked out but was back in minutes. He placed
a mug on her desk.

Sam nodded her thanks, sipped the coffee, and stared at the screen: crime strategy meeting, management meeting, this working party, that steering group. The list of notifications became a fuzzy blur.

Too busy for this shit...

She hit delete.

————

LESTER STEPHENSON PICKED up the two silver-framed photographs from the high mantlepiece above the wood-burning stove.

Two boys, two girls. His grandchildren. Three on one photograph, the eldest, a girl pictured alone, was his favourite: not because she was the eldest, but because he'd missed so much of her growing years.

He put the photograph back, whispered 'families,' shook his head and smiled.

'All set for today?'

Penelope walked into the sitting room; shaven head from sessions of chemotherapy, clothes now four sizes too big.

'Yes love.

'Your bag's packed. Dinner suit's back from the cleaners, apron's ironed.'

'You sure I'm okay to stay over? I can go without a drink you know.'

His wife dropped onto the leather armchair with the remote tilt control, the walk from the bedroom turning her frail legs to jelly.

She took a couple of shallow breaths. 'I know sweetheart, but you get away and enjoy yourself. You need a break from me. Go and see your pals.'

Lester Stephenson was convinced the police had

bugged his house.

Penelope looked at the photograph on the occasional table next to her chair, picked it up, raised it close to her eyes: her younger self, high on the back of black horse, caught mid-flight, blonde ponytail horizontal, taking a fence in the showjumping ring.

She rubbed her eyes at the memory, a time when her whole life stretched out in front of her, a time before her race was almost run. Now according to the medical staff, at best she was two months from the finishing line.

'Can I get you anything?' Lester asked. The text alert sounded on his phone.

'Just some water and could you pass the TV remote please.'

Stephenson handed it to her, returned to the kitchen, and read the text.

Party sorted. Big welcoming committee. Weather over here mild. See you and your partner in crime very soon.

He returned to the sitting room, kissed his sleeping wife's forehead, and re-read the text.

How long had he known him now? Must be over forty years.

He tapped the photos icon on his phone, chuckled at the suntanned image of the sender... bald in summer top and shorts, the flowing perm, flowery shirts and wide-lapel pinstripe suits consigned to history.

Lester Stephenson liked to plan everything but had left the flight plan and refuelling scheduling in the hands of someone who had the expertise: the pilot.

The aviator had spent his time in prison preparing for the Private Pilot Licence theory exams and completed the required flying hours on his release.

All Lester knew was that from the first airstrip he

would fly to the south of England, then across the Channel into France and from there, Spain and a waiting car.

Whatever checks the police had at ports and airports wouldn't affect him. He'd be enjoying paella and a cold Cruzcampo before Chief Inspector Parker knew he had even gone.

He looked at the photo on his phone again.

Marty Irons. Ex-detective constable. King of the timeshare. Time served for corruption.

It would be quite some reunion.

Chapter 47

ED HAD CHANGED into hiking boots, woollen hat and waterproofs and was walking towards a small field where an orange windsock was kinked at a 45-degree angle.

Overhead a light aircraft was coming in to land.

He pushed open the five-bar gate and walked towards the wooden building. One man was on the decking, sat on a white plastic chair at a white plastic table reading 'Pilot' magazine.

The other tables and chairs had a layer of water on them from the recent downpour, glistening now in the low November sun.

Ed stopped and watched the wheels of the Piper Cherokee come into contact with the ground.

'Any chance I can use your loo?'

The man put his magazine on the table and looked at Ed, bushy ginger eyebrows trying to meet the tight wiry curls of his hair. He stood up, ex-military written all over him, black shoes gleaming.

'Feel free young man. You walked far?'

No accent, clipped tones. Officer type, Ed thought.

Probably retired RAF pilot. He smiled at the 'young man' reference.

'Not too far. About five miles.'

'A gentle stroll,' the man grinned. 'Straight through there on the right.'

'Thanks.'

Ed walked into the building, saw the mic and some sort of log next to it on a small wooden table. Eyebrows had his back to him, nose back in the magazine that looked like a post card in his huge hands.

The log was open. An entry in fountain pen referenced the landing of the plane outside. A Cessna 152. The old boy outside was obviously duty officer, or whatever they called it.

He glanced down the list of incoming aircraft for the last few days, found what he was looking for, and walked past a long, dark, banqueting table to the toilet.

'Thanks for that,' he said, back on the decking.

'You're welcome.'

Ed walked away grateful to Brian Banks, back towards the gate, back towards 'Doris' in a horseshoe lay-by three hundred metres away, hidden from the road by trees.

Now all he had to do was drive.

Maybe he did have time to do Sam a favour.

BEV PUT her bag in the boot, glanced at her watch and turned to face Tara.

'Don't stray from the plan. Have a walk out this afternoon, pop into the Inn on the Lake if you want. Don't drink too much.'

Tara looked at the ground, scratched her ear. 'I won't. I'll be fine. Stop worrying.'

'I'll see you later. Have a good day.'

They hugged.

Bev drove out of the car park towards Pooley Bridge and the A66. Two hours from home. Back by 1pm.

Tara walked back into the White Lion, thoughts on three things – sandwich, stroll and SIM card.

She bought a sandwich in the shop, went back to her room, and got on her hands and knees to fish out the phone she had hidden under the wardrobe.

She had got lucky. Bev hadn't searched her.

Tara sat on the edge of the bed, staring at the phone, debating whether to turn it on.

She wanted to make a call, talk to someone who wasn't police, but she was worried The Man would have been trying to get in touch, wanting to know where she was, what was happening.

She rolled the phone in her hand, alternatively staring at the front and back.

The phone had the SIM card ending in the number 257.

When she finally powered it up the mobile pinged five times. Five messages, all from a number ending in 683. The Man's phone.

She didn't open them.

She had always been good with numbers. Maybe it ran in the family.

She made one call then went outside, the smell of wet grass and clean, clear air filling her nose.

What a place to live

LESTER STEPHENSON GLANCED at the case on the front seat, smiled at the thought of an unofficial Masonic reunion in the sunshine. Marty Irons and the other two detectives convicted of corruption had all been members of the same Lodge as Lester.

Their downfall had sparked a private outcry among their fellow Masons but hadn't stopped other police officers being allowed to join.

The Masons, though, didn't recognise police ranks. Junior officers often held higher positions within the organisation than their force seniors.

Some well-promoted officers had found it hard to handle.

Lester pulled into the outside lane and laughed out loud when he remembered a new member, a uniform superintendent, being outraged he had to wait on a detective constable at a Lodge dinner.

'I'm not here to serve mashed potato to him,' he'd said. Lester still remembered the indignation on the superintendent's face.

He was given a simple choice: conform or leave.

He served the mash and bit his lip when the recipient told him: 'Don't be stingy now.'

The detective constable had retold the story for months, a fly-fisherman reliving his best catch, the truth coated in ever-increasing layers of embellishment.

Ed Whelan always did tell a good tale.

JULIE TRESCOTHICK WALKED into Sam's office.

'Sorry Julie, but can you make it quick? I've got to leave for a meeting soon.'

Julie nodded as she began to speak: 'The sticky substance on the hands of the rabbit suit Zac Williams was wearing is a match for the sticky substance on the rifle barrel and butt. The scientist will write up her report about chemical compounds and the like, but it's a definite match.'

Sam leaned back into her chair and digested the information. Had the gun really been glued to Zac Williams' hands?

'The second rabbit suit has gunshot residue all over it,' Julie was saying now.

'The DNA results from it are back. DNA deposits all over the inside. Two profiles, consistent with both sets of DNA having worn the suit.'

Julie subconsciously paused, a conjurer building to the big reveal.

'One profile is Harry Pullman's.'

Sam exhaled, her mind racing.

Zac Williams has been set up.

'The other one?' she asked Julie.

'I did what you said. Got into Tara's house. Smashed through the loft hatch. Took controlled hair samples from her hairbrush in the bathroom for DNA comparison.'

'And,' Sam said, standing up, her excitement mounting.

'Waiting to hear from the lab.'

Chapter 48

He hadn't been too keen at the time but now Ed Whelan was delighted Sam had sent him for two days 'Open Source' training.

There was so much information available on the Internet; you just needed to know where to look.

People were fools, Ed told himself after he'd interrogated various search engines. Social media sites spewed back out as much information as the user had put in. The search options were endless, joining the so-called dots of any conundrum possible.

Ed's latest searches had led him to the driveway of a well-presented semi-detached bungalow in Northallerton, a market town at the northern tip of North Yorkshire.

He knocked at the door, glanced at the spotless silver VW Caddy parked close to the single garage. The neat garden and metal ramp gave access to a side door Ed presumed led into the kitchen.

'Mrs Lee?' he said, when the door opened, keeping the surprise from his voice.

He had expected a gaunt, disheveled alcoholic, not a

healthy woman in skinny, ripped jeans and tight cashmere sweater.

'Yes?'

'Hi. I'm Detective Sergeant Whelan. I'm involved in the investigation into the shootings at Seaton St George. You may have seen it on the news.'

'Oh my God. Is Tara okay?'

'She's fine. May I come in?'

'Yes of course.'

Valerie Lee didn't ask for any identification.

Ed stepped over the threshold, thankful that police dramas no longer had every detective wearing a suit.

'How can I help?' Valerie said, leading Ed through the wooden-floored hallway into the large orangery off the lounge. 'Please take a seat.'

Ed sat on the red tartan, rattan weave armchair, put one elbow on the cane arm, and crossed his legs.

'Tara was living next door to the shooter,' he said.

'How awful. But you said she's okay?'

She sat down on the chair opposite.

'She's fine. Obviously, it was all a shock to her. She's being looked after by a specially trained detective.'

'Dreadful. I don't know what the world's coming to.'

Ed guessed she was in her late forties, but she could have passed for someone much younger. Her skin had a glow that suggested Valerie Lee hadn't skipped on her daily care regime for decades. Her teeth, Ed noticed, were beautiful.

Whatever else she may be, Valerie Lee was no raddled alcoholic.

'Mrs Lee -'

'Please call me Val.'

'Val,' Ed said, staring into piercing blue eyes. 'As a matter of routine, we have to check out the backgrounds of those people in and around the scene of a tragedy such as this.'

'I thought the police shot the gunman?'

'I'm sorry but I cannot comment on that.'

Val Lee nodded.

'I'm trying to establish what type of person Tara is.'

Val leaned forward, put her hands on her knees.

'Where do you want me to start?'

She put her face in her hands, shook her head before continuing.

'Tara was difficult. Rebellious. Went off the rails as a teenager.'

She wafted thin fingers in front of her face.

Ed spotted the film of water over her eyes.

'It's okay,' he said, 'take your time.'

'As a young girl she was fine. Never knew her father and never asked. I've never seen him since I told him I was pregnant. Well not in the flesh. Seen him on TV, in newspapers.'

Ed looked at her. He could imagine a young teenager and an unwanted pregnancy, but a woman who must have been in her twenties at the time? Did that still happen?

Val smiled.

'I know what you're thinking,' she said.

That I'm a sexist pig expecting women to take all the responsibility for birth control. I didn't mean to come across like that.

'Frank was my first proper boyfriend. He was married, a few years older than me. I was still living at home. Classic combination of sheltered upbringing and puritan parents.'

Ed nodded. 'It's none of my business.'

'I know and to be honest I've no idea why I'm telling you. Maybe because it's some years since I've spoken about Tara, never mind seen her.'

Val sniffed and rubbed her nose. 'Not a day goes by when I don't think of her you know.'

Ed nodded. He couldn't contemplate not seeing his own daughter. Was that why he'd stayed with Sue all these years? Put up with all the shit?

'But Frank Worthington?' Val continued. 'I can't remember the last time he came into my head.'

Ed nodded again, said nothing. Did anybody's life ever run smooth?

Like Sam he followed the first rule of interviewing: don't interrupt their flow, let them fill the silences.

'Tara left on her sixteenth birthday. Never heard a word from her since, but I knew she was living in the Seaton St George area. A neighbour bumped into her once.'

Ed remained silent.

'Maybe I should have done more to find her?'

Val looked away, sniffed again, before turning back to Ed.

'When she was about ten, we both lived with my parents by the way, I met George at a church. Lovely man. We went out a few times, then I introduced him to Tara and within six months Tara and myself had moved in with him, into this house.'

'It's a nice house,' Ed threw a glance around the room.

'Thank you. When Tara hit twelve, she became very willful, the whole 'you're not my dad' scenario. It was pretty dreadful. George tried everything with her, but mostly she resented him, was absolutely awful towards him.'

Time to push, Ed thought.

'Awful in what way?'

Val Lee took a moment, composing herself, heading to a darker place.

'At thirteen Tara was very aware that she was attractive. Make-up, raising her school skirt, strutting around like she was on a catwalk. Then it was smoking and drinking. I blocked out thoughts she might be having sex.'

Now the words began firing out so quickly they barely had time to form.

'I'd gone out one night to visit my mum and dad. Tara and George stayed in. They were having one of their better spells. I got back and Tara started screaming, saying George had been watching her in the shower.'

Val Lee put her hand to her lips, looked at her knees, whispered: 'Awful.'

Ed let the silence stretch.

Val looked up, speed talking again.

'I told her not to be ridiculous. She shouted, and please pardon my language, 'you stop being fucking ridiculous.' Her language was appalling. I don't swear. And then…'

She started chewing her index finger.

'Then she accused him of trying to rape her, ripping off her towel, pushing her onto the bed. She said she fought him off.'

Val took a deep breath.

'And you didn't believe her?'

Val's mouth dropped open and her legs pushed her out of the chair. 'Of course I didn't believe her, and I didn't lower myself by asking George to defend himself.'

SAM PULLED over at a Costa and ignored the irritating woman on her SatNav repeating, 'make a U-turn when possible.'

Her next meeting was a couple of hours away, but so was the location.

ot/

She bought a flat white, sat at a picnic table and savoured a Marlboro Gold.

Nothing was certain in her mind with the exception that Zac Williams had been set up. He had not been the killer, had not shot anybody.

The whole crime scene had been staged, faked to give the impression the killer was a jealous young man with an interest in serial killers who died behind their own guns.

Sam slugged on the coffee and smoked.

But how would the real killer, whoever that was, keep Zac under control? Zac would probably be compliant as long as Lucy was alive, but once she was dead?

And if he knew Lucy was dead, why would Zac go to the window with the rifle in his hands? Why not scream out for help? Did he believe Lucy was still alive?

And what had he said to Ed? 'Help's not coming'. What did that mean?

Something, or someone, was keeping him compliant.

Tara?

The only means of leaving that house unnoticed once the siege began and before the rapid entry occurred was through the loft into Tara's house.

What if she was in Zac's house?

How much of the truth had she told? All of it? None of it?

Tara Paxman…

Sam was beginning to feel just a little out of control and that was never a good thing.

Chapter 49

'THAT WAS the end of the relationship with my parents,' Val said. 'They couldn't understand how I wouldn't believe Tara. She told them about the peeping and they were devastated. When she walked out of my life, she walked out of theirs too.'

'She uses the surname Paxman.'

'Really?' A sadness came over her. 'My mother's maiden name.'

'Why not use your maiden name?'

'Maybe she liked Paxman better, maybe she didn't want to use mine.'

Ed heard the back door open, a voice calling 'darling I'm home' and a whirring noise he couldn't place.

As soon as George Lee came into the orangery Ed understood.

'This is Sergeant Whelan,' Val said.

Ed stood up.

George maneuvered his electric wheelchair across the wood flooring and the two men shook hands.

Val explained why Ed was there and he sat back down.

'Tara was always difficult, but I never blamed her,' George said.

Val smiled at him.

'Tara was ten when she and Val moved in here. Big change for a young girl. New house, new school, no more getting spoilt by her grandparents. And looking back…well I was probably a bit hard on her.'

'No you weren't,' Val said, shuffling on her seat.

Ed kept his eyes on George, said nothing.

'I kept nagging her about the state of her bedroom. When she hit her teens it became worse. It was always a cause of friction.'

Ed nodded. 'I've got a daughter myself. I remember the teenage years well.'

George Lee gave Ed a weak smile.

'I was probably worse because of my background. Ex-military and all that. How I ended up in this bloody thing. Iraq.'

'I'm sorry,' Ed said, which seemed inadequate, inappropriate somehow.

George smiled more warmly this time.

'Not your fault mate. Blame the politicians. And me, of course, for being in the wrong place at the wrong time. IED went off and that was it for my spinal cord.'

Ed nodded.

'Could have been worse,' George continued. 'Mates died out there.' He shook his head slowly, the smile gone. 'For what?'

He spun his wheelchair around and headed for the kitchen.

Ed understood Val's tight smile.

Just give him a minute.

'I met George when he got back home,' she said. 'He came to a church service, and the rest as they say…'

'Brave man,' Ed said, noticing for the first time the small photograph of George in uniform. He was with two other soldiers, obviously somewhere hot.

'Very,' Val was saying. 'He could never understand why any woman would want to be with him, being paralysed, everything that it meant…called himself half a man. But I wanted companionship and I got that from George. More than I ever got from bloody Frank Worthington with all his flash and long hair.'

Ed nodded. 'Like the footballer from the 70s.'

Val Lee's mouth fell into a tight grimace.

'That's who he thought he was,' she said. 'A poor man's football star.'

Ed had instantly pictured the player as soon as Val mentioned the name – which football fan back then didn't know it?– but the Frank Worthington he was thinking of now wasn't famous…he was a Mason and a wanker, but he wasn't famous.

'I've put the kettle on,' George said coming back to the room, the smile restored. 'Do you want one Sarge.'

'I'm fine thanks,' Ed said, smiling at how easily George Lee had dropped back into rank structure. 'I should really get going.' Ed pushed against the cane arm and stood up.

'Did you have a specialty in the military, corporal?'

George returned the smile, acknowledged Ed's courtesy. 'Sniper.'

Ed whistled softly: 'Impressive.'

'You still do clays now don't you darling,' Val with pride in her voice.

Ed stepped towards the door then turned to George Lee.

'Gets me out in the fresh air,' George said. 'Not quite as scientific as taking a proper shot, no need to measure distance and wind speed, but it keeps my eye in and the legs that don't work don't stop me competing against the legs that do.'

'I'm still impressed,' Ed said.

George held out his arm. Ed shook his hand.

'It's just great to be able to compete, sarge, and it gets me out of the house. If the skeet's somewhere decent we make a long weekend of it.'

'Tara used to come with us didn't she darling,' Val said.

'She did. She was a really good shot.'

———

ED DROVE along the A19 until he reached the services at Exelby, a few miles north of Northallerton.

Tara can shoot?

He needed to write things down, join the dots.

Tara's mother was no alcoholic; George Lee was neither alcohol dependent or physically capable of raping Tara.

What did that mean, apart from the obvious?

He wrote 'liar' next to Tara's name and underlined it three times.

Next he wrote 'Frank Worthington'. He'd joined the Masons a few years after Ed, really loved himself.

Ed wrote 'full of shit' next to his name.

Ed could see him going for Val Lee: young, attractive and naïve. And in return, he could see Val falling for his brash bullshit.

Property developer? More like a front to launder drugs money although nothing had ever been proved.

He'd poshed up his name to Worthington-Hotspur after claiming he was a descendent of Sir Henry Percy, aka Harry Hotspur, the medieval Northumberland nobleman who took up arms against Henry 1V.

Had someone targeted his son to get at him? Make the father suffer?

After the siege, Tara said she'd introduced Marcus Worthington-Hotspur to Lucy Spragg.

Was that true?

Had Tara slept with Marcus?

Would she have known she was having sex with her half-brother? If that was a yes, what did that make Tara?

Would she want to kill Marcus to take revenge on a father who abandoned her before she was even born?

And what about Lester Stephenson, Harry Pullman, Hugh Campbell? Where did they fit in?

Ed typed out a text.

Tara is not what she seems. Be careful.

Before he pressed send a thought occurred to him. Facebook.

Something Val Lee said about Tara's grandmother?

It wasn't hard to find a picture. Tara and her gran Penelope.

Penelope Paxman until she married. Then Penelope Stephenson.

Ed added to the text.

She's Lester Stephenson's granddaughter

Chapter 50

Rain hammered against the windows, Ullswater hidden by darkness, but Tara didn't care. Sitting in one of the tub chairs she had admired the view of the barman for hours. The man was still fit.

Not that she had stared at him all the time; she was reading her Wainwright, the 'Pictorial Guide to the Lakeland Fells: The Eastern Fells', the first in the collection that covered the Patterdale Valley.

Her third gin and tonic was almost empty.

He walked over to her. 'Another one mademoiselle?'

She checked her watch. 7pm.

'No thank you Pierre.'

The great thing about name badges is you don't have to ask.

Pierre bent down, leaned in close. 'I finish in thirty minutes if you would like a walk.'

'Best not,' Tara said, fighting her instincts. 'Busy day tomorrow. But thanks anyway.'

Pierre didn't push it. He'd probably already stepped

beyond what the hotel would consider appropriate guest/staff boundaries.

Tara finished her drink, walked out of the bar, through reception and stepped outside.

Light glowed from the huge orangery and the driveway was well illuminated, but across the road Helvellyn was barely visible, a 950-metre mountain reduced to a dark, foreboding outline.

Tara took a deep breath.

Walking to the hotel had seemed a good idea at 3pm when it was still daylight; the bar in the White Lion had been quiet and she was glad of a change of scenery. But now, in the darkness…

People who spend their lives in towns and cities under streetlamps have no idea how dark it gets in the country.

Tara was about to find out.

———

THE MAN in the corner of the bar folded up his broadsheet newspaper, placed a disposable coaster over the pint of lager he'd spent an hour sipping and walked through the French doors onto the patio.

He didn't think any of the older residents scattered around the place were taking any notice of him, although you could never be sure.

He was meticulously unmemorable: black polo shirt, black jeans, black trainers; short brown hair, no tattoos, no distinguishing marks. At 5'8" he was one of life's grey men and that's how he liked it.

He took a cigarette, lit up and hastily blew out the smoke. He didn't inhale. He despised cigarettes, but needed an excuse to be outside and the most natural reason to leave the warmth of a hotel lounge was to smoke.

He walked away from the window and sent the text he'd typed earlier.

She's on the move

BY THE TIME Tara got to the end of the drive her jeans were soaked. The lights from the Glenridding Hotel were on, the shops opposite in shadow. Beyond, it was as dark as the ghost train she'd enjoyed as a child, in the days before her mother got in tow with the cripple.

It was less than a mile to Patterdale and the White Lion but in the dark, in the rain, twenty minutes would be an eternity.

The street was deserted and silent but Tara's imagination found shadows and noises behind every bush, around every corner.

Tara started singing under her breath, although Michael Jackson's 'Thriller' probably wasn't the best choice to calm the knot of fear tightening in her stomach even though it was nowhere near midnight.

Her heart banged so fast she thought it was going to burst clean out of her chest and make its own bid for freedom.

When she saw the soft-focus glow of the mini-market 100 metres ahead the relief made Tara laugh out loud, like the moment the doors would swing open at the end of that ghost train and the demons were left behind in the darkness.

Then as the distance closed, she saw him.

Someone was outside the mini-market standing statue still and silent.

Who the fuck's that? In this weather.

Head bowed and eyes flicking to her right, she fought the urge to run or call out, concentrated on breathing with the panic running like ice water through her veins.

Maybe he would cross the road, cut her off.

She narrowed the gap between them and thrust her hands into her coat pockets, her head still down.

She summoned the courage to glance quickly sideways as she drew level.

The figure stayed motionless in the rain.

She was relieved and angry at the same time, mind playing tricks on her.

Get a grip you stupid cow.

She smiled at the red post box – the motionless figure - and gulped in breaths of relief.

HIS MOVING lips touched the yellow Motorola walkie-talkie gripped in his right hand.

'She's approaching the Glenridding Hotel, heading towards Patterdale.'

He put the device, so much more reliable in the mountains than a mobile, on the passenger seat, grabbed the wheel with his left hand, and shuffled himself into position to drive off.

His window was open just enough to keep the air circulating and the windscreen clear. The rusty Land Rover Discovery, stationary in a line of parked cars on a side road opposite the hotel, was as common in the Lake District as a baked bean was in a tin of Heinz.

His left foot depressed the clutch, right foot hovered over the accelerator.

The noise of another vehicle caused his thumb and

index finger to freeze around the ignition key.

He slumped down behind the wheel and watched the car drive past the Glenridding Hotel towards Patterdale.

There was no rush. Let that one get out of the way. He knew where she was going.

He stared at his wrist, watched the second hand tick through sixty seconds before moving off.

He didn't put the headlights on.

Tara, Tara, Tara. What's your game?

Finding her in that hotel had been easy. His accomplice, a man she had never met, walked into the handful of bars in the area and found her by the window reading a little green book. After that, it was just case of waiting.

Of course, finding her without any idea where she was hiding would have been impossible. They had that bent bastard Whelan to thank for that.

He turned right at the mini-market, emerged onto the main road and grabbed the walkie-talkie.

'Where the fuck's she gone?' he said into the Motorola.

The second man was in the car park to the driver's left, behind the Glenridding Hotel, next to the steamer station.

'How the fuck do I know?'

The radios hissed crackling static.

'I'm walking up towards the road now. It's fuckin' pitch black here.'

'You were supposed to be hiding near the road waiting for her, you dick,' the driver said, slowing the Discovery, turning on the headlights at full beam, looking left and right.

'It was pissing down so I went to find a tree for shelter,' the second man said. 'Found one near the boat thing.'

'Well get up here quick. She can't just vanish. We need to find her before she gets back to the pub.'

Radio static was replaced by the sound of light, rapid footsteps, the man sprinting towards the road, finger still on the transmit button.

He was breathless in seconds: 'I'm running up to the road,' he panted.

The Discovery headed into Patterdale, the driver watching the road and trying to look over the dry stone walls at the same time.

'Fuck,' he shouted, the palms of his hands slamming the steering wheel.

He turned around in the White Lion car park, headed back towards Glenridding.

'No sign of her,' he said through the window to his wet, breathless accomplice.

'She can't have just vanished.'

'Well she has. Something's spooked her. She's hiding. No way did she have time to get to the White Lion. She's got to be close. Jump in.'

He drove down the driveway onto the car park, parked up by the steamer station. They both got out.

'She can't have come too far down here or she'd have run into you. She's definitely come off the road though, so let's start at the top and work our way back down here.'

The rain was getting heavier.

'Fuckin' weather,' the second man groaned.

'Least it means nobody will be hanging about. What would you prefer? A summer night, sunshine and wicker picnic baskets?'

They heard a vehicle and ducked down by the public toilet block, their black clothing melting into the shadows.

The vehicle didn't drive past.

'Must have turned off,' the second man said.

They crept back towards the road, eyes searching, ears listening, two poachers stalking human prey.

Chapter 51

LEISURE AND TOURISM in the Lake District means two things to most people: walking and water sports. Ullswater had both.

Lying face down under the leaking, long-abandoned carcass of an upturned wooden rowing boat, nose pressed into the gravel, forehead resting on her forearms, she shivered, clothes soaked by rain, surface water, and the rotting hull that was wet to its core.

She tensed her whole body, fighting to control her shivers, frightened she'd make it too easy for them by shaking the boat, scared they would hear her pounding heart.

James Fenimore Cooper's book 'The Last of the Mohicans' flashed into her head. She had no idea why. She hadn't read it since school. Maybe the boat resembled a canoe? Not that she was going on the lake in this leaky death trap. Even Sam Parker couldn't make this thing float.

Daylight was still hours away, and she knew in this pissing rain, passers-by would be rarer than rocking horse shit.

Rainwater dripped through the leaking hull onto the back of her head, but neither the rain nor the sound of her own breathing blocked out the whispers she could hear getting closer.

'BE quiet and watch where you're walking,' the driver hissed. 'Christ you're making enough noise to wake the dead.'

'These stones are soaking. I'm going to break my neck.'

'Well do it fucking quietly.'

They stopped and looked around; eyes already adjusted to the blackness.

Under the trees and bushes adjoining the road they could make out two upturned rowing boats about twenty metres apart.

The driver tapped his associate on the shoulder, put his forefinger to his lips, pointed at the boats.

The second man nodded.

On tiptoes they reduced the distance with each careful step.

Twenty metres from the nearest boat the driver tapped his accomplice's shoulder again and put his mouth against his ear.

'Let's fan out,' he said. 'You go to the left. I'll go the right. We'll get to opposite sides of the boat together, then she has nowhere to run.'

'What are we going to do with her?' the accomplice whispered back.

'I was just going to drive her away, find out what she said to the police, ask her what's she playing at. No point now. They've put her in hiding. That can only be because she's filled them full of shit.'

'So?'

'Dangerous place this in the dark. People get lost. She's going to take a long walk off a short pier. Tragic accident but I suppose there's worse places to drown. Fell off a jetty, bashed her head on the rocks and game over. Now let's get her found and get the hell out of here.'

They split up, hunting dogs in a pincer movement closing in on a rabbit. They stopped after each step, eyes glued on the boat, bodies ready to sprint if she made a run for it.

They reached the bow of the boat and crouched opposite each other.

The driver raised three fingers on his right hand.

The second man nodded, ready to grab the front of the boat.

Two fingers.

One finger.

The last finger folded over and four hands grabbed the boat and threw the front up.

Sound travels further and clearer in the country than the city.

His 'fuck' was muttered but it cracked like gunfire, the sound of a boat crashing back down an explosion.

They ran to the second boat. No need for stealth now. No need for a finger count.

They yanked up the hull, lifted it to chest height and pushed it backwards.

She threw her hands around her face and shielded her eyes from the fierce, bright white light.

'What the fuck?' said the driver, hand dropping to his leg, torch shining on his black trainer.

Two types of light hit the men: vivid white illuminated them like actors on a stage, ominous red dots peppered their torsos.

The combination of dazzling roof-mounted spotlights from the roaring BMW X5 and the ear-piercing repeated shouts of 'armed police' left them frozen.

'Get on the floor! Hands on your heads! Now! Do it now!'

Harry Pullman and his accomplice hit the ground quicker than the discarded boat.

Eight figures dressed in combat black and pointing MP5s emerged from their hiding places in the trees and encircled the two men.

'Stay where you are. Don't move.'

A gloved hand reached for the woman, pulled her to her feet.

'About bloody time. I'm in the early stages of hypothermia here.'

Bev Summers winked at the AFO, walked past the inner cordon and got into the back of the waiting car.

'Turn the heater up before I catch my death,' Bev said, slamming the rear door.

Sam turned up the fan speed. 'Better?'

Bev nodded, pulled a soggy cardboard box from her coat pocket and snatched a cigarette. It snapped just above the filter, shreds of tobacco fluttering in the warm, blown air towards the floor.

'Brilliant!'

She threw the packet with such force it bounced off the gearbox tunnel, ricocheted from the dashboard and hit Sam before the floating strands of tobacco had landed on the carpet.

Bev sat back, stared at the roof lining, counted loudly to five. 'Don't suppose anybody can spare a fag?'

Sam and Tara, who spent the count focused on the windscreen fighting to keep straight faces, burst out laughing.

Sam passed her a cigarette. 'You okay?'

Bev steadied her shaking hands, lit up, inhaled.

'Apart from the fact I'm half frozen to death, pissing wet-through and my nicotine levels are dangerously low, I'm absolutely fine and dandy.'

Smoke drifting from her nostrils formed a thick, low-level, eye-stinging fog.

'And I never got to see the look on their faces because of all the lights. First their torch, then the main show. Who was it?'

'Harry Pullman and one of his mates,' Sam said.

'As expected,' Bev looked with something like devotion at the glowing cigarette end. 'No show without Punch... you okay Tara?'

Tara shuffled forward, half turned, watery eyes blinking at Bev through the cloud of smoke.

'Good thanks, although I was shitting it when I thought the post box was one of them.'

Sam laughed, more relief than humour, explained the significance of the post box to Bev.

'I must have been under that bloody canoe for an hour or more,' Bev said. 'Absolutely Baltic. Poor buggers who are homeless. Makes you wonder. I'm going to volunteer at a shelter when this all gets sorted.'

'Very public spirited,' Sam said.

'And I'm going to read The Last of the Mohicans again.'

'What?' Sam's head snapped left in surprise.

'Last of the Mohicans. Got to thinking about it when I was under that bloody canoe.'

Sam shook her head, smiled. 'It was a rowing boat.

Look, I'll drop you two off. You can get a shower and a cuppa.'

Bev leaned forward, her head between the front seats, exhaled smoke from her puckered lips.

'Don't know about you Tara but warm shower, warm clothes is a must.'

Tara nodded, lit her own cigarette.

'But you can stick the tea Sam, I need a drink...a proper drink.'

Smoke and woody damp latched onto Bev's hair, clung to her clothes. She was a herring being kippered in a Northumberland smoke house. The coughing fit began.

Instinctively, everybody opened their window.

Bev stuck her head out and gulped fresh air before settling back into the seat and the cigarette.

'How was everything when you left the hotel Tara?'

'Wet, but all good.'

'All good?' Sam said. 'Clockwork more like. Went like a dream.'

'I just got past the Glenridding Hotel,' Tara said, excitement in her voice. 'Jumped in the back of Sam's car when she drove past.'

'You should have stayed there,' Bev said. 'The front seats are for police officers only.'

'When I've dropped you two off,' Sam said, ignoring the jibe, 'I'll go to the local nick, thank all concerned and see what we've got. The spotter in the hotel did a good job, giving us the heads up when Tara left, so I need to thank him.'

Bev shivered. 'Least he was warm and dry.'

This time she blew smoke through the window but it still kick-started another coughing fit.

'Those firearms lot sent the willies up me,' Bev said, 'when they started bawling and shouting and they're on our side. God only knows what Toot and Ploot made of it all.'

'Toot and Ploot?' Tara was thrown.

'She means Harry Pullman and his mate,' Sam said.

'Shit themselves I bet,' Tara grinned. 'Good enough for them.'

Sam looked over her shoulder.

'I'm leaving a couple of AFOs outside the White Lion just in case there's any more of Pullman's mates in the area.'

Tara's smile vanished. 'Do you think there's more?'

'Just a precaution, Tara. Don't worry, but make sure you stick to Bev.'

Harry Pullman, arms cuffed behind his back, walked towards the lock-up van, firearms officers by his side. He saw Sam in the driving seat of her vehicle.

'Parker,' he shouted.

Sam stuck her head out of the window.

'Everybody's been played here, you included.'

She got out of the car and stood with her left arm on the roof.

'Bent bastard Whelan told me where to find that lying slag.'

He nodded towards Tara in the front seat.

'I came here to find out what shit she had told you lot. I've got fuck all to do with any shootings.'

'Save it for the interview,' Sam said, ducking back into the car, the signal for the AFOs to put Pullman in the van.

'I'm telling you Parker,' he shouted. 'We've all been played here. Ask yourself who by. Bent cop's my bet.'

Pullman was still shouting when the back doors of the van slammed shut.

Chapter 52

SAM PARKED CLOSE to the only vehicle at the far end of the White Lion car park.

Bev jumped out, jogged towards the VW camper, towards Ed Whelan leaning against its bonnet, the thick-trunked trees and their huge branches sheltering him from the rain.

'You're a sight for sore eyes,' she said, stopping short of throwing her arms around him.

He smiled; arms outstretched. 'Disgraced and abandoned.'

Sam and Tara caught up.

'What's he doing here?' Tara demanded.

Ed Whelan smiled again.

'You okay?' Sam said.

'Never better,' Ed said. 'You lot want a brew in Doris before you go?'

'Not got anything stronger?' Bev said, the cold and the soaked clothes temporarily forgotten.

'You're on duty,' Ed said.

'Not for much longer I'm not.'

'Go on then, get the kettle on,' Sam said.

Tara's head swivelled from one police officer to another, hands on hips, legs bent at the knee. She was oozing indignation.

'Will somebody explain what's going on here?'

'Already boiled,' Ed said.

'Cup of tea and a few extra minutes won't hurt,' Sam said. 'I called round to see Sue this morning.'

'Went well did it?' Ed sighed.

Tara turned up her volume and glared at him. 'Which one are you shagging then?'

Ed ignored her as he stepped into the van, filled four plastic mugs with boiling water and put them on a plastic tray.

'Well as you could expect,' Sam said. 'I told Sue everything would work out, but the fact that you'd never answered her calls and were splattered all over the papers didn't help.'

'The last thing I needed pulling this together was outside distractions and that included the soon to be ex-Mrs Whelan.'

Steam rose towards their faces as they each lifted a mug.

'You made your mind up then?' Sam said.

'Sure have,' Ed said. 'I'll be the talk of the Gurdwara. Corrupt and seeking a divorce.'

Tara nodded towards Ed, sipped on the tea. 'I thought it was Bev but maybe it's Sam...or are you doing them both?'

Nobody responded, just carried on as if Tara was nothing but empty space.

'What's Harry said?' Ed asked.

'Just that her ladyship here is full of the proverbial,' Sam slurped the tea.

'Well he would say that wouldn't he,' Tara snapped, straightening her legs, planting her feet.

'I want everything boxed off tomorrow Sam,' Ed said. 'Reputation restored.'

'Hello,' Tara shouted. 'I am here. I'm not a tree.'

Sam nodded. 'Appleton will be livid. Bad enough you're not bent, but when he finds out the suspension was all fake...'

Tara's eyes flicked around the group, brain trying to compute what was unfolding.

'Will somebody tell me what the fuck's going on!'

Bev lit a cigarette, offered them around. 'He's livid? I was only told the suspension was all a set up just before I climbed under that boat and I'm supposed to be your mate.'

'Appleton's a knob,' Ed said. 'No idea how close I was to knocking his lights out. As for you not knowing Bev, sorry, but needs must. If the likes of you were genuinely shocked, no one would think the suspension wasn't for real'

'I give up,' Tara said, inhaling on the cigarette, stepping closer to Bev. 'Have your private police conversation.'

Ed closed Doris' sliding side door and stepped backwards from the cloud of smoke hovering above him, away from the smokers spewing their pollution into the Lakeland sky.

'So Tara,' Ed said, acknowledging her at last. 'Now we get to hear what Harry thinks about all of this, although I can tell you when I spoke to him, he was saying what he's saying now, that you're full of shit.'

Tara drew deep on the cigarette, blew more smoke into the darkness. 'And?'

The word hung in the rain.

'He's bound to say that isn't he. He's the gangster, not me.'

Ed stepped towards her. 'But some of what you told Bev is shit, isn't it?'

Tara straightened her back, inhaled deep on the cigarette and forced smoke through her oval mouth towards Ed.

'Such as, Sherlock?'

Ed ignored the smoke, didn't give Tara the satisfaction of a reaction. 'Like how your mother was an alcoholic.'

'She is.'

Ed poured as much sarcasm into his smile as he could.

'Didn't look like it when I spoke to her.'

Tara's contorted face echoed the cold aggression in her voice.

'Whatever. More faces than the town clock that woman. Trust you to believe her.'

Ed backed away from the next plume of smoke that was forcefully and deliberately blown towards him.

'And I spoke to your war hero, wheelchair-bound stepfather. Not exactly your archetypal rapist.'

Tara threw the mug into the bushes with a sudden swing of her arm.

'You have absolutely no idea what you're talking about.'

'I think I do. Your stepfather is paralysed. He can't have sex.'

Tara stepped towards Ed, her tone poison.

'You're all the same aren't you. No wonder victims don't come forward, don't want to report.'

She raised the cigarette to her eyes, examined it before speaking again.

'Doesn't mean he can't look. Doesn't mean he doesn't

want to try, does it? Doesn't mean he can't use his hands or let his mates have a go.'

'Is that the part when they came upstairs?' Ed paused, a barrister preparing to deliver another verbal blow. 'Even though you lived in a bungalow.'

It was Tara's turn to grin.

'I never said we didn't live in a bungalow.'

'You lying cow,' Bev spat out the words, anger shooting through her pointed index finger.

Tara shrugged her shoulders. She drew on the cigarette again, savouring the nicotine hit, relishing the verbal fist fight.

'I trusted you Parker,' she turned to Sam. 'Now you're prepared to believe Harry Pullman on this bent bastard's say-so. I told you not to trust male coppers.'

'You can go and get that mug back,' Ed said.

Tara leaned forward from the waist, raised her wrists to her face and wobbled her hands from side to side.

'Oooooo. Let's all change the subject because the detectives have got it wrong.'

Sam spoke: 'Lester Stephenson described you as a commodity.'

'Charming,' Bev said.

Tara stood up straight. 'He can say what he wants, free country.'

'Of course he can say what he wants Tara,' Sam said. 'He's your grandfather.'

'Jesus,' Bev said, looking up at the rain leaking through the trees. 'I've missed out on all sorts whilst I've been stuck up here in the sticks.'

Tara put the cigarette between her lips, stepped closer to Bev and blew a mouthful of smoke in her face.

'About time you retired. You're past it. Even your mates kept you up here, out of the loop. Ask yourself why.'

Bev ignored the smoke, didn't bite. 'What, because I'm not a manipulative cow? Just want to see the good in people?'

Tara flicked the cigarette towards the bushes, towards Ed's mug, glared at Bev.

'All you saw was a tight arse and firm tits. Don't think I didn't see you looking, drooling like a bitch on heat.'

Bev grinned. 'Don't kid yourself.'

Sam examined the Marlboro, took one last drag before speaking.

'Get used to it Tara. Plenty will be looking in jail. And that's where you're going. We know Zac didn't kill anybody, Tara. And Harry Pullman's wasn't the only DNA profile on the inside of the second rabbit suit.'

Tara pouted. 'But I'm not on your precious database.'

Sam leaned back against the campervan, flicked the cigarette into the air and crossed her outstretched legs.

'You're not on the database but we could easily have got a controlled sample of your DNA from your house. You know, from a hairbrush or something.'

Tara wagged her finger at Sam.

'Naughty, naughty. I hope you got a warrant.'

Sam straightened, moved away from the campervan towards the finger.

'That's what bothered me right from the start Tara. I heard a noise in your house. You were a lone female, your most recent sexual encounter had just been fatally shot, your neighbours killed, carnage outside and yet you wanted me to get a warrant to check out your loft. That was your first mistake.'

She lit another cigarette, didn't offer Tara one.

Tara took her cigarettes from her coat pocket, opened the box.

'Like I wanted you people roaming all over my house,

planting things faster than a gardener. Course my DNA's in
that suit. It's my suit.'

She put a cigarette to her lips.

'I had a client who liked me to dress up. Haven't seen
him for ages, which is why it's in my loft. No need for it
now. Hardly makes me a killer.'

Sam ignored her. 'Your second mistake was treating us
all like idiots.'

Tara smiled, nodded towards Bev.

'Didn't have to try too hard with her.'

Sam studied Tara, the posture, her arrogance and
scorn.

'It might be that Bev's brief was to let you tell more
lies, catch you in your own web.'

Tara slowly shook her head.

'Harry Pullman came here to kill me and I bet you any
money that bent bastard,' she pointed her cigarette at Ed,
'told him where I was. They're the gangsters, not me.'

'Believe me we'll be asking Pullman all about it,' Sam
told her. 'But if you're involved…all sorts of opportunities
arise.'

'Like?'

Tara's fingers tried two pockets before they found the
lighter. She lit the cigarette.

'Kill your half-brother?' Sam already had a list. 'Get
back at the father who abandoned you before you were
born? Get rid of Paul, the Skinners' man in the police. Get
rid of Harry Pullman?'

Tara threw out her hands. 'If what you say is true, why
would I do that?'

'That bothered me,' Sam told her. 'Then the Skinners
got killed in jail. Did Hugh Campbell want to take over
their business? Lester visits you. He's Campbell's
accountant. Knows some bent police officers.'

'Yeah, like him,' Tara said, pointing at Ed.

'Unfortunately for you, Ed knew your father and grandfather socially.'

Tara tilted her head, blew smoke upwards and looked back at Sam.

'Another Mason?' the words a sneer. 'Another member of the men-only secret society? Keep their women in check, never allow them to better themselves. What's that saying? Women should be obedient, grateful and tied to the kitchen sink?'

'Bev,' Sam said, nodding towards Tara.

Bev moved and took hold of Tara's left arm.

'I'm arresting you on suspicion of...'

Tara's free right arm was a blur as it shot towards Bev's face.

The deafening sound of the gun boomed like dry summer thunder.

Chapter 53

FOR A NANO second Sam and Ed were frozen in the moment, shock and disbelief chiselled onto their faces.

Tara had grabbed Bev around the neck, fired the pistol into the air and now had the smoking barrel pointed under Bev's chin.

'Either of you two move and the old perv gets it.'

Bev flinched as the end of the hot barrel was pressed against her temple.

The two AFOs, MP5s raised into the firing position, ran from the front door of the White Lion onto the car park.

'Stop! Armed police!'

'You stop,' Tara shouted. 'Or this one's the first to die.'

The AFOs pulled up but kept their guns raised.

Tara shouted again: 'Tell them to back off, Parker. I'm warning you. She gets it otherwise.'

Sam raised her right arm.

'This isn't helping, Tara,' she said.

Tara backed towards the car park's retaining wall, dragging Bev with her.

'Turn around and sit,' Tara ordered as they reached the wall.

'Get ready to drop over. You try to run and I'll shoot you in the back. Understand?'

Bev nodded.

'Remember. I know how to use these things.'

Ed glanced at Sam and flicked his eyes towards Bev but Sam shook her head. Too much ground to make up.

Tara pushed Bev off the wall and jumped the four feet after her.

Bev landed awkwardly on her ankle but Tara grabbed her by the hair, yanked her head back and pressed the gun against the side of her head.

The AFOs ran back to the road. Ed sprinted to the wall and jumped.

'Shoot the fucker,' Ed screamed as he dropped onto the road inbetween the AFOs and Tara, all sense and reasoning abandoned.

No doubt he would be back in the shit later; no unarmed officer should put themselves between a fleeing armed suspect and chasing AFOs.

Tara, ten feet away, pointed the gun at him.

'All I need is one excuse and you get it Whelan. I'll take you both out before they shoot at me.'

Sam appeared at the top of the wall.

'Ed!' she shouted.

Tara looked up, pointed the gun at her.

'Back off,' Sam shouted. 'Everybody, back off.'

The Firearms Commander course she had done some years previously was kicking in. She needed to diffuse the situation, not escalate it. Bev's life was the priority, negotiation not confrontation the maxim.

Tara put the gun back against Bev's head.

'Best listen to your boss, Ed.'

Sam heard the fallen leaves rustle behind her, turned briefly and saw an elderly man.

'Sir. For your own safety please walk to the back of the car park and stay out of sight until a police officer comes for you.'

She turned her focus back to Tara and Bev.

That old man looked familiar

Ed picked up Sam's lead and slipped into negotiator mode:

'Tara, what do you want to happen now?'

'Save your psycho-babble,' she pressed the gun barrel just a little harder into Bev's head. 'I've heard it all before. It won't work with me.'

'How far do you think you'll get?' Ed said.

Tara grinned, pulled Bev tighter into her.

'Far enough.'

Behind them tyres squealed, burning rubber drifting on the damp air. A big, dark Jaguar roared out of the car park and swung hard right, narrowly missing the red telephone box on the opposite side of the road, the driver fighting to keep the snaking back end under control.

Sam visualised the old man, her memory flying through its stored names index, frantically searching for a match.

Lester Stephenson.

Ed glanced over his shoulder but identifying the vehicle, all high revs, low gear and dazzling headlights, was impossible.

The AFOs darted to the left towards the drystone wall but weren't quick enough.

The Jag swerved towards them, front nearside ploughing into their legs, knocking them into the air like circus acrobats.

The car, in front of them before the AFOs crashed

back to the road in distorted heaps, screeched to a halt alongside Tara and her prisoner.

Tara yanked open the back offside door and pushed Bev onto the back seat.

'She'll get a bullet in the head if you follow,' she shouted.

Ed concentrated on the registration number as the Jag powered past then sprinted after it, hoping the driver would lose control.

Breathing hard, lungs bursting and thighs on fire, he lurched to a stop after 50 metres; his hands grabbed his shaking knees and he launched into a coughing fit, firing spittle into the darkness before his churning stomach heaved his 4pm pasty over the road. Pieces of undigested carrot, swede and potato peppered his shoes.

He gasped for breath, wiped his mouth and glanced at the wall; his chest felt it was being crushed under the Lakeland stones like a medieval torture.

As quickly as he could he went back to the stricken AFOs.

Witnesses who came running from the pub would later describe it as a jog, but Ed just couldn't move any faster.

He reached the first officer, knelt down, and pressed the transmit button on her radio.

GUNSHOT AND SCREECHING tyres had staff and punters alike running from the pub. Sam ran through the car park, by now filling with staff and customers, scanning the small crowd, seeking out the owners.

'I need to use your phone,' she shouted.

She didn't want to risk her mobile and a dodgy signal.

The White Lion was now the Forward Command post.

One of the owners rushed inside with her. The phone was behind the bar.

She punched 999.

'Emergency. Which service do you–'

'Police,' Sam said.

She knew Ed would be doing what he could for the injured AFOs.

A non-believer, she still mentally prayed, asking God to prevent any fatal injuries tonight.

As she waited to be connected, she placed her hand over the mouthpiece and spoke with the owner.

'Look I'm sorry, but I can't run this from here if you're selling beer. I need privacy. It's a big ask, but I really need you to close the pub. Just for half an hour or so. Until Cumbria take command.'

He nodded.

Sam spoke into the phone.

'This is Detective Chief Inspector Parker, Eastern Police. I need to speak with the control room inspector immediately.'

As soon as she was connected she gave the inspector a rapid overview of the situation.

'You need to notify the on-call chief officer, the on-call SIO and your hostage negotiator. We need firearms back-up, ambulance, air ambulance if available. Air support, road policing at the bottom of Kirkstone Pass, both Ambleside and Bowness end. The registration of the Jaguar is…'

Sam closed her eyes. Thought of Bev in that car.

A mobile hostage.

A worse scenario was hard to conjure.

'DETECTIVE SERGEANT WHELAN, EASTERN POLICE, URGENT,' Ed said, gasping into the radio.

'Go ahead…Sergeant Whelan?'

The confused radio operator knew there wasn't a Whelan in her force, but she was aware of a joint operation with Eastern Police.

'Two officers down, White Lion, Patterdale. Hit and run.'

The female AFO groaned. Ed ripped off his coat, put it under her head.'

'Suspects made off in a large saloon, registered number…'

Ed rattled off the registration. The AFO gently squeezed his arm. He smiled at her.

'You'll be okay,' he said. 'Help's on its way. Try and keep still.'

He stroked her forehead, a small act of human kindness that focused his mind on her plight.

Ed wondered if she had kids, hoped she would recover, hoped she wouldn't be left like George Lee.

He stood up and shouted in the direction of the pub.

'Over here. Bring some blankets.'

'Sergeant Whelan,' the radio crackled.

He knelt down again.

'Sorry. Two suspects. One Tara Paxman. Armed and dangerous. Driver unknown. Responsible for mowing down two local firearm officers. Eastern police officer kidnapped.'

'Sergeant Whelan. I've just been informed that your DCI is speaking with my inspector.'

'Roger.'

Ed bent forward, grasped the AFO's hand, relayed her collar number over the radio.

'Suspects made off towards Patterdale, possibly heading over Kirkstone Pass.'

'Roger that Sergeant Whelan. For your information: ambulance dispatched, AFOs en route, ETA five minutes, air support may not be able to fly due to low cloud cover. Same applies to air ambulance.'

'Roger.'

Fucking weather.

He smiled at the officer. 'I'll just go and check on your colleague.'

Her lips moved but nothing came out.

'It's okay,' he said, smiling at her. 'Control room will give me his name.'

PC Malcolm Epsom was unconscious, each shallow breath a ragged moan.

Ed instructed the owner of the pub and a member of staff in White Lion livery to place duvets over both AFOs.

'Can you each get a torch? I need one person stood outside the pub and one further along this road to stop any traffic. Just wave the torch in front of you. The traffic will stop. If you can get a couple of people at each location, that would be even better.'

They nodded.

'Thanks,' Ed said. 'I know Health and Safety would have a dicky fit, but for now it's needs must. I don't want these officers getting hit by another vehicle.'

The two men ran to find torches and organise volunteers against the backdrop of distant sirens.

Chapter 54

'YOU OKAY?' the driver asked, looking in his rear-view mirror.

Tara kept her eyes left, fixed on Bev.

'This daft bitch was going to arrest me.'

Bev inhaled slowly. Caution was king. One wrong word...

'What happens now Tara?'

Ask the question. Use her name. Show her she's in charge.

Bev wasn't a trained negotiator, but over the years she'd had a few chats with Ed on the subject.

Lester Stephenson concentrated on the narrow, winding road and the encroaching dry stone walls as the car climbed towards the summit of Kirkstone Pass.

'Stop the car,' Tara shouted.

He pulled over in one of the passing places.

'Turn to face the window,' Tara ordered, sticking the gun into Bev's ribs.

Defiance flashed through Bev's mind, fighting for the gun suddenly seeming an option.

Stephenson shuffled in his seat, turned to face Bev and pointed his right hand. The gun was small and black.

'You heard her.'

Bev had no choice but to comply. She couldn't disarm both of them.

Tara's words were quiet, authoritative.

'Put your palms on the window. I'm giving him my gun. Any sudden movement and your brains will decorate that window.'

Bev leaned forward, put her hands on the window.

'Tara, you still haven't told me what happens now.'

'In a minute you'll ring Parker and providing she calls her dogs off, you'll be released.'

Tara bent down, took off her boots and socks, put her boots back on and tied the socks together.

Bev gasped when the grey, cotton socks went around her eyes and were pulled tight at the back of her head.

Tara's warm breath floated into her ear.

'Where's your phone?' she whispered.

'Coat pocket.'

Tara rifled through Bev's pockets until she found the Samsung S6.

The car accelerated away.

'We can't drive far,' Stephenson said. 'They'll have the number.'

The automatic gearbox changed down as he negotiated another of the pass's tight bends.

'When we get to the top, there's only two roads down and they'll block them both off,' he said.

Tara rubbed her eyes.

'What do we do then?' she asked.

'There's a pub up there.'

'I know. We both went in it. I was talking about the history to the barmaid. This philistine just sat by herself.'

'We could dump the car,' Stephenson said. 'Head up the fells behind the pub and hide, but…'

'But?'

He stopped talking, slowed down as headlights came towards them. The vehicles squeezed past each other.

'It's freezing. First light, they're after us with dogs.'

'Okay. Stop by the pub. Cuff her and leave her blindfolded on the fells.'

She dangled Bev's handcuffs above her head.

'Only when we're away will we tell them where she is.'

THE FLASHING blue lights reflected off walls and buildings as the Land Rover sped towards Patterdale. Ed was pleased the driver hadn't put on the two-tones: there was no traffic on the road to warn and more importantly, Ed always believed when you were injured the last thing you wanted to hear was a siren.

He remembered how he felt when he'd been stabbed. The two-tones made him feel worse, as if his injury was more life-threatening than he thought.

Three firearms officers got out of the vehicle. Two rushed to their colleagues, the driver, a PC, spoke to Ed.

'Nigel Hunter. You okay mate?'

His southern accent was strong.

Ed nodded. 'Whelan. Ed Whelan. Detective Sergeant. Eastern. I'll survive…thanks for asking.'

He briefed the AFO who looked over Ed's shoulder towards his stricken colleagues.

'Hopefully they'll be okay,' Ed said. 'Just a few broken bones, but they may have internal injuries, head injuries. The car drove straight at them.'

Nigel Hunter nodded, said nothing.

'The lad's unconscious, breathing steady but weak,' Ed said, 'The lassie…'

'Charlie.'

Ed paused, mind playing catch up.

'Charlotte when she's giving evidence,' Hunter said. 'Out here, Charlie.'

Ed nodded. 'She's conscious. Struggling to speak. Maybe rib injuries, but it's her legs that look the worst.'

Right on cue they heard the ambulance, siren blaring. It could have been a hundred metres away; it could have been three miles.

'Jesus,' Ed said. 'I'm sure they put those bloody things on when they're going for their bait.'

Nigel's initial grin faltered. His turn to be thrown.

'Bait. Food,' Ed explained.

Hunter dipped his head in apology. 'I've only been up here a few months. Transferred up from Thames Valley.'

'You'll soon learn the language,' Ed patted his shoulder. 'Bit different for you up here I expect. I would have said quieter but after tonight…'

Ed shook his head, exhaled loudly, spoke again.

'No shortage of firearms on duty have you? More than us and we're townies with our fair share of gun-carrying shit-bags.'

In different circumstances Ed might have made a quip about poachers, but not tonight.

'Plenty out because of this planned operation,' Hunter said. 'Not normally this many of us on shift.'

'Listen, if you need anything else from me just shout, but right now I need to get back to my boss.'

Ed wanted to sprint but his legs and lungs insisted otherwise.

Small groups were scattered on the road, watching, speaking in whispers.

Ed wanted to tell them to move back, wanted to tell them there was nothing to see, but decided to leave that to the local uniforms.

The decision lasted as long as it took him to spot the tall, skinny, forty something with blond dreadlocks, friendship bracelets and sockless, thick-soled walking sandals even in all this rain. He was filming the injured AFOs on his mobile.

Ed's anger went up like a bonfire night rocket.

He chopped hard on the skinny tattooed forearm holding the iPhone.

'Jesus man, what's your game?' Dreadlocks said, turning to confront Ed as the phone skimmed across the Tarmac.

'They're my colleagues you sick bastard.'

Ed picked up the phone, scrolled through to the photo and video library and deleted everything that showed the scene.

'Hey, you've got no right to do that man. That's a breach of my civil liberties.'

'Really,' Ed said, handing him back the iPhone. 'Tell someone who gives a shit.'

Ed turned, walked away.

He had taken three steps before Dreadlocks shouted: 'You won't get away with it, fascist. I'll be complaining to your superiors. I know my rights.'

Ed hid his balled fists in his trouser pockets, carried on walking and thought about Bev.

Behind him he heard a deep Cumbrian voice telling Dreadlocks – already filming again – his iPhone was going up his arse if he didn't put it away.

Ed glanced back to see Dreadlocks scuttling away.

The send-off got Ed's full approval and a cheer from what he guessed were stalwarts of an old-school farming community.

'And think about getting some meat down you. Do you the world of good.'

Ed walked into the pub.

SAM GRABBED the ringing mobile from her pocket and on the illuminated screen read the name.

Bev Summers.

'Bev?' Sam said quickly.

She didn't dare move in case she lost the signal.

'Sam it's me. Don't speak. Just listen.'

Sam cursed herself for leaving her coat on one of the chairs.

Behind the bar she scrambled frantically for something to write on and something to write with. Underneath the small window with its daylight view of Place Fell she found a small food order pad and tiny blue pen.

She glanced at the phone and exhaled relief. She still had a signal.

'I'm okay. I'm out of the car, blindfolded. They're still with me.'

Bev was obviously trying to control her words but their speed told Sam she was failing.

'They're going to dump me somewhere on the mountain. If you don't try to stop them when they drive away, they'll tell you where I am. They need four hours.'

Chapter 55

ED WALKED TOWARDS THE BAR.

Sam held her arm up, palm facing towards Ed.

He got the message, said nothing, walked towards her.

'Bev,' Sam said for Ed's benefit, putting her device on speakerphone, face up on the bar. 'Let me speak to Tara.'

Seconds later and she recognised Tara's voice.

'What is it you want?' Sam asked.

'No Whelan? I thought he was the trained negotiator.'

'I can get him.'

'What, he's stopped running after cars like some deranged dog? Don't waste your time. I'll talk to you.'

'What do you want?'

'Safe passage. Then you can get her back.'

'Can I trust you?'

Ed gave Sam the thumbs up. He was now the Number 2 negotiator, offering encouragement. The words, 'can I' were much less aggressive than 'why should I', but the question needed to be asked.

'You have no choice. I'll ring you at 1am with her

location. You arrest me before then and I'll not say a word. She'll die alone and very cold on the side of a mountain.'

Ed pulled the pad away from Sam, scribbled 'TOO LONG'.

'Four hours is too long,' Sam said. 'She'll not survive.'

'She'll be fine. Now call the dogs off.'

Tara terminated the call.

'What now?' Ed said.

'I need to get in touch with their control room again. We need to get their on-call SPoC out.'

Each Force has a number of accredited Communications Data Investigators, who are designated SPoCs –Single Point of Contacts – for telephone service providers.

'We need a trace putting on Bev's phone.'

THE THREE-LITRE ENGINE accelerated down The Struggle, the road steep, narrow and winding, hurtling the Jaguar towards Ambleside.

As dry stone walls flashed by, beads of sweat broke out on the driver's forehead.

Even a rally star would find it a battle on The Struggle at speed. Passing a basic test gave you no chance.

When he lost control on a right-hand bend, the crash was like something a TV movie director might film in slow motion, the Jag suddenly airborne, two tonnes of metal and three jerry cans of aviation fuel in the boot flying over a sloped grass field.

The front seat passenger screamed and didn't stop. The driver, knuckle-white fists clenching the steering wheel, said nothing, silent even as the flames consumed them in a fireball that lit up the sullen night sky.

AFO Nigel Hunter walked into the White Lion.

'How are they?' Sam asked.

'We'll find out in a few hours. Hopefully they'll be okay. I just popped in to tell you that there's a report of a vehicle on fire somewhere near the top of Kirkstone. Called in by someone leaving the pub up there.'

'Shit,' Sam muttered.

'That'll be them,' Ed said. 'Where are the fire bobbies coming from?'

Not a phrase Nigel Hunter had heard before, although he guessed Ed meant firefighters.

'Ambleside.'

'Tell them to be careful,' Sam said. 'We know Tara Paxman's armed. The driver may be as well.'

'Will do,' he said, walking towards the door.

'We need to find Bev quick,' Sam said. 'Problem is, can we believe anything Tara says anymore?'

'Let's hope Bev's still got her phone and they've sorted the trace,' Ed told her.

'They have,' the confirmation from the tall, bald, broad- shouldered detective superintendent stepping through the glazed door.

'Barry Harrison. You must be Sam,' he said, walking towards her, hand extended, the sleeve of his bottle-green overcoat rising up his arm.

Introductions over, they all sat, Sam and Ed opting for the long fixed seats.

'Don't worry about your colleague. We'll find her,' Harrison said, his back facing the bar, shuffling to get comfortable on the low, red-topped stool. He unbuttoned his coat.

'A search team coordinator is drawing up plans. He'll liaise with the Patterdale Mountain Rescue.'

'We're in your hands,' Sam said.

It wasn't a position she enjoyed.

'I'm already aware of your operation tonight and our cooperation regarding the firearms aspect,' Harrison continued. 'Things obviously took an unexpected turn once you got back here.'

'You could say that,' Sam said, putting her arms, tired and heavy like the rest of her body, on the dark wooden table.

She relayed the events from the car park.

Harrison looked at Ed. 'Thanks for running to help our people.'

Ed said nothing, nodded.

'I'm waiting for an update on the burning car,' the superintendent continued. 'The brigade is there now. The heat is ferocious. Anybody in the vehicle won't have survived, but the fire itself...'

Sam leaned back against the backrest before speaking, the beginnings of a headache gathering, guessed what he was thinking.

'Patterdale isn't Hollywood,' she said.

'Exactly,' Harrison had leant forward. 'Cars in the real world don't just explode. You could fire bullets straight into the diesel tank and it wouldn't go up, wouldn't just go bang.'

Sam nodded, told them how years earlier a driver had died in his burning car because bystanders were too scared to approach.

'They'd all seen too many exploding in the movies,' she said.

'It didn't and the poor guy burnt to death when he could have been saved.'

Stop blabbering Sam. Blabbering is a sign of stress.

Harrison's phone rang.

'If you'll excuse me,' he said.

Sam nodded, picked up a steaming mug of tea courtesy of the owner and looked at her watch. 9.11pm.

'I can't just hang around here doing nothing,' she said. 'What if Bev's in that car?'

Sam sipped the tea, considered her words, her thoughts. She spoke slowly, carefully composing each sentence.

'The car exploded. That doesn't happen in an accident. Barry's right. So how has it gone up?'

Sam stared into the bar's coal fire, the swirling, hypnotic flames dragging her towards a blackness she desperately wanted to resist.

'Cars burn when somebody torches them,' she said.

Ed bowed his head, covered his eyes with his hands, tried to push away the images playing in technicolour through his head.

'Let's just pray it was torched after everybody got out.'

They both looked towards the door as it opened.

'The phone is on the move,' Barry Harrison said, bursting in, broad shoulders slumped.

Neither Sam nor Ed spoke. Whatever Barry Harrison had to say, he wasn't finished yet.

'And it's moved too far to be on foot.'

Chapter 56

DRIVING through the market town of Kendal towards the M6, Tara Paxman obeyed the speed limits, traffic signals and road markings. She hadn't seen any police cars but there was no point in risking attention. Not every police resource would be at Kirkstone Pass, although she suspected the place was keeping most of the Force busy.

Assumptions, like attention, were dangerous but it was reasonable to believe it would be some time before the fire was out and the vehicle declared safe enough for examination. Identifying the bodies would take even longer.

Add in the fact the police had no idea about the car she was now driving and Tara felt her cautious optimism wasn't misplaced.

Bev Summers had been only too willing to visit the Kirkstone Inn last night, presenting Tara with the opportunity to check if the car was parked up ready for her in case Plan B was required.

She'd seen the black VW Golf, knew the keys would be

taped to the inside wheel arch. Bigger than her VW Polo and very nice.

The initial plan had been to get tonight over with then sneak off into the waiting Jaguar with Lester Stephenson.

Everything changed with the exchange in the car park. Parker and Whelan were no fools, but she was still taken aback by the accuracy of their deductions.

Lester did a good job knocking over the armed police and Summers had been easy to get into the car. She was blindfolded, handcuffed and once in the car park, put in the front seat of the Jaguar.

Driving through Kendal was a circuitous route. The quickest way would have been to drive along the shores of Ullswater towards Pooley Bridge and head up onto the A66, but that would have meant driving through Patterdale.

Tara checked her coat pocket, searched for some Kendal Mint Cake.

She pulled out a phone.

Bev's phone.

'Bollocks,' she shouted.

Had Bev Summers put up more of a fight she might still be alive.

'I'VE GOT A REALLY bad feeling about this,' Sam said.

Sam, Ed and Barry Harrison were in the bedroom that Tara had been using.

Asking the owners of the White Lion to close temporarily was one thing, asking them to close for the night altogether different.

Sam had given them forty pounds, told them to buy everybody a free drink for their inconvenience. She wouldn't get the money back – imagine trying to submit that 'expenses form' – but it would buy her good will.

The phone signal wasn't great, but it was enough and Harrison had a police radio. Not that they were much better than phones.

Sam, itching to discover what was in the car without room to pace the floor, began systematically searching the bedroom and Tara's belongings.

'I've got things to coordinate,' Harrison said. 'As soon as I know anything.'

He left without waiting for a response.

'God, I feel so useless,' Sam said, dropping onto the edge of the bed.

'You and me both.'

'We don't know if Bev's on the fells or not,' Sam said, staring at the oatmeal coloured carpet. 'Let's hope for the best, plan for the worst. If one of them from the car has done a runner we need to think about where they're running to.'

Ed put his mind to it while Sam went on.

'Firstly, why four hours?' Sam asked. 'That's how long Tara said we'd have to wait to discover Bev's location.'

Ed nodded. Four hours was a whole heap of time.

'How far could you get in four hours and where would you safely go?' Ed said. 'The possibilities are endless in reality.'

'But they need to get away and hide,' Sam trying to work it through. 'Me, I'd be out of the country as soon as I could. Maybe drive to Cairnryan. We're on the right side of the country. Get the ferry to Belfast. You could get to the ferry port in well under four hours from here.'

Ed shook his head. 'You could, but I once took Doris on that ferry. No sailings after midnight. Need to wait until tomorrow morning. And surely she'd expect us to put out an 'all ports' warning. She'd know we'd have agencies checking at the borders.'

Sam flopped backwards onto the bed, eyes looking at the ceiling.

Where are you Bev?

'I'm thinking about a small airfield just outside York.'

Sam shot up into a sitting position as Ed carried on speaking.

'You could get there in less than two and a half hours. In four you could have flown anywhere.'

Sam, hands on knees, leaned forward.

'Why would you think of something so off the wall Ed Whelan?'

'I checked out a small airfield near York.'

'What?'

She was on her feet now.

'More a field with short grass really.'

Sam walked to the window, watched the reflection of the blue lights, considered the revelation.

'You could have told me earlier.'

'I was trying to piece it together.'

'And what did you piece?' she asked, turning to face Ed.

Ed told her about the man he guessed as an ex-RAF pilot and the log book.

'On Thursday 29th a Cessna 152 landed there. Nothing unusual in a plane landing on a private airfield but Brian Banks told me about this one.'

'Brian Banks. You still talking to him?'

'I am. And just as well…you okay?'

Ed watched Sam sit back on the edge of the bed.

He'd seen bodies with more colour on the mortuary slab. Sam's face was drawn, skin translucent, stretched tight as cling film.

'Tired and I'm really worried about Bev. Not being able to do anything to get her back isn't helping.'

Ed unwrapped a packet of complimentary shortbread biscuits, handed one to Sam.

'It'll be good for your blood sugar.'

Sam thanked him, took a small bite and rubbed her blood-shot eyes.

Ed filled the kettle in the en suite, sat on the chair while it boiled.

Sam nibbled on the biscuit.

'Brian Banks knew about the plane. He knew who was coming in on it. It was a dry run.'

He stood up, poured two teas, gave Sam the other biscuit.

She put it between her lips, waited for him to continue.

'Marty Irons.'

'Who?'

Ed explained. Ex-DC Martin Irons who had done time for corruption and now lived in Spain. The Marty Irons who had trousered a fortune out of the timeshare boom.

'He kept in touch with Banksy and they met up for a drink when he flew into the airfield near York. That's what I wanted to check. I thought I was going to have to ask around but the flight log, or whatever it's called, meant I didn't have to.'

Sam picked up the small white tea cup, stared at the white wall.

'Wonder who Bev had a date with? She never did tell me who the toy boy was.'

A knock at the door.

Barry Harrison popped his head into the room.

'We're following a car in Kendal. We suspect Bev's phone's inside it.'

Chapter 57

THREE UNMARKED ARMED RESPONSE UNITS, BMW X5s, were in convoy behind the target vehicle, poised to conduct a 'hard stop.'

Inside the vehicles, AFOs mentally visualised the next few minutes: hours and hours of practising this tactical option combined with previous experience would soon culminate in a few seconds of potentially life-threatening action.

The intelligence indicated at least one occupant was likely to be armed and dangerous.

Each AFO asked themself the same question.

Would the suspect shoot if cornered?

The unknown ramped up the tension.

Silence. Deep breathing. Concentration.

The car, travelling within the speed limit towards the M6, appeared to have only one occupant.

'Can you see anyone else?' the driver of the lead police vehicle asked, leaning towards the windscreen, trying to answer his own question.

A combination of darkness and poor streetlighting wasn't helping.

The AFO beside him squinted ahead. 'Not sure whether I can see a front seat passenger or whether it's just a headrest.'

Was there a passenger? Was the passenger armed?

The uncertainty only cranked up the tension.

The firearms operational commander, a well-respected sergeant on the Firearms Unit, was in the lead vehicle. He had already agreed a plan with two other officers: the on-call superintendent, who had now assumed the role of strategic firearms commander, and a firearms tactical advisor.

He notified control room that they were now able to implement the 'hard stop'.

All three BMWs were in position. No other vehicles were in the vicinity. No visible pedestrians.

Authorisation was granted.

'Go, go, go,' the operational commander shouted into his radio.

Speed and coordination were key now.

High-pitched sirens shattered the silence of the night; flashing bright blue lights, secreted in the X5s' grilles, pierced the darkness.

The first BMW roared past the target vehicle, swerved in front of it, screeched to a halt. The armed officer, hanging out of the front passenger door, jumped out before the vehicle stopped, before the tyres finished smoking.

'Armed police!' he shouted, running towards the driver's door.

His colleagues leapt from the car, dashed towards the front of the target.

The driver of the second police vehicle accelerated

aggressively then stood on the brakes, the front end nose diving as it lurched to a stop alongside the target vehicle, all four doors of the X5 shoved open simultaneously, the AFOs inside star-bursting from the vehicle.

The third BMW sped towards the rear of the target, stopping inches from its bumper before the officers dived out.

The first AFO out of the lead car smashed the driver's window of the target with the butt of his weapon.

'Armed police,' he shouted again, MP5 now pointing at the driver. 'Hands on your head.'

AFOs surrounded the car, all shouting, 'armed police.'

The driver, the lone occupant, was totally compliant.

The operational commander spoke into his radio.

'Target vehicle stopped; driver detained. Repeat, target vehicle stopped, driver detained.'

Tea forgotten, they both stood in the small bedroom, parade square rigid.

'It's the waiting I can't stand,' Ed said.

Sam felt sick with nerves. 'I'd feel better if I could listen to the firearm operation. At least I'd get an immediate answer if Bev's inside once they've stopped the car.'

'If Bev's not in the car where is she?' Ed said. 'On the fells?'

'We can speculate all night. We'll just have to wait. I don't like it any more than you do.'

Sam walked back and forwards, gathering her thoughts.

'If Bev is in that car, she's not alone. If she was alone, she'd have contacted us. If she's in the car she must be incapacitated otherwise she'd be looking to escape from the driver. Very hard to control a car and control an individual.'

'Agree.'

They fell into a heavy silence, the seconds and minutes stretching.

When Sam finally spoke, her words hit Ed like a boxer's body shot.

'I forget to tell you,' Sam said. 'Chris Priest has put his ticket in.'

Like a winded heavyweight Ed's intake of breath was audible.

'Priest's retiring?'

Sam nodded.

'I'm going to nip downstairs,' Ed said after a moment. 'I'll get us some cold drinks. Why don't you jump in the shower? You might feel better. It's going to be a long night. I'll give you twenty minutes.'

He gave her twenty-five.

The shower had transformed her: shiny, damp hair, skin somewhere near normal, eyes not exactly sparkling but the tiredness gone.

'Any news?' Ed asked.

Sam shook her head.

'So, Marty Irons?' she said, bending forwards, rubbing her hair dry with a towel.

'Here, take this,' he said.

He handed her an ice-cold Coke in a small, glass bottle; regular coke, regulation pub mixer.

Ed watched her run her tongue around dry, cracked lips.

'It's full fat. Get some more sugar into you.'

Sam thanked him, tied the towel around her head and walked to the window swigging from the bottle.

'Marty Irons met up with Brian Banks,' Ed said behind

her. 'As I was saying, they kept in touch, although I didn't know that until the last few days.'

'Okay. But what was so important about Chris Priest putting his ticket in?'

Two steps and Sam stood next to the bed, about turn, two more back to the window.

'Marty told Brian that a couple of his associates were leaving Britain and joining him over there. It was all very vague, but he said a bent cop from the old days was joining them. At the time I wondered if it was Don Mulrooney, the other surviving member of the 'Seaton Three', but Brian wasn't sure and I always thought he went out there with Marty when they were released from prison.'

Sam kept up the two-step pacing.

'So, what are you saying?'

'I think it might be Chris Priest.'

'Chris Priest? Head of Professional Standards?' Sam was stunned. 'Based on what?'

'Rob Conlon, Paul Adams' cousin, didn't think Paul was corrupt.'

Sam sat on the edge of the bed, put her hands on the mattress.

'Sixty grand in a shoe box suggests otherwise.'

'It does, providing it wasn't planted there.'

'That's a big leap.'

Ed shuffled in the tiny chair.

'First things first,' he said. 'I've called Tucky Walton. He's on his way over here to collect us.'

'What?'

'If the locals get Tara, fair enough. But if they don't, I think she'll be headed for that little airstrip. We should be there waiting.'

Sam was back on her feet.

'If you're right, and it's a big if, we need to share that

with Cumbria. Plus, any arrests will be a firearms job and if the airport is near York, that's a North Yorkshire operation. We can't do this ourselves.'

Ed nodded. The idea of keeping it to the two of them appealed but he knew it was impossible. There were protocols to be followed in cross-border jobs.

Sam stood at the window. She wasn't happy about leaving Bev.

'Tucky's also going to contact the detective who was sitting with Paul's wife, the family friend,' Ed was speaking again. 'Tucky will get him to ask Erica Adams if Chris Priest was ever at the house.'

'Why have you got a bee in your bonnet about Priest?'

'Priest would have contacts,' Ed answered. 'He could find out where Harry Pullman was. Ray Reynolds always believed the 'Seaton Three' was the 'Seaton Four'. That was the reason Harry Pullman and Hugh Campbell bought into my suspension. I worked with the bent bastards. I lived for years under that cloud. It was one of the reasons I left when I did.'

His phone rang.

'But remember,' Ed said, ignoring the mobile. 'Priest worked with the bent bastards too.'

He answered the call.

'Ed, it's Tucky.'

The background noise indicated he was driving.

'Heard anything?' Ed said.

A pause.

'Is the boss with you?'

'She is.'

'Can you put her on please. Her phone's not ringing for some reason.'

'Did you do what I asked?'

'I did.'

'And?'

'I need to speak to the boss.'

Ed thrust his phone towards Sam.

'Tucky Walton for you. Put him right will you. He obviously didn't get the memo about my suspension being bogus. He's not happy sharing information with me.'

'Sorry Ed,' Walton said after a brief word with Sam. 'Someone did visit Erica on Saturday.'

'Time?'

'About the time Paul was with Tara.'

'Who.'

'She doesn't know. Nice man she said. Old. Talked his way into the house, said he was an old boss of Paul's. Gave Erica some cock and bull story about Paul passing information to organised criminals.

He did leave the room to go to the loo. Erica thought she heard the front door open but wasn't sure so she didn't ask any questions or challenge him. After he left, she rang Paul twice to tell him, but he never answered his phone and...'

'What?' Ed snapped.

'Paul had already told Erica and his DC friend he had stumbled across a bent senior police officer.'

'Who?' Ed pumped with adrenalin, desperate to know.

'Never told them. Said it was too dangerous. Said he was going to confront him.'

Ed swallowed on the disappointment and considered what they had.

'Confirms it's a man I suppose. When was this?'

'Few weeks ago. He can't remember when.'

Sam looked at Ed, raised her eyebrows.

'Why didn't he tell us? Come to see us?'

'He didn't know who to trust,' Walton said. 'Only told me because he started panicking, thinking he might be at risk, being Paul's mate, and he didn't think I was high enough up the food chain for Paul to refer to me as a senior police officer.'

'Look I'll see you when you land. Ring when you're five minutes' away. Save waking everybody up.'

'Well?' Sam said, after Ed ended the call.

He brought her up to speed while they waited.

Chapter 58

TEARS WERE STREAKING HIS CHEEKS, tears born out of fear and frustration.

Fear because he'd never been arrested before, least of all at gunpoint.

Frustration because he didn't think the detectives would believe him.

'Look,' he shouted, forgetting the interview was being recorded.

'Stop shouting,' DC Manners interrupted, his soft tone matching his name. 'Calm down.'

'Sorry.'

Rhys McKenzie, 23 years old, top lip smeared in sweat, tongue darting around his lips, thighs bouncing, began rubbing his wrists where he'd been handcuffed.

'But you've got to believe me,' he pleaded. 'I told the armed police the same. I don't know anything. You've got the wrong person.'

'Because?'

'Because I'm not a criminal. Because I live at home

with my parents. Because I've never been in trouble with the police. Please check.'

'We have,' DC Manners said. 'Let's say for now we believe you. Why did you have a phone on the front seat of your car that does not belong to you?'

'Like I tried telling the armed police, I was in the pub. Tuesday is darts night. There's a few gets in.'

'Go on,' Ian Manners said.

Rhys lowered his head, lowered his voice.

'I went to the toilet, bumped into this lass. She was proper fit.'

'Do me a favour Rhys, look up while you're talking and speak up so the tape can record what you're saying.'

McKenzie nodded.

'She bumped into me. I said sorry even though it was her fault. We got chatting in the corridor outside the toilets. She says she's here overnight on business. Asks if there's anywhere decent she can get a drink.'

'And?'

'I said, here. Like I said, she was proper fit.'

'Then what happened?'

'She asked if I'd do her a favour. Said her boss tracks her phone. Said she was shattered. Asked if I'd mind driving around Kendal for an hour or so with her phone, make her boss believe she was still working. Then when I got back, she said we'd have a drink and see what happened.'

'And you agreed?'

Rhys looked down again, nodded.

'Can you describe her?'

Another nod.

Rhys McKenzie was terrified but he wasn't a liar. Manners already had a report that told him that.

He had already read through the key points...

The car was registered to McKenzie.

Another detective had confirmed he was in the pub and according to his friends had just vanished after throwing his darts, saying he was going to the toilet.

Nobody had seen him talking to a female but the toilets are near the side entrance door and he was recorded on internal CCTV talking to a girl by the toilets.

Nobody saw the girl in the bar but the CCTV in the pub car park recorded her walking through the side door.

The CCTV also showed Rhys McKenzie getting into his Ford Fiesta and the girl walking out of the pub. There was no footage to identify any vehicle that she may have been using.

DC Manners rose from his chair, opened the interview room door and scrolled through his phone for the boss's number. Detective Superintendent Barry Harrison wanted answers quick.

Manners glanced over his shoulder and asked his final question.

'How long did you drive around for?'

'Twenty minutes maybe. Not long.'

'Paul might have been set up,' Ed said. 'Once he's with Tara, someone goes to his house.'

'Plants the cash?' Sam sighed, dropped back onto the edge of the bed.

'Possibly.'

'Where would he get that amount of money?'

'Tara's grandad. Lester Stephenson. Accountant to Hugh Campbell.'

Erica Adams had said it was an old man who came to the house. Could it be Lester?

Sam ran a hand across her forehead. 'Get someone to show her the photograph of Lester going into Tara's. The one Steph Crosby took. Is it starting to fit now? Or are we forcing the pieces together? Chris Priest? He's the one that fits the least.'

'Why not Chris Priest?' Ed said, making no effort to hide the annoyance in his voice. 'Maybe that's how he's got away with it for so long, he seemed above suspicion.'

Sam was on her feet again.

'But how would Paul Adams find out? And when he does, why not report it? Why not come straight to me?'

The second hand on the wall clock completed a full revolution before Sam spoke again.

'Let's think this through...what if Paul's motivation wasn't taking down a corrupt senior officer. Erica said he looked after the money and they were never short.'

Sam's words were now turbo-charged.

'What if he Paul was always bent? What if this time, blackmail was his motivation? What if the sixty grand wasn't a plant but a pay-off or an instalment?'

'If that was the case, why mention anything to his wife and his mate?'

Sam exhaled loudly, pushed her hands through her still damp hair and raised her voice.

'Will anything fall into place in this crock-of-shit of an investigation?'

She watched the clock again, letting her anger and frustration subside.

'Tell me about Priest and the two of you in the CID office,' she said, sitting down on the bed.

She drank a mouthful of the coke, tepid now in the heat of the room and her sweating hand.

'He was on shift with me. Worked with Marty Irons and Don Mulrooney. Our detective sergeant was worse than useless. Let Irons and Mulrooney get away with murder.'

When Sam asked who was paying them for information, Ed shook his head.

'They weren't fussy as it turned out. Took money off anybody. The Skinners. Campbell. Whoever. They'd do anything if it paid.'

'And you never suspected?'

'Not at all. It's not like they were waving the money in your face. Good thief takers, arrested loads of people, but afterwards, when you thought about it, you realised it was quantity not quality, that mostly they were locking up the small fry.'

Sam nodded.

'And then there's the phone call,' Ed went on. 'Luke Skinner asking if Pugsley can help.'

'The reference to the Addams family, reference to Paul.'

'Easy conclusion to jump to,' Ed told her. 'Except of course when he joined, Chris Priest was overweight and nicknamed...'

Sam jumped up. 'Chris Priest! Overweight?'

'Lost four stone in his first year in the job,' Ed said, shaking his head. 'I totally forgot about it. Never gave it a second thought. It was years ago. The nickname vanished with the weight.'

'Surprised they took him in the first place if he was that far out of shape.'

'Different times,' Ed said. 'I joined in '78. Edmund-Davies was just completing his review into police pay. As long as you didn't wear glasses and reached the minimum height requirement you were in. Huge staff shortages then. Poor pay. Low morale. I knew a lad who got in and he had a criminal conviction.'

Ed sipped tonic from the small, glass bottle, saw Sam's eyebrows arch for the second time in as many minutes.

He raised the bottle, toast-like. 'Always been a Pepsi boy, don't like Coke,' he grinned. 'Imagine people getting in today with a record. And what a great man Lord Edmund-Davies was. Welsh mining stock.'

'Really?' Sam said, allowing Ed a little time off-piste. He would be worried about Bev too.

'Talk about making the best of yourself,' Ed continued. 'QC before 40, Lord Justice before 60. Trial judge for the Great Train Robbers, presided over the inquiry into the Aberfan mining disaster. What a legal brain. Those sentences for the Train Robbers? Thirty years. Was that because they'd robbed the establishment? And those poor children at the school in Aberfan. I wasn't much older. My mam told me all about it.'

Sam decided that was enough of memory lane.

'So, Priest's nickname?' she asked.

Ed nodded. 'Given before political correctness and touchy-feely snowflakes took over the Job. When name calling was just having a laugh and something that had to be put up with.'

He took another mouthful of tonic water.

'When the school of thought was, if you can't put up with having the piss taken out of you in the office, how could you cope with being slagged off on the streets.'

He put the bottle on the table next to him.

'Did he know my suspension was bogus?'

'He had to,' Sam said. 'The Deputy wouldn't countenance it without him being involved. Appleton thought it was real. Priest knew it was bogus…'

'What?' Ed asked, staring at Sam, her face deep in thought.

'If Priest is bent, why didn't he tip off Pullman and Campbell?'

'No need,' Ed said. 'I don't think Harry Pullman knew who Priest was. Harry would have bartered him into the deal when he was running scared from the Skinners if he had known, especially if he thought Priest could track him down for the Skinners. He never mentioned Priest. He was convinced I was suspended. That wasn't an act, where he knew the real bent cop was Priest.'

Ed stood and stretched, arms above his head.

'But Campbell? He's different. That could have been an act,' he said.

He dropped his arms, put his hands in his pockets.

'Let's be right. If he was in on it, he knew Tara was setting up Pullman.'

Sam was still trying to see Chris Priest as corrupt, the scale of the damage he would have done over the years, the fall-out when he was exposed.

Christ he'd risen to be in charge of Professional Standards. He was the Deputy Director of Intelligence before that…. 'Come on then. What's his nickname?'

'For one year, back in the day, the fat, bent bastard was called Pugsley.'

Chapter 59

Tara Paxman was now travelling north on the M6, heading for the junction that would see her join the A66 east.

The pale blue lights of the instruments were relaxing, but she was concentrating. She did not want to be stopped for speeding and she needed to think through her next move.

She had already made one massive mistake tonight which could have been catastrophic. A stupid oversight, speaking with Parker and then putting the phone in her pocket without thinking, a sub-conscious slip that could have ruined everything. Summers hadn't said anything. No doubt hoping the police would track her phone.

Tara let a smile become a broad grin.

Problem solving was never an issue, no matter how little time she had.

Her self-preservation was born out of necessity, but ingenious even if she did say so herself. Thinking on her feet was second nature.

She turned the temperature down two degrees, a

cooler setting would help keep her alert, and settled back into the seat.

Why did so many men fall for the three-card trick?

Flick, flutter, flash.

Flick your hair, flutter your eyes, flash anything that grabbed their attention.

Her lecturers fell for it all the time.

She had stood by the pub door, waited for someone suitable to go to the toilet, then walked into him.

Flick, flutter, flash: do me a favour; I'll have a drink with you; let's see where it goes from there.

It had been so easy; he couldn't wait to take the phone; couldn't wait to get to his car.

She wondered if the police had stopped him yet, grinned again as she conjured up the moment.

Imagine if it was armed police.

What did they call him? Welsh name. Didn't matter. She laughed out loud, pictured him shitting it.

And the police? She wished she could have seen their faces when they pulled him over, discovered the phone.

She thought of Lester Stephenson and the smile faded.

It had been her grandfather's idea to burn the car.

'It'll give the police something else to think about, buy you some time. My wife's dying. I was going to leave that life behind, stop looking over my shoulder, enjoy my remaining days abroad with you and Marty, but that's not happening now.'

Tara wiped away a tear. He had given his life for her.

Tara was following as he sped along The Struggle, saw the Jag crash through the wall, fly through the air and cartwheel over the field.

She had walked towards the twisted metal, crushed roof, shattered glass. She didn't check on Lester, hidden amongst the exploded airbags. He had made her promise not to look.

She lit a marine distress flare, stolen from Bill Redwood's boat, threw it into the car and ran away.

Once the car ignited, she dropped the yellow Ocean Safety container holding the rest of the flares by the roadside.

She was already driving towards Bowness-on-Windermere before the emergency services had been notified.

She had come off the M6, driven towards Kirkby Stephen, a small market town in the Upper Eden Valley. She had pulled over, checked her phone for a signal, and made the first call to the number ending in 683. The Man.

He seemed to answer before it rang.

'You okay?' he said, no hello or other greeting.

'I'm fine. We're on our way now. We'll see you at the airfield at six.'

'What car are you in?'

'In the Jag. With Lester.'

'What about the Golf?'

'Still on the car park. Never had to use it. Everything went off just as planned. Maybe Parker's not as good as everybody thinks she is.'

'Put Lester on the phone.'

'He's in the bushes. Toilet visit. You know what these old men are like.'

'I'll see you at six,' he said.

Tara had replayed the conversation. Had he believed her? Why wouldn't he? Still...

She had made another call.

'Marty, it's Tara.'

'Everything okay?' Marty Irons, disgraced detective, convicted criminal, timeshare king.

She snatched up a breath and began to cry.

'No Marty. It's not. Lester's dead.'

Through her fake tears she had told Irons what had happened.

'How did they get onto you?' he had demanded.

'Pugsley. Pugsley's betrayed us. We need to get out quicker than planned.'

WEDNESDAY 4™ NOVEMBER

'IT WASN'T HER.'

Barry Harrison closed the hotel room door behind him and leaned against it, facing Sam and Ed.

Sam glanced at her watch. 12.10am.

'The phone was given to a lad called Rhys McKenzie. That's who we pulled.'

'Bev's not coming back,' Sam said quietly, sitting down on the bed.

'I'm afraid it doesn't look that way. Two bodies in the car. Burnt beyond recognition. Both in the front seats. Clothes disintegrated. Not yet known whether they're male or female.'

Sam clasped her hands together, focused on the wall.

'I guessed that. If Bev's phone was on the move, and Tara and the driver were in the car, Bev would have contacted us.'

Harrison continued. 'They've had a better look in the car. The front seat passenger has their hands cuffed behind them. They look like police issue rigid handcuffs.'

Sam and Ed said nothing. They knew what that meant.

Ed walked to the window, stared into the darkness, heard Harrison saying it was too early to be sure how the fire started but small fragments from a marine flare had been recovered.

'Jesus,' Sam said, moving her gaze from the wall to the carpet. 'They throw off an incredible amount of heat.'

'Over a thousand degrees centigrade according to the Chief Fire Officer,' Harrison said.

'Anything else?' Sam tried to push away an image of the inferno.

'A yellow bottle with more flares in it, on the verge near where we suspect the car left the road. We'll make some inquiries tomorrow with boat owners and Chandlers to see if any have been stolen.'

Sam stood, spoke quietly.

'We've had a guy on a yacht killed. I'll check with his daughter. They may be off his boat. Is it the square-sided bottle with a red screw top lid?'

Barry Henderson scrolled through the photos on his phone, showed the picture of the bottle to Sam.

'Yeah, that's what I thought,' she said. 'Anything else you think we should know about from the scene?'

'The Brigade crow-barred the boot. Looks like metal jerry cans in there. We'll know much more when we can get it into a forensic bay. It's covered by a tent for now.'

'I'll get you details of Bev's dentist,' Sam said, eyes glazing over.

'Thanks,' Harrison said, looking down at the carpet, relieved Sam had brought the subject up without him having to ask. 'That would help.'

Ed turned around: 'It's a long shot, but the jerry cans may be filled with aviation fuel.'

Harrison's eyes flicked between the two detectives while Sam told him about the airfield.

'There's nothing we can do here,' she said. 'We'll head off, go to the airfield. We've got a lift coming.'

'Will you keep me posted?' Harrison asked. 'Under normal circumstances I'd send someone with you, but I haven't got the staff.'

'Of course. We'll need to link in with North Yorkshire. That's why we've got a lift coming. I wanted a car fitted with comms.'

'Thanks. Obviously if you get Tara, arrest her on suspicion of murder.'

Sam nodded. 'Don't you worry about that...can you tell me about Bev's phone?'

Harrison outlined the interview with Rhys McKenzie.

'She used the phone to speak to me, after I'd spoken to Bev,' Sam said. 'It's just a case of whether she deliberately kept it knowing she was going to send us on a wild goose chase...'

'Or?' Ed jumped into the pause, seeing where Sam was going.

'Or she made the best of a bad job,' Sam went on. 'She inadvertently put the phone in her pocket after talking to me then had to come up with a plan.'

'Shows she's resourceful,' Ed said.

'Resourceful's the least of it,' Sam said, locked on a memory, her and Bev sipping Tanqueray gins and giggling like schoolgirls, grading the young barmen one to ten. 'She's a cunning bitch.'

Chapter 60

WHERE TO?' Shane 'Tucky' Walton asked, as Sam and Ed got into the car.

'Head to York,' Sam said, stretching her legs across the back seat, the dashboard digital clock displaying 1am. 'Ed will keep you right.'

'We need to end up on the old A19 into York. Your call how you get there,' Ed said.

Shane nodded, face blank.

'I'll direct you to the airfield when we're closer,' Ed said.

Sam leaned her head on the offside rear door, closed her eyes.

'Turn the heater up please,' she said.

She couldn't sleep in cars and tonight would be no different. But she needed a few minutes; focus on the job in hand, forget about leaving Bev behind, alone and scared in a place she didn't even like, the end horrific beyond belief.

Except she couldn't forget.

Sam bit her lip, pleased that those in the front couldn't

see her tears, hoped that Bev was dead before the car was torched.

They drove in silence.

Shane had driven towards Pooley Bridge, now he took a left towards Dockray.

'Am I allowed to know what's happening?' he said at last. 'Why are we going to an airfield near York?'

Ed opened the glovebox. 'Is there a phone charger in here?'

Shane dropped his hand into the driver's door pocket. 'Use mine.'

'Cheers,' Ed said, putting his phone on charge. 'We're going to York because I think the plan is to get Tara abroad. I also think a bent cop is being whisked away.'

Shane gripped the wheel a little tighter, eyes fixed on the headlight beam and the narrow road.

'Tara?' he said, shaking his head. 'I thought she was on our side?'

'So did we.'

'Where is she now?'

'Driving to the same airfield I hope,' Ed told him. 'Only she's got a head start so you need to get your foot down.'

Shane wanted to drive faster but it was impossible on the poorly-lit, twisting roads. Putting them all in a ditch would help nobody. He'd accelerate hard when he hit the A66.

'What happened then?' Shane said.

'Everything went to rat shit when we all met on the pub car park.'

Ed told him everything from meeting up to Tara being driven away.

'Now you know as much as we do,' Ed said.

Once they joined the A66 the speedometer needle headed right.

Sam sat up, leaned forward inbetween the front seats, turned to Ed. All that mattered now was justice for Bev.

'Tell me more about Chris Priest. What was he like when he joined the CID?'

'Quiet. Didn't have informants. Didn't arrest burglars.'

Ed tilted his head, looked up at the roof lining.

'Did he belong?' he pondered aloud. 'Was he dynamic enough to be a 1980s detective?'

'What do you mean?' Sam said.

Ed looked at Sam.

'Different times Sam. Different expectations. The go-getters were the glory boys and everybody was expected to be a go-getter, expected to run informants, but it didn't work out like that. Not everybody could. Chris Priest couldn't. Didn't fit the go-getter profile.'

'Meaning?'

'He was never the centre of attention. Never the one other detectives were jealous of because he'd been the one behind a really good job.'

Ed turned back to face the windscreen, the car zipping along the quiet carriageway.

'He was the type who in the Christmas party debrief would never be mentioned. He was a grey man at a time when CID offices were filled with colour.'

Sam shuffled, sat back; Shane concentrated; Ed looked over his shoulder.

'Some older detectives definitely believed in 'noble cause corruption,' he said. 'Using dirty means to achieve noble ends. The academics even came up with a name for it, called it 'Dirty Harry' syndrome.'

Irons and his bent pals weren't interested in 'noble ends' for the department, Ed knew. Everything had been for personal gain...the tip offs, stealing cash from prisoners, burgling premises. They had been a law unto themselves.

Ed was back in the CID room, the rivalry infectious.

'All the time you'd see the office superstars trying to outdo each other, getting information on burglaries, robberies, recovering stolen property, making arrests,' he said. 'They'd have competitions who could get the most TICs.'

Offences 'Taken into Consideration' weren't charges but that didn't matter; accepting a TIC meant it went on the punter's record and was a no-fuss way of scratching unsolved cases from the crime log.

'Priest on the other hand would grab a theft report from the pile we'd get off the gas board. Breaking into gas meters and stealing the cash was just what happened in those days in some communities.'

Ed remembered how Priest would work... arrest the householder in the morning, get a quick admission, charge and bail them to court, prepare the file in the afternoon. Job jobbed.

Sam leaned forward again.

'If you're right, how did he become involved in corruption?'

'No idea,' Ed told her, stomach twisting when he thought about the corruption inquiry that had thrown the whole CID office under a cloud of suspicion, everyone tarred with the same dirty brush.

He turned away, breath fogging the passenger window, and watched the air-con melt it away.

'Irons and his cronies had taken thousands of pounds,' he spoke again. 'So every detective in that office thought they were being followed, lifestyles under scrutiny, bank accounts being checked. Everyone was paranoid, whispering in corridors because we thought the office was bugged.'

'And you think Priest was involved?' Sam still couldn't see it. 'Christ he's that clean he squeaks.'

Ed turned around to face Sam again.

'That's how people melt into an organisation and get away with it. I can't even remember if Priest was ever interviewed by Complaints.'

Ed thought about Chris Priest and remembered another nickname, this one whispered behind his back, spoken with a crude laugh when the after-match pints were flowing.

'Priest the Beast,' Ed said it out loud.

'Priest the Beast?' Sam thrown again.

'Always going on holiday to Thailand,' Ed said. 'You know how the thinking goes...single, middle-aged bloke, trip after trip to Thailand, must be a sex tourist after young ones. So Beast, as in paedo, rhyming with Priest.'

Sam shook her head, a veil of disgust on her face.

'I've heard that's all a load of bull.'

Shane had been silent behind the wheel but now he spoke up.

'Paul Adams told his best mate that Priest always went to Cuba. Never set foot in Thailand. That's just a ruse.'

Ed was about to argue the toss when Sam told him to contact the North Yorkshire control room, give them enough advance warning to call out whoever they needed.

Sam sat back, closed her eyes again, contemplated the new information about Chris Priest as the car sped further east.

No extradition from Cuba, probably lax banking regulations.

Could Priest have been stockpiling money there?

Chapter 61

CHRIS PRIEST PARKED HIS CAR.

5.30am; dark, damp and depressing but at least he was early.

He shoved his hands into the pockets of his reefer jacket, sunk his neck into the collar and walked towards the clubhouse, surprised to see a dim light illuminating the end of the building nearest the entrance. Maybe he could get a hot drink.

He pushed the door open, stepped inside and breathed in the seductive aroma of percolating coffee.

'Morning Chris,' Sam said, moving from behind the door as he closed it. 'Going somewhere nice?'

Priest jumped, spun around.

'Bloody hell, Sam. What a fright!'

Two North Yorkshire AFOs, Ed a step behind them, emerged from the shadows at the far end of the club house.

'Thank God,' Priest said. 'I thought he'd got away.'

He moved towards Sam.

'Stay exactly where you are Sir,' one of the AFOs shouted.

Priest raised his arms above his head.

'Sam, I don't know what you think is going on here,' he said, slowly letting his arms drop, 'but Whelan's the subject of an ongoing investigation into police corruption and needs taking into custody right now.'

'You cheeky bastard,' Ed stepping forward before the AFO barked the same warning he'd given Priest.

'This is ridiculous,' Ed shouted. 'He's the bent one not me.'

'The only thing ridiculous is how you've got away with this for decades,' Priest fired back.

Priest rocked back on his heels, put his hands in the pockets of his dark blue jeans, turned to Sam.

'Think about it. I'm a Superintendent. Over thirty years in the job. Access to sensitive material. I've passed the highest standards of vetting, every background check, financials, the lot. Can you say the same about Boy Wonder here?'

Ed didn't move, blood flooding his cheeks, his anger alive and prowling like something hungry in a cage.

Sam looked at the AFOs.

'Relax, but I need you to stay here for a little longer.'

The AFO with blonde hair in a pony-tail nodded; the other, black beard surrounding lips that were a line pressed tight together, kept his eyes fixed on the three of them.

'What did you think had kick-started the new corruption inquiry Sam?' Priest said, cool and confident.

Sam said nothing. Waited.

'I'll tell you what started it. Paul Adams, that's what?'

'Before we do anything else,' Sam said, 'I need to speak with the firearms commander, give him an update.'

'At least you won't need a negotiator,' Priest said, the sarcasm lead heavy. 'Ed's already here.'

Sam's next sentence was an order: 'Both of you sit down opposite each other and keep your hands on the table where the AFOs can see them.'

Ed's eyes blazed, the anger scratching at the cage bars.

'You're not seriously listening to this bullshit, are you?'

He yanked out the wooden bench and sat facing the AFOs, palms on the long, dark, wooden table.

Priest put his left leg over the bench opposite, sat down, hoisted his right leg and turned to face Ed.

'Ever wondered why he changed his on-call that night?' Priest said, looking at Sam.

Ed jumped to his feet, the table squealing; two MP5s moved like lightening to the shoulders of the AFOs.

'Sit down Ed! Now!' Sam shouted.

She waited until he was back on the bench.

'If I have to I'll cuff the pair of you.'

'Paul Adams found out about Whelan being corrupt,' Priest keeping up the attack. 'Paul was a whistleblower who ended up dead, his killer shot by the police, and Boy Wonder here is the negotiator making sure Zac Williams takes the rap.'

Sam looked at Ed, shook her head.

Ed didn't move.

Priest kept talking, a fighter firing jabs, using his speed.

'Then when that's not quite working to plan, he gets suspended so he can go and speak to whoever he wants without anyone checking up on him.'

Sam walked to the door, stepped outside and rang the inspector commanding the firearms team.

Priest had started to hum Gloria Gaynor's 'I Am What I Am.'

'You coming out the closet then?' Ed spat, leaning

across the table, backing off before the AFOs could react. 'Going to tell the truth about yourself? Admit it's all been a sham?'

Priest grinned. 'Your time's up Whelan you bent bastard.'

'Right,' Sam said, back in the room, 'as soon as transport arrives, we'll all go to the local nick.'

Priest had started humming again but now he stopped.

'You know Sam,' Priest said, Ed watching, listening.

'Back in the day, Ed here mixed with criminals, paid for information, was renowned as a good thief taker. But so was Marty Irons. He was older and some younger detectives, impressionable detectives, tried to emulate him.'

'Jesus, Sam,' Ed's voice loud and strained.

Sam silenced him with a look, let Priest punch away.

'Not one of them confessed you know,' he went on. 'Bent coppers sent down without saying a word in the interviews.'

Chris Priest paused, held Sam's gaze before continuing.

'The anti-corruption squad recovered a few hundred pounds in cash from their houses, some electrical equipment, TVs, microwaves, video recorders, that sort of thing, but not a lot. They had got away with thousands.'

'What happened to the rest of the money?' Sam asked, glancing at her watch.

'Who knows? The mid-80s was a different world. Banks were still relatively private places and the Proceeds of Crime Act was years away. Not hard to launder ill-gotten gains.'

He turned his eyes to Ed.

'That's right isn't it Ed?'

Ed stared at him, eyes on fire, but didn't move.

'Tell me Sam,' Priest back in the centre of the ring, punching and punching. 'Was it his idea, the bogus suspension? Fill you full of nonsense about how he could visit Harry Pullman and Hugh Campbell. Find the leak?'

Sam didn't respond.

Priest smiled, an easy smile that showed his teeth and reached his eyes.

'He did, didn't he? And you let him. Told you about this place as well I suppose? Did it not cross your mind he was planning to fly off from here? Him and that little tart Tara Paxman? Maybe you're getting too old for him. Maybe he fancies a younger model.'

Ed felt an invisible force pushing him to his feet, sensed fingers tightening on triggers.

'Sit down Ed! Now!' Sam shouted.

That's two strikes. A third and the fingers won't just be tight.

'How do you know about Tara?' Sam asked.

'I'm Head of Professional Standards. Courtesy call from Cumbria. And it's not like Edward here has never chased the women is it?'

'Meaning?' Sam bit back on her own emotions.

Don't be fucking jealous, not now you stupid cow

'Ask him about a blast from his past by the name of Susan Street.'

'Who?' Ed said, nose scrunched, head shaking, voice quiet.

'I had an interesting conversation with her recently. Seems Edward here was close to Susan in the 1980s. Still at least he wouldn't whisper the wrong name in his sleep. How is your wife by the way Ed?'

Ed clenched his fists, the veins straining in his neck. 'Is that transport here yet?'

'It's why I never married,' Priest continued. 'I wanted to avoid the emotional, invisible prison of the three Cs: commitment, communication and compromise. Way too complicated for me.'

He paused, considered his last sentence and grinned.

'Complicated. I've just come up with the fourth C.'

He looked over his shoulder, spoke to the AFOs.

'All right to stretch and rub my knees? They're a bit stiff.'

Blackbeard raised his weapon but nodded.

'Like I said Sam, too complicated for me,' Priest standing up, bending at the waist and moving steady hands over his knee caps. 'Looking over your shoulder all the time when you're playing away from home. It's why I could never be corrupt. I couldn't cope with the double life.'

Priest sat back down.

'Seems Edward –'

Ed unclenched his fists, spread his fingers across the table and dropped his voice to a menacing whisper.

'Stop calling me Edward you irritating piece of shit.'

'Many years ago, Edw…' he stopped and grinned. 'Ed was out late one night, early hours late, parked up on an industrial estate with Susan Street, like him married at the time.'

'I never had a thing with Susan Street,' Ed growled.

'Least he remembers who she is now. What did Shakespeare say? Something about protesting too much.'

Sam frowned, wondered where this was going.

'Sadly, Susan's gone downhill,' Priest said, 'but back in the day…'

He pursed his lips, whistled long and steady.

'What a looker.'

He shook his head, the grin wider.

'Let's just say everybody wanted their typing done by Susan Street. Some were lucky enough, blessed even, to have those fast fingers to themselves in private.'

'This is utter bollocks,' Ed said. 'We need to get out of here. I'm not listening to anymore of this fucker's garbage.'

But Priest had no intention of stopping, a fountain that couldn't be turned off.

'A bit of a CID groupie was our Susie in her time. I spoke to her, not long back,' he said.

'She remembers you two being parked up on an industrial estate, doing whatever you were doing.'

Another grin.

'When you saw Irons and his cronies coming out of an electrical goods storage depot. Ring any bells?'

Ed didn't move, stared at Priest.

'You sat in the darkness and watched them load a van. She says you didn't do anything. Just watched. And after they left, you just drove off.'

Ed's fists were white-knuckle balls when he spoke through clenched teeth.

'I…never…had…a…thing…with…Susan…Street.'

Priest leaned a slow inch across the table, white spittle forming in the corners of his mouth.

'She would be really disappointed to hear you don't acknowledge the relationship.'

Ed began to push the bench away with his backside.

'Ed!' Sam shouted again. 'Ten count. I'm warning you. We can easily check out Susan Street's version of events.'

'You could,' Priest said, the grin now a permanent feature, 'but unfortunately she died last week. Cancer. She did say that the burglary all those years ago was reported but Ed here kept telling her to leave it, that he had it under control.'

Ed sat still. He didn't need another of Sam's warnings, but it didn't stop him speaking.

'If they weren't here,' he glanced towards the AFOs, 'I'd rip your fucking head off.'

Priest's smile didn't slide.

'When Irons and co. were arrested,' he said, 'she was so

425

scared, she handed in her notice. Went to work someplace else.'

All heads turned when the door opened.

Shane Walton walked in, a pair of bushy, ginger eyebrows and highly-polished black shoes following him.

Even without the copy of 'Pilot' magazine, Ed clocked him immediately.

Was that only yesterday?

The voice had no accent, clipped tones, just as Ed remembered it.

'Yes, that's him,' retired Wing Commander Leonard 'Lion' Moorcroft said.

Chapter 62

TARA PAXMAN HAD GONE to the Hoppings as a child and hated it. Europe's largest travelling funfair, a descendent of the Blaydon Races, had been rolling up at Newcastle's Town Moor every June since 1882.

But the memory of soaring above the ground, spinning at speed in what she was certain were cobbled together death traps meant that first visit was also her last.

Now, stiff with terror, she concentrated on breathing, forcing herself to think of something, anything other than the fact that the buffeting metal between her and eternity seemed no thicker than a tin of beans.

Nose pushed against the cold passenger plexiglass, eyes staring at the swathes of orange lights below, she wondered where they were, how long they had before they would have to refuel.

The distraction was brief; fear rules everything once your imagination invites it to the feast.

The padded headphones blocked out most of the noise when they were speaking, but Tara's mouth was too dry for conversation, and in the cold, pre-dawn darkness, the drone of the groaning engine seemed ready to give up the fight against the headwind.

She moved her head away from the window, hands on knees, terrified of knocking something in the cramped cockpit and sending the plane into a tailspin.

White shapes danced behind her tightly-closed eyes.

Her headphones buzzed. 'You okay there?'

She answered, then remembered the switch for the mic.

'Fine,' she lied, speaking into the mic jutting from the headphones, not wanting to be ridiculed at some pilots' annual dinner or worse, the dinosaur detectives' piss-up.

Reluctantly she opened her eyes, looked out the front window. The sight of the single, whirling, yellow-tipped propeller, the only thing keeping them airborne, sent a rapid 'oh shit' signal to her brain which snapped her eyes back shut.

She wiggled her toes, dug her nails into the palms of her hands.

'You sure you're okay?'

This time she didn't turn her head, didn't speak, just raised her right thumb in his direction.

The aircraft bucked on a pocket of turbulence and she jumped in synchronisation.

'Nothing to worry about,' said the voice in her headphones.

She thought she caught the hint of a smile behind the words.

Oh you're enjoying this...

She felt blindly along her headset and flicked the mic switch.

'How much longer?'

'About an hour.'

She breathed out slowly, tried to settle nonchalantly back into the seat.

Another hour. Refuel. Then over the channel.

The thought of flying over the sea brought a new level of fear.

What if we crash into the freezing water?

How would we die?

On impact, drown or hypothermia?

None were particularly appealing.

'I'm really sorry about Lester,' the pilot's voice somehow alien over the headphones. 'After all these years I can't believe Pugsley betrayed us.'

'I didn't know him like you did, so maybe I wasn't as blinkered.'

No one fools me.

Tara Paxman had looked at herself many times and constantly liked what she saw – too cunning to be caught out, too clever and crafty to stumble into the traps. Like the animal she admired most, she was sly and sneaky and a survivor in a world stacked against her, an animal who hunted alone.

I am the vixen.

I am the urban fox.

THAT's the man who was here with Marty on Sunday,' Leonard Moorcroft said, pointing his banana-thick index finger.

'Hello there,' Leonard said, looking at Ed. 'We meet again. How are you young man?'

Ed stood up.

The AFOs tensed.

Sam mouthed, 'It's okay.'

'I'm very well thank you sir,' Ed said. 'Sorry we dragged you here so early.'

Leonard smiled. 'Bit of excitement's good for the soul. I don't get much these days, not since Barbara…'

His words trailed away.

Sam stepped towards Leonard, held out her arm, shook his hand.

'I'm DCI Sam Parker. Pleased to meet you.'

Her hand was doll-like in his.

'I'm sure this all looks a little out of the ordinary,' she said. 'Armed police officers in your clubhouse.'

Leonard smiled. 'I've seen plenty of out of the ordinary in my time young lady.'

Sam turned to Priest.

'You see Chris, when we got here earlier, Ed and myself hid outside while Shane dashed around to Mr Moorcroft's to get the key. Then we waited in here. Shane brought Mr Moorcroft to the clubhouse once I'd spoken to him on the phone.'

Chris Priest's face didn't move and he wasn't humming.

'I rang Shane when I went outside,' Sam told him. 'You thought I was speaking to the firearms commander. All we needed was some time together in here to see how you would play it, hear what nonsense would come out of your corrupt mouth.'

She grinned.

'I thought Ed played his part very well, didn't you?'

The faces of two AFOs were expressionless, although unlike Priest, they had been fully briefed before they reached the airfield.

'All we had to do Chris was wait to see if you turned up. You did. Unfortunately for you, Tara didn't. Mr Moorcroft has confirmed nobody's landed here since yesterday afternoon.'

Sam looked at the smart old flyer.

'And you know Marty Irons, don't you Mr Moorcroft?'

'Spoke briefly to him on Sunday when that man there,' he nodded towards Priest, 'got in the aircraft with him.'

Leonard 'Lion' Moorcroft adjusted his RAF blue, red and white striped silk tie, glanced at his Breitling wristwatch.

'Nice chap, Marty. At least he seemed to be. I knew he had been a policeman, but we all thought he'd left to start his own business. We knew nothing about prison. The members will be shocked, I can tell you that.'

'They can form a queue Leonard,' Ed said. 'Superintendent Priest here can enjoy his place at the front.'

Chapter 63

CHRIS PRIEST SAT in a tiny interview room in a tiny North Yorkshire police station. He'd not spoken a word since 'Lion' had identified him.

Sam sat opposite him; Ed was at his side.

'You want a solicitor?' Sam asked.

Priest shook his head.

'We'll make custody arrangements in a little while,' Sam said.

Priest nodded.

It was standard practice to take arrested police officers to custody suites where they would be unknown. In Priest's case, as a senior officer, that meant in reality going to a different force.

The sound of the 'hunting horn' interrupted them as Ed's message alert blared.

He strolled out of the interview room, made a call to Shane Walton in response to the text and walked back moments later.

'Seems Tara left you high and dry.'

Ed paused to savour the moment.

'Marty Irons too,' Ed said, sitting down. 'No honour amongst thieves.'

Priest said nothing, stared at the small, child-size desk as Ed went on.

'Leonard Moorcroft, let's just call him Lion, such a great nickname, has made some checks with his mates at other small airfields.'

Priest looked up, eyes glazed.

'Marty's plane landed at 5.30am at a field about twenty miles away. Picked up a young, dark-haired girl. No bonus points for guessing who that is.'

Priest, grey as the weather, wore the ashen 'I'm fucked face' a thousand detectives had seen a thousand times.

Ed continued: 'The girl arrived in a VW Golf...that's still there. We'll get it dusted, but I'm sure we'll find Tara's prints. A witness saw her fiddling with a mirror, checking her make-up.'

Priest licked his licks, his Adam's apple pulsed.

'I want protection,' he said, 'and immunity from prosecution.'

'You're a long way from that,' Sam said. 'Start talking.'

Priest began a staring match with Sam.

Sam won.

Priest looked away and started talking.

'In the early days, Ray Reynolds suspected the 'Seaton Three' was a 'Seaton Four' and of course he was right. He just kept barking up the wrong tree.'

Priest glanced sideways at Ed.

'Constantly barking up the Ed Whelan tree,' Priest said.

Ed's mouth said nothing, his face said less.

'Whelan's wife had plenty of money and his lifestyle, especially in the early days, was always subject to rumour and innuendo. He was the perfect suspect for the fourth man.'

'Why did Ray think there was a fourth?' Sam said.

'No idea. Maybe he had a grass who told him. Who knows? I never directly said anything to Ray, who I have to say was always charm personified towards Ed, but I dropped little seeds whenever the opportunity arose.'

'You bastard,' Ed said, pouring all of his hatred into the words.

'How did you get involved with Irons and Co?' Sam said.

Priest was like the dam that slowly cracks, his own words a trickle building to a torrent, nothing left to save but his own skin.

'Good question,' he said. 'I certainly didn't fit the corrupt officer profile, but of course that's how I got away with it for so long. Flying under the radar, so to speak. Your RAF man would like that.'

'How did it start?' Sam said, hiding her disgust. She despised corruption but she wouldn't do anything to risk Priest clamming up. Now that he was talking, he was almost enjoying the process.

'It was me with Susan Street, not Whelan,' Priest said. 'I saw them coming out of the warehouse. Told them I wanted in or I'd have them arrested. They had no choice.'

Priest saw Sam's face, read her thoughts.

'You're wondering why,' he said and shrugged.

'Greed...excitement...a sense of belonging, becoming a member of a secret club...and I was loyal to them, had their backs when the shit hit the fan.'

Priest sat back in his chair. He was as laid back and chatty as a man talking football in the pub.

It was another movie Sam and Ed had watched before... 'The Happy Confessor.'

'And did Susan quit for another job or was that another lie?' Sam said.

'No she quit,' Priest oblivious now to the put down. 'Wanted nothing to do with me. She didn't know anything, but she suspected something was going on.'

'Had you spoken to her recently?'

'Haven't seen her for years. Read in the paper she'd died.'

Sam looked at him. Not even the hint of sadness for an old flame extinguished. Another narcissist who couldn't think of anyone but himself. Her contempt soared.

Priest carried on talking, the crack widening, the water gathering pace.

'While the lads were in prison I rose through the ranks and the higher I went, the more sensitive the information that came my way. My price to the likes of the Skinners and the Campbells went up and up.'

Priest paused, smiled. 'I like to think I was good value though.'

Sam didn't want a long interview, wasn't interested in asking lots of questions. She couldn't decide whether her skin was crawling because of Priest's flippant admissions or the lack of air in the cramped room.

Either way she would make do with the gist for now.

'Luke and Mark Skinner could have informed on me when they were arrested, but they were gambling on me giving them Harry Pullman's location and their people silencing him.'

'Conspiracy to murder, Chris?' the words out before Sam could stop them,

Priest didn't miss a beat, showed no remorse.

'Without Harry's testimony they felt they'd be acquitted, a better option than trying to negotiate a lighter sentence for exposing me. No jail being better than less jail.'

Ed reached behind him and opened the door, the heat stifling in the room not much bigger than a broom cupboard.

'Twice the Skinners botched the hit on Pullman after I tipped them the location,' Priest in full flow. 'Fortunately Hugh Campbell, or at least his sons, came in with a better offer. A hostile takeover in business terms.'

Priest smiled: 'Very hostile as far as Mark and Luke Skinner were concerned.'

Cooler air had drifted into the room alongside the sound of a cleaner's mop and bucket.

'What about Paul Adams?' Sam asked

'Struck lucky with the name,' Priest said brightly. 'I was hoping anybody hearing Pugsley would put two and two together and get five.'

'But I remembered,' Ed eyed him as he spoke. 'I remembered you when you were a fat nobody, remembered your nickname.'

Priest sighed, carried on with his script.

'All those years and nobody had a clue,' he said, a respectable man remembering happier times. 'Then one young detective somehow stumbles across my indiscretions. Phoned me when I was in my office. Asked to see me. I thought he was a whistleblower. I couldn't believe it when he sat down and said he knew I was bent. Bent. That was the word he used. Told me had proof safely tucked away, but I always suspected that was a bluff.'

'Sums you up,' Ed said, bitterness rising like bile in his mouth.

Priest ignored the jibe as if Ed had said nothing.

'He wanted money. Five thousand a month. I've been paying him for six months now. I didn't know what he had done with the money so I arranged for the sixty thousand to be planted to make sure you two took the bait.'

'Lester Stephenson?' Sam asked and regretted it, the flame-ravaged wreckage of the Jaguar and Bev Summers handcuffed and helpless a blinding image behind her eyes.

'Very loyal,' Priest said.

Ed couldn't resist, couldn't hold back, wanting Priest to hurt.

'No loyalty in dead men,' he said. 'Burnt to death on a Lakeland fell.'

Priest shrugged, remained impassive.

'He had a good innings.'

Ed got out of his seat, looked out into the corridor. The cleaner was getting closer. He shut the door.

'Tell me about the money you gave Paul,' Sam said.

Priest couldn't have smiled more broadly if had watched a longshot win with his hard earned on the nose.

'Every £20 note he ever received was counterfeit. He was a test purchaser but he never knew. When he spent the money we knew the notes were good enough to go into circulation.'

Priest stopped, looked around the small room, and then let the torrent run again.

'When I decided 34 years was enough and it was time to retire, a decision had to be made whether Paul took over from me. It was tricky. With me, Hugh Campbell had become used to information a young detective like Paul Adams just couldn't provide. That made him useless to the Campbells and a danger to me. Hence the plan.'

'What plan?' Sam asked.

'Hugh and I knew what Tara had been, what she was. Prostitutes are actors and we knew Tara would play her part, from setting up Paul to throwing herself into the helpful arms of the police.'

'How did that work out?' Ed sneered.

'You always had a good investigative gut Whelan and Sam, well, she's one of the best. Two variables we couldn't cater for. Plenty of investigators would have taken everything at face value, not you two. But we had no choice; we had to take our chances.'

He means that, the sanctimonious prick.

Ed popped his head into the corridor, saw the cleaner had gone. He left the door open.

'Lester wanted to retire,' Priest was saying now. 'His wife was terminally ill. So Lester and Tara get the big pay-off and as a bonus she has the chance to kill the son of the father who abandoned her. The perfect storm really.'

Sam remembered what Tara had told her, that she had slept with Marcus.

'Did Tara sleep with Marcus?' she asked.

Priest laughed. 'It all helped her story. She befriended him but set him up with Lucy straight away, as she was told. Tara never slept with Marcus. Even she drew the line at having sex with her brother.'

The interview was already running longer than Sam had wanted, but she knew even the sketch of Priest's plan wasn't finished. Exhaustion and the crushing effort of keeping a hold on her grief were sapping her, though.

'Zac Williams had to die, so did Lucy,' Priest's voice dragged her back from the edge.

'Why were they selected?' Sam asked.

'They lived next door. Lucy was a good-looking girl. Zac was the jealous type. Ticked all the boxes.'

'And Sanderson?' Ed's turn to prompt.

'Wrong place, wrong time,' Priest said, 'although not exactly society's loss.'

For the first time, Ed had to agree with him.

Fatty's excuse all of his life. Wrong place, wrong time.

'I needed all the loose ends tied up,' Priest went on. 'Nothing left to chance.'

Priest had met Bill Redwood a few times, been seen with him, so he needed to go. He had every faith Inspector Mick 'Never' Wright would happily sign it off as an accidental slip from the jetty.

'That's why I chose a night he was on duty,' Priest volunteered.

Sam shook her head, craved a Marlboro.

'And Scott Green?' she said.

'Should have been simple. Suicide note and off the multi-storey car park. Except of course he escaped.'

Priest grinned, shook his head.

'And to make things even more damaging I find out he couldn't write. I still can't believe nobody told me that. Always the last to know, sadly.'

'Maybe if you'd been a proper detective,' Ed said, 'instead of locking up meter thieves.'

Priest let that barb bounce off him like all the rest.

'Anyway, I couldn't risk Davy Swan and Jimmy Marshall getting arrested, especially if the old guy in the shop identified them. I met them after I finally got away from Tara's, made their deaths look like a suicide. Not that it fooled anyone but it was another smoke screen, another drain on dwindling resources.'

'Where did you go when you left them?'

'Tara dropped me off in York. I can give you the name of the hotel, Sam. Nice place. No questions asked if you happened to be checking in with a married man.'

Sam examined the back of her hand; aware he was playing mind games.

She looked up, stared at him and thought again about Bev.

Not a cat in hell's chance you'll get immunity you corrupt bastard.

'Were you hiding in Tara's loft?'' she asked, eyes giving nothing away.

'I needed to be in the house with Tara. She couldn't overpower Zac and Lucy by herself even with a gun. She needed me there as insurance.'

'Who did the killing?'

'Tara of course. Scampering back and forward through that loft hatch like a lunatic.'

Sam would explore that in more depth in a further interview.

Was it all down to Tara?

'And the Skinners?' Sam asked.

'The work of Mr Campbell. But of course, having them dead did me no harm. Another loose end.'

'And Marty Irons?'

Priest told them they had met a few times since Irons was released, mainly in Spain and always away from the tourist hotspots. They had met on Sunday to discuss the final arrangements.

'Where's Tara now?' Sam asked him.

'If she's following the plan, with Marty; they're flying to Spain then a chartered yacht from the Canaries across the Atlantic. Amazing what pockets full of cash buys without questions.'

Ed summoned up his sarcasm.

'Couldn't buy you a seat in the plane could it?'

Priest was a man past caring, the water almost spent.

'Is that the extent of the plan?' Sam said.

'Apparently, just to be on the safe side as they'll be in the tail end of the hurricane season, they'll sail south to the Azores before turning west towards the Caribbean and

Cuba. Then it's sunshine, salsa and cigars. I know Marty likes a big Havana these days.'

There was no bitterness in Priest's voice. The dam was empty.

SAM AND ED were back at headquarters, their third mugs of coffee on the desk.

Priest had been 'housed' in the cells at a police station in West Yorkshire.

Sam looked at the wall clock. 8.05am.

'There's a lot for the interviewers to get stuck into,' she said.

'Too right,' Ed stifled a yawn. 'Lot of planning to do. I want to know what happened to Marcus. Did they tell him to make a run for it and then shoot him in the back?'

'That would fit,' Sam said. 'We'll just have to wait and see. Let's grab some sleep whilst there's a lull. Dream of lazy days on a Cuban beach, drinking mojitos and reading Hemingway.'

'Maybe a nice cigar as well,' Ed mimed lighting up. 'If it's good enough for Irons...'

'When did you start smoking?'

Sam paused, Bev back in her head.

'Me and Bev promised each other we would stop smoking when this job was over.'

'Really?'

'Yep, cough's getting worse.'

'I never thought I'd see the day,' Ed could feel her pain. 'You maybe, but not Bev.'

He hesitated.

'About sleeping. Am I okay at yours?'

Sam forced a smile that was weak but from the heart.

'Of course. I'll let everybody know we'll be back here at 1pm.'

She reached for her coat, fumbled in the pockets for her cigarettes and flicked open the packet.

Empty.

Maybe now was a good time to keep that promise.

ACKNOWLEDGMENTS

I would like to thank everyone at Cheshire Cat Books for publishing Lies that Blind.

A huge thank you as always to Paul Jones, Head of Publishing, for his insightful ideas and help in plot development.

Thanks to Garry Willey, Head of Editorial, for a line by line forensic examination of the text and the sprinkling of his 'literary magic dust'.

Thanks to the other 'Cats' without whom none of this would be possible:

Adam Maxwell for his IT wizardry; Laura Swaddle for another great cover; Helen Long for her fabulous sub-editing skills; my son Ben for another tremendous cover photograph (Ben Thomas Photography will go far).

For all the support and encouragement when the end seemed a long way off, my thanks go to my father Ken, my mother Jean, sisters Tania and Tanis, sons Ben and Flynn, and last, but by no means least, my partner Saphron.

And finally thank you, the reader, for taking the time to

read this book. I am always humbled. Without readers, books are just words on a page.

Printed in Great Britain
by Amazon

23669178R00260